Say Yes

A Sons of the People Novel

LUCY VARNA

Say Yes

A Sons of the People Novel

LUCY VARNA

Bone Diggers Press
www.bonediggerspress.com

For Jackie and Trey, who deserve a Levi
For Suzan and Marissa, who found theirs
And for my dad, who's always been one

Cover design © L.J. Anderson, Mayhem Cover Creations.

Published by Bone Diggers Press, Clayton, Georgia.

ISBN 978-1-943465-00-2

TITLES BY LUCY VARNA

THE DAUGHTERS OF THE PEOPLE SERIES
Book 1: *The Prophecy*
Book 2: *Light's Bane*
Book 3: *The Enemy Within*
Book 3.5: *Tempered*
Book 4: *In All Things, Balance*
Book 5: *Sanctuary*

THE SONS OF THE PEOPLE SERIES
Book 1: *Say Yes*

THE CULLOWHEE HERITAGE SERIES
Book 1: *A Higher Purpose*
Book 2: *A Wicked Love*

Notes from the Fab Four

Notes on the People compiled by Tom Fairfax, Phil Walters, George Howe, and James Terhune, known at the IECS unofficially as the Fab Four.

Aenkanien. A tattoo inked into the left-hand shoulder blade of a Son who becomes the husband of a Daughter. Once approval has been granted by the mothers of both parties and the tattoo is in place, a formal marriage ceremony is unnecessary; the two are considered married in the eyes of the People, though many couples choose to undergo a civil or, less frequently, traditional ceremony.

Amaetien. The tattoo Sons receive on their sixteenth birthday (the day they become men under the traditions and laws of the People) to indicate their maternal lineage. Usually inked onto the upper left arm, the *amaetien* is a symbol of the mother's eternal protection and devotion, and a warning to any who would harm the Son.

Ankana. Woman. Also refers to the Woman with No Face.

Council of Seven. The People's ruling body, consisting of seven women, one representing the line of each of the Seven Sisters.

Daughter. A direct descendant of one of the Seven Sisters, Daughters may be either immortal (if they have not yet broken their own curse) or mortal (if they have broken their own curse or are the daughter of a mortal Daughter).

Eknon. Student.

Eternal Order. A supposedly mythical group devoted to undermining the ultimate goal of the People, to break the curse of immortality for every Daughter through the fulfillment of the Prophecy of Light.

High Guard. Seven Daughters devoted to eradicating the Eternal Order. A highly secret and deadly group.

Institute of Early Cultural Studies (IECS). Located in Tellowee, Georgia, USA, the IECS is the main historical research branch of the People and serves as a repository for much of its history.

Kaetyrm. Sister, usually used in a formal situation, though not always.

Maetyrm. Mother, usually used as a term of respect for an elder Daughter and not necessarily as a reference to one's own mother. Teachers, for example, are referred to as Maetyrm.

People, The. The name used by the descendants of the Seven Sisters to describe themselves. The People include all immortal and mortal Daughters, Sons, and the mortal descendants of all submitted Daughters to the second degree (i.e. through the grandchildren of Daughters who have submitted their wills and become mortal). Other descendants are not counted among the numbers of the People.

Prophecy of Light. Issued by an unknown person at some distant point in the past, the Prophecy of Light portends a way for the curse of immortality to be lifted from all of the People, and not solely the Daughters who submit their wills and become mortal.

(See the Daughters of the People website.)

Seven Sisters. The progenitors of the modern People. The seven women, all sisters, avenged the deaths of their parents by killing the men of the People (the original band) and were cursed by the god An to live immortal lives without the ability to bear sons. The curse was tempered by the goddess Ki, who decreed that the curse could be broken by each one if she would submit her will, in whatever way (except sexually), to the man she loved. (See the Legend of Beginnings on the Daughters of the People website.)

Shadow Enemy. The traditional enemy of the People.

Son. Usually refers to the child of a Daughter who has broken the curse and become mortal, but may also reference the child of a Son or another male descendant of a Daughter.

Tellowee, Georgia, USA. One of the centers of the People, located in rural northeast Georgia.

Prologue

PETEY NOLAND stared up at the waterslide and wished for his mama. Dale had already gone down it twice and Matty once, but they were both older. That's what MawMaw said when Petey held back. *Dale and Matty are bigger than you. Let them go first and then you'll see there's nothing to be afraid of.* She'd hugged him hard, like he was a little kid or something. Even away from home, she smelled like cookies and flowers.

It reminded him of Mama and made the funny ache in his chest worse.

When he was eight like Matty, maybe the slide wouldn't scare him. Maybe he could climb up to the tippy top and sit down and just go, like it was no big deal. Eight wasn't that far away, but it'd be too late for him. They'd be home a long time before his birthday and he'd miss his chance to have fun on the waterslide. He knew he'd like it, if he could only bring himself to make the steep climb.

Dale jogged over and slung a wet arm around Petey. At eleven, Dale was already a whole head taller and had muscles in places Petey only dreamed about. His big cousin could hit a baseball nearly to the fence on the Rec Department's fields. *Reliably,* Uncle Jack said, which meant he could do it almost every time he came up to bat.

Petey knew he was doing good just to make contact with the ball.

You'll hit your growing spell soon, Petey, Mama said. *Things will be different then. You'll see.* She said it a lot, so he figured she believed it. Or maybe she just wanted to make him feel better because he was scrawny and short and whatever the opposite of athletic was. Dale and Matty could do anything. Petey wished with all his might that he could, too, but it never happened. If a ball was involved, he sucked at it, doubly so if he had to run. Maybe if he had a dad to do things with him like his cousins did, he'd be a great ball player, too, but he didn't. All he had was his mama. He loved her and all, but she didn't know diddly about man stuff.

"You gonna come up, Petey?" Dale said.

Petey shrugged. No way was he admitting he was scared of the steps. *No. Way.* Dale wouldn't make fun of him or anything. He was cool like that, unlike the guys at school. Nope, Dale would laugh it off and coax him into trying it anyway, and then Petey would get stuck halfway up and they'd have to send somebody up to carry him down.

Dale and Matty would never want to play with him again.

"You sure? It's a lot of fun. Man, that slide feels like greased lightning under your butt."

"I'm ok here," Petey said in the soft lisp he was stuck with until his front teeth grew back. He prodded the gap with his tongue and slumped. No teeth yet.

Dale squeezed hard. "Ok, then. I'll be back soon."

Petey watched his cousin jog back to the line forming behind the waterslide. A hard knot of something that kinda hurt lodged in his stomach and his eyes felt all funny. He swiped the back of his hand over them and stared after Dale. Someday, he'd be big, as big as the slide, and he'd never be afraid of it again. He'd learn how to throw a ball and run around the bases without wheezing and shoot a basketball straight enough to hit the rim.

He fingered his inhaler through his shorts. Maybe the ball would even go in, if he practiced hard enough. Uncle Jack offered to help him all the time, but it felt funny, almost wrong. Maybe if Petey had a dad, it'd be different. A dad would be around all the time, just like Uncle Jack was for Dale and Matty. He'd make pancakes and teach Petey how to throw a ball and not make fun of the all the posters on his walls just because they were from dorky movies. A dad would tuck him in at night and tell him stories and...

Petey let the thought trail off. No way would he ever have a dad. Mama didn't even date. That's what Aunt Candi said, and everybody knew you had to date before you could fall in love and get married.

He screwed up his face and tried to remember what else grown ups did when they liked each other. Kissing, maybe. Holding hands for sure. Aunt Candi and Uncle Jack got all gooey eyed when they held hands. One time, Petey had caught Uncle Jack with his hand on Aunt Candi's butt.

Which was kinda gross, so maybe Mama could skip that part and stick to holding hands.

First, though, she had to meet somebody. If she did, they could go out on a date, and then he'd have a dad, a real honest to gosh dad with a truck and a pancake pan and everything. And he wouldn't have to wait until he was big to climb that slide. *No way.* A dad made you unscared of everything, like Dale and Matty were. *They* didn't care that the steps to the waterslide were really high. *They* knew how to throw a ball and catch it and hit it without turning away first.

They didn't wheeze every time they ran around too much.

His hand clenched tight around his inhaler, so tight it dug into his fingers, pinching the skin until it hurt. He needed a dad. That was the ticket. All he had to do was figure out how to get Mama to meet a guy. Not any guy, though. They needed a guy that was nice to Mama and brought her flowers, like PawPaw brought MawMaw, and one that'd teach Petey all about sports, like Uncle Jack did for Dale and Matty.

They needed a guy that loved them enough to stay, not like his dad, who'd died before Petey was born. The way he figured it, dying wasn't something you did to your kid. It really kinda sucked when your dad died, so a real dad would stick around, no matter how bad it was, and he'd never give up, not ever.

Petey stared up at the waterslide and smiled. A dad. That's what he needed.

He settled down to think it over as Dale slid down the slide again, screaming laughter out the whole way down.

PART ONE

Falling

One

THE WAY SERAFINA NOLAND figured it, a woman deserved a vacation every once in a while, especially a woman whose biggest obligation outside of work was, at that moment, being spoiled rotten by his grandparents in Orlando.

At seven, Petey had declared himself too old to be chaperoned by his mother. Sera's parents had agreed. "He'll be fine," her mom had said, and her dad had added, "Man's gotta grow up sometime."

Sera had let that one pass without comment.

So off the lot of them had gone, Mom and Dad, Petey, and Sera's two nephews, for a *glorious, fun-filled week* at Walt Disney World followed by another week at Daytona Beach.

Sera had decided to do something different. As soon as her parents had approached her about taking their grandkids on vacation without their parents, she'd started looking for her own getaway. Her books were doing well and she had plenty of money in the bank, so she'd picked a spot on the map and decided that *there* was where she'd be while Petey enjoyed the thrills of Orlando with his cousins. To justify the expense, she'd called a local bookstore and arranged a mid-week signing, and brought along her latest work in progress so she'd have no excuse to deviate from her writing schedule.

And now here she was, on her way to Kill Devil Hills, North Carolina, ready for her own fun-filled week in the Outer Banks. If the weight of loneliness pressed against her, she ignored it. So what if she was twenty-nine and had never been married? So what if most of the women she'd graduated from high school with already had their two point seven children and were working on husband number two? Big deal. She and Petey were doing just fine on their own. They had a good life and, more importantly, they had each other.

Sera sighed as she pulled off Highway 158 onto a side street, following it until it dead-ended onto Highway 12 where her rental apartment was located. Maybe it would've been nice to share her vacation with somebody, a friend from her old job, if she'd made any real friends there, or a nice older man with a stable life and not a lot of baggage. Probably an impossibility, but a girl could dream.

Such was not her lot in life, though, so she determined to make the most of what she had. She'd already planned sight-seeing trips to the area's attractions, and when her schedule was clear, the beach was a quick walk from her apartment. Her Kindle was packed with unread books and her skin called out for a nice tan to wash away its indoor pallor. What more could a woman want?

She rolled into the parking lot with a careful eye on the pedestrians darting here and there, automatically playing Petey's car tag game as she did. Massachusetts. Texas. Three tags in a row from Georgia. Ohio.

She did a double take on the Georgia tags and sighed out a laugh. Two were from Rabun County and the other was from Towns County. The joke back home was that no matter where you went, you'd see somebody from Rabun County while you were there. Unfortunately, she probably knew whoever it was. The county just wasn't that big and her family was fairly well known. As Wendell and Barbara Noland's daughter, she'd be expected to socialize, leaving less time for sight-seeing and reading.

Oh, well. At least she wouldn't be lonely.

Sera located her building, parked several spaces away from the folks from home, and checked in at the manager's office. When she came out, the roar of waves breaking against the beach called to her from behind a line of sand dunes. Through a path winding between two mounds of sand, she caught a glimpse of the Atlantic's vast, blue-gray waters. She glanced between her car, the building, and the dunes. Screw it. The drive out had been long and tiring, even with an overnight stop midway. A short walk on the beach followed by a nice, relaxing hour reading would go a long way toward helping her unwind.

She grabbed her beach bag out of the car, glad she'd had the foresight to pack it with a clean beach towel, a bottle of water, and sunscreen, and tucked her Kindle in it before heading out. Humid heat rolled off the pavement in waves, coating her with each step. After a short walk, Sera hit sand, and smiled when it shifted under her feet. She hadn't been to the beach in years, not since she was a little girl. Petey would love the sand crunching between his toes and the seagulls flying down to peck at detritus. She inhaled the salty air and turned her face into the light breeze blowing off the ocean, and the tension slid from her shoulders like butter melting off a steaming cob of corn.

As soon as she passed through the barrier dunes, she mentally marked her spot on the beach, a reminder of where her car was parked. To her left, four buff young men in their early twenties were playing volleyball. They were tall and handsome and fit, and looked like they hadn't a care in the world between them.

Sera bit back an appreciative sigh. What hunkdillyiciousness, and on her first day, too. They were too young for her, but no harm in looking. And they made a great landmark, or a memorable one, at least. Lifeguard chairs and sunbathing families all looked alike after a while, but those four would be hard to forget.

The line of water beckoned. She pulled off her Chuck Taylors and dipped her toes into the ocean, hissed in a breath. Lordy, the water was cold, and it July. A wave rolled ashore, higher than she'd anticipated, and soaked the lower hem of her capris. She laughed and danced out of the way, and since they were already wet, she skirted the edge of the ocean as she walked, stepping hastily away when waves washed in too high.

The late-afternoon sun beat down and the clear azure sky floated above her, a fairy tale blanket protecting the landscape under its weight. In the distance, two boats cruised across the choppy water, one hauling a water skier. The other was a larger pleasure craft with tiny people moving across its deck. The noise of the engines drifted in, mingling with the sounds of children playing in the surf and the crash of waves against the shore.

What a great day.

She shrugged her bag onto her shoulder and stuffed her free hand into her pocket as she turned and headed back. Sand scuffed out from her toes as she trudged through it and, without conscious thought, her mind picked up the thread of her latest work in progress. A scene played out in her head, rewound to the beginning, and spooled out again. She studied it from every angle, reworking and refining it until she was satisfied with its flow.

By the time she finished, she'd lost track of her walk. She glanced around and shook her head, pursing her lips around a rueful smile. She'd passed the volleyball game by at least a hundred yards. After a quick backtrack, she picked out a spot not far from the game and laid down on her towel facing away from the ocean, propped up on her elbows with her Kindle open to the latest Patricia Briggs novel.

As she delved into the story, the real world faded away. Gone were a mother's worries over her son and the knot that had developed in the plot of her own manuscript. Gone were the sounds of other people gathering their things together in readiness for an early supper and a night out on the town. The roar of the ocean, the squawk of birds flitting from sky to sand, the sounds of the four young men and their game, all disappeared, overshadowed by the story unwinding on her Kindle.

A gentle tap against her hip broke her concentration. She glanced around and saw a volleyball, and automatically reached out, stopping its sluggish roll across the churned up sand. One of the young men, a handsome redhead with close-cropped hair and a square chin, jogged lightly toward her, his mouth twisted into a smirk below sunglasses and a straight nose.

As he came near, she looked up and up, taking in the hard muscles of his legs below baggy swimming trunks, the flat abdomen, the faint line of ginger hair disappearing into the low-slung waistband of his trunks, and the broad expanse of his chest and shoulders. He bent, retrieved the ball, and unfolded to his full height of *really tall*.

"Hey." He stared down at her and flipped the ball back and forth between strong, capable hands. "Sorry about that."

She smiled, couldn't help it. It wasn't every day a sun god spoke to her, especially one with a hint of an exotic accent underlying his Southern drawl. "No problem."

"Quit flirting, Levi," one of his friends called. "Time's a-wasting."

Levi smirked and walked backward a few steps. "See you around."

"Sure," she said. What else could she say? *It was a pleasure seeing all six-foot something of you,* or *Hey, thanks for the heat, you shining star, you.* She grinned as she watched him jog back to the game, admiring his easy stride and the muscles bunching and flexing with each step. If that was the view she'd have all week, then she was glad she'd picked this particular beach to vacation on. Too bad Levi was half a decade too young for her.

She turned back to her book and fell into the story, letting it block out the heat of his gaze where it lingered on her from across the narrow beach.

LEVI EWART HAD KNOWN a lot of women in his time, from the many women in his family to the many women hoping to bed him. A Son didn't make it far past puberty without having at least one woman throw herself at him, though he learned early on how to deal with it.

Levi had learned earlier than most. As the great-grandson of an immortal Daughter who was a respected elder of the People, he was heir to a sizeable fortune, accumulated over the lives of his foremothers. From the time he'd taken his first step, responsibility, loyalty, and duty had been pounded into him, including learning how to deal with women who might prey on him because of his wealth and standing among the People.

He'd carefully hidden the side benefits of being a Son from the women who loved him; the Daughters who pursued him *because* he was a Son, the women who wanted to bed a strong, attractive young man. A Son's sexuality was an open secret among the People, one everybody knew, but nobody discussed.

That suited Levi just fine.

Like most Sons, he knew he'd have to settle down one day, probably with a woman hand-selected by his great-grandmother for her political connections, if he wasn't lucky enough to find love on his own. He *wanted* to fall in love, wanted a wife and children, and looked forward to the day when his wife's mark would be tattooed over his shoulder blade, a symbol of the love and respect between a

Daughter and her husband.

But not just yet.

At twenty-two, he wasn't ready for that life, and sure as hell didn't want the responsibility. He was content in his work and more than happy to play the field until the woman of his dreams came along.

He'd come to Kill Devil Hills for a week and a half of fun with three long-time buddies, and had been prepared to flirt and play if the right woman came along. The petite brunette with slender arms and gentle curves who'd stepped through the sand dunes near their game seemed like a promising candidate. She drew a second look, and then a few more. He was intrigued by her tinkling laugh as she tiptoed into the ocean, and kept a subtle eye on her as she wandered up and down the beach, apparently lost in thought.

When she settled nearby, he deliberately overshot a serve. It hit the sand near her, exactly where he'd aimed it. Three pairs of male eyes rolled skyward.

"What?" he said.

Jordan propped his hands on his slim hips and narrowed his dark eyes to slits. "Cut the innocent crap, Levi. There have to be better ways to meet women."

Heath grinned, his teeth white against his natural tan. "I bet..."

Colin bumped his large shoulder against Heath's. "You know the rules. No bets on the first day."

Levi smirked at Heath. "Bet me tomorrow. I'll still be up for it."

"Just go get the damn ball," Jordan said, his tanned face pulled into a scowl.

Levi jogged over and retrieved the ball. The woman's honeyed Appalachians accent piqued his interest, and he took a great deal of pleasure in eyeing her curves up close. When Jordan called him back to the game, he could've sworn she watched him go, though by the time he took his place behind the net, she'd already turned back to her e-reader.

Tomorrow, he'd take Heath up on that bet. It was guaranteed to involve the pretty brunette with her silver eyes, wide smile, and firm, round arse, if she was still around. He'd take the bet and he'd win, and then he'd make a point of getting to know her on a personal level, maybe one involving stripping her down to her pale skin, his hands skimming over her curves, and his mouth discovering the pleasure of hers.

Two

SERA SETTLED EASILY into the cozy apartment she'd rented for the week. It suited her, with its narrow living area, tiny kitchenette, and double bed with a trundle built into it. Just what a woman on her own needed and no more. She put the last of her toiletries away in the bathroom and looked around, satisfied. It was perfect for a week of fun in the sun with a dash of work thrown in to stave off madness.

She took a quick shower, washing off the sweat of travel and sand from her walk along the beach, and let her mind drift to the hunky Levi with his cocky grin and beautiful physique. She couldn't wait to tell Candi about the foursome when she got back home. Her sister-in-law would be green with envy over Sera's brush with such a handsome young man.

Maybe Levi and his friends would pose for a snapshot.

Naw. Sera grinned and got a mouthful of water for her trouble. Though she'd grown a lot over the years and nearly conquered the painful bashfulness of her youth, she'd never approached a man on her own, not outside of work. Apprehension slithered down her spine. Never had, never would. God bless her introverted soul. Her innate shyness had kept her out of a lot of trouble growing up, that and having her nose buried in a book.

If it had kept her that way, Petey might not now be living without a father in his life.

But at least something good had come out of her one miserable failure. Petey was a good boy, sweet and kind, his mind keen and intelligent, even if his sense of humor was raunchy, as only a seven-year-old boy's could be. They had grand adventures and sometimes not-so-grand disagreements, but she never worried about the love. That would always be there between them.

Petey would always be her little boy and only hers, and nobody could say otherwise.

She ate supper at a nearby steakhouse, then returned to her apartment and caught up on work, setting it aside when the long day of driving caught up with her. After a sound night's sleep, she woke bright and early and heeded the call of the ocean. A long walk on the beach as the sun tipped over the horizon would be just the way to start the day.

She pulled on a sundress and twisted her hair into a knot on top of her head, snagged an empty plastic grocery bag, and headed for the beach. The soles of her shoes smacked against the pavement, then sank into the sand. High tide had left seaweed and seashells scattered along the beach. She chose a path near the water's edge, far enough away that she wouldn't get wet, close enough to have her pick of the seashells, and trudged through the damp sand.

Petey would love the fragile shells. He'd hold the larger ones to his ear, listening for the ocean's echo, and incorporate the smaller ones into one of his games. The rest would serve as a memento of her first solo vacation, a reminder that she didn't have to be part of a couple in order to have fun.

She'd nearly reached her turning point when the sounds of feet hitting wet sand approached her from the rear. She peeked over her shoulder and bit back a grin. Levi and his friends were running in a loose pack toward her, all of them wearing running shorts and tennis shoes and the skin they'd been born in, stretched taut over well-formed muscles.

Oh, yes. The scenery on the beach was well worth the trip from Georgia.

They ran silently past her, their easy grace stirring her envy. Levi slowed and faced her, walking backward in front of her, a small smile tugging at his mouth.

"Hey," he said.

She stopped, half afraid if she didn't, he'd trip trying to keep pace with her. Up close, he was nearly a foot taller than her with a leanly muscled form. His eyes were the color of warm whiskey and held a heat that baffled her as they slid slowly down her body and up again, settling on her face.

"Hi," she said, and prayed her tongue wouldn't twist into knots in her mouth.

His smile stretched into a grin flashing strong, white teeth, the front ones slightly crooked. It was a charming flaw and made him seem almost approachable. He flicked a finger down her cheek, surprising her with the quick gesture and the punch of tingling heat it left behind. "Nice," he said, and then he was gone, loping after his friends. She stood rooted to the beach, one hand over her cheek holding in the feel of his skin against her own as her heart pounded and her nerves fluttered.

Her eyelids slid closed and heat rushed into her cheeks. Oh, God. She didn't have on a speck of makeup and hadn't bothered to put on a bra before sliding the strappy sundress on over her head. What must he think of her?

Later, she laughed over the silliness of worrying about how her lack of a bra would appear to a stranger, but not until she'd stumbled her way back to her apartment. In the bathroom, she eyed her makeup-less face and the swell of her breasts under the thin material of her dress. What had Levi seen that was so nice? The woman looking back at her wasn't plain, but she wasn't extraordinary, either. Medium brown hair atop average features. Boobs that were big enough to notice, but not so big they stood out.

Her mouth twisted into a grimace. She was still carrying an extra five pounds around her hips, weight she'd tried to lose after Petey's birth and never had. The only remarkable thing about her was her eyes, the light gray, almost silver color she'd inherited from her father framed by thick, dark brown lashes. They were her best feature, but they weren't enough to attract the attention of a man like Levi, and she wasn't stupid enough to believe otherwise.

She shrugged it off and put on a bra under her sundress, not bothering with makeup before she tucked her camera into her purse and set out for her first adventure in the Outer Banks.

Well, her second adventure, if she was being honest. Her brush with Levi definitely counted as an adventure, no matter how brief it had been.

She hummed to herself as she headed out in her car, grabbed

breakfast at a drive-thru, and made her way to the Wright Brothers National Memorial. She spent the entire morning there, wandering through the exhibits, hiking up the steep hill to the memorial, and taking loads of pictures to show Petey. Next summer she'd bring him out, separate vacation with the grandparents or not, and they'd have a grand ol' time exploring the Outer Banks, exactly the way a mother and son should.

AFTER LUNCH and a leisurely nap, Sera hit the beach again, this time wearing a bathing suit under her sundress, a modest, cranberry colored maillot with spaghetti ties at the neck and around the back, chosen more to cover the handful of stretch marks on her lower abdomen than anything. It wasn't sexy or daring, more's the pity, but it served its purpose.

She regretted not having the body for sexy and the bathing suit to match when she spotted Levi and his friends playing Frisbee on the beach. A woman was entitled to one wild fantasy in her life. Hers was apparently having the body of a twenty-year-old in the presence of a group of hunkdillyicious young men.

She tried to muster shame for the frivolous wish and came up with a whole lot of *meh*. Practical was for the fifty-one weeks of the year when she wasn't on vacation.

Before she'd done more than lay her towel on the sand and pull out her Kindle, Levi jogged toward her. He plopped down on the beach beside her and propped his forearms on bent knees, settling in as if he meant to visit for a while.

She eyed him, torn between exasperation and suspicion. What could a man like that possibly see in a woman like her?

"Look," she said. "I get that you're bored and your friends have probably put you up to something..."

"Who says I'm bored?" He dug his bare toes into the sand. "Maybe I just wanna get to know you."

"Or maybe your friends put you up to something."

He grinned. "Ok, you got me there."

"So what was it? Get my number, cop a feel?"

"Can't say."

"Why?"

"'Cause then I'd lose and they'll never let me hear the end of it."

Her jaws snapped shut. He'd actually bet on getting close to her? Good grief. "You've never lost before?"

"Nope." He turned his whiskey eyes on her. "Don't intend to lose now."

"I should leave just to break your streak," she retorted.

"Comes to that, I'll leave," he said, surprising her. "But as long as you're here, I figure we can help each other out."

A red flag popped up in her mind. "Right. Help each other out. Gotcha."

He laughed, flashing his endearingly crooked teeth. "So suspicious. You're here alone, right?"

She carefully blanked her expression. "My husband's waiting in the apartment for me."

"Get real. My nana owns this building. How hard do you think it was to find out there's only one person booked in your room?"

Not as hard as believing he'd gone to any kind of trouble trying to track her down. "How do you know what room I'm in?"

He lifted one shoulder in a casual shrug. "Saw you come out of it this morning."

She huffed out an exasperated breath. "So now you're stalking me?"

"Suspicious." He flicked the end of her nose with the tip of his finger. "I was curious, that's all. I didn't even look to see your name or where you're from."

"And I'm not telling you either."

"Yes, you will." He stuck out his hand. "But I'll go first. Levi Ewart, Tellowee, Georgia, northeast of Atlanta."

She eyed his hand, twin thoughts running through her head as her heart sank into her toes. These were the people with Georgia plates? And, with his build, coloring, and name, he could only be one person, the son of Iain Ewart, a gregarious mechanic who kept her Volvo running like a top. Levi's parents and hers had known each other for decades, though Sera had only nebulously been aware that the Ewarts had children.

Just her luck the one she met was as handsome as the devil and had a smile twice as sinful. "I know where it is."

18

"Yeah?" He wiggled his fingers until she gave in and shook his hand. "And you are?"

"Serafina Noland." She slid her hand out of his and curled her fingers around the sparks shooting through her. God, she needed to get out more if the handshake of a barely-legal man rattled her. "Sera to non-stalkers."

"So, Sera of the Nolands from an unknown place. Need help putting on sunscreen?"

"Does this have anything to do with why you're sitting next to me?"

"It's more of a tit for tat thing. You don't want a sunburn, do you?"

"Uh-huh." She bit her tongue, holding in the less polite responses building up in her mouth. "I'm not stupid."

"Never said you were," he said mildly. "Doesn't mean you don't need help, and I don't believe that line about the husband. Come on. Take off your sundress and let me help you."

He had a point. Sort of. It was hard for a person on her own to apply sunblock to those hard to reach areas. After a lengthy debate, she'd come to the conclusion that she'd simply have to limit her full-body exposure to the sun to a few minutes a day and use sunblock to cover areas she could reach the rest of the time. He was giving her a way out of that predicament, though she didn't trust his motives, not for a New York minute.

"What's the catch?" she asked.

"Tit for tat." His grin was unrepentant and just a tad rakish. "I do you, you do me."

Her eyes drifted down his pale skin, over the freckles sprinkled lightly across his shoulders and the well-defined muscles of his arms and back. It would be no hardship to touch him, none at all, and absolutely not horrible to have those strong, slender hands caressing her back.

And she *was* on vacation. A woman deserved a little treat every once in a while, didn't she?

She closed her eyes against her own neediness. Lordy, she was easy, and she was probably playing right into his hands.

She opened her eyes and pinned him with a stern glare. "No funny business," she said in her firmest mommy voice. "I mean it."

His whiskey eyes went hot. "Mmm. Can't promise that."

"Try."

She rose to her knees and pulled her sundress off over her head, folding it before stuffing it into her beach bag and snagging her sunscreen. A flush heated her cheeks. Here she was not even a full day into her trip, and already some strange man had talked her out of her clothes. A really hot stranger and one her family likely knew, given who he probably was, but still. She should be ashamed.

Strangely, it was the one emotion not running through her as she switched places with Levi, giving up her place on the towel so she could kneel behind him. Breathless anticipation mingled with the first glimmer of desire low in her gut and her hands trembled as she squirted sunscreen into them. She rubbed them together, trying to control the sheer need racing through her. Maybe she could try treating him like Petey. Yes, that's what she'd do. If she thought of Levi as a really large friend of her son, it wouldn't be so hard to touch him.

She exhaled a shaky breath. Right. Because the sexy man in front of her resembled a scrawny seven year old.

Not so much.

She rubbed sunscreen gently over the tops of his ears, then ran her fingers behind them and down the sturdy column of his neck, across the firm planes of his shoulder blades, using long sweeps of her hand and a lighter touch down the length of his spine. More sunscreen in her palms before she covered his ribs, applying it as close to the sensitive area around his armpits as she dared. He never flinched, even when her fingers tickled lightly along the skin there.

She ignored the smooth feel of his skin, the play of muscle and sinew against bone, and kept her strokes brisk and impersonal.

As an afterthought, she inched the waistband of his trunks down and quickly applied the protective lotion to the area around his hips where his shorts rode down while he jogged.

His wide shoulders lifted on a silent sigh. "Go a little lower."

The words were husky and low, and a tendril of heat wound through her.

"Forget it." The words came out breathy and a tad too needy for her peace of mind. She scowled at his back. Drat him for being so sexy. "It's bad enough I'm doing this at all."

"I like it." He peered at her over his shoulder, his gaze warm and heavy. "Wouldn't mind if you went a little slower."

Of course, he wouldn't. He was a man, wasn't he?

She tackled the tops of his long arms, admiring the definition and feel of his hard muscles under her fingers, and puzzled over the tattoo on his upper left arm, a harp of some kind with musical notes dotted artfully around it "What's this?"

"A tattoo."

"Wise guy." She traced the symbol, pressing the tip of her finger lightly to each note. "What does it mean?"

"It's a rite of passage, a mark of my lineage." He caught her finger and held it against his arm. "My mother is a musician."

"So you got a tattoo of a harp thingy." She tilted her head, considering him. "I always heard the folks in Tellowee were odd."

"Not odd, just different."

Different was one way to put it, but not the word she'd usually heard used for that bunch.

She let it go. It was none of her business how other folks chose to live their lives.

"I'm done back here." She tugged her hand gently out of his grasp, rubbed her fingers against her bathing suit, and completely failed to eradicate the tingly heat left behind by his touch. "Want me to do your face?"

"Yeah." He unfolded his long body, spreading his legs wide, and patted the space he'd made with one hand. "Come on, Sera. Don't be shy."

"I'm not shy," she said, and crossed her fingers, negating the lie. "That's not exactly an appropriate place for me to sit."

His rakish grin flashed. "Sera, honey, I'd love to show you inappropriate."

The irreverent statement sparked a bubbling laugh and, oddly enough, put her at ease. "I bet."

"Come on. I won't bite."

Against her better judgment, she knelt between his legs with her knees primly closed, uncomfortably aware of his thighs bracketing hers, the brush of his swim trunks against her bare skin, and the bump of his dormant sex underneath the cloth.

He leaned back on his hands and closed his eyes. She stroked

21

sunscreen lightly over his face, unconsciously memorizing the curves and hollows of his strong features. Her hands drifted to his throat, and his eyes slid open, watching her with an unnerving intensity as she covered the area around his collarbone and shoulders.

She eased back, and his left hand shot out, catching her right one in a gentle grip, easily halting her withdrawal. "Finish me."

She sucked in an uneven breath. "That's a bad idea."

"Why?"

"Ah." Her eyes dropped to the juncture of his thighs, where his sex lay as dormant as it had been before she'd started. Disappointment shot through her. He was completely unaffected by her touch. *Silly Sera*, she chided. *Like he could possibly be aroused by you.*

His utter lack of interest tweaked her ego. For just a moment, hurt flickered through her. This attractive young man had absolutely no interest in her, and that stung.

She shook the hurt away. It wasn't like she *wanted* him to be interested, was it? And since he wasn't, there was no need to be afraid of him or how he might react, no need to fear that things might get out of control. Tension bled from her shoulders and she relaxed. It really *was* like being around Petey's friends. To them, she was just another nagging mom. To Levi, she must be just another woman in an endless string.

She reached around him for the sunscreen and squirted more into her palm, warming it between her hands, then resumed her exploration. His pectorals were firm under her palms, his nipples taut nubs as she brushed across them, taking her time now that she knew he didn't care. Why not please herself a little, show appreciation for his well-built body? There was no harm in that, was there? And surely he'd tell her if she hurt him or if he wanted her to stop.

As her fingers smoothed over his skin, a heated ache settled into her groin and she shifted restlessly. Too bad touching him bothered her. Darned if she'd show it, though.

Talk. That's what she needed. She poured out a dab more sunscreen and swiped her fingertips slowly over his sternum and abs, lingering longer than she should've. "What do you do when you're not stalking strange women?"

He hesitated for so long, she thought he might've gone to sleep. "This and that," he said at last.

She laughed lightly, and his stomach muscles clenched beneath her fingers. She gentled her touch, sliding her hands over him in long, slow strokes. "That's nice and vague."

"It's true enough." He dropped back to his elbows. "I work for Nana, go where I'm needed, filling in or taking over if I have to. Sometimes, I take outside jobs, but usually I'm too busy for that."

Her fingers skimmed along his bellybutton and lower, tracing the line of his waistband, testing the slender line of ginger hair angling downward. It was crisp and silky at the same time. She rubbed a thumb over it, tempted to follow it underneath his trunks. Which was bad. Bad, bad, bad. Her eyes followed the line anyway and widened. His sex, dormant moments before, wasn't anymore. An erection pushed against the thin material of his swimming trunks, firm and long and completely undeniable.

Sera sat back on her haunches and jerked her eyes up to his. "All done."

He shook his head slowly. "A little lower."

Heat rippled through her, strong and insistent, and the muscles of her thighs tightened. She bit her lip and kept her gaze firmly on his. "Levi, really."

"I want your hands there." She snorted, and he sat up and bent his legs at her sides, curling his hands around the backs of his thighs, holding himself upright. "You thought I wasn't getting worked up."

"It's ok. I mean, I didn't expect you to..."

She clamped her lips together. Some things didn't need to be said, how a man like him couldn't possibly be interested in a woman like her, and how hard it had been not to give in to temptation. How hard it was to ignore a man as attractive as him when he'd spread himself out in front of her like a tasty buffet, waiting to be sampled.

"React," she finished lamely.

He breathed out a laugh. "Any other time and I'd take your hand and show you what you do to me."

"But you weren't, ah." Her eyes dropped to the rigid length of his sex and her fingers curled in her lap. He was so beautiful, so deliciously real. What she wouldn't give to touch him there, but she couldn't, no matter how tempted she was. "Before, you weren't," she breathed.

"I was reciting Virgil's *Aeneid* in Latin," he said, his grin wry. "Otherwise, it would've taken a lot longer, but yeah, I'd have still gotten hard."

"Sorry," she said faintly. "I had no idea."

"That's what happens when a woman touches a man, Sera."

"I know that." Boy, did she ever, and she had the kid to prove it. Speaking of. "I should give you some space."

"Damage done." He held out a hand. "My turn." She hesitated, and his mouth firmed into an uncompromising line. "Don't even think about backing out."

"Wouldn't dream of it," she murmured, and put her back to him, facing the ocean. He tugged on the strings holding her bathing suit together, and she twisted around, eyes narrowed at him over her shoulder. "What are you doing?"

"It's in the way. I'll tie it back later."

She turned back around, choosing to believe him when she really shouldn't. Here she was letting a strange man touch her, a strange gorgeous man with bright hair and a sensuous mouth and sexy tufts of ginger hair under his arms and scattered across his body.

Candi would be so jealous.

His hands cupped her shoulders. Sera closed her eyes and relaxed under his light touch. He slowly worked sunscreen into her skin, exploring her body more thoroughly than she had his. His thumbs skimmed along her spine, his fingers brushed her ribs. Unlike her, he didn't hesitate to delve under her suit, stopping well shy of touching her intimately. Need tangled through her anyway, pooling between her legs, hardening her nipples into tight, sensitive nubs.

He tied the strings around her back together. "Turn around."

She did without hesitation, scooting around to face him, and was surprised to find him kneeling with his knees spread wide, his arousal clearly visible through the thin material of his swimming trunks. He grasped her right arm between his hands, coating it with sunscreen from shoulder to fingertips in slow, methodical strokes, then did the same with her left one. It should've been impersonal, the way he touched her, the way he looked at her with his expression a blank mask. His hands skimmed up her arms and his thumbs stroked under the edge of her bathing suit, teasing the tops of her breasts, and the impression she got from the way he touched her was a far cry from impersonal.

"That's probably good," she said. "I can..."

His hand slipped around the nape of her neck, startling her into silence. "I want to do this when we're alone and I can touch you all over for as long as you'll let me."

Her breath left her in a rush. "I don't... We just met."

"I know. That's why I'll settle for a date."

"A date?" she said, and was appalled at the girlish squeak in her voice. "With me?"

He laughed gently and his breath feathered over her skin. "Yes, with you. I'll take you anywhere you wanna go. Just say you'll be with me."

"Wait, no." She shook her head and it jogged her memory, dampening the heat he'd built as easily as if he'd thrown cold water on her. "You're just trying to win a dare."

"Already did," he said bluntly. "And lost it, too."

"What?" She shook her head again, trying to dispel the confusion. "How can you win and lose at the same time?"

"Heath thought you'd chase me off before five minutes were up. Colin bet I couldn't get you to touch me willingly." His expression shuttered abruptly. "Jordan said I couldn't make it without getting hard. Win, win, lose."

"Oh." A grin fought its way out. "That's kind of juvenile."

He shrugged. "We're guys. What do you expect?"

He had her there. "Sorry I broke your concentration."

"It would've happened sooner or later. If you'd touched my back the way you touched my stomach..."

Heat crept into her cheeks. "I thought I was hurting you."

"In the best way possible."

Her eyes slid closed on a wave of mortification. She forced them open and met his gaze evenly. "I had no idea you liked it, not, you know, like that."

"You don't know men very well, then. Any man in his right mind would crawl over hot coals to have your hands there." His thumb stroked over her pulse and his eyes dropped to her mouth.

"Go out with me tonight."

He was thinking about kissing her. Even as long as she'd been out of the game, she could see that. Worse, she wanted him to kiss her, wanted to have his mouth claim her the way his hands had, with the slow, easy touch of a man who knew how to please a woman and took his time doing it.

How could a man his age have accumulated that kind of experience?

"How old are you?" she blurted out.

"Twenty-two. Does it matter?"

The hand of regret squeezed tight around her heart. He was so young, so very, very young. "I need to think about it."

He released her nape, rolled back on his heels, and pushed himself into a stand, towering over her. "Don't think too long or I might have to do something inappropriate."

He pivoted away and jogged back to his friends, and she gaped. He wouldn't dare. Would he?

He glanced over his shoulder and raked her body with a hard stare.

Excitement rippled through her and she swallowed it down. Yes, he would. He definitely would.

The idea didn't bother her nearly as much as it should've.

Three

I N BETWEEN HANGING OUT with the guys and playing in the water, Levi spent the rest of the afternoon keeping a casual eye on the lovely Serafina sunbathing on the beach. Her pale skin glistened in the sunlight, a stark contrast to her deep red bathing suit.

He'd bet hard money she thought the one piece suit was modest and sedate, and that she had no idea of her potency.

Her gentle touch, as brief as it'd been, had pushed him shockingly close to the edge of his control, a place he hadn't been since his last broken bone more than a decade before. Even during sex, he only loosened the tight grip he kept on his body, never lost it. No woman had ever pushed him beyond that line, not even close, not until Sera Noland.

The skin below his navel still tingled where she'd touched him. Every time he remembered her kneeling between his legs with her soft hands on him, desire rushed through him, heating his blood and hardening his body. The way she'd looked at him was seared into his mind, as if she'd never touched a man before and now that she'd found out what it was like, never wanted to stop.

His grip tightened on the chilled bottle of water in his hand. What would it take for her to look at him like that again?

Ruby jogged over, her wispy blonde ponytail swinging with each step. She'd been shopping for the past two days and had missed his interludes with Sera. Otherwise, she would've already ragged him about the *mundane mortal* that had caught his eye.

"Hey, cuz," she said. "We're heading in to get ready for supper. You coming?"

He shrugged and dug a toe into the sand. "Got plans."

She followed his gaze and frowned. "Does Nana know about her?"

"Does Nana know about Jordan?" He allowed his mouth to curl into a snarky smile. "How about Jordan's mum?"

Her scowl deepened. "You wouldn't dare."

"Try me." He sipped his water, savoring its chill as it slid down his throat. "You know any Nolands back home?"

"Wendell Noland. He owns a construction company, one of the few that made it through the recession without tanking. Why?"

"He have a daughter, say, twenty-five to thirty?"

"Yeah, I think he does." She nodded toward Sera. "That her?"

"Maybe. You know anything about this Noland's daughter?"

"Writes romance novels, has a son. Single parent, as a matter of fact." Ruby's storm cloud gray eyes fixed on him. "I'm trying to remember the last time you showed this much interest in a woman."

Probably never. "It's no biggie."

"Yeah, sure." She tucked her arm through his elbow and rested her head on his shoulder. "Don't let her hurt you."

A smart remark died on his tongue. "I'll try."

"Wow. You're all serious. Is it *twue wuv*?"

He grinned and elbowed her. "Cut it out, Ruby."

Her wide-eyed innocent look didn't fool him for one minute. He knew his cousin. She worried at a problem until it broke apart under her sledgehammer-like attention. He could almost hear the gears in her brain turning as she tried to figure out how to either keep him away from Sera or make sure Sera fell head over heels for him.

Which one depended entirely on how much Ruby wanted to stay in Nana's good graces.

Sera sat up and gathered her things, putting each item into the colorful canvas bag she carried with precise, efficient movements. She stood and shook out her towel, draped it over her arm, and a few moments later walked past, her gaze carefully averted.

"Five thirty," he called.

Her stride hitched and her eyes flicked over him and Ruby, and then she disappeared up the path leading through the barrier dunes.

Ruby clucked her tongue. "I see you've impressed yet another

28

woman. Such a charmer you are."

"She wants me," he said in an easy tone, and mustered a grin he didn't quite feel.

"Uh-huh. You sure you don't want to eat with us?"

"Positive." He brushed a kiss over her cheek. "Later, cuz."

He jogged after Sera, heading toward the suite he shared with Jordan. So she needed a little convincing. He didn't mind. Something good would come from knowing her. He could feel it in his gut, or maybe that was the aftereffects of her touch. Either way, he was game.

Half an hour later, he'd showered and shaved and changed into a brown and green plaid shirt, khakis, and matching dress shoes. A few minutes more put him in front of her door, knocking firmly. She opened it, and he bit back a sigh. She'd pulled her yellow sundress over her bathing suit and that was as dressed as she'd managed to get since walking off the beach.

"You're not ready," he said.

Her gaze met his head on. "I never said I'd go."

He leaned a shoulder against the door frame. "Mind telling me why?"

"As a matter of fact, I do."

He stifled a grin. She was using her mum voice. If she knew how hot it made him, she'd never use it again. "Let me guess. I'm too young, you're not interested in a fling, you don't have time for a man. Which one?"

She relaxed against the door, her lips curving into a smile. "All of the above."

"So think of me as a friend. You're Wendell Noland's daughter, right?"

"You've been stalking me again."

She sounded more exasperated than worried, so he shrugged. "My cousin Ruby told me." She raised an eyebrow, and he added, "The woman I was standing with on the beach."

"That gorgeous, hard-bodied blonde was your cousin?"

"Don't tell her that. It'll give her the big head."

"Must run in the family," she muttered.

He ignored her. "Your dad does a lot of work for Nana, has for a long time."

"Small world. And?"

"What kind of man would I be if I let the daughter of an old family friend eat alone?"

She eyed him, her smile growing wider by the second. "You're going to keep talking until I go out with you, aren't you?"

"Planned on it, yeah."

"Do you always get your way?"

"When it's important." He slid a finger down her cheek, and her beautiful eyes went dreamy. Triumph surged through him. "Say yes."

She sighed and opened the door wide. "I must be out of my mind."

No, but she would be, as soon as he could get his hands on her. After that, all bets were off.

WHEN SERA EXITED her bedroom, Levi was sitting on the upholstered sofa reading her Kindle, exactly where she'd left him when she'd gone in to shower and dress.

He'd insisted on reading one of her novels while he waited and it had worried her the whole time she'd been getting ready. What would he think of them? Would he like the romance? Hate the sex?

No, scratch that. He was a man. Of course he'd love the sex.

Why she cared what a man she barely knew thought of her work escaped her, but there it was. She did care and shouldn't, was nervous over the evening ahead, couldn't seem to help it, and should never have indulged Levi when he'd stood at her front door looking so handsome and sexy and mature that she'd given in.

Damn her greedy hide. She wanted to spend time with him, wanted him to make her feel the way he had on the beach, as if she were beautiful and desirable and attractive. What woman wouldn't, especially when the man doing it was Levi?

As soon as the bedroom door snicked shut, he closed her Kindle and put it away, and did a flattering double-take at her outfit, a clingy black halter dress that hugged her body to mid-thigh. She'd paired it with strappy black heels and piled her hair on top of her head, showing off the dangly silver earrings she'd slipped on.

He rose slowly and tucked his hands into the pockets of his slacks. "Turn around."

"Why?"

"Just do it."

She rolled her eyes and turned in a circle as quickly as she could without breaking her ankle. By the time she faced him again, he'd crossed the room and stood next to her.

"Slower," he said, his low, husky voice shivering across her skin. "Please."

Her cheeks heated as she turned again, slower this time, and though he kept his hands in his pockets, his gaze burned across her skin wherever it landed on her. When she'd made it all the way around, he slid his hand down her arm, caught her hand, and lifted it to his mouth, pressing his lips lightly against the back of her hand, then her palm.

His eyes were hot, his slow smile promising, and her knees trembled. Holy cow, he was potent.

"You need a wrap," he said. "Nights on the ocean can get chilly."

"Um." She stared at him blankly. He'd said something, hadn't he, but whatever it was, it had been drowned out by the ripples of heat running through her, by the gentle skid of his skin along hers. His lips twitched into an almost familiar smirk, and she blushed. God, she had to get herself together. "Right. A wrap. Just a sec."

She snagged a sweater and a clutch with a wrist strap, tucked her wallet and lip gloss inside, and followed him out of the apartment, locking the door tight behind them. He placed his hand low on her back, a polite gesture that somehow became *more* when Levi did it. His fingers grazed her suddenly sensitive skin, leaving a trail of heat behind.

He helped her into a shiny white Jeep Rubicon with Georgia plates. "Ruby's," he explained. "I left my car in Tellowee and rode out with Jordan."

"Jordan?"

"One of the guys I'm here with. Couple inches shorter than me, tanned, short brown hair?" He shut her door, slid behind the wheel, and cranked the Jeep. "Stick around. You'll meet him."

He drove competently and carefully, seemingly aware of

everything going on around them, and took her to a nearby restaurant. Once seated, she studied him from behind the cover of the menu. Fully dressed, he seemed so mature, much less like the irresponsible, fun-loving kid she'd taken him for and more like the man he so obviously was. Young, yes, but polite, charming, thoughtful.

And very, very yummy.

After a waitress came by and took their orders, Sera said, "Where are you really from?"

"Tellowee."

She arched a single eyebrow.

"Really. Before that, Scotland, where Da was born."

"I know your dad." She fidgeted with the hem of her dress. "He works on my car."

"Does he now? Small world, eh?"

Wasn't it, though. "How did your mom end up in Scotland?"

"She travelled for a while there, met him, fell in love."

"She was a musician then?"

His mouth curled into a smile. "You remembered."

"Your tattoo. It's..." *Sexy. Mouth watering. Hunkdillyicious.* "Distinctive."

His smile widened. "That's not what you were gonna say."

"It's all you're getting," she said tartly. "You were born in Scotland?"

"Yeah." He sat back in his chair and threaded his fingers together in his lap. "Ran wild there until I was about six, then my parents moved here."

"Do you miss it?"

"We go back, visit my grandparents, Da's family. What about you?"

"I wasn't raised in Scotland." His steady, even stare unnerved her, and she relented. "Georgia peach, born and bred. Lived in the same house my whole life until I went to college, and then came back to the mountains to raise my son."

"You didn't bring him with you?"

"Not this time. He's in Orlando with my folks."

"Walt Disney World or Universal Studios?"

"Disney. Probably getting sick on roller coasters, though he swore he wasn't when I talked to him this afternoon."

Their dinner arrived, shrimp scampi and a salad for her, a medium rare rib eye with broccoli and a baked sweet potato for him. They ate without speaking for a while, surrounded by the noise of diners coming and going, and the restaurant's staff sliding through the nearly full room serving guests. After a while, she relaxed, allowing him to draw her into a light conversation about their favorite books. He was surprisingly well-read in everything from Shakespeare and Arthur Miller to modern genre fiction.

At one point, he leaned forward and said quietly, "You keep looking at me like you're surprised I have any depth. That's gonna get old really quick, Sera."

She flushed and glanced away. "I don't know what you're talking about."

"Right. Let's get this straightened out now so it won't be a problem later, ok? I was raised to be an educated gentleman and a responsible one. I have a degree in finance, a healthy investment portfolio, and enough work to keep me busy." He covered her hand and squeezed gently, waiting until she met his gaze before continuing. "I'm a man, not a kid, with a man's appetites and the maturity to handle a relationship, if that's what I want."

"I didn't think you weren't."

His expression hardened abruptly. "Don't ever lie to me."

"Ok, you're right. I do think of you as a kid, and I'm sorry for that." Her hand twitched under his. She curled her fingers into a fist against the temptation to turn her hand over and meet his palm to palm. "You're a lot younger than me and it's a little unnerving."

"Age isn't important. Trust me. I know a lot of couples who have stable, loving relationships where the woman is much, much older than her mate."

"Is that what you're looking for here, a stable relationship?"

A rakish grin lightened his expression. "I'm looking for a healthy flirt with a good woman."

A laugh bubbled up and over, filling the air between them. "Honestly, Levi. How can I take you seriously when you say things like that?"

"You want me to lie?" He shook his head as if to say, *Not gonna happen.* "If it leads to more, I'm open, but if not, we've had

33

fun, yeah?"

She tilted her head, considered the casual honesty. "I have a feeling you were a handful when you were young."

"I'm still a handful." His whiskey eyes glimmered as his thumb brushed across the skin of her hand, stirring an answering warmth within her. "Stick around long enough and you'll learn how to handle me."

LATER, AFTER a sinfully delicious chocolate pound cake topped with fresh strawberries, Levi drove Sera back to her apartment and coaxed her into a walk on the beach. The sun had dropped below the horizon while they were at dinner, leaving a full moon and a star-bright sky to light their path. A breeze blew in from the ocean, cool in spite of the humidity. Sera shivered and pulled her sweater on, glad Levi had reminded her to bring it.

He took off his shoes and socks and rolled up his slacks, then unbuckled her shoes and slid them off her feet. She held his with one hand and rested the other on his shoulder for balance. His hands were slow and gentle and warm on her ankles, lingering longer than was polite, though they never strayed higher than her calves. That didn't keep her from thinking about it. For once, she couldn't find the energy to chastise herself for wanting his touch. After the blunt set down he'd delivered over their meal, she wasn't sure if she *should* be wary of him.

She glanced at him out of the corner of her eye as they strolled hand in hand down the beach. It was such a sweet gesture, as if he'd known exactly what to do to undermine her defenses, to please her.

To treat her like a woman.

A man's appetites. A shiver raced through her, accompanied by a vision of his bare chest, the rich smoothness of his skin beneath her fingers, the erection pushing against the fabric of his swimming trunks.

She'd expected a token dinner and a full-court press for sex. He'd given her a mostly healthy meal, good conversation, and a romantic walk along the beach under a shining moon.

If he were a little older, she'd already be half in love with him.

His hand tightened on hers, pulling her around a clump of

seaweed. "Careful."

"Thanks."

"Seemed like you were miles away."

"I was daydreaming. Gets me in trouble sometimes," she said, laughing.

"Is that why you write?"

"I write because it allows me to support my son, and because I enjoy it." She turned her gaze to the beach, memorizing the feel of the sand beneath her bare feet, the warmth of his hand holding hers. "When I went to college, I had this dream of going off to the city and landing a job with a major newspaper, working my way up through the ranks, becoming a household name."

"You're a household name now, I bet. Think my mum reads your books."

"Does she?" Pleasure fluttered through her. There was nothing like hearing that someone enjoyed your work. "Good to know."

"So instead of becoming a hotshot journalist you became a hotshot author."

"Not overnight, no. I started out as a journalist back home with the local paper. They were the only ones who'd take me fresh out of college and..." She bit back the word *pregnant* and rushed on. "Anyway, in my spare time when Petey was young..."

"Your son?"

The carefully casual interest behind the question was hard to miss. She tucked it away for later thought. "Yes. When he was young, I'd write for an hour or two at night after he went to bed. Pretty soon I had a whole drawer full of manuscripts. I thought about finding an agent, but something always held me back. It was never the right time, the stories weren't ready, I didn't have the energy to deal with it."

"What made you change your mind?"

"The e-reader boom. Long story short, when I realized how popular they were becoming and how easy it was to self-publish, I polished a handful of manuscripts and published them all at once."

"And now you do it full time."

"While Petey's at school. It's really been a godsend."

"I bet." He nodded toward the pier, still a good distance away. "Turn around now or up there?"

"Oh, wow." She glanced behind them, judging the distance they'd walked. "I didn't realize we'd come so far."

The corners of his mouth tilted into a sly smile. "Good company."

She squeezed his hand. "Yes. Sorry for babbling like that."

"You weren't. Besides, I was curious."

They turned and headed back, and strolled in comfortable silence for a few minutes. Sera gathered the courage to be as openly curious as he'd been. "What was it like, growing up in Scotland?"

"Wild. I loved it. My grandparents have a farm there. Sheep, though I never had much to do with them. Mostly, my parents set me loose in the countryside, let me run as I pleased as soon as I was old enough to leave the house on my own."

"And then you came here?"

"For school, in Tellowee. Nana wanted to spend time with me."

"Nana?"

"My great-grandmother, the matriarch of my mother's family. Hawthorne?"

Sera shook her head. "I've never met her."

"Be glad. She's a tough woman."

"But you love her."

"I do. There's no one like her, thank the Goddess, but I wouldn't give her up, even when she meddles."

The exasperation underlying his words tickled her. "She does that a lot?"

"Whether we want her to or not. You'll like her, though. She's a writer, too."

Maybe she would, but it was a moot point. Sera's time with Levi would end as soon as she left Kill Devil Hills, if not before, and she'd never meet his great-grandmother unless they ran into each other back home.

When their walk ended, he insisted on carrying her across the pavement to save her shoes from the sand on her feet, though he was barefoot himself. He lifted her into his arms so effortlessly, her breath caught in her throat. She held still in his embrace as he walked, pressed against the hard breadth of his chest, surrounded by his clean, spicy scent, and reveled in the way he made her feel. Safe, protected. As if he'd never let her fall.

He set her down on the stairs leading to her apartment and tugged her around until they were face to face. His gaze met hers, that whiskey warm gaze, so serious now. The intent she read there shuddered through her, raising a wave of heat that slid down her spine and pricked every nerve in her body into awareness. He slid a hand around the nape of her neck, rested the other on her hip, and lowered his head, brushing his lips across hers once, twice.

The teasing touches stole her breath, and she yearned. "Levi."

He touched his forehead to hers and drew her closer, melding her to his hard form. "Don't say no."

How could she when she wanted his kiss so badly?

"I'm saying yes," she said, and then his mouth was on hers, tasting her, taking her with a thoroughness that pushed her into achy need. It raked across her nerves, settled low in her gut. She kissed him back and, emboldened by his hands tightening against her flesh, darted her tongue out, tasting the firm curve of his lower lip, and moaned when he flicked his tongue against hers and nipped gently at her lips with sharp teeth.

It was heaven, the way he touched her, slowly, like a man who had all the time in the world and nothing more he wanted to do. His mouth claimed hers with a barely restrained ferocity, ratcheting the need ever higher. It burned through her, taking her breath and her reason and leaving her with nothing but the hard press of his body, the warm strength of his touch, and the stars shining down above them.

He gentled the kiss, sucked lightly on her lower lip, buried his face in her throat while his quietly panted breaths blew across her pulse. "I've wanted to do that all day."

She tried to laugh, tried to gather the thoughts that had scattered in the wake of his touch, tried to find herself in the desire consuming her inside and out.

"Come on." His lips skimmed her throat, a final slide of gentle heat. He drew back and slipped his hand into hers. "I'll walk you up."

She pivoted on shaky legs, leaning into him as much for balance as for his touch. At her door, she pulled out her keys with hands trembling from tiny aftershocks of Levi. He took them from her gently and unlocked the door.

"Do you..." She inhaled a steadying breath and met his gaze over her shoulder. "Do you want to come in?"

"Sera, love, if I come in, I'm not leaving until morning." He slid a finger down her spine over her sweater and kept going, cupping her bottom through the thin fabric of her dress. "Are you ready for that?"

Yes, she thought, and then, *No.* She dropped her forehead to the door. Its coolness seeped into her reasonless brain and did not a thing to steady her.

"That's what I thought." His hand skimmed up her hip and curved around her stomach, pulling her back against him. "How long are you staying?"

She stifled a groan. His body was so hard behind her. The skin-warmed fabric of his clothing brushed gently along her skin, a stark contrast to the rigid length of his erection pressing into her lower back. "Until Friday."

"Spend the week with me."

"I have plans."

"Change them."

"I can't..." His mouth found her throat and, God help her, she angled her head, giving him better access. The slow slide of his lips created delicious tingles along her skin, and she bit back a moan. "Wednesday, I have a book signing."

"What are you doing tomorrow?"

"Roanoke." She grabbed hold of the destination with a desperation born of need. "Cape Hatteras on Tuesday. You can come, if you want."

"Me and the guys and Ruby are taking a boat down on Thursday to see the lighthouse. You should come with us instead, do something else with me on Tuesday." He rested his chin on the top of her head and sighed. "Wouldn't mind seeing Roanoke with you tomorrow, if we can do it in the morning."

"Yes." *Anything.* She bit her lip against the thought and gathered her practical nature back from the four winds where it had taken a nice vacation during Levi's kiss. "Can we play the rest by ear?"

His hands tightened on her skin. "That sounds like a no."

"It's a firm maybe."

He laughed. "Is that what you tell Petey?"

A smile curved her own lips upward. "When he's really persistent."

"I bet you're a good mum." He tugged her around, putting them face to face. "What time tomorrow?"

"After your run?"

"Weights tomorrow, upper body. There's a gym in the building, if you wanna use it."

"Are you trying to tell me something?"

"No, absolutely not." He squeezed her hips, digging his fingers gently into her skin through the knit material of her dress. "I love your body. It's soft and ripe and beautiful, and begging to be touched."

"Oh. Well." Her heart thumped in her chest. That was *not* what she'd been expecting. "Um."

"Serafina Noland, romance author, at a loss for words." His mouth quirked into a half smile, softening his expression. "Eight o'clock too early?"

She shook her head, remembered the shoes she still held. "Here. Sorry."

He took them from her, dropped them to the ground. "One more?"

"God, yes," she said, and lost herself in his kiss.

Four

AT 7:59 THE NEXT MORNING, Levi knocked on Sera's door, and knocked. Her car was still in the parking lot. Maybe she'd taken a walk or gone to the communal laundry room. He rolled the tension out of his shoulders and knocked again. So help him, if she'd changed her mind again...

The door opened on a yawning Sera, dressed in a white man-sized t-shirt and barely visible underwear, her curly, sable hair disheveled.

His stomach muscles clenched and the desire he'd barely banked the night before roared back to life in a mad clamor of heat and need.

"Levi, what're you..." She smothered another yawn, shook her head. "Sorry. What're you doing here?"

"It's eight o'clock." With a great deal more effort than it should've taken, he dragged his eyes away from the sway of her loose breasts under her t-shirt and met her sleepy gaze. "We're going to Roanoke, remember?"

"We are?" Her eyes went wide and she slapped her hands over her mouth, dropping them to say, "We are. Oh, crap."

A flush heated her cheeks. She whirled and raced through the apartment past the coffee table where her laptop sat among scattered pages of a manuscript and an open spiral-bound notebook. He stepped inside and shut the door behind himself, admiring her nearly-nude curves as he followed her into her bedroom.

He leaned against the frame of the bedroom's door while she yanked open drawers and pulled out shorts, a tank top, and clean underpants.

Bikinis, pale pink with a wide lace band at the waist.

"I'm so sorry. Won't be long." She dropped the clothes on her bed and started lifting her t-shirt, then released the hem and shoved him out. "God, you've got me so rattled. Go read or something."

"Yes, ma'am," he said, smirking, and let her push him out of her bedroom.

When she'd shut the door on him, he rubbed a finger across his lower lip, savoring the tantalizing glimpse of flesh he'd caught. His eyes slid shut. He'd woken her, pulled her out of sleep, and been rewarded with her fresh from bed, her hair down, her full breasts unbound.

By the end of the day, he'd have his hands there, cupped around her firm flesh, teasing her nipples into hard little peaks.

By the end of the week, he intended to have all of her, maybe even to wake up beside her, but for today, touching her would be enough.

He'd gone to bed the night before with her taste lingering in his mouth, with the feel of her sweet curves imprinted onto his flesh and into his mind. If he'd had the slightest hint she was ready for more, he would've taken her then, but she wasn't, not even close. He was content to wait until she felt comfortable with him, for a while, anyhow. He had the patience to tease her out of her shell, to bring out the woman that had kissed him so passionately his control had wavered enough to push her for another taste, another touch.

She'd gone willingly down that path again, opening for him like a rare, night-blooming flower, too shy to seek the light of day, and her touch had stripped him of his strength and sense.

He dropped onto the sofa and rummaged through her manuscript, careful to put the pages back precisely where they'd been when he'd finished reading them. The process behind revising the story fascinated him, evident in the scribbles and notes she'd left on the printed draft and in the notebook. By the time she came out of her bedroom wearing the tank top and shorts she'd picked out, he'd developed a healthy respect for her mind and the stories she created.

And was wise enough to have her Kindle in hand so she'd never suspect he'd sifted through her work without permission.

"Sorry about that." She dropped a gauzy long-sleeved shirt onto the couch beside him and bent over the coffee table, straightening her work. "After you left last night, I had a great idea for the story I'm working on and stayed up too late developing it. Forgot to set my alarm."

"There's no rush." He cut off the Kindle and set it on the coffee table, snaked out a hand and caught her wrist in a gentle grip. "Come greet me proper like."

Her eyes fell to his mouth and her breath shallowed. "I, um. Levi."

He grinned and reeled her in, drawing her carefully into the cradle of his thighs as he scooted to the edge of the sofa. She rested her hands on his shoulders and looked down at him with a gentle smile curving her lips.

"Good morning," he said.

"You pulled me over here for that?"

He wrapped his hands around the backs of her thighs below the rolled edges of her shorts. Her skin was soft, smooth, warm from her shower, and smelled subtly of almonds. "I pulled you over here to get my hands on you."

She pressed her lips into a disapproving line, though her silver eyes sparkled. "You're incorrigible."

"What can I say? I need a firm hand." He squeezed her thighs lightly, skimmed his hands over her hips, resting them on her waist. "Wouldn't mind a kiss, if you have one to spare."

"I bet." She stepped closer and wound her arms around his neck. "What is it about you?" she murmured, and then her mouth met his, a light, teasing dance of her lips against his. Her tongue darted out, testing the seam of his lips, and he opened for her, savoring the quick licks and rubs of her tongue. Heat surged through him, primal, raw. He willed his hands to stay where they were, reined in the need with a tight grip.

She stroked her nails through his hair and slid a hand down his back, and his control fractured. He clamped down on it, hard. Patience. He really needed to find his patience.

She nibbled her way out of the kiss and touched her forehead to his. "I think I'm awake now."

"Glad to help." Really, *really* glad, so glad he had to tamp down on the need still writhing within him before it raced out of control.

"Ready?"

He fed her breakfast at a nearby fast food restaurant, then spent the morning exploring the remnants of the lost colony of Roanoke and the nearby Elizabethan gardens with her.

She seemed to absorb even the tiniest detail of the Roanoke exhibits, *oohed* and *ahed* over displays of artifacts, and collected enough brochures and souvenirs to weigh down a small pack elephant. As they walked through the nearby formal gardens, she took picture after picture and bounced along the pathways with the exuberance of a child at the circus. Her cheeks flushed and her eyes shone, and her fingers threaded through his with an ease that comforted as often as it surprised.

They caught a quick lunch before she drove them back. She parked near Ruby's Jeep and twisted toward him in her seat, happiness beaming out of her like a light flashing through the deepest dark. "Thanks for letting me drag you around."

"Thanks for letting me tag along. It was fun."

"Well." She blew out a breath and tapped a finger on the steering wheel. "Maybe I'll see you later?"

"Maybe you'll see me now."

She glanced at him from beneath lowered lashes. "I thought you had plans."

"Me and the guys and Ruby have commandeered the pool for the afternoon, closed it off to strangers. We can only do it once, though." He tugged on a curl that had escaped her ponytail. "We'll hang out by the pool, maybe throw something on the grill later. Have a bonfire in the fire pit once the sun goes down. It'll be fun."

Her hands tightened on the steering wheel and she glanced away. "Maybe your friends won't want me horning in."

"They'll get over it," he said easily. "And they've probably already picked up women of their own by now, so..."

"I'm not your woman," she said primly, and he grinned.

"You will be." He tugged at the curl, ran a finger down her throat. She shuddered under his touch, and he bit back a grin. She gave herself away, every single time. "Come on, Sera. What do you have to lose?"

"My sanity," she retorted. She opened her door and yanked her purse out behind her. "My dignity. My self respect."

He got out and closed his door, smirking at her across the roof of her car. "Hey, don't hold back."

She paused with her hand on the car door. "Does nothing keep you down?"

"Not much," he admitted, though he was beginning to suspect she might be able to. "Coming?"

She shot him a sour look and slammed the car door. "Oh, all right."

Half an hour later, after changing into bathing suits and grabbing beach towels, sunblock, and Sera's Kindle, they headed down to the pool. Heath and Colin were already there, staked out on beach chairs with a cooler full of beer between them, listening to classic rock blasting from a portable radio. Levi introduced them to Sera, then led her to the opposite side of the pool, away from his friends.

Not that he thought Sera would defect, but it was never wise to dangle temptation in front of a woman, not when the temptation was another Son.

She set her things beside a lounge chair and shimmied out of the shorts she'd put on over her bathing suit.

"Do that again," he said.

"Fat chance."

He shrugged. "Had to try. Give me the sunblock."

She paused in the middle of uncapping it. "Why?"

"Why do you think?"

Her eyes went round and she nibbled on her lower lip. He could almost see the memory of the previous day flashing through her mind, of his hands on her skin, of their legs brushing together, of his fingers skimming under her suit, caressing the flesh hidden from the sun.

She slapped the sunblock into his hand and settled herself face down on the lounge chair, offering her back to him. "No funny stuff."

He laughed and earned a stern glare from her. No way was he promising not to try something. Seeing how far she'd let him go was half the fun, though he had no intention of going far at all, not in public.

He started with her legs, smoothing sunblock from her slender ankles over the curve of her calves and up the back of her thighs, brushing his thumbs across the tender folds behind her knees and in the creases under her rear. When she didn't protest, he slid his fingers under her suit, skimming them along the bottom curve of her firm arse and down her inner thighs.

"Watch the hands," she said.

Strike one, he figured, and squirted sunblock into his palm.

He loved the lower curve of her back, the hollow of her spine. Her back was like the rest of her, small but strong. He started under her suit this time with the dimples of her pelvis and moved upward, untying the two bows holding her suit together as he did, leaving her skin open to his touch.

She shifted restlessly on the chair. "What are you doing?"

"I like that dress you wore last night." He spread sunblock over her shoulders, kneading her muscles until she relaxed. "Tan lines will ruin the look."

"No they won't," she grumbled.

"Humor me."

She snorted. "You seem like the kind of man who'll take a mile if I give you an inch."

Well, she had him there. He slid his hands over her arms, spreading the thick, white protective screen over her skin. She pushed herself up so he could protect her face, holding the top of her suit to her chest as she did.

And denying him a glimpse of her beautiful breasts.

Jordan and Ruby exited the building together and plopped into chairs near Heath and Colin.

Levi kissed Sera's nape. "I'll be back in a little while to do your front. Will you be ok?"

"Grown woman." She closed her eyes and rested her head on her folded arms. "Go away."

He stroked the curls she'd piled into a knot on top of her head. "Don't go to sleep."

"Too late," she said, and he laughed, full of the scent of her skin, the feel of it under his hands.

He left her alone for a while, kept a close watch on her, making sure she didn't burn as she dozed under the sharp rays of the coastal sun. Heath pulled out a Frisbee and challenged Colin to a game.

Levi was content to sit on the sidelines sipping a cold beer, soaking in the sun, and listening to his friends rough horseplay.

Sera stirred restlessly in her sleep. He set his beer down and padded across the concrete, sat on the edge of the lounge chair at her hip, and touched her shoulder, keeping her from turning over. He tied the top strings of her suit into a loose bow. "Feel better?"

"Mmm. A little." She shifted onto her side and curled around him, her thighs against his lower back, her torso against his thigh. "Thanks for letting me sleep."

"You seemed to need it. Here, let me do your front."

She shifted again, settled onto her back, and frowned when he undid the top bow of her suit and tucked the strings out of the way. "Why do you keep doing that?"

"I like seeing you in dresses." He dabbed sunblock on her throat, smoothed it along her collarbone, and tamped down the temptation to taste her there. "Maybe a strapless dress next time, a deep blue to bring out the color in your eyes."

"So now you're dressing me."

"No," he said patiently and slid his hands to her chest. "I'm telling you what I like."

His thumbs dipped down her breasts, skimming an inch and a half above her nipples. Close enough to tease, far enough away to satisfy propriety.

Her eyes grew wary. She caught his hand between hers and her chest. "You're kinda grabby. I don't think I like that, especially when we're out in public."

He drew back, stung to the quick, and rose to his full height. "You think I'm grabby."

Her gaze slid from his and her brow furrowed. "Well, yeah, but..."

He slashed a hand through the air, and she fell silent, her beautiful lips clamped around whatever she'd been about to say.

She didn't like his touch, didn't enjoy having his hands on her, didn't want the slow, sensual slide of skin on skin. He'd kept it mild, touching her only where the sun could reach and a little more to make sure she was safe. To tease her, yes, and test her limits, but not much more. He was a man and he wanted her, wanted to feel the sweet curve of her arse under his hands, wanted to taste every inch of her skin and send her soaring as high as she could go.

Apparently, the attraction only went one way. Why had she spent time with him if she didn't feel it, too? Why had she given him the sunblock if she didn't want him to touch her?

What the hell was she doing with him if she didn't want him?

She held her suit to her full breasts and sat up. "Levi, wait."

He leveled a cold, impassive stare at her, unmoved when she flinched away. The day before, she'd accused him of being a child, of playing with her. What had she been doing but toying with his feelings, stringing him along for ends only the Goddess could know? He turned his back on her, as much to quell the raging hurt welling up as to gain distance, and dove into the pool, letting the water soothe him as it always had.

SERA SLUMPED against her chair and slung a forearm across her eyes, blocking out the bright sun and the memory of the hurt that had crossed Levi's face, just before his eyes had gone cold and hard.

Why had she blurted that out?

Damn it, he'd gotten her all stirred up while she was half asleep and her defenses were down. She'd been dreaming of his hands roaming over her body, of having him buried deep inside her, filling her as they made slow, sweet love to the rhythm of the waves beating against the shore. When she'd woken, he'd been there, his touch gentle, insistent, and far too arousing for her comfort. He'd slipped under her guard with his kindness, and she'd repaid him by lashing out.

Why did he have to be the one to make her feel that way, as if he were the only man in the world for her?

A chair squeaked nearby. "He's always had a temper."

Sera lifted her arm away from her eyes. Ruby lay on her back on a lounge chair a few feet away, her eyes closed, her body golden against the scanty lines of her lemon yellow bikini.

Sera tied the top strings of her suit around her neck. She was tired of holding the damn thing up. "I think I hurt his feelings."

"Shouldn't've called him grabby."

"You heard that?"

Ruby's mouth curved into a familiar, snarky smile. "We all

did."

Well, crap. "I didn't mean it."

"Then you shouldn't've said it." Ruby rolled onto her side, propped her head up on an elbow, and pinned wide, gray eyes on Sera. "Levi's like a brother to me, so I'm gonna tell you something I'd never tell another woman."

Sera eyed her warily. "Why would you do that?"

"Because I love him and I want him to be happy," Ruby said bluntly. "Levi never loses control, never, and he never touches a woman in public who's not family, not even innocently. No hand holding, no kissing, no sunblock spreading."

Sera sat up and wrapped her arms around her bent legs. Levi was still in the water, ignoring the game of Frisbee Heath and Colin were playing. He swam in long strokes from one end of the pool to the other, slicing through the crystal clear water as if the very devil were on his heels.

"You think he's interested in me," she said.

"I know he is." Ruby stretched her leg out and pushed gently against Sera's lounge chair with one toe. "I'm not going to warn you away. He's a grown man and perfectly capable of deciding what he wants, but be careful with him. He's not as tough as he looks."

Sera exhaled a shaky breath and his hard, cold stare flitted through her mind. "I don't know. He seems pretty tough to me."

"On the outside, we all are. It's the inside that's the problem."

Wasn't it always? "Thanks for telling me."

"He deserves a little happiness." Ruby rolled over onto her back and closed her eyes. "Just, for the love of all that's holy, don't let him introduce you to Nana. You'll never get your life back if you do."

"I'll keep that in mind."

Sera watched Levi as he crossed the length of the pool, flipped in the water, and pushed away from the side with a strong shove of both feet. He swam like a man born to it, moving swiftly through the water, his strokes clean, efficient.

She turned, intending to ask Ruby if Levi had ever been on a swim team, and let her curiosity die. Jordan had taken a seat at the other woman's hip and was caressing her shoulder with slow, sensual touches, a gentle smile softening his stern features.

Sera glanced away from the intimate scene. Was that what she and Levi looked like when he performed the beach-time ritual of sunblock spreading for her?

No wonder Ruby thought he liked her.

A shadow passed over Sera a moment before Heath flopped down in the chair on her other side. He'd turned his ball cap backwards over his soft brown hair and his nearly black eyes twinkled mischievously.

"Hey." A slow grin slid onto his face as he flexed his massive pectorals. "How you doin'?"

She bit back her own grin. "Hello, Heath."

"So, I noticed you're all alone over here, pining away." He leaned forward and waggled a thumb at Levi, still swimming laps. "You ready to ditch Red there and hang out with a real man?"

A laugh bubbled up. Were all of Levi's friends as outrageous as he was?

"Cut it out, Heath," Jordan said. "You know what he's like."

"Hey, you move, you lose." Heath raised his eyebrows and raked his dark gaze over Sera from head to toe. "And he moved. So, whaddaya say? Me, you, and a bottle of wine on the beach later, testing the sand."

"Ah." Did *testing the sand* mean what she thought it meant? "Well, I..."

A rush of water caught Sera's attention and she glanced around. Levi braced his hands on the concrete lip of the pool and shoved himself out. Water sluiced off of him as he stood and scraped his hands over his head, rubbed a hand down his face, shaking the water off. His trunks rode low on his hips, baring the ginger hair trailing downward from his bellybutton, a path she'd taken the day before and itched to explore again. The thin material of his suit was molded to his narrow hips and muscled thighs. He looked like a god, a child of the water and the sun, the two combining to create shimmers of light along his alabaster skin.

Sera's heart tripped in her chest and her mouth watered as heat slid down, settling between her legs in a low, persistent throb.

"Get your own woman, Heath." Levi's whiskey eyes held a dangerous glint. "Stay away from mine."

Heath stood and held his hands up, palms out. "I was just

asking."

"Ask somewhere else."

Levi's gaze followed Heath as his friend sauntered away. He rolled his shoulders, then sprawled into the chair Heath had vacated, not once looking at Sera. He draped his forearms over the chair's arms and closed his eyes, ignoring her.

She couldn't let her earlier grumpiness come between them. Ruby's belief that Levi had developed a small crush wasn't nearly as important to Sera as their budding friendship. She enjoyed being with him, liked talking with him and having him near.

And she really hadn't meant the grabby remark, or wouldn't have if she hadn't been so damn vulnerable and needy. He hadn't done anything she hadn't expected or, truth be told, wanted him to do. If she'd asked him to stop without being snarky, he would've. On that, she was absolutely certain. Levi was a gentleman, a young gentleman with a penchant for pushing boundaries, but still a gentleman.

She laid a hand on his arm. "I'm sorry."

"No big." He shrugged without opening his eyes. His hand covered hers in a touch so fleeting, her skin barely had time to warm under the contact. "I pushed too hard, you said no. End of story."

Her stomach sank like a rock in the ocean and she withdrew her hand. *End of story.* Surely that wasn't as final as he made it sound.

She settled back in her chair and watched Heath and Colin horsing around in the pool, silently worrying over the whole incident. After a while, Levi joined them, diving in behind Heath and dunking the larger young man. The sun fell toward the ocean and shadows lengthened in its wake. Levi barely acknowledged her. Oh, he was polite enough, offering her a beer, bringing her a snack, but he'd closed himself off so completely, she felt like she was spending time with a stranger.

Which she was. Two days did not a friendship make, no matter how strong the attraction.

Her throat tightened around a lump the size of Black Rock Mountain. There was no need for her to be there, distracting him from his friends, holding him to an obligation he no longer wanted any part of. She gathered her things together, said a quiet goodbye to Ruby and Jordan, and slipped away from the pool as unobtrusively as she could, heading into the apartment complex.

She was halfway down the first floor hallway when the door leading to the pool opened behind her.

Levi fell into step beside her, rubbing a beach towel over his hair. "I'll walk you up."

"I can make it on my own."

He slung the towel around his neck and held the ends, one in each hand. "I shall walk you up," he said, carefully enunciating every word, his whiskey eyes boring into her.

"Ok." What else could she say? *Gee, Levi, don't know why you'd bother when it's obvious you don't want to be with me,* or *Hey, I apologized, what more do you want?* She pressed her lips together, keeping the words in her mind where they belonged. Maybe she deserved the cold shoulder and maybe she didn't, but he didn't deserve to have her lash out at him again.

He opened doors for her, regarding her with that cold, amber stare, and never so much as accidentally grazed her arm with his. When they reached her door, she unlocked it and turned to him. His gaze dropped to hers, as hard and impassive as it had been since she'd accused him of being grabby. He brushed a gentle kiss across her lips, touched his mouth to her forehead, and then he was gone, padding silently away without looking back.

Her heart tightened painfully in her chest. That had felt an awful lot like goodbye, not a *Hey, I'll see you tomorrow goodbye,* but a *Nice knowing you, have a good life* goodbye.

She entered her apartment and sagged against the closed door. A careless word, that's all it had taken to break their budding friendship. Already, a keen sense of loss crept through her. Why hadn't she thought before opening her mouth?

On the other hand, if that's all it took to chase him away, maybe it was better she'd found out early on how flighty he was.

She touched the place on her forehead where he'd kissed her and swallowed the tears clogging her throat. Damned if she'd cry over another man, especially one she'd only known two days. She pushed away from the door and tried hard to ignore the guilt and sorrow gnawing their way through her.

Five

S ERA SPENT a restless evening trying to work, gave up around
supper time, and walked to a nearby restaurant, came back to
the apartment and tried to work after. Half an hour spent
staring at her blinking cursor, and she closed the lid of her laptop.
Lordy, she was a mess if she couldn't even work.

A restless energy pushed her away from the couch. A walk on
the beach. That would do the trick, but when she went outside, the
sounds of Levi and his friends drifted to her from the pool area,
along with the voices of half a dozen or so women. Her heart
squeezed into a painful knot. Maybe those were Heath and Colin's
women and maybe they weren't, but if Levi had found somebody
else, she didn't want to know.

She slipped back into her apartment, settled onto her couch
with her Kindle, then set it aside after it turned itself off the third
time while she stared blankly at it, moping over Levi.

After a nearly sleepless night, she woke early and waited for
Levi's knock on her door. They hadn't made plans, but still. He'd
wanted to do something with her. When nine o'clock rolled around
and no knock had sounded, she dragged herself out of bed, changed
into a thin, coral colored sundress with a button-down front, and set
out for Cape Hatteras.

The drive down was a nightmare. Between her own lack of
sleep, the narrow, sand-clogged roads, and the low speed limits, it
took entirely too long to travel from Kill Devil Hills south to the
famous lighthouse. Sera made the most of it, taking her time
climbing the steps to the top, filling her camera with pictures from
every angle and location, absorbing the historical notes scattered on

plaques and exhibits around the site. She found a cheesy souvenir stand nearby and bought t-shirts for Petey and her nephews and baseball caps embroidered with an Outer Banks logo for her father and brother.

A local at the souvenir stand directed her to a seafood restaurant with good food. Sera couldn't have said if it was or not. Her taste buds had quit working around the time of her and Levi's disagreement. She ate anyway, left a good tip for the waitress, and trudged out to her car for the long drive back to her rented apartment.

Once there, she said *screw it*, stripped off her clothes, and fell into bed and a deep sleep. A gentle tap at the door woke her what felt like five minutes later. She shoved a handful of curls out of her face and peered blearily at her alarm clock. 4:43. Ugh. A cotton fog floated through her head accompanied by a sharp pang in her temples. An afternoon nap hadn't done her a bit of good, and she'd really needed the sleep.

The knock sounded again, a little more insistently, and she buried her face in a pillow.

"Sera," Levi called. "It's me. Open up."

Well, drat. She hefted a sigh and rolled out of bed. Made it halfway across the living room before she remembered she was in her underwear, and backtracked to pull on a t-shirt. He'd seen her before in a t-shirt with no bra on underneath. No big.

A sudden stab of pain pierced her heart. Yeah, Levi was no big. *Way to fool yourself, Sera.*

She opened the door and glared at him, all six foot something of gorgeous male flesh wearing nothing but damp swimming trunks and a wary expression. "What?"

"Hey." His eyes skimmed down her body and clenched shut, and he rubbed a hand over his face. "Sorry. I keep waking you up."

Yes, he did, and it didn't bother her at all. Hardly any. Especially when she noticed the bump of his penis lengthening under his swimsuit, one tiny increment at a time. Why, it made her plum happy to see that. "I guess you want to come in."

"No. Yes." He sighed, hooked his hands to his hips. "I'm sorry."

She opened the door and stepped back, closing it behind him

after he entered. "For what?"

"For everything. You were right." He stopped three feet into the apartment and crossed his arms over the broad plane of his chest. "I was way out of line yesterday."

"Not so much," she murmured. "I overreacted just a tiny bit."

A corner of his mouth curled up and his whiskey eyes glinted. "Maybe a little. Guess I don't blame you, though."

"Touching my breasts was a little much, Levi."

"Yeah." He looked away, scrubbed a bare foot against the carpet. "Can't promise I won't do it again, though."

Well, at least he was honest.

The silence stretched between them. He sighed and shrugged. "The guys are waiting for me."

"Ok."

He coughed, cleared his throat. Shrugged again. "You're welcome to come, too."

"I have to get ready for tomorrow's book signing," she said gently.

"Oh. Ok, then." He hesitated, then pressed a soft kiss to her forehead. "I'll see you around."

"Sure." She tilted her head, considered the carefully closed expression, so at odds with the half erection tenting his trunks at the juncture of his thighs. "Supper?"

The corner of his mouth quirked up again. "We're grilling. Wouldn't mind having you along, though."

"What time?"

"Maybe an hour, hour and a half?"

"I'll be there. What should I bring?"

"Just yourself."

She walked him to the door, all two steps. He touched her elbow with gentle fingers and brushed his lips over her cheek, then left. She closed the door and rested her forehead against the cool metal as a weight she hadn't known she carried lifted from her heart. They'd be ok. Maybe they'd never be able to reclaim the easy attraction from before, but at least when they met on the streets back home, they could be polite. And if that politeness developed into something more, well, maybe that wouldn't be such a bad thing.

She tugged her t-shirt off as she padded toward the bathroom for a quick shower, and set her mind to preparing for the next day's event.

LEVI KEPT a close watch out for Sera, a bad habit he'd developed since spotting her coming through the barrier dunes a few days before. She'd forgiven what Ruby had bluntly called his sulk with little more than a good-humored shrug.

He hadn't been sulking. Hurt wasn't sulk no matter what Ruby said. So he'd pushed a little too far and Sera had pushed back, and her rejection had touched a nerve. It was an understandable reaction.

He jostled the chicken on the grill, testing its doneness. And why was he standing around explaining away his own actions? He could've handled it better, yeah, could've been the man he'd told her he was instead of the kid she thought him to be.

He, who prided himself on his maturity, had resorted to a childish sulk.

Damn it, Ruby was right. He dropped the lid on the grill and glared at the hapless metal dome. She'd never let him hear the end of it if he admitted it, so he wouldn't, but it rankled all the same.

So Sera didn't want him to touch her. He'd work around it, at least try to establish a friendship, maybe ease her into something more.

He pushed the idea away. Goddess help him, who was he kidding? If she didn't want him, he needed to let it go, not pursue her. She'd been pretty clear about it, hadn't she? Though she'd enjoyed his touch before, seemed to enjoy touching him back.

And had kissed him willingly enough the morning before.

He knuckled the furrow between his eyebrows. Talk about your mixed signals. Either she wanted him or she didn't, but which one was it?

And why did he care so much one way or the other? She was just a woman, a sexy woman with soft curves, a gentle touch, and the sweetest mouth he'd ever tasted, but she was just a woman.

Ruby slouched into a nearby chair. "You're burning the chicken."

"Am not." He lifted the lid on the grill and turned the *not burnt* chicken over. "Why aren't you bugging Jordan?"

"He and Colin made a beer run. I swear, you boys drink like fish."

"I'm not a boy," he snapped, then pinched the bridge of his nose. "Sorry."

"Missing Sera?"

He dropped his hand and stiffened. "Why would you think that?"

"Because you've been walking around like a bear with a thorn in its paw since she left yesterday." She lifted the bottle in her hand, downed a swallow of beer, and gazed at him, her mouth curled into a smirk. "Did you apologize for sulking?"

"I wasn't sulking." Not that he'd admit to, anyway. "She as good as told me to bug off."

"She asked you to quit pawing her in public, you dolt."

"I wasn't pawing her." He enunciated the words carefully on the dim hope Ruby would pay attention. "Her skin's too fair for her to be out in the sun without protection."

"So you put sunblock on her breasts?"

"I want to see her in a low-cut dress without tan lines." He jabbed at the chicken. "Is that a crime?"

Ruby opened her mouth, probably on a smart retort, and was interrupted by Heath, who held his hand out for the tongs. "Dude. You're killing the chicken. Go fight with Ruby some place else."

"We're not fighting," Levi said.

"Yeah?" Heath cocked an eyebrow and jerked his head toward the doorway leading to the pool. "That's not what Sera thinks."

Levi exhaled slowly. Great. She'd caught him bickering with Rubes. His sins kept piling up. Pretty soon, they'd be so big, Sera wouldn't want to have a thing to do with him. He pivoted around, sought her out. She stood half in and half out of the doorway, worrying at her lower lip with sharp, white teeth.

He handed the tongs to Heath without another word and jogged lightly to her. "You made it."

"I said I would." A furrow appeared between the high arches of her eyebrows. "I wasn't eavesdropping."

He drew back, considered her guilty expression. "Ok."

"You were fighting over me."

"Ruby was being a pain and I was being a pain back. It happens."

"But you..." She looked away and blinked rapidly. "I wasn't telling you to bug off yesterday."

"We settled this already."

"No, we didn't. I apologized and you apologized, but we didn't really settle anything."

He clamped down on the temper winding up through his gut. Damn thing had already gotten him in trouble once. "I don't see the problem here."

"The problem here," she said carefully, "is that you think I don't want to be around you, which isn't true, by the way. You were the one who stopped touching me."

He breathed out an exasperated laugh. "Because you asked me to."

"You were being grabby."

"I was protecting your skin and got a little out of line. That's not being grabby."

She scowled. "You touch me all the time."

His eyebrows snapped down. "Sera, love, you've got to make up your mind. Either you want me to touch you or you don't."

"I want you to, of course I do." She glanced at Ruby and Heath, and lowered her voice. "Just not so much in public, ok?"

"No, it's not ok," he said flatly. "I'm not following some arbitrary rule just because you're ashamed to accept my touch in front of other people."

Color burst into her cheeks. "I'm *not* ashamed of you."

"Yeah? So what about that whole thing with me being too young for you, huh? How about that?"

"Wow, this is better than Wimbledon," Ruby called from across the pool.

"Butt out, Rubes," Levi said.

Ruby stood slowly, her body tense. "Don't call me that."

"How about you make me stop?"

"Honestly, Levi." Sera shook her head. "And you wonder why I'm worried about your age."

"Don't even go there." He leveled a flat gaze at her. She returned it with one of her stern good-mum stares, and he bit back a raw stab of humor. "Arguing with Rubes doesn't make me a kid."

Ruby shrugged and cracked her neck. "I told you not to call me that."

"Cut it out, Levi." Sera glanced at Ruby and hunched her shoulders. "She looks like she's about to slug you."

"And?" He shrugged. "If she does, I'll slug her back."

Sera gaped at him. "You'd hit her? Oh, my God, how could you do that? You're bigger than she is and no matter what she's done, she doesn't deserve to be hit."

"Says someone who doesn't know squat about Ruby." He rolled his eyes skyward. This is what he got for picking up a mortal. "Hey, Rubes. Sera thinks I can kick your butt."

Ruby's face went blank, then she doubled over and laughed so hard, tears streamed from her eyes.

"Um, why is she laughing?" Sera asked.

"Why do you think?" He shook his head. "I can't believe you think I'd hurt somebody weaker than me."

"You were going to fight with her." She slid a sideways glance at the laughing Daughter. "Though she is kind of annoying."

"I heard that." Ruby straightened and wiped tears from her face. "Twenty bucks says I can take you."

"Ruby, come on. I'm not stupid."

Sera placed a gentle hand on his arm. "No, wait. Y'all have done this before?"

"Sera, love, you know all those rumors you've heard about Tellowee? Well, some of them are true." He drew her hand into the crook of his arm and held it there, savoring the feel of her skin on his. "As soon as children can walk, they learn how to handle themselves."

"Like martial arts?"

"And other things."

She glanced between him and Ruby, her gaze speculative. "What chance do you have of beating her?"

"Not much," he admitted. "She's older, faster. And she's got a mean right hook."

"Hmm." Sera turned to Ruby. "No hits below the belt or above the neck."

A slow smile spread across Ruby's face. "What's the bet?"

"Twenty dollars says he can take you," Sera said promptly.

"Hey, now, maybe I'm not inclined to be Ruby's punching bag."

"So, ante up." She tilted her head, her smile coy. "You said you wanted to slug her."

"I said I'd slug her if she slugged me first. Big difference there."

"He's still sore from the last ass-whooping Rubes gave him," Heath said from the grill.

Sera peeked around Levi. "Oh, really?"

"Oh, yeah. She beat the..."

"Heath." Levi snapped. "I was seventeen. Give me a break."

"So consider it a rematch," Sera said. "Now that you're a big, strong man."

He narrowed his eyes. Did she really think needling him would make him give in? On the other hand, maybe he could trade a fight with Rubes for something he really wanted. "I'll do it for a kiss."

"Done."

"Not so fast." He placed his mouth close to her ear and said softly, "A kiss in public, any time and any way I want."

She shuddered and her eyes slid shut. "Levi," she breathed.

"That's my price."

She squinched her eyelids tightly together. "Ok, then."

"Woot!" Ruby shouted. "Beach time, cuz."

He shook his head and pinned Sera with a sour look. "When she kicks my arse, you have to play doctor."

She fluttered her long, brown eyelashes at him. "Aw. Want me to kiss your booboos?"

"That and a few other things," he muttered.

He followed Ruby down to the beach, resigned to spending the next little while deflecting her lightning jabs and sneaky punches. Underhanded, that was Rubes.

On the other hand, when it was over he could put his hands on Sera any way he wanted to, at least for a little while.

He helped Ruby draw out a rough circle in the sand, spared a single glance to make sure Sera had stayed behind the railing separating the pool from the beach.

And ducked. Ruby's first swing whistled past him, a solid right hook aimed at his mouth.

He snorted. Of course, she wouldn't play by the rules.

"No bet for cheaters," Sera called, and earned a disgruntled glare from Ruby.

He grinned and fell into a defensive posture, danced out of the way of a punch to his ribs, blocked two hits aimed at his stomach. Man, he shouldn't have called her names. It had put her in a vicious mood.

They moved around the circle, two warriors who knew each other's fighting styles too well for either to land a solid hit. A crowd gathered around them, staying well back, their quiet comments rolling past him without denting his concentration.

To shake things up, Levi caught Ruby's arm during her next swing and pulled her over his shoulder, and yelped when she bit him on the back. He lifted her legs and leg go, then scrambled out of the way. She tucked into a roll as she hit the sand and came up swinging.

They went at it in earnest then, using whatever body part was handy to jab, punch, or kick. Sweat coated Levi's skin as he moved faster and faster, trying to keep up with Ruby's immortal reflexes. His guard slipped fractionally, enough for her to sneak in a hard punch to his ribs. The crowd murmuring sympathetically. Before he could retaliate, three sharp whistles sounded. Levi glanced toward the lifeguard running across the beach. Ruby popped him in the mouth, cracking his lower lip, and his head snapped back under the force of her blow.

Well, shite. There went his kiss with Sera.

He glared at Ruby as the lifeguard pushed through the crowd. "You can deal with him," Levi said, and stalked away, probing his throbbing lip gingerly.

Damn it. He'd been so close, too.

Sera ran up to him, alarm and guilt warring for dominance in her expression. "Oh, Levi. I'm so, so sorry. I can't believe she really hit you."

"That's what happens in a fight, love."

"I know, but she wasn't supposed to hit you in the face." She pulled his head down, ran gentle fingers over the cut on his lip. He hissed out a breath, and she winced. "Just look what she's done to your beautiful mouth."

"You think my mouth's beautiful?"

"Oh, hush, you. Why didn't you say no?" She ran a hand down his ribs over the bruise already forming there. "And look at this. Oh, I could just get her for hurting you like that."

"I told you she could take me."

"Well, how was I supposed to know she really could?"

"Because I told you so," he said drily. "There's a reason I don't step into the ring with Ruby."

"And you did it anyway." She glared at him. "And for what?"

"A kiss."

Her eyes widened and her cheeks went pink. "Oh. That."

"Yes, that. Which I can't do right now anyway, so quit looking so nervous."

"Who's nervous?" She gave a breathy laugh and tugged him toward the pool. "Where's the first aid kit?"

He followed along behind her, let her doctor his lip, though it was barely a scratch. Ruby had made sure to hit him hard enough to break the skin, not hard enough to do lasting damage. Damn her hide. She'd purposefully popped his mouth to keep him from gaining his reward.

He hunkered down on a chair and held ice wrapped in a towel to his mouth while Sera prodded his ribs gently, arousing him more than anything. Not that he could do anything about it, not for at least a couple of hours while his mouth healed, but at least now he knew she didn't hate his touch.

Six

I F GUILT HAD A NAME, right at that moment it would be *Sera.* That thought ran through her mind while she pressed gently on the bruise blossoming across the pale skin over Levi's ribs. Prodding him into fighting had been dirty and low and selfish. She'd wanted to watch him move, knew he'd be just as beautiful exchanging blows with Ruby as he was running or playing volleyball or walking hand in hand down the beach under the light of the full moon.

Sera *knew* better, for cripes' sake. Wasn't she a parent? Didn't she tell Petey that fighting never solved anything, that talking a problem out made for a more satisfying resolution? And here she was egging Levi into a fight with his cousin, who would've kicked his rear if the lifeguard hadn't come along.

Sera blew a wayward strand of hair away from her face and scowled at the bruise. No broken ribs, thank goodness, but drat Ruby anyway. She'd done her level best to hurt Levi, though *she* wasn't the one who'd pay for it. Oh, no. Sera peeked at him, caught the heated weight of his whiskey eyes, and glanced just as quickly away. What a fool she'd been to wager a kiss for a chance to watch him fight.

It had totally been worth it.

After Ruby the Cheater's first underhanded swing, Levi had gotten this dangerous glint in his eye. He'd fallen into a fighting stance so naturally, Sera figured it must be ingrained, and then he'd reacted, flipping away a complicated series of blows Ruby threw at him as if he were brushing away air. The two had danced around the sand, their bodies sharp and efficient as they attacked and countered. For a while, Levi had kept pace, his body moving effortlessly. Though Sera readily admitted that she knew nothing of fighting as a sport, it was clear he knew what he was doing, and equally as clear that, as good as he was, Ruby was far, far better.

But Levi. A shiver ran along Sera's skin at the memory of what he'd done, the strength of his body, the way he'd moved. Graceful, powerful, and so, so hot.

Sera had stood at the fencing around the pool, gripping the rail tightly, watching the two opponents dance around the temporary fighting area they'd scratched into the sand, only peripherally aware of Jordan and Colin's return, and of Heath quietly defusing the tense crowd and discouraging onlookers from calling the police. Her focus had been on Levi and that look he'd gotten, a hard look that said he could handle any takers and then some, the same one he'd had when Heath had plopped down beside her the day before. At that look, her breath had shallowed and heat had strummed through her blood. Her toes had curled as something primitive and rich throbbed low in her gut, echoing in the secret place between her thighs.

She'd gained a few beautiful moments of pleasure and paid for it in the damage Ruby had done to Levi's nearly perfect form.

Sera glanced at him again and sighed. His lips curled into a slow smile and need stirred in his eyes. Drat him. He knew she felt guilty about pushing him into that fight and he fully intended to use it against her. Kissing him in public? Probably not that big a deal, but what price would he extract in exchange for the guilt?

Her heart tripped and bumped in her chest and heat wormed its way up her cheeks. She could deal with whatever he dished out. What worried her was the fact that she *wanted* him to do something. She, a grown woman with a half-grown child, wanted a man seven years her junior, a man she'd known less than a handful of days and would probably never see again, in spite of living so close to his family. It was crazy and needy and, sweet God in Heaven, she wanted him anyway.

"I've got another bruise for you to doctor," he said.

She brushed her fingers over his ribs a final time and *did not* enjoy the feel of his skin. Hardly at all. "Mmm. Where?"

He smirked as he snagged her hand and slid it slowly down his flank, trapping it between his hand and his hip.

She tugged against his grip, all too aware of his erection blooming a few inches away from where he held her hand. "I'm not looking there."

"Chicken." His voice was soft and gravelly, and scraped over her nerves as if he'd licked her skin. "You promised you'd tend me."

Well, that hadn't taken long. "Within reason."

"Quote *Want me to kiss your booboos?* unquote. Your exact words." He shifted onto his side and tucked a thumb into the waistband of his trunks. "And I said yes and had a go with Ruby, which makes our arrangement a verbal contract. Time to pay up, love."

"We could at least do this in private."

"Sure, we can," he said with an easy shrug. "And after you kiss my booboos in private, I'll be more than happy to do the same all over that gorgeous body of yours."

Well, if he put it that way. "Was negotiation part of your finance degree?"

He grinned, and the wicked curl of his lips did wicked things to the heat roiling through her. "Learnt that from Nana. Come on, now. Get along with it."

"Oh, all right," she said on a huff. "At least hold your trunks up so you don't flash half the beach."

"You want the trunks up, you hold them there."

If his voice had been anything but soft and warm and lilting, Sera would've refused, but the need there was her undoing. She slid her hand around and tucked her fingers into the waistband of his swimming trunks, grazing the line of ginger hair under his bellybutton. The back of her fingers caressed his skin and his stomach muscles flexed inward, as they had the day she'd coated him with sunblock.

The urge to press her lips there tumbled through her. She shook it away. Crazy, what this man did to her.

As careful as she was to maintain a casual grip, her fingers tightened and her skin tingled and awareness of exactly where her hand rested, inches from his manhood, bled through every cell in her body. She deliberately relaxed her tense muscles. Touching him was the closest she'd been to having sex since early in her pregnancy. After that, she'd had a few dates, fewer kisses, and one memorable night that had ended when her date had had one beer too many and let his hands wander.

A knee to the privates had done the trick, though it would've been nice to know some of Levi's moves then.

Levi wound his finger around a curl that had escaped from the barrette holding her hair up and tugged. "Keep going."

"You are the very devil, Levi Ewart."

She glanced over her shoulder. Levi's friends were fixing plates, the onlookers had dispersed. It was just her and Levi and temptation. When had it gotten so hard for her to stay on the straight and narrow?

Right. That would be the Sunday just past when this man had sauntered up to her with a smirk on his face and three bets to win.

She eased his trunks down, exposing the alabaster skin of his hip inch by glorious inch. He was softer there, smooth. The top of the bruise was already a deep blue. Sera pulled the fabric down, exposing the whole thing along with a good portion of his bottom. A nearly four-inch circular patch of mottled skin marred his flank. She inhaled sharply and swayed toward him, then jerked back. Her first instinct had been to press her lips there and ease the pain, and in public, no less. Wouldn't that have been a sight to see?

"Knee strike, a hard one," he murmured.

"She didn't have to be so rough." Sera prodded the area gently with her thumb, then eased the fabric back up over the bruise and the uncovered portion of his flank. "I think you'll be fine. No more fights for a while, ok?"

"No more wagers on your part, then."

Even if she wanted to, she wouldn't. The guilt alone would be enough to stop her, that and the odd little upset in her heart every time she saw the bruise over his ribs.

No, no. That was guilt, *only guilt*. She absolutely, positively wasn't upset that he'd gotten hurt. Nope, not a bit.

She stared at the bruise and her heart did an awkward flip and she sighed. *You're a terrible liar, Sera.*

And she still owed him a kiss *in public*, not at night on the bottom step of their building or in a darkened hallway when no one was around to see.

He dropped the curl he'd been winding around his finger and cupped the nape of her neck. His hand was as warm and heavy as his regard, and filled with promise. "Ready to eat?"

He kept surprising her, with his attention, with his maturity and thoughtfulness, and now... "You don't want to collect your kiss?"

"Not yet." His thumb stroked the skin above her thready pulse. "All things in their time."

Her breath caught in her throat. "That sounds like you're planning something."

"I'll never tell."

His reply didn't reassure her at all. He stood and held his hand out to her. She took it and allowed him to pull her up. Food first. Worry later. His hand fell to her waist, a touch that would've been casual and polite from any other man. Levi made it feel like another step in his courtship, if that's what he was doing.

Was he courting her? And to what end? If all he wanted was sex, surely he would've asked for it by now or moved on to an easier conquest. She was caving quickly, for her anyway, but probably not quickly enough for a sexually active young man, especially not a young man who could have his pick of women. So if not sex, what did he want from her?

LATER, AFTER they'd eaten and cleaned up, the whole group returned to their separate quarters and changed into street clothes. They met back on the beach to watch the sky darken above the ocean as the day ended. Sera had only paused long enough to grab a light sweater to throw on over her sundress, in case the strong breeze blowing inland grew chilly. Levi and his friends had pulled on dry shorts and t-shirts, though all of them were still barefoot, including Ruby.

The men each brought down a lounge chair and set them up several feet apart facing the ocean. All but Levi settled onto a separate chair with their women sitting snug between their legs, Jordan with a dreamy-eyed Ruby, and Heath and Colin with their women *du jour.*

Levi tugged Sera's hand. "Come sit with me."

She stared at the three couples, soft, feminine backs molded to hard, masculine chests. "You expect me to do that."

"I want you to. Hope you will." He dropped a fleeting kiss to her mouth and another to her forehead. "It's kind of a tradition."

"Does this tradition involve groping and fondling?"

His mouth twitched into one of his trademark smirks. "If you insist."

"You may hold me," she said primly, and bit back laughter when he said, "You're a hard woman, Sera Noland."

Levi sat on the chair with his legs straddling the seat and pulled Sera down. She leaned against his chest and curled her legs up in front of her under the skirt of her sundress. His arms slid around her, firm and warm, and she blew out a shaky breath. When was the last time she'd let a man hold her like that? When was the last time she'd trusted a man enough to want him to hold her?

"Relax." His cheek brushed her temple, then his lips. "I won't bite, not unless you want me to."

"Ha. Right."

He surrounded her. Heat rolled off his chest through the thin t-shirt he wore, from the hands he rested on her stomach and the hard muscle of legs he'd stretched out on either side of the chair. Gradually, it relaxed her, enough that she could enjoy the twilight chasing the sun across the sky, the first twinkle of stars, and the clouds dotted across the far horizon. The stiff ocean breeze lifted humid air over them and the waves crashing against the sloping beach drowned out the voices of the people passing by.

After a while, the rest of the world faded until only she and Levi existed under the endless expanse of sky. Her hands found his and memorized the elegant length of his fingers, the neatly trimmed edges of his fingernails, the fine bones of his wrists. She traced the muscles of his arms as far toward his elbows as she could reach, then reversed her touch and learned the shape and size of them from the other direction. For a long while, she brushed her fingers across the soft hair of his forearms, contrasting its texture with that of his skin. Curiosity pushed her into boldness and she tested the hair above one knee. It was coarser, denser, and no less sexy.

"Is there anything about you that's not perfect?" she asked. When he didn't answer, she shifted, meeting his perplexed gaze with her own. "What? It's an honest question."

"You think I'm beautiful."

"I don't think, I know."

"And perfect, which I'm not, but you think I am, and you still hold back."

"We haven't known each other that long," she explained gently, and pressed a kiss to the rapidly healing cut on his lip, just because she could. "And I know you don't want to hear this, but you're really young."

"Not in the ways that count," he insisted. "Age isn't that big a deal."

"Isn't it?" She shrugged and turned toward the waves and the wind and the stars. "Anyway, it doesn't matter. In a few days, I'll go home and you'll do whatever it is you do and it won't be an issue."

He stiffened against her and his heart thudded so hard, it pounded into her back. "You don't want to see me again."

"I didn't say that."

"You assumed this week would be it."

The hint of accusation in his tone baffled her. What had she done but follow the logical path of their relationship, such as it was, to its natural end?

"I didn't look beyond the week," she said, and it was nearly true. She'd only once considered what would happen if they carried whatever it was they were doing beyond her short vacation. "You're an attractive young man. Once I'm gone, you'll find another woman and..."

"Turn around."

The flatly spoken words startled her. "Levi, really, it's not that big..."

"Turn around now."

He didn't wait for her to shift, but did it for her, lifting her by her waist with his graceful hands, so much larger than hers, and pulling her onto his right thigh with her back cradled in his arm. "Look at me, Sera. Is this the look of a man who wants another woman?"

"I..." Her gaze caught on the warm glow of his whiskey eyes and her hand drifted to his chest, resting over the thump of his heartbeat. It took her breath, the need she saw there. She'd learned its twin well over the past few days, learned it, memorized it, bathed in it so often she was drenched in a near constant ache, from bone to skin and everywhere in between. "Levi."

"I want you, Sera. You, with your ripe body and sharp mind and that soft touch that drives me wild." He gripped her hand and slid it down his sternum until it rested low on his belly. "Touch me, love. Feel what you do to me."

Her eyes widened and her fingers curled into his t-shirt. "Touch you how?"

He touched his forehead to hers. "There. Touch me there."

"Levi, I can't. We're on a public beach and..."

"No more excuses, Sera. Please." His hand released hers and skimmed slowly up her arm, burning a trail of heat along her skin. "Just touch me. I don't care where or how as long as I can feel you."

His lips brushed gently across hers, slow and easy, and he settled there, kissing her with the heavy need of a man, not the fumbling want of a child. Her own need rose abruptly, the cacophony of sensation warring with her good sense. Part of her was lost in the feel of him, in the way his mouth moved over hers, in the hard strength of his arm around her back and the push of his erection against her hip.

Another part of her, a dwindling dot of reason, screamed at her to back away. *He'll hurt you*, it said, and though she knew it was true, it was difficult to hold on to the warning with his tongue tracing the seam of her lips and the backs of his fingers brushing over her breast through her sundress and bra, teasing the nipple until it hardened into a tight, aching peak.

She had a choice. For one brilliant moment, it beamed at her with an unusual clarity, fixing itself in her mind. She could push her fingers into the waistband of his shorts and discover the precise scope of Levi's desire, or she could withdraw her hand and let whatever was between them continue to build. Either way, the end would be the same. Levi would walk away with some piece of her. The only question was, how big of a chunk would he take? Which path would bring the most heartache? It was coming, like a train steaming down the tracks, a frightening rush of noise and smoke and unstoppable momentum. Her only choices lay in the when and the how.

Levi's hand drifted down her leg, then pushed up under the skirt of her sundress and splayed across her thigh. He broke the kiss and leveled a hard stare on her. "There'll be no more talk about us going our separate ways. No more, you hear? Not until we've discovered if what's there is worth having."

His words echoed in the hollow of her heart as the native burr he'd slipped into shivered across her skin. *Nae muir.* As if it were that easy to talk her 'round.

Her fingers twitched against his stomach, poised between one path and the next. What would it be like to have him, all of him, for as long as he would have her? To feel him moving in her and loving her, to be perpetually surrounded by his heat and light? How many times had she imagined just that, never believing she'd have a chance to know? And now, he offered himself to her freely, as if there *were* no choices, simply one path to the truth of what could be.

Nae muir.

"Levi," she murmured. "You don't know what you're asking."

"Only what I ask of myself."

They stayed entwined for what could've been hours, with her hand on his stomach and his on her leg, comforting her with his steadfast grip while the choices whirled around in her head.

Seven

CROWD PUSHED into the narrow confines of the bookstore, eager to hear Sera read from her latest book. Or maybe they were just interested in the four young men ranged protectively around the group of attendees.

Earlier that morning, Levi had let it slip to Ruby that Sera had a book signing that day. Before he'd known it, his cousin had roped everybody else into going, too. *The People stick together,* she'd said, and he'd understood what she'd left unspoken. Sera wasn't of the People, but he was. As long as Sera was under his protection, she'd be under Ruby's, too.

Levi caught Colin's eye across the room and stifled a grin. Two white-haired ladies near the back tittered and snuck coy glances at Colin. He endured it the same way he tolerated the antics of the people he guarded when he was at work, with a flat stare and casual indifference.

Which didn't deter the ladies in the crowd at all, or a couple of the gentleman, either. Young or old, straight or not, all had quietly speculated on the presence of the four young men. Were they cover models? Bodyguards?

Sera's lovers?

Thank the Goddess Sera hadn't overheard *that* comment. No telling how she would've reacted, though it might've been fun to watch.

She paused in the middle of reading and sipped from the bottle of water at her side. Her silver eyes glanced toward him from under lowered lashes and pink colored her cheeks. She'd been doing that all day, from the time he'd picked her up that morning through the drive to the bookstore and while she and the bookstore's owner were finalizing the setup for the book signing.

Maybe he was growing on her after all.

Their kiss the night before had been a catalyst. As he'd held her under the deep sky of night, touching her the way he'd needed to for what felt like an eternity, something had shifted in her. She hadn't touched him back, not the way he'd wanted her to, but she'd melted sweetly under the pressure of his mouth and curled her fingers into his shirt, innocently adding fuel to the desire boiling in his blood.

On the walk back to her apartment, she'd taken his hand, not waiting for him to make the first move. Her thumb had rubbed gently over the backs of his fingers, learning their shape, filling him with a longing to know her touch in every way a man could know a woman. At her door, she'd stood on tiptoe and tugged his head down and kissed him as if it were the first time all over again, and his control had nearly shattered.

Around her, he stayed breathless and needy, and yeah, he was beginning to like it. No, he loved it, loved that every shy glance from her silver eyes shot straight through him.

Polite applause reminded him where he was, at a bookstore surrounded by strangers, not alone with Sera under the starry sky. Ruby rose from her seat on the front row and removed Sera's stool while Sera settled behind a table full of books and knickknacks she called *swag*. To everybody's surprise, his cousin had volunteered to act as Sera's assistant during the signing, opening books to the correct page, ensuring that each attendee received only one piece of swag.

The only exceptions were members of Sera's street team. The two young women each received gift bags full of swag and a signed copy of Sera's latest work as a thank you for their help getting the word out. Katie had driven in from Raleigh and Sandra from Wilmington, just to see Sera. It was a whole new world for him, the dedication those women showed for a woman they knew primarily through her books.

Though who could blame them? Sera's sincere appreciation of their efforts had the young women beaming and giggling, the same way others reacted to movie stars. Who knew romance novelists could inspire that kind of fandom?

He and Sera spent the rest of the day together, chasing each other down the beach, hanging out with his friends. After another supper cooked on the grill, he waited politely on her couch while she chatted with Petey on her cell. When she was through, he took her to the movies, wrapped an arm around her shoulders, and held her close. He'd never wanted to protect a woman before, not like this, not a woman who wasn't kin, but with Sera, the need to shield her rose as easily as the desire she teased so effortlessly from him.

Early the next morning, he knocked on her door and followed her inside her apartment. Her notes had been carefully packed into a portable file holder and her suitcase lay open on the couch.

He slipped his hands into the pockets of his shorts and jerked his chin toward the suitcase. "You're packing."

"I have to be out of here by eleven tomorrow." She stuffed her Kindle into a messenger bag with her laptop, her smile absent-minded. "Lots to do before then."

He considered her, measured his need against hers, ran a shaky hand over the erratic thump of his heart. "We're supposed to stay another week."

"Oh?" She stood on tiptoe and bussed his cheek. "That'll be fun."

"I have to go back next Thursday. Business." He lifted one shoulder in a casual shrug. "You could stay with me until then."

"Ah. Um." Her brows furrowed and her fingers plucked at the strap of her bag. "I really need to get back home. No, really," she said when his expression turned skeptical. "This week will be my only chance to catch up on chores before Petey comes home. If I hadn't already made plans..."

"I get it. You've got a life to get back to."

"I'm sure you do, too. Maybe when you get back to Tellowee, we can do something together."

He tucked a stray strand of hair behind her ear and lingered on the soft skin of her cheek. "I live in Atlanta, love."

"You said you were from Tellowee."

"I am. It's my home, always will be, but I don't live there."

"Oh. Well. Ha." Her eyes went round and her teeth worried at her lip. "Still, that's not too far."

"Not so very," he agreed. "We'll work something out."

"Sure. I'm sorry."

"No reason to be." He pulled her close and buried his face in her hair and surrounded himself with her sweet scent. How could he tell her he'd be so busy when he got back, he wouldn't be able to see her again for weeks? "You ready?"

They joined the rest of the group in the parking lot and piled into two cars for the drive to the marina. Their guide, the captain of the boat they'd rented, met them on the dock, and not long after, they launched and set sail for Cape Hatteras.

The day was overcast, the ocean choppy, though that didn't keep Sera from plopping down on a chair on deck and unpacking her laptop.

Levi scooted a chair up next to her and dropped a bottle of water into the cup holder embedded in the arm of her chair. "Does anything keep you from working?"

"Not a thing," she said cheerfully. "Well, except when Petey's sick. I know I shouldn't admit it, but I hover when he's not feeling well."

"It's what mums do." He sipped from his own bottle of water and eyed her over the rim. "So, where's Petey's da?"

Her face went blank and her fingers stilled in the middle of opening her laptop. "He died before Petey was born."

"I'm sorry."

"Don't be." Her voice was as hard as the deck beneath his bare feet. "It was a long time ago. Anyway, Petey does fine without him."

"And do you?" She arched an eyebrow, and he added, "Are you fine without Petey's da?"

"Is that jealousy I hear?"

"Curiosity," he corrected, though maybe she had the right of it. The thought of her with another man did terrible things to his heart, the soft bastard. It ached and pinged in a way that would've been embarrassing if anybody else could witness it. "Is it wrong for a man to ask a woman about her last love?"

"Who says he was my last?" Her silver eyes were coy and shone with a secret light. "Eight years is a long time between lovers."

He stretched out in his chair and smirked. "So I'm your lover now."

"If you play your cards right, I might think about it."

"You're a hard woman, love."

"So you say." She nudged his leg with the side of her foot. "How many lovers have *you* had in the last eight years."

"Enough to know what I'm about when I put my hands on a woman."

Her breath whistled out in a rush and her cheeks flushed pink, and he laughed, tickled by her reaction.

"None I've had a child with, though," he said.

"Really? You've never been serious about a woman?"

"Not yet." Though he suspected he was getting close to serious with her, or would if they had more time. "Why didn't you ever remarry?"

She looked away, rubbed a finger over the pucker in her brows. "I never married the first time 'round."

His hand went slack around the bottle of water and he bobbled it. Of all the mortal women he'd met, Sera seemed most like the marrying kind. He would've laid money on it. "Why not?"

"It's a long story."

"Tell me."

She exhaled sharply and leaned her head against the chair's back. "The night I told Petey's father I was pregnant, he stormed out. Ended up in a bar and got plastered, and wrecked on his way home. He died. End of story."

Son of a bitch. If Petey's da were alive, Levi would beat the hell out of him, just on principle. No man should abandon the mother of his child while she was pregnant. He scooted his chair closer and lifted her hand to his mouth for a comforting kiss. "That sounds like the short version."

"Yup. Abridged are us." She sighed, rolled her head against the chair's back, and met his gaze evenly. "Most men either run when they find out Petey's illegitimate or they think I'm easy."

"And you're wondering which one I am?"

"Yeah, I guess I am."

"My mum's illegitimate. So are Ruby and Colin and a lot of the women I grew up with. Illegitimacy's not that uncommon among the People. Frankly, I don't see what all the fuss is about."

"You don't."

"A government-sanctioned ceremony doesn't make you a good parent."

"True."

"It doesn't make you stick, either, doesn't guarantee love or loyalty." He rose and knelt on the deck with her feet between his knees and her sweet face cupped in his hands. "I'm not one to run when things get tough. Might back away until my temper cools, but I don't run."

"I don't..." Her hands circled his wrists and her fingers bit into his skin. "What are you saying?"

"You can count on me, Sera." He touched his forehead to hers and their breaths mingled. "Don't be afraid of what's between us, just because one man left when life threw a curve."

"It was a good curve," she murmured. "Why didn't he get that?"

"Some people never see the silver lining."

"Do you?"

The odd spark of hope in her sweet gaze touched him at his core. He brushed his lips over hers, a gentle reassurance of his promise to her. "I do, love. His loss, my gain."

She laughed and squeezed his wrists. "Only you would say that."

Bare feet pounded on the deck. "Ew," Ruby said. "Get a room, y'all."

"Ignore her." Levi cupped his hands over Sera's thighs and settled back on his haunches. "She's just jealous."

"Am not." Ruby flopped into Levi's chair and closed her eyes. "I've got my own man, thank you very much."

"He must have the patience of a saint," Sera muttered.

"I heard that."

Sera rolled her eyes.

"Heard that, too." Ruby's lips curled into a smirk. "Geez, you guys are predictable."

"About as predictable as you cheating," Sera retorted. "They should call you Ruby the Underhanded instead of Rubes."

Ruby's eyes popped open on a low gasp. "Don't say that!"

"Ruby. The. Underhanded." Sera waggled her eyebrows. "Fitting name for a woman who can't fight fair."

"Well, that one's gonna stick." He'd make damn sure it did, even if his lip had healed. "Looks like you earned your first nickname, cuz."

"Shit." Ruby closed her eyes and shook her head. "That's what I get for encouraging you to date a mundane mortal."

"Who's the mundane mortal?" Sera whispered.

"You are. It's a People thing. Means you're not one of us."

She opened her mouth on a question he was sure would be difficult for him to answer, so he did the only thing he could. He claimed her mouth in a demanding kiss that chased the questions right out of her head.

AFTER THEY'D TOURED the Cape Hatteras lighthouse, eaten lunch, and turned back toward the marina in Pirate's Cove, Sera sat next to Levi, taking in the sun. They'd all gathered on the deck, Jordan and Ruby cuddled together on one chair with Heath and Colin ranged out to the side, sipping chilled bottles of beer and debating the merits of soccer versus football versus rugby.

During a lull in the conversation, Sera quietly asked Levi, "What are you doing next week?"

"Pretty much the same thing we've done this week. Grill out, play in the water, catch the sights. Why?"

She hesitated for a long moment, her lips pressed into a thin line, her fingers tight around his hand. "I can't stay, but I wondered if you'd like to..." Her grip eased and she shook her head. "Never mind. Sorry."

His heart tripped over itself. Was she trying to ask him if he wanted to cut his vacation short and spend time with her? "Tell me."

"No, it's silly. Stupid really. Forget I said anything."

He lifted her fingers to his lips, nibbled the racing pulse in her wrist. "Say it, whatever it is."

She squinched her eyes closed and blurted, "Come home with me."

"You mean tomorrow or...?"

"Yes, tomorrow." She opened one eye and peeked at him warily. "It's a long drive. Company would be nice."

"You're not gonna try to drive back in one day, are you?"

She opened the other eye. "Um, no, actually. I was going to stop in Winston-Salem and spend the night, maybe visit a couple of historical sites the next day."

He leaned toward her and lowered his voice to a near whisper, well aware of the silence on the deck and four pairs of interested eyes following their conversation. "Are you ready for what might happen if I tag along on an overnight trip?"

"I don't know. I want to be."

"Wanting and doing are two different things, Sera. You have to be sure."

"I am. I will be," she amended hastily. "I want to spend time with you and I get the feeling that if I don't do it now, it'll never happen."

"It'll be a while. Work is pretty hectic right now. That's not a reason to rush into anything." He pressed her hand to his lips, savoring the taste of her skin and the faint tremor running through her. "You don't have to have sex with me to hold me to you."

"I know that. That's not what this is about." Her lips curved into a faint smile. "Mostly, anyway."

"So you don't want to have sex with me?"

Her smile widened into a grin and her silver eyes sparkled. "I didn't say that."

"Woman, you drive me wild." He pressed a hard kiss to her mouth, and lingered, memorizing the sweet taste of her mouth and the soft hitches of her breath. Ruby let out a wolf whistle, and Levi pulled away, more to keep Sera from being embarrassed than anything. "I need to make some calls, but yeah, I want to go, if you don't mind me hanging out for a few days."

"I'd like that."

It was the first time he honestly believed she wanted to be with him, and it sent an unreasonable hope soaring through him.

He made his calls, first to Yvette, Nana's frighteningly efficient assistant, and had her cancel his meeting with his great-grandmother, scheduled for the upcoming weekend. He called his own assistant, asked her to cancel his flight from Raleigh to Atlanta, make reservations at Nana's hotel in Winston-Salem, and rearrange his schedule. The Winston-Salem property was on his agenda for later in the month, a routine check. It wouldn't take up much of his time, so he might as well get it out of the way while he was there, and maybe have more time for Sera later on.

If she still wanted to see him then.

Sera watched him as he juggled and shifted his schedule, her head tilted to one side, her silver eyes gleaming softly under the harsh Carolina sun.

Between one call and the next, he said, "Can I have somebody leave my car at your house?"

"If it's in Tellowee, I can take you to get it. Otherwise, yes."

He debated the most efficient path for a moment. "If you don't mind taking me, it'll be easier for us to get it."

"I don't mind," she said, smiling sweetly.

"Thanks. Do you like berries?"

At her puzzled nod, he placed a call to his berry farm and cancelled the tour he was supposed to make of it on Thursday evening after a quick flight home. He could take Sera earlier in the week, introduce her around, help her pick berries if she wanted to put some by for Petey.

A few more calls and his schedule for the week was mostly clear. The only thing he couldn't cancel was a meeting early Friday morning. It wouldn't last much past lunch, and after, he'd have the rest of the weekend free. "Wanna go shopping on Friday?"

"Sure." Sera curled up on her chair and faced him. Her expression had gone from puzzled to an odd mix of curiosity and desire. "That whole take charge thing you're doing is kinda hot."

"Yeah? How hot?"

"Like, so hot I'm about to come over there and nibble on you."

Heat flooded through him and his skin tightened. Sera with her mouth on his skin. *Mmm.*

"So, what exactly do you do anyway, besides this and that?" she asked.

"A lot of things." She flashed a sour grimace at him, and he laughed. "It's true. Mostly, I work for Nana, helping out when problems pop up in her holdings, that sort of thing."

"Which is pretty much exactly what you told me the first time I asked." She tilted her head and her expressive silver eyes seared right through him. "Are you being evasive out of habit or because

79

you don't trust me?"

He met her gaze evenly. "Habit. It's complicated and not the kind of thing I usually discuss with women."

"You'll have to tell me eventually."

"I will," he said, and tugged one of her stray curls. "When I know you won't hold it against me."

It was near supper time when they arrived back at the marina. They loaded up and grabbed a noisy meal as a group, then headed back to their separate rooms. Levi left Sera at her door with a scorching kiss and a promise to meet her early the next morning for the trip home.

He slipped quietly into his suite. Jordan was sitting on the couch in the living area between their separate bedrooms, watching ESPN.

"Hey, man," Levi said. "Where's Rubes?"

"Shower." Jordan cut the TV off and tossed the remote onto the coffee table. "She delegated the *Do you know what you're doing?* talk to me."

"Butt out, Jordan," Levi said flatly.

Jordan held his hands up, palms out. "Don't kill the messenger."

Levi snorted. "Like you wouldn't lecture me on your own."

"Ok, you're right, I would. I like Sera. She's a nice woman, comes from a good family, but she's also mortal. Hawthorne'll have a shit fit when she finds out you're dating outside the People."

"Nana can't force me to choose a Daughter as a mate."

"No, but she can make your life a living hell if you don't."

"Only if I let her." Levi stalked into his room, Jordan hot on his heels, and yanked his suitcase out of the closet. "Anyway, I'm not dating Sera. We just met."

"Get real, Levi. You've been following her around like a lovesick puppy all week, drooling over her, sulking when she's not around, and now you're rearranging your life so you can spend a few extra days with her. This isn't like you."

"Yeah, well, she's special."

"That's what worries us." Jordan propped his hands on his hips. "Ruby especially. She doesn't want you to get hurt."

"Can't say that I won't be, but I'm not gonna dwell on it." He set the suitcase on his bed and unzipped it. "You ever think about how hard it'll hurt if Ruby dumps you?"

"Not if I can help it." Jordan's mouth twisted into a wry smile. "With Ruby, it's a hit or miss kinda thing, depending on whether or not she's willing to take on a Son."

"Seems to me she's already made that decision."

Something dark flickered across Jordan's expression. "She won't submit, refuses to even consider it. I know she'll leave me one day. I just hope it's not too soon."

Levi paused with his hand on the drawer of his dresser. "You're in love with her. Shite, man, what were you thinking?"

"About the same thing you're thinking with Sera. Do yourself a favor. Don't wade in so deep you drown."

Probably too late for that. Jordan was right. He'd never put off business for a woman before, not for anybody outside of family and friends or an emergency among the People. It should worry him. Strangely, that was the last thing on his mind. Going back with Sera the next day seemed like the most natural act in the world, and not just because he knew she'd be in his bed by the time Petey came home. He wanted her, Sweet Goddess did he ever, but sex was only a part of it.

The rest of it, he refused to analyze.

He finished packing, called his mum for a quick catch up, and stretched out onto his bed with a copy of Sera's latest novel, his heart thumping as he anticipated the week ahead.

Eight

FRIDAY MORNING, Sera woke to the soft drizzle of rain falling outside the bedroom window. The dark clouds that had threatened foul weather the day before had finally followed through on their promise. She rolled out of bed, peeked around the curtain, and sighed as contentment rolled through her, and with it the soft tingle of excitement.

Levi was coming home with her. For the first time in her life, she'd scrounged up the courage to approach a man first. So what if it hadn't been entirely her idea? She'd done it and her reward was having two whole days of Levi, all to herself. Well, except for the meeting he had to attend the next day, but that was a minor blip, or so he'd led her to believe. The rest of the time was theirs, him and her and the open road, a quick trip through the historic Moravian settlements around Winston-Salem.

And a night at a hotel room with a big, soft bed.

She hugged herself tight as the tingling grew into heat and her imagination took over. The covers would be down. Those always got in the way, so she'd pull them down first thing, and then coax Levi into stripping down to his drawers. Her heart leaped and thumped and butterflies flitted around in her tummy. Or she could take his clothes off, push his shorts off one inch at a time, trail her mouth over the bruises Ruby had put on him and down the thin line of hair under his navel.

Oh, God, yes. Would he let her have her way there, let her touch him and taste him and learn him, the way a woman should know her lover?

Would he want to do the same to her?

Her alarm clock buzzed at top volume, startling a yelp out of her, and her heart thumped so hard she put her hand over it to keep it in her chest. Here she was daydreaming when there was work to do. Levi would be down soon. There'd be plenty of time to moon over him during the long drive home.

She rushed through her morning routine, showering and blow drying her hair as quickly as she could. A dash of mascara, a touch of lip gloss. The cranberry sundress Levi seemed to like, worn over a matching bra and panty set. Thank goodness the building had a laundry room.

She stuffed her heels into her suitcase and slid on her Chuck Taylors. So they weren't very feminine or romantic. Travelling for hours in the car demanded at least a nod to comfort, especially since she'd be driving, and her canvas tennies were comfortable.

Levi knocked on her door at ten thirty sharp. She opened it and studied the forest green polo and khaki slacks he wore with dress shoes. "You're all dressed up."

"The casual executive look is all the rage in Winston-Salem." He dropped a kiss to her mouth and forehead as he came in, and set his suitcase and garment bag inside the front door. "Ready?"

"Almost." She shut the door and frowned. "Why are you all dressed up?"

His lips twitched into a half smile. "I'm not. This is what I usually wear on a business trip."

"Oh." Her gaze lingered on his sharply pressed slacks. They were very nice, but they covered his legs. Levi had really great legs, muscled and firm, the legs of a man that used his body the way he was supposed to instead of sitting behind a desk all day. And now, those legs were hidden. Darn it, summer was for naked legs. Everybody knew that. "But your business meeting's not until tomorrow."

"I'm still Nana's representative tonight."

"Oh," she said again, and winced. What was it about being around an attractive man that made women stupid? "Should I wear something fancier?"

"Not on my account." His gaze heated as it slid down her body. "On second thought, yeah, you should change, as long as I get to help."

She pulled a sour face, and he laughed.

"Had to try," he said. "If you'll give me the keys to your car, I'll start loading stuff."

They ended up loading her aging Volvo station wagon together while the rain tapered off. She did a final run through the apartment, made sure it was clean and nothing had been left behind, then locked it up and dropped the key off at the manager's office.

Levi took her to the Black Pelican in Kitty Hawk for lunch and refused to let her pay. It was becoming a habit she needed to find a way to break. Honestly. She was a grown woman and made decent money, but every time she suggested they split the bill or, Heaven forbid, she pay, he gave her his patented *I'm the man* look.

After lunch, he wiggled his fingers at her. "Give me the keys and I'll drive if you want to work or watch the scenery going out."

Best to set this line now. "I'll drive," she said firmly. "You can navigate and handle the radio stations."

His smirk shot a warning across her nerves, like he was up to no good. She shrugged it off. What mischief could he possibly make while strapped into the passenger's seat?

The roads from Kitty Hawk off Nags Head Island and through Manteo were clogged with vehicles. Sera concentrated on navigating the bumper to bumper traffic, her hands tight around the steering wheel. Levi set the radio to a classic rock station, then pulled out his cell phone and typed. His thumbs moved rapidly over the keypad for so long, her curiosity roused.

A red light on the outskirts of Manteo caught them and she eased the Volvo to a stop. "What are you doing?"

"Answering an e-mail from my assistant."

"You have an assistant?"

"They're fashionable in Atlanta these days," he murmured, his gaze fixed on his phone.

That was the second time he'd made light of his work, after twice refusing to tell her exactly what he did. He'd made his job sound haphazard and casual, not something he would need an assistant for. And then on the phone the day before while he'd been *making calls*, he'd used a no nonsense, take charge voice. Once she'd shaken down the goose bumps shivering over her from his sexy tone, her curiosity had taken over. He'd sounded more like a boss than an employee, a far cry from the feckless image he'd portrayed during the past week.

Though, maybe that was the impression she'd gotten because she *wanted* to see him as young and irresponsible. The way he handled himself, the dangerous glint he sometimes got in those beautiful whiskey eyes, and the fact that he'd had to call his *assistant* and rearrange his schedule to spend time with Sera were completely at odds with the Levi she'd built in her mind.

The light turned green. Sera eased the car forward, matching its speed to the flow of traffic.

Once upon a time, she'd thought of herself as open-minded and tolerant. Where Levi was concerned, she'd apparently built a wall and cherry picked the parts of him that were young, combining them into a false image to keep him at something close to arm's length. It was wrong and unfair, and she couldn't believe she'd done that to him after the sweetly considerate way he'd treated her.

Why hadn't she listened to the inner voice telling her what a great guy he was? Why did she still have her misgivings about his age, especially when his secrets were a much bigger concern? All along, she'd been fixating on the wrong thing.

By the time they reached the Virginia Dare bridge, traffic had thinned enough for Sera to relax her grip on the steering wheel.

Levi closed his phone and placed it in the console between the seats. He splayed his hand over her thigh just above her knee, a heavy, comforting weight. "I love these bridges, always have. You can see for miles across the water."

"Mmm." His thumb made tiny circles on her skin, inching the skirt of her dress up, and her muscles tensed beneath his hand. "You come out often?"

"More when I was a kid. Mum used to bring me out for the summer, after we moved across the pond. Now, there's too much going on for a long visit."

Her skirt hitched up another inch under the caress of his thumb. Surely he wasn't doing that on purpose. "Too many tourists. I can't believe how crowded it is."

"It's better in the winter. Fewer people. Harsher weather, though."

"I don't think I'd mind."

Though she was beginning to mind the hand on her leg. His thumb found bare skin and created tiny ripples of heat wherever it touched. By the end of the next bridge, her skirt was halfway up her thighs and his fingertips caressed the sensitive skin above her knees. A tremor stole through her with every shift of his hand along her skin. She stifled a moan and tried to focus on the narrow road running parallel to the Alligator River.

"It's beautiful through here," he said.

His fingers slid along her inner thigh, drawing a gasp from her. "What?"

"The swamp. It's beautiful."

His smug amusement should've infuriated her. All she could think about was his hand on her thigh. "Are you trying to drive me crazy?"

"I'm occupying my time. Why? Am I bothering you?"

"Nope, not a bit," she blurted, and winced. What a whopper. "Ah, maybe you could pull my skirt back down, though."

"I like it where it is."

Ha. Of course, he did. What man wouldn't? She caught sight of a blue sign out of the corner of her eye and nearly shouted, her relief was so huge. Refuge, if a rest area could be called that. "Time for a pit stop."

"We've been on the road less than an hour."

"Oh, well, you know. Girls," she said on a breathless laugh, and ignored his knowing smirk.

She pulled over and parked, dashed inside the women's bathroom, and locked herself inside a stall. God, his touch was lethal, and he'd only gone halfway up her thigh. How would she react when he...? She cut that thought off before her imagination could run with it. No need to borrow trouble, and it would be. Just the thought of what he might do to her was enough to prod her into a tizzy of hot, breathless need.

She used the restroom, washed her hands, and, calm at last, exited the bathroom. Levi was waiting in the wide hallway between the men's and women's rooms, studying the map of North Carolina pinned to the wall behind a glass case.

His gaze met hers and flicked down her body, and the heat there reignited the need she'd just quelled. He rested a polite hand on her waist as they walked to the car, and when he held out his hands for the keys, she handed them over without a whimper of protest.

One day, though, she needed to find a way to keep him from getting his way so often. A woman had her pride, after all.

Once on the road again, he drove carefully and competently at precisely five miles per hour over the speed limit, with one hand on the top of the steering wheel and the other resting on the edge of her seat next to her thigh. His fingers kept time with the music on the radio, tapping out a sometimes complicated rhythm.

She watched him for a while, sifting through the pieces of the puzzle that was Levi. "So the whole hand on the thigh thing."

"Idle hands make the Devil's work." His fingers pressed against her thigh through the thin fabric of her sundress. "Anyway, I think better when I drive."

"Lot of thinking to do, then."

He shrugged, a casual lift of one shoulder. "I like to drive. It's a guy thing."

"Because you don't trust me, the little woman, to get us there safely."

"Because I'm a guy and I like to take charge. Yesterday, my take charge attitude made you hot."

"Yes, well, today it's kind of annoying."

He grinned, flashing his slightly crooked teeth. "Only because I rattled you."

"Pfft." She waved a dismissive hand. "You didn't rattle me."

"Mmm. So that wasn't your body trembling under my touch."

"That was your imagination," she said primly.

"How about we pull over and try again, this time with my mouth there?"

Her fingers curled together in her lap and her breath hung in her throat. Levi with his head between her legs, trailing hot kisses up her inner thigh. Holy Mother of God, he was trying to kill her.

He squeezed her thigh. "That's what I thought. Might do that tonight, though. If you want me to."

Sera stifled a breathy moan. How could she possibly think of anything else between now and then?

THE MILES ROLLED steadily by under the Volvo's tires, eating up the distance between the Outer Banks and Winston-Salem. Acre after acre of sandy farmland planted with sweet potatoes, soybeans, and corn flashed past the windows, broken by long stretches of forests and the occasional jumble of towns dotting the eastern Carolina landscape.

Levi fixed his attention firmly on the road, and when it strayed, he filled it with the classic rock his da loved. He did *not* think about the night ahead or what might happen when they reached the hotel in Winston-Salem, and he absolutely did *not* wonder what Sera was wearing under her dress.

That way be dragons.

The simple act of teasing her into handing over the keys had cost him plenty of control, and now, it wavered and fumbled on the flimsiest excuse. A whiff of the almond-scented lotion she coated all over her body every morning left his heart thundering in his ears. The smooth skin of her thighs under his fingers had made him tremble and ache. The catch in her breath when he'd threatened to put his mouth on her skin had nearly sent him over the line he'd been toeing since she'd walked onto the beach a week before, all woman and sunshine and laughter, wearing the same outfit she'd chosen for their trip.

What *was* she wearing under her sundress, anyway?

He snuck a glance at her out of the corner of his eye. She sat quietly in the passenger's seat, gazing out the window at the passing scenery. Less than ten minutes after he'd taken his place behind the steering wheel, her hand had drifted down and covered his where it rested next to her thigh.

As if she couldn't help herself, as if she *needed* to touch him, even in this small way.

Now, her fingers circled softly over the back of his hand, tracing the bones, dipping into the space between each finger, sliding to his wrist, brushing through the hair on his forearm, then starting all over again. Skin, bones, fingers, wrist. Her touch soothed and comforted and aroused in equal measures, and his imagination slipped unbidden to other, hidden places she could touch.

She hadn't touched him nearly enough. Tonight she would, all over, right after he made her come so hard she forgot about everything but him.

He inhaled through his nose, exhaled through his mouth. Need clawed at him, fierce and demanding, and he breathed again and again, reaching for a calm he couldn't feel around the sensations she aroused, around the mere thought of her touching him. Sera's hands on his bare skin, her palm trailing down his chest, her fingers toying with the line of hair leading from his navel down. Heat eddied through him, settling between his thighs, stirring him as it did every time he remembered the way she'd touched him that day.

He yanked his attention sharply back to the road. Goddess above, what was he thinking? If he couldn't clamp down on his control, he wouldn't last a minute inside her, wouldn't have the fortitude to do half of what he wanted to do to her.

She shifted in her seat, turning toward him, and lifted his hand onto her thigh. "You ok?"

He checked the rearview mirror, glanced at the speedometer, anything to keep her from seeing how not ok he was. "Yeah. Why?"

"You're fidgeting, and you're not a fidgeter."

"Just thinking."

"About what?"

He slanted a glance at her. "What do you think?"

"Do you really want to know?"

"Yeah, I do."

She turned solemn eyes on him. "I think you're wondering what you've gotten yourself into."

He snorted out a laugh. "I know exactly what I'm into, love. What I'm wondering is what else I can get into with you."

"Oh."

"Yeah, oh."

Her quiet, shallow breaths filled the air-conditioned interior of the car. "You have ideas."

"A whole imagination full."

"Like what?"

"If I tell you now," he said, enunciating each word carefully, "we'll both get stirred up and I'll have to pull over."

"Oh."

"Or you can wait until we get to our hotel and I can show you."

"Oh." She drew the word out into a low, breathy moan. "I see."

"Any objections?"

"I don't..." Her fingers clamped down on his hand, biting into the bone and tissue. "Do you think I'm desperate? You know, for wanting you?"

"Why would I think that?"

Especially when he was edging so close to desperation himself, he wasn't sure he could hold out that long once he had her naked under him.

"Because you're so much younger than I am." She rushed through his objections, her voice soft and thin. "Because you're so much *more* than I am."

He turned that over, trying to figure out what she meant, and came up completely clueless. The only thing he understood was the insecurity she'd inadvertently revealed. Somehow, he'd made Sera, with her luscious body and keen intelligence, feel unsure about herself.

A blue sign caught his eye. He signaled for a merge into the right lane and exited into a rest area, parking well away from the other vehicles.

"The only more here is what's ahead of us, Sera." He undid his seatbelt and leaned toward her, slipping his hand around her nape, pulling her close enough for her breath to feather across his lips. "Haven't I made that clear?"

Her eyes were wide in her face, pale against the tan she'd acquired over the week, her nod jerky. "I feel like I'm in way over my head with you."

"No, you're not. Whatever it is about me that makes you feel small, get it out of your head right now."

Her lips twitched and her eyes sparkled. "There's that take charge voice again."

"Yeah? Are you getting hot?"

"Maybe. Maybe I like your size, too."

"That's not what I was talking about."

"I know." She pressed a fleeting kiss to his mouth, just long enough to tease him with her taste. "It's true, though. You're so..." She blinked and bit her lip. "*Mmm.*"

He couldn't quite stop a smirk from spreading across his face. "So you're with me because you think I'm hot."

"That, and other things."

"Yeah?" His stomach muscles clenched into a knot. What other things had caught her interest? Had she found out about the money, his status among the People? Was she just another gold digger looking for a strike?

Sweet, innocent Sera.

He had to be wrong. She didn't seem the sort to care about money and status, not like that. Maybe she'd think the worst of him for the wealth he and his family had accumulated, but surely she wasn't after him because of it. Was she?

He cleared his throat. "Like what?"

She cupped his cheek and rubbed a thumb over his lower lip. "Hey, now. What's wrong? You kind of went all cold on me."

"Just answer me. Please."

She huffed out a laugh. "Ok. What were we talking about?"

"You said you were with me because of other things."

"Right. Other things." She smiled and kissed him again, lingering a little longer, sliding her lips across his in a slow, easy glide. "Mmm. Wow. You're potent." She blew out a soft breath. "Other things, like the way you take my hand when you think I need you or the way you ask after Petey every day, even though you don't know him from Adam. The way your face goes hard but your eyes are hot and you sort of run them down my body like you're undressing me in your head."

The tension slid out of his gut. "I am."

"Things like the other night when you were talking and your drawl faded out and this brogue crept in. *Nae muir.*" She shuddered as her eyes fluttered closed. "Mmm. Sorry."

If a little brogue turned her on, what would she do when he slipped into Gaelic?

"And the fact that you love music and you're well read and you can talk intelligently about whatever comes up. Do you know how hard it is to find a man like that?" She laughed and her breath feathered across his mouth, feeding his desire, stoking it higher. "I guess you wouldn't, what with being a man and all."

"I know how hard it is to find a woman like that outside of the People."

"Yeah? Hunh. Want me to keep going?"

"I think I get the picture."

"That's good. In a minute, I was gonna start in on your body, and that would've been uncomfortable."

He laughed, the way he figured she'd intended him to. "Maybe we'll get to that later."

She slipped her seatbelt off and curled toward him in the seat. "So. Are we gonna neck in the car or get on with our trip?"

"Maybe a little of both."

"Hey, I'm game."

And since she was, he couldn't resist. He hauled her closer and captured her mouth in a slow, gentle caress, letting his relief push him into taking as much as she'd give, exploring her when she blossomed for him, storing up her sighs and whispers and shy touches.

Soon, he'd have to tell her about his life, about the work he did for Nana, about his personal wealth and the hefty trust fund he'd never touched. About the People and the Seven Sisters, about the Prophecy of Light and a Son's importance to his family. Not yet, though. Until then, he would enjoy her, bring her pleasure while they learnt one another, and see if there was anything to the spark between them aside from the flash of light and heat.

Blessed Goddess, please let her not care about the money.

They hit the road again, and Sera dragged out her laptop and worked while he hummed along with the songs on the radio. Traffic steadily increased as they passed through Rocky Mount, merged onto I-40, and skirted Raleigh. Not long after, Levi took the Cherry Street exit toward Nana's hotel. Once inside, he checked them in to the family's suite.

The young woman at the desk smiled and flipped her golden curls over a slender shoulder. "Oh, Mr. Ewart. Ms. Carnahan wanted to speak with you when you arrived."

Levi smiled politely and waited while the clerk fetched Angela Carnahan, the hotel's manager. She strode into the lobby a few minutes later looking as fresh as she probably had when she'd arrived at work early that morning.

Her eyes flicked to Sera as she held out her hand. "It's so good to see you, Levi."

He shook her hand firmly, exactly as she expected him to.

"Angela, this is my companion, Sera Noland. Her family lives near Tellowee."

"Ah. I see." Angela nodded toward Sera, her smile professional. "I hope you enjoy your stay with us."

Sera smoothed the skirt of her sundress down and murmured, "I'm sure I will."

"Don't hesitate to ring me if you need anything." Angela's gaze held only the slightest hint of speculation as she turned back to him. "What time shall we begin in the morning?"

"Is seven too early?"

"That's perfect. I'll see you then." Angela held her hand out, accepted Levi's for another firm shake. "It was a pleasure meeting you, Ms. Noland."

After Angela pivoted and returned to her office, Levi ushered Sera into the elevator and punched the button for their floor. "You ok?"

"Fine." Sera's hand ran down her sundress again. "I wish you'd let me change into something more appropriate before we left."

"I like the sundress."

"It's not exactly a white pants suit, though, is it."

"A white pants suit." It took him a minute to figure out what she was talking about. "Sera, come on. She's the manager. If she didn't dress like that, it wouldn't be very professional."

"You didn't tell me your meeting was with the manager. I thought..." She wrinkled the fabric of her sundress between her fingers. "Your work isn't as haphazard and uncomplicated as you made it out to be, is it?"

He shrugged. There wasn't a lot he could say that wouldn't give her exactly the right idea about who and what he was. "It's not that big a deal."

Her laugh held equal portions of humor and disbelief. "She kowtowed."

"Angela Carnahan wouldn't know how to kowtow if her life depended on it."

"Oh, that was definitely kowtowing. And the clerk." Sera shook her head, her silver eyes glittering. "I think she has a crush on you."

"Yeah?" He waggled his eyebrows. "Do you have a crush on me?"

93

"You wish."

Yeah, he did, and therein lay the problem. Serafina Noland wasn't nearly as enamored of him as he'd like. That could change, though, would change if he had his way.

The elevator doors slid open. Levi led Sera to their room and locked them inside. Time for him to court her the way he'd wanted to since the first moment she'd touched him.

Nine

SERA STEPPED into the hotel room and clutched her shoulder bag with nerveless fingers. The door shut behind her with an ominous click, locking her into the suite with Levi. Alone with Levi, just him and her and a comfortable couch, a gargantuan bed, and other assorted furniture of the perfect height, shape, and size for sex.

She rubbed her eyes and sighed. Over the years, how many characters had she deliberately placed into situations just like the one she faced? Was it some kind of poetic justice that she should be here, nervous as a cat on a hot tin roof, about to embark on the very kind of sexual journey she wove into her stories?

The wheels of the baggage cart squeaked. Warm hands slid around her waist and pulled her back against a hard, muscled torso. "Second thoughts?"

"Not exactly," she muttered.

"We don't have to do anything, if that's what you're worried about." He rubbed his cheek over her hair and kissed her temple. "Do you need a little more time?"

"Ha. Well." Much more time and she was pretty sure she'd run screaming in the opposite direction. "Maybe a shower first."

"Hmm. A shower." His hands tightened on her stomach. "Can I watch?"

Oh, God. Levi watching her in broad daylight, *her*, with her nearly thirty-year-old body and stretch marks and nowhere to hide. What was she thinking, running around with a man seven years her junior? Levi was perfect from head to toe, firm and male and beautiful, and she was short, soft, and so deeply flawed.

"Nope," he said.

His voice startled her out of her thoughts. "What?"

"I know what you're thinking."

"You do?"

"And the answer is *no* and *I don't care.*"

"Erm." She relaxed into him, couldn't help the humor swelling up over her panic. "That's two answers."

"I'm covering all the bases."

"So you didn't really know what I was thinking, then."

"Not exactly. I could feel you tensing up, though, getting ready to run or turn me down. Here. You don't need this." He slid the bag off her shoulder and set it on the ground beside them, then surrounded her again. "I told you. We don't have to do anything you're not comfortable doing, but I do want to spend time with you. Can't do that if you skitter off like a scared rabbit."

She huffed out a breath. "I wasn't going to."

He turned her around with firm tugs and pulls, and wrapped a hand around her nape. His whiskey eyes held that dangerous glint he'd gotten when Heath had hit on her, and again when he and Ruby had been fighting. "I warned you about lying to me."

"Levi, really, that wasn't..."

His fingers dug into her waist as he hauled her up against his chest. "There you go again. Guess I'll have to teach you not to."

"Wait. I..."

His mouth came down on hers, claiming hers in a surprisingly tender kiss. She'd expected ferocity, harshness, anything but the gentle rub of his lips over hers. His hand skidded down her back and cupped her bottom, melding them together. She could feel him through the thin material of her dress and his slacks, every inch of him, long and hard and already ready for her.

Her fingers curled into his shirt and her breath left her in a rush. How could she even think of turning away this man who wanted her so much, a simple kiss stirred him to arousal?

His tongue flicked along the seam of her lips and she opened for him, and moaned when he dipped inside her mouth and tasted her. He ravaged her then, consuming her as if he couldn't live another second without her, as if her acceptance had been the only barrier between her and his hunger.

He broke their kiss abruptly and touched his forehead to hers, his eyes closed, his expression rigid. His breaths puffed in quick strokes over the remains of their kiss on her mouth and his whole body tightened around her, wrapping her in his desire. "Don't run from me, from this."

His eyes flashed open, hot, yearning, and his need trembled through her, melting the last of her resistance even as it threatened to swallow her whole. In that moment, he was huge to her, the embodiment of every restless night, of every longing to have someone else's heat filling her lonely bed. Another mind to share her day with and shoulder the responsibility of raising a child. Was this what he was becoming to her, and in such a short time?

The possibility fluttered in her chest, interrupting the steady beat of her heart and the quiet rhythm of her breath. She cupped his face in her hands and met his gaze evenly. "How could I?"

"You won't regret it," he said, soft and low. "I swear."

"Levi." She kissed him, lightly at first, slowly pressing into him, just as slowly letting him go. "Make love with me."

He lifted her high against his chest, easily holding her in the strength of his arms. She wound her hand around his neck and explored the sturdy column with her fingertips as he carried her to the bedroom. He was soft there, the skin smooth, and it was too tempting to ignore. She leaned forward and tasted him, cool masculinity flavored by the faintest hint of salt.

His moan vibrated under her lips. "You keep that up, I won't last five minutes."

She laughed against his skin, and his shudder rippled through them both.

He laid her on the bed, cradling her head against the pillows, and backed away. His eyes held hers as his hands tugged his shirt out of his pants and stripped it over his head. She shifted onto her side and watched while he folded it carefully and set it on the lone chair in the room, then took off his undershirt and did the same, leaving his torso beautifully bare. His shoes went next, toed off and placed under the chair, and then his socks.

"Do you remember the day we..." She bit her lower lip and followed the movements of his fingers as he undid the fastening on his slacks and slid them slowly down his legs. Oh, she'd missed those legs, every muscular inch of them. She sighed and patted her chest over her fluttering heartbeat. "Ah. The day we had our misunderstanding?"

"You mean the day you called me grabby." He smirked and stepped out of his pants, folded them precisely along the seams, and laid them on top of his other clothing. "Is that the misunderstanding you're referring to?"

She grimaced and ignored the pings and twitters growing inside her. Levi in swimming trunks? Awesome. Levi in skin-hugging boxer briefs? Magnificent, especially with his erection clearly outlined by the clingy fabric. Maybe he'd walk around like that the rest of the night. "You went for a swim, lapping the pool like the devil was on your heels."

"That's one way of putting it." He crawled onto the bed, taking her with him, and braced himself above her with his hips cradled in the juncture of her thighs. "Swimming clears my head."

"Mmm. Good to know." She lowered her gaze to his chest and scratched her nails through the crisp ginger hair scattered there. "Then Heath came over..."

"The bastard."

She pursed her lips, containing her laughter. "And you pushed yourself out of the pool and water dripped off you, clinging to you as if it were reluctant to leave, and then the sun hit you and you sort of sparkled under its touch. I thought you were a god, a child of fire and water. You were so beautiful then."

He nuzzled her throat and the flat of his tongue rasped across her pulse. "You're making me blush."

"Hardly," she said, and tilted her head to the side, making room for him and the delicious heat he licked into her. "You're one of the most self-contained people I know."

"It's called control. Hard won, too, mind you." He nibbled his way along her jaw and nipped her ear. "You'll like my control. Trust me."

"Oh? Um. Ha. Sounds..." *Delicious. Wonderful. Mind-numbingly blissful.* "Promising."

"I love it when you do that."

His breath feathered along her ear, pulsing into her. She rubbed her fingertips into the taut muscles of his chest, searching for her own control. "Do what?"

"Start a sentence and pause half-way through, like there are a million things going through your mind and you're trying to find the most innocuous thing to say."

"You've got me there."

He shifted over her, touched his nose to hers. "Ready?"

"I still have my shoes on."

He grinned. "I know. Some men dream of making love to a woman wearing heels. Me, I've got a thing for Chuck Taylors."

Her sputtered laugh morphed into a giggle. "That's so *wrong.*"

"Maybe." He touched his nose to hers again, then dropped a kiss to her mouth. "It's kind of a recent development."

She sighed out the last of her humor, though her smile refused to fade. "Oh?"

"You don't think Chuck Taylors can be sexy?" He shook his head and clucked his tongue, and his whiskey eyes glowed in the soft light filtering through the curtains. "With the right woman..."

Her heart thudded so hard, it nearly bounced out of her chest. "Am I the right woman?"

His lips curled into a slow, knowing smile. "Here we go, love."

He shifted his weight onto one forearm and captured her mouth in a devastatingly gentle kiss. His fingers trailed down her neck and along her collarbone, sliding slowly along the edge of her sundress and across the top of her breast, lingering there in a feather-light caress. Back and forth his fingers skimmed as his mouth explored hers, his lips soft, giving under the pressure of his kiss until they were melded together, man and woman, dark and light.

She clung to him, arching into his touch, moaning into his mouth when his finger dipped into her bra and found her nipple. He plucked it, rolled it between his fingers, then slid his hand inside, cupping her flesh. His palm was warm and the need he stirred a liquid heat shimmering through her veins.

His weight pressed her into the bed as his body slid against hers, nudging his erection against the core of her body with every shift of muscle and bone. He broke the kiss and dragged his mouth down her neck, down, down, and captured her nipple in his wet heat. She gasped and clasped his head in one hand, holding him

99

there, offering herself to the sweet suckling of his mouth, the lash of his tongue across the hardened nub of her nipple. Her fingers skidded through his hair, silky cool, a stark contrast to the passion burning under her skin. She could feel it in him, under her other palm where it rested on his shoulder blade, in the desperate beat of his heart, in his sharply inhaled breaths and the ripple of muscle as he touched her.

His fingers drifted to the buttons running down the bodice of her dress, opening them with quick, agile flicks, and then his hand ran along her ribs. His mouth trailed lower, teasing her stomach for only a moment, and he licked his way to her other breast and showed it the same torturous care he'd given the other.

She slid a leg over his thigh and her hips found their own rhythm, grazing her sex along his erection through the barriers of their clothing, stoking the languid need swirling through her. He shifted his weight, moving the delicious friction out of her reach, and she moaned. "Please, Levi."

"I want to do things to you." His voice was rough and shaky, his native brogue thick, and his fingers were no longer gentle on her skin, but needy, demanding. "I want to taste you, every single inch of you, and make you beg for my touch."

"Oh, my God," she breathed.

"I'm so close, so fucking close." He shifted again and flexed his hips into her, rubbing himself across her exactly where she wanted him to be. "It was supposed to be slow, easy. Hours of me touching you and making you come over and over again, not you shattering my control ten minutes in with those soft little noises you make and the feel of your skin on mine."

He pushed himself off of her, off of the bed into a stand, and stared down at her with his face a hard mask and his eyes hot and greedy, raking over her as if he owned her, all of her, from skin to bone and back again. "Let your hair down."

Absent his heat, the air chilled her skin. She curled her fingers into the bedspread. This Levi wasn't the gentle lover that had carried her into the room. No, that man was gone, lost to the one standing in front of her. This Levi wouldn't be tender. He'd be rough and ravenous and wild, and he'd soak up every ounce of passion she could give, all the while demanding more. She shivered and inched her hands up to her hair, lifting her head up to remove the barrette. Her curls sprang free and she spread her hair out beneath her head.

He took the barrette and set it on the nightstand. "Show me your panties."

Her breath hitched in and her thighs clenched together. "Levi, please."

"Show me them," he said, and his eyes raked over her again, pushing her to do his bidding. She dug her fingers into the fabric of her sundress and, as slowly as she dared, pulled the skirt up, exposing her underwear. His gaze dropped there and lingered, and her heart hammered in her chest. If she'd ever had a doubt, just one single doubt that Levi wanted her, that look told her differently.

His thumbs hooked in the waistband of his briefs. "Take them off. Shoes on."

A laugh escaped through the heavy heat seeping through her limbs. She shimmied out of her panties, tugged them off around her shoes, and tossed them at the chair where he'd left his clothes. By the time she finished, he'd pulled off his briefs and had his back to her as he rifled through his slacks.

God, he was beautiful, from the broad reach of his shoulders along the inward curve of his spine and the outward curve of his firm bottom, down the long, long lengths of his legs. He had a faint tan line around his hips, fainter ones above his knees, and then he turned and she forgot all about the sun's touch on his skin. He walked to her, unashamed of his nudity or the hard length of his erection jutting from his body, surrounded by thick, silky curls shades darker than the hair above it, under his navel.

She sucked in a breath. Had she thought him beautiful? How wrong she'd been. He was magnificent, stunning, breath-taking, and he wanted *her*. She closed her eyes against the doubts shooting through her. She'd been there before, lost in the sanity of a woman who knew her own limits. This man had none and he would never acknowledge hers.

The mattress shifted under his weight and his hands clamped onto her ankles, spreading her legs wide. "Don't go there."

She squinched her eyes tightly closed. "What, are you a mind reader now?"

"Something like that."

A moment later, his breath blew gently along her inner thighs. He licked the flat of his tongue up the seam of her body and sucked her clitoris into his mouth, surrounding her for one glorious moment with wet heat and the roll of his tongue. Her eyes popped open and her gaze landed on his smirk.

"Thought that might get your attention." He knelt between her legs and rolled a condom on. "Later, I'm gonna spend some time there. Lots and lots of time, using my tongue and teeth and lips and fingers, and you're gonna squirm and scream and beg me to let you come."

She bit her lip and moaned. "Levi, God. Why do you say those things?"

"Because they're true. Now, though, I need to be deep inside you."

He covered her slowly, pinning her to the bed with his weight as his erection nudged her sex. She lifted her knees, inviting him in, and he filled her, easing into her so slowly, so tightly, it was as if he were a part of her. He kissed her temple and flexed his hips, and then they moved together in a nascent storm of need, his hips thrusting steadily against her, hers rising urgently to meet him, skin sliding on skin as their breaths mingled.

"Sera, sweet Sera."

His murmured to her, a slow torrent of unfamiliar, lilting words. Their music chimed within her, striking the desire until it reverberated through her, an endless chord hanging on the wind, never diminishing, echoing into itself. She traced her fingers along his tattoo, dug her nails into the notes marking his skin, and sighed his name into his throat as his passion resonated within her.

"That's it, baby," he said, his voice thick and rough. His hand jerked her sundress up and found her hip, skidded down her thigh and pulled her knee up, anchoring it against his ribs. "So tight."

Her hands scrambled over his sweat slicked skin in a frantic rush to know him everywhere, ending with the fingers of one hand splayed over his firm bottom and the other cupping his head, pulling him down into a fierce, needy kiss. His hips thrust against hers, hard, so beautiful, and the desire he'd strummed within her burst in a wild crescendo, sweeping her breath and sanity away in a mad chorus of sighs and groans amid the sweet friction of skin on skin. She panted her release into his mouth, and he pushed into her one last time, his own release throbbing through her in a dazzling finale of heat and light.

THE WORLD SLID SLOWLY 'round, settling into a new rotation. Levi held himself above Sera, resting only a little of his weight on her. She was limp under him, her silver eyes closed, her heart hammering beneath his. It marked a steady beat, forcing his own heart to match her quicker rhythm.

Pleasurable aftershocks rippled through him, reborn with every pulse of her pussy around his dick, every sigh of her breath on his chest. He thrust into her again, leisurely, unwilling to break free of her hold and the passion they'd shared, needing it to last a little longer.

He nuzzled her throat, pressed an open mouthed kiss over the rapid flutter of her pulse.

She stirred and rolled her head to the side, leaving herself open to his touch. "If I'd known it would be like that, I would've dragged you back to my apartment that first day."

He snorted out a laugh. "No, you wouldn't have."

"You're right, I wouldn't. Sounded good, though."

"It did." He dropped a hard kiss to her willing mouth and levered himself off of her, out of the warm cling of her body around his. "Be right back."

He padded into the bathroom and disposed of the condom, cleaned himself off and wet a washcloth. When he re-entered the bedroom, she'd pulled her sundress down, covering her lower body. He sat beside her and eased it up again, tugging when she put her hands down, holding it in place. "Let me clean you up."

Her eyes fluttered shut. "I'm not letting you do that."

"I've already seen whatever it is you're trying to hide."

She covered her face with both hands and groaned into her palms. "Levi, God. Leave me some dignity."

He smirked. "Be glad it's not my mouth down there, licking you clean."

Her fingers parted and a silver eye peeped out. "You wouldn't."

"I'm gonna do that later, when I show you some of that control I promised you."

He slid her dress up and nudged her thighs apart. Her pussy glistened in the light streaming through the window, firm and beautiful, perfectly formed. Desire stirred in him as he ran the washcloth gently over the labia, along her inner thighs and over her mons, stirring the dark curls protecting her sex. He deliberately dragged the cloth over her clitoris. "Do you like that?"

Her hands fell to the bedspread and her fingers dug into its fabric. "Is nothing off limits to you?"

"Not a thing." Though he knew when to back off. He folded the washcloth into a square and tucked her sundress carefully around her thighs. "Supper's still a ways off."

Her eyes slanted warily toward him. "And?"

"There's a pool if you want a swim or the gym."

"I've had enough exercise today, thanks." Her hand crept off of the bed onto his bare thigh. "What do you want to do?"

"Hold you, touch you. Talk." He shrugged. "Spend time with you."

"Really? You don't want to, ah, do that again?"

"I think we should wait until you're comfortable being naked around me, or at least until you're sure you're not too sore."

"Ah. Um." Her gaze slid from his and landed somewhere over his left shoulder. "Maybe we could cuddle?"

"Sure. Want a t-shirt?"

"One of yours?"

Sera wearing one of his t-shirts, her luscious body draped in something that had touched his skin? "I'll get one for you."

Her hand tightened on his thigh. "You're so confusing."

"How so?"

She blinked and shifted on the bed, curling around him. "We just had fantastic sex, you're still hard as a rock, and you're willing to let me put clothes on and cuddle with me. What sane man does that?"

"The kind that wants to stick around."

Her eyes widened and her mouth formed a perfect, silent *oh*.

"Yeah, oh. I'll get you a t-shirt."

He dropped the washcloth onto the bathroom floor and

retrieved her panties, then padded into the suite's living area and rummaged through his suitcase for a clean t-shirt. She'd slipped into the bathroom by the time he found one and returned to the bedroom. He pulled the covers down on the bed and propped pillows up against the headboard, settling against them while he waited.

She'd broken his control.

He'd always prided himself on the disciplined response of his body, earned through years of struggle and work. Nana had pushed him to his limits time and again, testing him, stretching his will to the breaking point and, more often than not, well beyond. She'd tempered him, molded him, hammered the need for control into him over the years of his childhood until it was second nature. Never had he thought the day would come when it would break again.

One week with Sera, a few minutes of having her under him. That's all it had taken to shatter his hard earned control.

Sera, lovely Sera, with her sweet voice and shy smile and enough reservations to last them both the rest of their lives.

The toilet flushed, water ran. She stepped out of the bathroom wrapped in a towel, her shoes gone, her hair loose around her bare shoulders. Her gaze fell on him and skittered away, and her skin flushed pink. Did she regret having sex with him or had her innate shyness won out in the aftermath of their passion?

"My dress was soaked." She inched closer to the bed, her steps hesitant and light. "Mind if I borrow that t-shirt now?"

"Here you go." He held it out to her along with her panties, waiting for her with the patience of a man tempting a wild doe to feed from his hand. "Want me to help you?"

She shook her head in a quick no, then pursed her lips and nodded.

His firmed his lips against the smile that threatened. "Come here, then."

She stepped into his reach, bowed her head as he tugged the t-shirt onto her. He pulled her long curls out, fanning the fine locks through his fingers. "You have the most beautiful hair. Soft and springy."

"Drab and dull." She slid one arm after the other through the sleeves of the t-shirt, holding the towel tight against her breasts until he'd smoothed the shirt down over it. "A stringy mess."

"Beautiful," he said firmly. He pulled the towel away, letting it pool onto the floor, and helped her step into her panties, then tugged her onto the bed next to him. "Like the rest of you."

"You don't have to keep flattering me. We both know I'll have sex with you again."

"How could such a sweet woman be so cynical?"

"You call it cynical. I call it realistic." She tucked her arm under her head and curled up facing him. "Like knowing that as soon as you crook your finger, I'll come running."

"And here I was pondering what a shy, retiring creature you'd become."

She laughed. "Only for a minute, and only while I was naked and fresh from truly magnificent sex. You have a way of stripping away my defenses."

"It's mutual." He gave in to temptation and entangled himself with her, sliding one of his thighs between her legs and his arm around the indent of her waist. "So, here we are, all alone in this big bed with an hour to kill before we have to get ready for supper."

"You said we could cuddle."

The mild reprimand in her voice tickled his humor. "Sex is a form of cuddling."

She huffed out a sigh. "I just got dressed."

"I know. Sorry. You're so easy to tease."

"Hmm, right. That's what you call it." Her fingers found his sternum, stroking lightly. "Can I ask you something?"

"Anything, love."

"What happened to the bruises from your fight with Ruby?" Sera's eyes swept up and pinned him in place. "As hard as she hit you, you should still be black and blue, or at least ugly shades of yellow, and yet, there's barely a mark left on your skin."

Shite. He'd been so desperate to be in her, he'd forgotten all about those damn bruises. "I'm a quick healer, that's all."

"Nobody's that quick, and besides." She cupped his jaw, forcing his gaze back to hers. "You went all cold again. You only do that when you're hiding something from me."

His heart turned over, quick as a snap, taking his breath with it.

"Maybe we've spent a little too much time together."

Her eyes shuttered and her hand dropped away, leaving him as cold as she'd accused him of being. "I see."

"No, wait. I didn't..." He blew out a breath and scrambled for the control he hadn't been so long without since he was a kid. "You see right through me, every single time."

"You say that like it's a bad thing."

"It could be," he murmured. If she ultimately rejected him, especially after learning all his secrets, her being able to read him so well could lead to serious trouble for them both.

"Aren't lovers supposed to be open with each other?"

"Lovers implies a long-term relationship." He tucked a stray strand of her hair behind her ear, lingered on the graceful column of her neck. "Is that what you want?"

One corner of her mouth quirked up. "Maybe."

"Do I get a say?"

Her lashes swept up in a flirtatious tease. "What if I said no?"

"I'd find a way to convince you."

"And if I said I wanted you to stick?"

"I'd fall at your feet and worship you until the end of time."

She laughed and snuggled into him. "You say the most outrageous things."

"I do not." He rubbed his cheek over her temple, savoring the weight of her thigh draped over his and her breath caressing his skin. "You're just not used to a man being plain about what he wants."

"You've got me there." She yawned and stretched, a kitten settling in for a nap. "I don't think there's another man like you on God's green earth."

"Yeah?"

"Yeah." Her eyes fluttered shut on another yawn. "I think I like it."

He wrapped her in his arms and held her as she drifted into a light doze, his mind twisting through the wonders that were Sera.

Ten

A FTER A SHORT NAP, Sera showered alone. Levi had pulled on his underwear and settled on the suite's couch with his laptop, getting ready for the next day's meeting, she supposed.

With a kowtowing woman whose body was trim enough to wear a well-fitting, white pants suit.

Sera turned her face into the water and scrubbed it with both hands. She was not jealous. To be jealous, she'd have to have a reason, and Levi hadn't given her one. Even if they were in a real relationship, which they weren't, he'd done nothing to stir the green-eyed monster. In fact, he'd been nothing other than sweetly attentive the entire time she'd known him, save the rare occasions his temper stirred, and even then he'd retreated into that cold shell of his instead of lashing out.

He wanted to stick.

She lathered soap into a washcloth and scrubbed her arms. Him saying that outright wasn't the first clue he'd given that he wanted something more from her, something deeper and lasting. He'd edged around it all week, lightly at first, more sternly when she'd let it slip that she fully expected him to forget about her as soon as her vacation ended.

And in retaliation for her doubts he'd...gone to a book signing with her. Gotten down on his knees and told her he wasn't a quitter. Rearranged his entire schedule to have another week with her, made love to her with a tender regard usually reserved for someone you loved, and then committed the grave sins of dressing her in his t-shirt and cuddling with her.

Why was she so hesitant to continue a relationship with a man who so obviously wanted to be with her?

The shower curtain screeched as it was yanked back. Levi stepped into the tub and yanked the curtain back across the opening, and Sera's startled shriek morphed into outraged laughter. She turned her back on him and nearly melted when he slid his arms around her and pulled her firmly against him, molding her softer body to his hard form.

"What are you doing in here?" she asked.

"You were taking so long, I was afraid you'd use up all the hot water."

"It's a hotel. There's an endless supply."

"Ok, you caught me. I was lonely for you."

She snorted out a laugh. "More like you were bored and decided to stir up trouble."

His lips brushed her ear. "Think you have my number now, do you?"

"I'll never tell."

He snagged the soap and rubbed it between his hands in front of her. "Hold still now, love."

"I've already..."

He smoothed his soapy hands down her chest and over her breasts, lingering there. "You have an objection to me washing you?"

"Um. Ha." His fingers splayed across her breasts, teasing her nipples, massaging heat into her skin. "If you put it like that, then no."

"Didn't think so. Spread your legs for me."

"Levi," she breathed. He slid his soapy hands down her stomach and delved into the secret heat between her thighs, and she trembled.

"Not too sore there, are you?"

Her voice stuck in her throat, lost in the wave of need washing over her. She shook her head and clutched the arm he held around her midriff under her breasts, all too aware of his erection pressing into her lower back, the rush of his breath on her neck, and his fingers circling leisurely around her clitoris.

"Good, then. I'm of a mind to pleasure you for a while." He

rinsed his fingers off under the shower's spray and brought water to her sex, rinsing it with light splashes and rubs. "Open for me."

She swallowed the moan rising in her throat. "Shouldn't we do this in bed?"

"Where's your imagination?"

"I save it for my books."

He tsked and nudged her thighs apart. "What fun is that?"

"I can honestly say it's never been an issue before."

His laughter tickled the side of her neck, and then his teeth nipped her earlobe. She gave in to his touch, opening her thighs for him, resting her head against his strong chest. His arm around her midriff shifted and his hand cupped her breast. Lightning shot between those points, the insistent press of his arm holding her upright while he strummed her nipple with his thumb and the light, teasing rub of his fingers on her clitoris. It seared and writhed within her, cleansing her doubt, burning it out of her, leaving only the need. She arched into his touch, a live wire held taut by a sharp electric current, and panted as he brought her high, higher.

"That's it, now," he whispered. "Almost there."

She reached back and dug her nails into his shoulder, pinning him to her, unable to contain the heat on her own. "Levi, please."

His mouth latched on to her neck, sucking hard as he pinched her nipple and pressed his fingers firmly against her clitoris, jerking sharply, and the heat released abruptly in a flood of throbs and spasms, sweeping through her, all of her. She gasped and the strength seeped out of her limbs, and he kissed her neck and snuggled her into his embrace, holding her upright as the water rushed over them.

"My God." She let go of his shoulder and curled her hands around his arms. He was firm under her touch, rock solid and steady. It was the best thing about him. One of the best things, anyway. "That has to beat the record for the world's fastest orgasm."

He choked on a laugh. "I'll give you a better one later."

"A better..." The words wheezed out of her. "Any better and I might die from it."

"You act like you've never had an orgasm before."

"Not quite like that," she admitted. That one had been intense and fulfilling, for all its speed. "Thank you."

"Any time. Later, definitely." He propped his chin on the top of her head and rubbed lightly. "I think I made a couple of promises when you had me in your thrall earlier."

"Ha, right. I had you in my thrall." She squeezed his arms and settled against him with a contented sigh. "I've barely touched you, not the way you've touched me."

His hips shifted, grazing his erection across her skin. "Don't."

"Don't what?" She twisted in his arms and leaned back, and was surprised to find his expression tense and his eyes tightly shut. "What's wrong?"

"I'm hanging on to my control by a thread as it is. If I even think about you touching me, I'll lose it."

She cupped his jaw and, when that didn't work, pinched it. He opened his eyes, those beautiful whiskey eyes, and stared down at her with something close to helplessness.

"Don't you think I feel the same way?" she asked.

"It's not the same for you. I was raised to control my body, my emotions, to discipline myself."

"Nobody has that kind of control, Levi, not during sex."

His brows furrowed and his eyes shuttered, and it hit her then that he had at least the capability of controlling himself during the wild heat of really great sex.

And that he hadn't been able to control himself with her.

Levi had phenomenal control, from what she could tell, and what had Ruby said about him? That he never touched a woman who wasn't family, not in public, not even accidentally. Yet from the start, he'd sought Sera out, offering himself to her, touching her in ways that were barely decent, and sometimes not even that.

Even though she was supposed to be, as he put it, a healthy flirt.

Maybe he'd simply gotten tired of controlling himself for so long. Maybe having a family member around to hold him in check hadn't been enough this time.

Or maybe the fact that she had an illegitimate son had made her an easy target in his mind, just like all the other men she'd dated since Petey's birth.

A heavy knot burst into her heart, fully formed. She dropped her hand, weighed down by the ugliness of that thought. "How often do you have these light little flirtations, Levi? A couple of times a month? Or do you wait until you're strung so tight, you have to give in to it?"

His expression hardened into a granite mask and when he spoke, his voice was low and thick. "You're not a light flirtation."

"Aren't I?" She turned away from him and shut her eyes, willing the tears welling up through the heat of shame to stay put, safely hidden behind her eyelids. "It's ok. I was willing enough."

"Not so much," he murmured. "And for the record, I'm never strung so tight I have to force myself on a woman."

"I didn't say that."

"Sounded pretty damn close to me." His laugh caught a note halfway between humor and disbelief, and his arms dropped away from her. "Is that what you really think, that you're just another warm body to me? That I'm using you for sex?"

No, she wanted to say, but wasn't that what she'd been thinking?

"By the Goddess, Sera, how could you doubt..." He inhaled sharply and eased away from her. "I'll leave you to your shower, then."

He stepped out of the tub with far less noise than he'd entered it, sliding the shower curtain back and forth so quietly, the sound was lost under the spray of water cascading down around her. A moment later, he snagged a towel and slipped out of the bathroom, leaving her cold and empty and lost. She wrapped her arms around herself and bowed her head, sniffing back the tears sliding down her cheeks.

How could he have fooled her so thoroughly?

She forced herself to pick up the soap and wash again, cleansing herself by rote, her mind numb, her heart raw and open. He'd been so kind to her, so attentive. Was it all part of his game, a dare from one of his buddies? Coax the single mother into bed and fuck her senseless, but to what purpose? None of them had struck her as being cruel, not even underhanded Ruby, who'd seemed genuinely friendly in spite of her snark.

Sera scrubbed her hair, rinsed the soap and shampoo away, and cut the water off. Why would Levi do that anyway? He was handsome enough that he shouldn't have to chase women. She'd seen how women watched him when they were in public, the way their gazes lingered on his athletic form and on his bright hair and whiskey eyes. He could have his pick of any female between the ages of eighteen and forty, minimum, and he was young enough to...

Her hand halted halfway to a towel.

He was young.

A tremor of misgiving hit her, followed by a sinking dread. Had she totally misread the situation? Was he simply so young that he hadn't yet met a woman that didn't fall immediately under his spell, swayed by the wild charm hinted at in his smirk and innate self-assurance? Had he pursued her precisely because she hadn't fallen into his bed, and his lack of control was simply a consequence of the sexual tension that had stretched between them all week?

She buried her face in the towel. Crap. Why did her fallback reaction always have to be defensiveness?

And why, oh why, had she ever thought she could handle two days alone with a man she found so attractive, the slightest hint of wrongdoing cut her to the quick? How could she have forgotten how steadfast and mature he was, how he'd done everything he could to reassure her? He'd flat out told her he didn't think less of her because Petey had been born outside of wedlock. How could she have allowed her own insecurity to push that out of her mind?

She dried off hastily and finished her ablutions as quickly as she could, leaving her hair to air dry. She stepped into the bedroom half expecting to find him sprawled out on the bed, hoping so, anyway. Her shoulders drooped. The room was empty, the door to the outer living area snugly shut, and his clothes were no longer draped over the chair. She pressed a trembling hand to her mouth. Surely he hadn't left, not without saying goodbye.

He'd taken the time to make up the bed and had set her suitcase and laptop bag on top. She fumbled through her clothes, threw on a t-shirt and shorts, and raced into the living area. He was sitting on the sofa dressed in the clothes he'd worn earlier, laptop open on the coffee table, and was talking on his cell in rapid bursts of an unfamiliar language. His eyes flicked to her and returned just as quickly to his work.

She bit her lip and rubbed her hands together, and called herself ten kinds of fool for hurting him. At least he hadn't left, though. She could still fix this, lay it all out for him, ask for his forgiveness. He was patient and reasonable. Surely he'd understand how her mind had drifted into irrational, how hard it was for her to trust a man, any man, after what Petey's dad had put her through.

She perched on the edge of the plush, matching armchair and waited him out.

A few minutes later, he closed his phone and dropped it on the table. "After supper, I'll be moving to another room."

Her heart dropped into her knees and she slumped into the chair's cushioning. "Levi..."

"I'll arrange for a rental in the morning, once I see you off."

"That's really not necessary."

He speared her with a gaze so coldly impassive, she flinched away from it. He had a way of looking right through her as if she weren't even there, and it hurt so much to have him direct that empty stare at her again.

"Would you like to eat in the restaurant downstairs or would you rather go out?"

She swallowed the misery clogging her sinuses and closing off her throat. "I'd rather we talk this through."

"You've made your feelings clear." He closed his laptop and stood, hands in the pockets of his slacks, his blank stare boring into her. "And I have nothing further to say to you."

His words stabbed into her, bruising and tearing their way with blunt precision through the last shred of her ego. Had her heart been raw before, when she'd thought he was playing with her, using her because she'd given birth without the benefit of marriage? She bowed her head and closed her eyes, dug her nails into her palms, and still, his disdain ate through her, turning in on itself until it consumed her and not a single cell in her body remained unscathed.

"I'm sorry," she whispered. The words hung in the air, echoing in the room. A door snicked shut, and when she looked up, he was gone. She wound herself into a ball on the chair and rested her head on its arm, her gaze fixed to his laptop and phone, her breath shallow around the wad of sorrow lodged in her chest. He'd come back, and when he did, she'd explain and apologize and make it right, and he would listen. He just had to.

LEVI SLUMPED against the wall outside his and Sera's room, breathing through the pain wrapped like a vise around his chest.

How often do you have these light little flirtations, Levi?

He huffed out a humorless laugh and scrubbed his hands over his face. Damn Sera and her doubting heart. How many ways did he have to show her that she meant more to him than that? Sweet Goddess, he'd given her so much, as much as he was able for the short time he'd known her, and she'd all but accused him of playing her.

As if she hadn't a clue as to what kind of man he was.

He beat the back of his head against the wall. That's what he got for opening himself up to her, for chasing after her in the first place, knowing how reluctant she was to be with him. She'd even hinted that she might not feel the same way in her comments about how grabby he was, her request for him not to touch her in public, her belief that he was too young for her.

Why had he overlooked all of her misgivings?

His stomach muscles tightened. She'd touched him once the way a woman touched a man she wanted. Just once, she'd lost herself in sensation and touched him freely. Soft and slow, her fingertips running gently over his lower abs as those beautiful silver eyes went hot and her teeth nibbled on her lower lip. She'd touched and she'd looked and she'd *wanted*, and his body remembered what his heart wished it would forget.

The heat of her caress lingered nearly a week later, a mark invisible to others, but no less permanent than the *amaetien* inked into his arm. In school, his classmates had whispered the rumor to each other that a Son only gave his heart once, and when he did, it could never be given again, as if a man had any control over where his love landed and for how long.

He had more discipline than that. No, he hadn't given his heart to Sera, fickle Sera whose emotions shifted with the wind, couldn't have. He'd only known her a week, and though they'd spent a lot of time together, learning one another, he'd foolishly thought, he wasn't rash enough to leave himself vulnerable to her whimsy.

He rubbed a hand over the ache in his chest. Fuck all. Surely he hadn't already started that slide into love, not with her. He wanted her, yeah, with a fierceness that hammered at him to walk through that door, pin her to the nearest surface, horizontal or not, and make love to her until she saw reason.

'That wasn't love. It was lust, pure, unadulterated lust.

He dropped his hand and sighed. Yeah, right. The urgent need he had to bind her to him was only lust. Maybe if he told himself that enough, he'd even believe it.

He pushed away from the wall. It wasn't quite love yet, no matter what his heart said. There was still time to stop it, still time to pull himself back from the brink and reclaim himself. He couldn't halt the need he had to take care of her, to make sure she ate and had a decent night's rest, to see her safely off toward home the next day. A Son was trained from birth to take care of his woman. It was one duty he could never shirk, but he sure as hell didn't have to give in to his other needs. Holding her through the night, protecting her as she slept. Burying himself in her, making her come over and over again. Anything to please her.

And she'd rejected that, pushed him away without giving him half a chance to prove himself to her. He glared at the hapless door, the only barrier between him and the woman that had come to mean so much in such a short time. Hell with that. When a woman toyed with a Son's affections, there were consequences.

He yanked the keycard out of his pocket and slid it into the lock, and caught an odd sound coming from behind the door. Sniffles, a quiet cough, an even quieter sob. The anger drained abruptly out of him. He rested his forehead on the door and listened to the nearly silent sounds of Sera crying.

Because of him.

Her sorrow wormed its way through his heart, burrowing and twisting, carving away any thought he had of binding her more closely to him.

He didn't want to hurt her. Sure as rain, he didn't want her to hurt him again. Maybe the friendship they'd begun wasn't strong enough to endure her doubts, and if it wasn't, the love following it would never last, not on her part.

For his part, once he gave his heart, it would be hers always. It was simply his way. He wasn't ready to risk that, not without assurances on her part that she could love him equally.

He marked off time, waiting for her to calm, ignoring the stares of guests as they walked past. When her sniffles had been quiet for a while and he was sure he wouldn't intrude on her privacy, he unlocked the door and walked in. She was curled up like a kitten in the chair across from his laptop, her eyes closed, her hands tucked between her thighs. He stared down at her for long moments, waiting out the breathless ache gripping him on seeing the tear tracks on her cheeks and the cold chills spreading across her skin. She left him helpless and weak, vulnerable to her slightest whim, and unable to fulfill even the simple task of caring for her.

How could such a small woman have such tremendous power over him?

Her lashes swept up, catching him off guard. "You came back."

She sat up and shoved her hair back, those long silky locks, still half wet from her shower. He inhaled around the memory of what they'd done there not an hour before, her skin under his fingers, her gasps of arousal and release. It wouldn't do any good to linger on what was good and right between them, even if memory left him aching to make it better.

"I'm so sorry," she said.

Her voice was tight and thin, the way it was when she was upset. He sat down on the sofa facing her, glad for the distance.

She exhaled slowly and rubbed her hands down her thighs. "Petey's dad was my last lover."

"Was he now?" he said, and winced when she bowed her head and threaded her fingers together in her lap. Why had he lashed out at her? That his fucking control was thread thin around her was no excuse. "Sera..."

"I dated." She lifted her head and stared him down, her gaze sharp and sad all at once. "A lot, once Petey was a toddler. For a while, anyway, and then the rumors started circulating back to me. How I was a whore for having Petey on my own. How no decent man would want me, though a few really good men asked me out. I went and tried, and in the end, it never felt right, so I stopped dating and learned how to be content with what I had. A son I love more than life, a steady job, and later, my stories.

"That didn't stop the rumors, of course, and it didn't stop men from trying things with me." She laughed, soft and bitter as the frost of winter after spring's first bloom. "Once, at church, the minister backed me into a corner and put his hand on my breast. Told me if I didn't fuck him, he'd run me out of town. His words, my hand to God."

A wild whip of fury lashed through Levi and his heart leapt into his throat, roaring at him to find that man and make him pay for touching her when she hadn't wanted him to, for hurting her, for making her feel no better than the dirt under their feet. She blanched and paled, and whispered, "Please don't look at me like that, like you don't even see me."

"I see you." He didn't bother clearing the anger lodged in his throat, thickening his voice. "Did you tell anybody?"

She shrugged and pinned her gaze to her knees. "Who'd believe me?"

"Your da and mum. Your brother and his wife."

"And what could they do?" She shrugged again, as if trying to brush the memory of it away, though it clung to her like a shadow. "I stopped going to church. That was about the time my books hit big, so I was able to quit my job and work full-time from home. It got better after that."

"You hid yourself away."

"No, I..." She exhaled a half laugh. "How did we get onto this? I was trying to apologize, not feed you a sob story."

"And what were you apologizing for, Serafina?"

"For being a complete idiot." She lifted her gaze, caught sight of his expression, and laughed. "Oh, Levi. You should see your face. Did you think I couldn't admit how wrong I was?"

He leaned forward, bracing his forearms on his knees, and met her gaze evenly. "I'm not even sure what happened between that record-breaking orgasm and the time I left the shower."

Her lips quirked into a grin that lasted only a moment before it faded. "You were right. I thought you were using me, for purposes unknown. Maybe to slake your need." She held up a hand, forestalling his reply. "You're young and have a very healthy libido. A blind woman could see that."

"I like sex, yeah. Doesn't mean I'd force myself on a woman."

"I didn't say you would."

"You implied it."

"You inferred a meaning that wasn't there."

He rubbed a thumb across the twinge in his forehead. "A lot of that going around, seems to me."

"Ok, yes, I've read a lot of meaning into this past week, things that might or might not be true, but that isn't the point here."

"Isn't it?" He slumped into the sofa. "Sweet Goddess, Sera, you've done everything but call me a player. I'm too young, too immature. Too grabby, too, what? Demanding? Needy? What is it this time? I mean, what is it that I've done to touch off this storm of accusations?"

"Nothing," she said quietly. "This is all on me."

"Don't even fucking go there." She winced and he rushed on, refusing to give in to the need to soothe her hurt. "You can't keep doing this to me, making baseless assumptions, jumping to conclusions because other men have hurt you. You want me to see you? Maybe I need you to see me, too, the real me, not this false image you've constructed because you're scared of being hurt again. I care about you, Sera."

"Levi..."

"No, you've had your say. Now you need to listen." He sucked in a breath, struggling to find the control that had always been second nature. "I care about you, enough to stick around and see if we could have something beyond friendship and a good fuck. It's not something I do lightly."

"I didn't think it was."

He slashed his hand through the air. "Whisht. My turn now."

She compressed her lips together and hunched her shoulders, and looked for all the world like she was hiding a smile.

Some of the tension slid from his shoulders, though he refused to soften toward her. These things needed sorting, and that wouldn't get done if he gave in to her. "I've never had anybody treat me the way you've been treated, so I can't say as how I understand what you've been through. What I don't understand is how you could possibly think I'd treat you the same after I've shown you over and over again that I won't. What more can I do to earn your trust?"

He leaned forward again and reached for her hand across the space between them. She took his fingers in her cold ones and squeezed.

"If you can't trust me, tell me now. End it before we're both in so deep we drown."

"I..." Her lower lip trembled and her gaze slid away from his. "I wish I could say that someday I'll trust you completely, but I can't."

Her words scored through him as easily as a knife through air. He dropped her hand and sat back, surprised that there was still a place in his heart left for her to hurt. Foolish him, he'd thought it too wounded to feel any more pain, and there she'd gone, proving him wrong. "That's that, then."

"We've only known each other a week. Can't you give me a little more time?"

His laugh was hollow, just shy of bitter. "Sometimes a man gives everything he has and it's still not enough."

"Does it help if I tell you I want to trust you? That if any man could earn my trust, it would be you?" She stood and skirted the coffee table, sat on his knee and cupped his face in her hands. "Don't let my insecurities ruin the possibilities."

"You have more control over that than I do."

"I do, yes, but I'm asking for your help." Her thumb brushed over his lower lip, tempting, teasing. "Please, Levi. Don't give up just yet."

He covered her hands with his own, gave in to the need to kiss her. Her mouth was soft under his, sweet and endlessly fascinating, much like the woman herself. He drew back and touched his forehead to hers. "Don't ever push me away again, not unless you mean for me to go. Promise me."

Her eyes fluttered closed. "I'll try."

"Don't try. Do. One more time, Sera, and I'll leave no matter what's in my heart, no matter how much it hurts. Do you hear?"

She nodded. "I don't want to hurt you."

"I know, love. I know." He kissed her again, a brief touch of his lips to hers, then scooted her off his lap. "Go get dressed now and we'll fetch supper."

He watched her go, certain in his heart of hearts that she'd hurt him again, and equally sure that he'd never be able to walk away from her, broken heart or no.

PART TWO

Claiming

Eleven

THEY ATE in the hotel's restaurant, and in spite of Levi's intention to put their earlier disagreement behind them, their conversation was stilted and stiff. By the end of the meal, his head pounded and misery clung to every line of Sera's pretty face.

In the elevator on the way back to their room, he stuck his hands in his pockets, away from temptation. She had on that clingy black dress she'd worn on their first date. It smoothed over her curves and, Goddess help him, her unbound breasts, and left very little to the imagination.

Or maybe the dress was perfectly respectable and he was filling in the gaps with what he already knew of her. Smooth skin, hitching breaths, slick heat. Fingernails digging into his skin and her mouth on his.

He stepped off the elevator into the hallway with his dick at half-mast, made it all the way inside their room without touching her, and stood there, uncertain, riveted to Sera's movements through the suite. Slipping off her earrings, unfastening the straps of her shoes as she walked, pausing in midstride to lift one slender foot at a time.

How did women do that so gracefully without twisting an ankle?

She padded barefoot into the bedroom, her skirt swishing around her thighs with every twitch of her hips. He followed her like the puppy Jordan had accused him of being, unable to resist the lure of her warm body and gentle heart. "I should probably go now."

She paused in the middle of rummaging through her suitcase. "What?"

"To my room. I should probably go now, give you some space."

"I thought..." She swallowed and clutched a t-shirt in her hands. "Couldn't you stay for a while longer? There's probably a movie on. Or we could talk."

Talking hadn't gone so well for them lately, and if he stayed long enough to watch a movie with her, he was pretty sure he'd have her naked by the end of the night. An hour in the hotel's pool seemed like a better idea, just him, the water, and as many laps as he could force his body to swim while he sweated her out of his system.

"How am I supposed to learn to trust you if we don't spend time together?"

He leaned a shoulder against the doorframe. "We've been together most of the day."

"That was before we argued." Her grip tightened on the t-shirt and her knuckles whitened. "You can't leave until we're ok again."

"We're fine, Sera." Or close enough. Maybe his heart was still a little tender and maybe he wasn't quite ready to open himself back up to her, but it would happen, eventually. "A little time apart won't kill us."

Her lips thinned and her gaze dropped to the floor. She whirled abruptly, putting her back to him. "Help me with my dress?"

"Sera..."

She peered at him over her shoulder. "What? It's hard to undo on my own and you're right there. It's silly not to ask for help."

Of course, it was. He blew out a breath. How hard could it be to unfasten a few buttons or whatever was holding her dress together? To slip the fabric off inch by inch, revealing tantalizing glimpses of her nude flesh. To breathe in her scent, to explore the graceful column of her neck and the sensuous curve of her spine with his fingertips, his mouth. His heart pounded, circulating raw heat through him, sliding downward where it pooled in his groin, and he hardened painfully, achingly aware of the distance between them. He could fix that, go to her. Bare her skin and bend her over the bed, nudge her panties aside and fill her. Love her slowly, coaxing her into a release so deep and thorough, she'd never doubt his desire for her again.

She slid the pins out of her hair and it fell in loose waves around her shoulders, covering the smooth skin he coveted. "It won't take a minute and then you can go, if you really want to."

He shuddered and clamped tightly down on the desire clamoring through him. "You're begging trouble, love."

She laughed, breathy and soft. "It's a dress, Levi, not sex."

Taking off her dress would damn well lead to sex. They both knew it, and still he found himself walking toward her, tangling his fingers in her hair, so soft and silky, and it was all he could do to brush it over her shoulder and not bury his face in it. He examined the fastening holding her dress around her neck, slipped the eyehooks out. The straps slithered down her front, taking the upper part of the dress with it, baring the tops of her breasts.

"This is the hard one." She reached between them and tapped the backs of her fingers along the zipper running from under her shoulder blades down her spine, stopping halfway along the luscious curve of her arse. "That eyehook is in the most awkward place."

He slid his fingers into the top of the dress, unfastened the eyehook, and slowly pulled the zipper down. His breath was gone, frozen in his lungs, and her scent surrounded him, the light, floral notes of her perfume combining with an undertone of almonds. Irresistible. He stepped away and tucked his hands safely into the pockets of his slacks. "All done."

"Thanks." She tossed a sweet smile over her shoulder and let the dress fall, turning to him wearing only her panties. They were black lace, cut high on her hips, and a perfect accent to the gentle slope of her hips and the firm length of her legs. She stepped out of the dress and picked it up, laid it on top of her suitcase, seemingly unaware of her near nudity. "You have no idea how many wiggling contortions you saved me."

He choked on what breath he had left, his imagination immediately caught on an image of her writhing under him, her expression rapturous, and the wet heat of her pussy throbbing around him as she came. His fingers clenched into fists in his pockets and his dick throbbed. Goddess above, was she trying to kill him?

She shrugged her t-shirt on and pulled her hair out of the neckline. "Are you sure you don't want to stay?"

He narrowed his eyes, not fooled for one minute by the innocence in her expression. "You did that on purpose."

"I needed help with my dress," she said firmly. "And you were here. So, movie?"

He laughed, couldn't help it. "I guess I can do that."

"Great." Her smile was an odd mix of relief and triumph. "Go get changed while I find something for us to watch."

He retrieved his suitcase and garment bag from the living area and changed in the bathroom, half afraid she'd spot the erection he sported and pounce on him. A man couldn't help being aroused by a woman as beautiful as Serafina Noland. Knowing what she felt like wrapped in passion, how she whispered his name when she came and clung to him with fierce abandon, only made it worse.

He stayed in the bathroom long enough to bring his wayward body under a semblance of control. When he re-entered the bedroom, she was curled onto the middle of the bed, remote in hand.

"It's a monster movie marathon." She patted the bed beside her and waited patiently while he turned off the lights. "Godzilla ok?"

He stretched out beside her, ankles crossed, back against the headboard. "Sure. It's a classic."

"Petey loves it, though I'm pretty sure he misses all the deeper meaning. Monsters tromping around he gets. Nuclear holocaust, not so much." She rested her head on his arm above the tattoo hidden under his t-shirt and handed the remote to him. "Here. This is the man's job."

"So we're gonna be sexist about this, huh." He set the remote on the nightstand, out of the way. And since they were, he didn't hesitate to pry. "Do you cook?"

"I'm a single mom. Of course, I cook." She rubbed her cheek across his arm, her smile illuminated by the flickering light thrown from the TV. "Sometimes not so well, but Petey almost never complains."

"I'll cook this week, then."

"Hmm. Well, I'm not sure which part of that to comment on first. You can cook?"

He wrapped his arm around her shoulders, pulling her close. Her hand settled on his lower abs, resting in exactly the spot she'd caressed the first time. Her touch zinged through him, undiminished by the layers of clothing between her hand and his skin.

He leaned his head against the headboard and stared resolutely at the TV. "Mum made sure we all could. The People are big on self-sufficiency."

"A wise philosophy," she murmured. "So, this all week thing. You're spending it with me?"

"Said I would, didn't I?"

"I thought you might've changed your mind."

He closed his eyes. Damn it. He'd never explained about his job, hadn't wanted to until he knew he could count on her. Now, as quickly as they were diving into serious, he had to tell her something, at least enough to explain why he wouldn't be around much for a while. "I have a lot of work, enough to keep me busy for months. This week is pretty much the only time I'll have to spend with you until September, maybe later."

Her fingers flexed on his stomach. "That's six weeks away."

"I know. I'm sorry." He brushed his chin over the top of her head. "My schedule was set a long time before I met you."

She exhaled a shaky breath. "It's ok. I can't expect you to change your life for a woman you just met."

He already had, more than he ever had for a woman outside of his family. "I'll try to come back before then, a day here and there when I can manage it, and you and Petey can come down. I've got a spare bedroom you're welcome to."

"We'll see."

They fell into silence, the movie a quiet backdrop. Her fingers crept under his shirt and lingered, caressing him in random lines and circles, trailing heat wherever she touched. He threw his free arm over his eyes and focused on "The Charge of the Light Brigade," reciting it silently while her fingertips grazed along the edge of his shorts, then delved into them under his briefs, following the line of hair angling downward from his navel.

"Sera..."

"Whisht," she said. "My turn now."

A laugh wheezed out of his lungs and morphed into a low moan as she encircled him with her fingers and explored him slowly, learning every inch of him with deliberate, teasing strokes from base to tip and back again.

"I can't even get my fingers all the way around you." She slid her hand out of his shorts and straddled him. "You fill me, all of me, and move so beautifully when you're in me. Do you know how wonderful that is?"

He dropped his arm and gathered her close. Her lips found his pulse, sliding over his skin with delicious ease, and he angled his head, granting her all the access she wanted. "I know how it is to have you wrapped so tightly around me I can feel every beat of your heart."

"I know you've been with a lot of women, more than I've..." Her breath feathered along his pulse, raising goose bumps. "It's not that I care. I mean, I do. Safe sex and all, but it's really nice to be with a man who knows what he's doing in bed."

He grinned in spite of himself. "Yeah? How nice?"

"It's definitely icing. Really scrumptious buttercream frosting over a rich, decadent pound cake. Chocolate. My favorite." She caught his gaze with her own, her silver eyes shining in the room's low light. "I'd have sex with you anyway, though. There's just no resisting you."

"Sera, love." He pressed her closer, tangled his fingers in her hair. "Be with me."

"I am," she whispered, and kissed him tenderly. He returned her passion tenfold, giving everything he could, and made sweet love to her through the long summer evening into the twilight.

SERA WOKE to soft kisses sliding across the top of her bare shoulder. She stretched and yawned and shoved her hair out of her face, interrupting Levi's gentle caresses. Light slanted at a low angle through the curtained windows, brightening the room. Morning, she guessed, really early. She shifted, facing Levi. He sat on the bed next to her wearing a crisp ivory shirt tucked into slightly sheened, medium brown slacks, paired with a forest green tie.

"Morning, sweetheart."

She blinked sleep out of her eyes and focused bleerily on him. "Time is it?"

"Six forty-five." His sensual lips stretched into a smirk. "Laze abed."

"Am not. Geez." She inched her hand closer to his thigh and snuggled into her pillow. "You kept me up until after midnight."

"I think you were the one keeping me up."

Yes, she had. She turned her face into the pillow, hiding a smile. Make-up sex with Levi had been awesome. Hours spent touching him wherever she wanted, giving back some of the pleasure he'd given her. Her heart skipped and jumped in her chest and something comfortable and warm settled low in her stomach. Not quite worth the fight, but it was awfully dang close.

"I have to go. Angela's probably already in her office waiting for me." He smoothed her hair back and pressed a kiss to her forehead. "I'll be back in a couple of hours."

"I'll be here, sleeping in like moms on vacation are supposed to do."

"Breakfast when I get back?"

"Mm-hmm."

His footsteps faded as he walked across the room, and a moment later, the outer door snicked shut. She rolled onto her back and smiled at the ceiling.

She'd taken a lover. Levi Ewart, sexy sun god, was her lover.

She tried it out in her head, liked it so much she said it out loud. "Levi is my lover." The sound of her voice echoing in the room sent her into a spate of giggles. "Levi is my lover," she said. "Levi is mine."

Her laughter died in her throat, replaced by a startling possessiveness. She turned it over in her mind, measuring the idea, examining it from every angle, and discovered it didn't bother her one bit. Shy, retiring Sera, single mom and former choir girl, had taken a lover.

And she didn't want to share.

Her smile turned smug. She stretched hard, energizing every muscle in her body, and buried her face in Levi's pillow, breathing in the scent lingering there. A whole nother week with Levi, filling their days with work and play, and their nights with wild passion. God, she couldn't wait.

She glanced at the clock and rolled out of bed, her mind

crowded with Levi and stories yet to be discovered, and the endless to-do list of a mother with a young child. She set the room's coffee pot to brew a single cup and showered, dressed in comfortable clothes for the day ahead, then settled onto the couch with her laptop and a steaming cup of coffee.

Levi returned to the suite two and a half hours after he left, wearing a matching suit jacket over the clothes he'd worn when he'd woken her. "I thought you'd still be in bed."

She glanced at him over the screen of her laptop and nearly melted. "Is that suit tailored?"

"Yeah. Why?"

She shook her head and tsked. "Crying shame you have to take it off."

"You'll see it again on Friday, or something like it."

"Oh?"

"I have a meeting in Atlanta. We're going shopping after, remember?"

"I remember," she murmured. "Are you ever going to tell me exactly what you do?"

His gaze drifted into the cold impassiveness he used as a shield. "You'll see on Friday."

She shivered, couldn't help it. "That sounds ominous."

"Hardly. I'll be back in a minute."

"Take your time."

She stared at the e-mail she'd been writing when he came in, not seeing it through the thoughts swirling around in her head. Levi had a meeting in Atlanta where he wore tailored suits to work and had an assistant. Her fingers tapped lightly against the edge of her laptop. Corporate, definitely, though what his exact capacity was, she couldn't say from what little she knew. He could be anything from a junior employee to a bigwig.

He'd said he worked with his nana, Hawthorne.

Sera glanced toward the closed bedroom door. Just a little peek into his life wouldn't hurt, would it?

She saved the draft of her e-mail, pulled up Google, and ran a search for Atlanta corporations owned by a Hawthorne. The results were both frustrating and illuminating. No corporations turned up, but there were a slew of returns for a fantasy writer using the pen name Al C. Hawthorne who lived in northeast Georgia. Tellowee maybe? Sera clicked on the link for images and found a scant handful of pictures of a woman in her mid-twenties with Levi's steady gaze staring out from the laptop's screen.

That woman was entirely too young to be Levi's grand anything. How common could the name be, though? And hadn't Levi said his nana was a writer?

Sera tapped her fingers and tried again, searching this time for Levi. The results contained half a dozen Facebook pages. She clicked through them all and finally found a picture of Levi and Heath standing on a dock, arms thrown around each other's shoulders, wearing matching mischievous smirks. She logged in and sent friend requests to both of them, then backed out and went through the other results one by one.

A few minutes later, she hit pay dirt. An article for *The Atlanta Journal-Constitution* included a picture of Levi, all seriously corporate, standing next to several people, one of which appeared to be the fantasy writer. Sera scanned through the article. It was dated the previous August and discussed a charity foundation for young writers funded and managed by Icenia, LLC. She bookmarked the link and googled Icenia, and was unsurprised to learn that it was headquartered in Atlanta.

"Hey, have you packed?"

Sera shrieked and bobbled her laptop, righted it and placed a hand over her racing heart. "Levi. *God.* You scared the life out of me."

He leaned against the frame of the door leading into the bedroom. His suit was gone, replaced by a thin, cream colored t-shirt with flat seams and olive green cargo shorts. "Sorry. Didn't mean to interrupt."

"It's ok. Just a little work."

She ignored the guilty flush staining her cheeks. Spying wasn't so bad, was it, if the man was as tight-lipped and mysterious as Levi? Especially if it was motivated by a relatively innocent curiosity. Shouldn't she know more about her lover before introducing him to Petey? She bit back a groan. That excuse sounded lame, even in her own mind. A few clicks and the incriminating evidence was gone, though her guilty conscience was not. She closed the laptop's lid and slid it off her lap, putting the whole thing out of her mind for later thought.

"Ready for breakfast?"

"Yeah," he said. "Thought we'd go ahead and pack the car so we'd be ready to sight-see as soon as we're done."

"Sounds like a plan."

After packing and eating a late breakfast, they spent hours wandering through the well-preserved remains of Old Salem and Bethabara, two historic Moravian communities established in the mid-eighteenth century in what at that time was a wilderness frontier. Levi acted as her tour guide, pointing out details she might've missed on her own and adding a depth not covered by the print literature she'd snagged.

While they were wandering through the cemetery attached to the St. Philips African Moravian Church in Old Salem, she said, "You've been here before."

"Lots. I'm here on business a few times a year and the hotel's nearby, so..." He lifted one shoulder in a casual shrug. "I like to soak in the history, remember times past and the people who lived here."

"That's almost romantic," she teased.

He slid an amused glance toward her. "Who says men can't be?"

Whether he was romantic or not, his patience held true during the humid heat of a mid-July day in North Carolina's piedmont. The streets of Old Salem were crowded with residents and sightseers alike, the sloping sidewalks barely cooler under the giant shade of the trees lining the roads. They paused at each marked spot on the tour, walking hand in hand in spite of the heat, and ogled every historic landmark in the tiny subsection of Winston-Salem.

Bethabara was an archaeological park, mostly open to the harsh summer sun. They took a guided tour through the historic church, still in good condition after more than two hundred years. Sera oohed and ahed over the strangely arched plaster ceiling in the sanctuary and the replica furniture and tiled wood stove in the minister's rooms. After the tour guide left, she and Levi explored the foundations uncovered by archaeologists nearly half a century earlier and ended up at the community and herb gardens, where she nearly filled her camera with pictures. A sunny corner of her backyard could easily house a much smaller version, and it would give her time outside away from work when her stories were driving her crazy.

Levi insisted on driving home. She rolled her eyes and gave in, and pulled out her work when he cut on the radio. They ate an early supper at the Mellow Mushroom in downtown Asheville, and nearly two hours later, after the sun had set and the stars had popped into the sky one by one, they hit Clayton, the closest town to Sera's house.

"Do you mind if we go ahead and pick up my car?" he asked.

"Nope." She stretched and yawned, then slid her laptop into its bag. "We're already out and it's early yet."

He signaled for a right turn, eased into the turn lane, and pulled onto Highway 76. "Speak for yourself. I've been up since five thirty."

She inhaled sharply. "Levi, really. Why didn't you tell me? I could've driven and let you rest."

"I like to drive," he said mildly.

She pinched his elbow. "Chauvinist."

He laughed. "Am not."

"Hmph." She dropped her hand to his thigh and held it there, soaking in his warm strength. "Tellowee's not far from my house."

"I know." His smile was faint and just a little knowing. "I googled you, too."

She sputtered out a laugh. "Sorry. I was curious, that's all."

"I was, too. Still am."

Twenty minutes later, he turned onto the side road leading to Tellowee, and not long after pulled up to the curb of a two-story home constructed of rock and wood.

Sera eyed the natural landscaping and the layout of the yard. "I think my dad renovated this when I was, oh, ten or eleven, maybe twelve."

"That would be about right." Levi switched off the ignition and opened the door. "That's about the time we moved here."

She gaped at him. "This is your parents' house?"

"Yup."

"You brought me to your parents' house."

"Relax. They're busy right now. Trust me. They won't appreciate being interrupted."

"Oh." It took Sera a moment to make the connection, and when she did, she slumped into her seat and cursed the blush heating her cheeks. "Right. I'll just drive my car now, the way I should've been doing all day."

He leaned over, slid his hand around her nape, and pressed a hard kiss to her mouth. "Give me a minute and I'll follow you."

She waited for his long legs to carry him up his parents' driveway before sliding into the driver's seat. She scooted it way up and bit her lip, containing a smile and the flutter of nerves and attraction ricocheting around her belly. Those long, muscular legs of his. A sigh escaped, then hitched at the muted roar of an engine. She twisted around and spotted the rear brake lights of a sleek, expensive sports car, and the butterflies in her stomach died a sudden, harsh death.

Why hadn't she been paying attention? Levi's parents lived in Tellowee, one of the most affluent neighborhoods in the county. He wore tailored suits, vacationed in the Outer Banks at property owned by a close relative, and drove a wickedly beautiful Mercedes that looked like it cost more than her house.

Whereas she was a single mom with a decade-old Volvo, a house that needed more work than she could afford, and a bank account whose balance fluctuated depending on how well her books sold, sometimes dipping low enough that she took side jobs working with her dad to make ends meet. She hadn't had to do that but a handful of times since going full-time as an author, and that in the early days, but it was still an option she kept in the back of her mind.

She started the Volvo's engine and clutched the steering wheel in a white-knuckled grip. Levi must be filthy rich, and if he was, she'd been so, so right. He was way out of her league, so much *more* than her in every way it was silly.

And he was her lover.

She eased onto the road and led him back to her house, her thoughts tangled in worry and an anxiety she hadn't felt since learning she was pregnant with Petey.

Twelve

THE NEXT DAY, Levi took one look at Sera's to-do list for the week and said, "No."

She gazed at him over the rim of her coffee mug, her silver eyes placid and slightly amused. "What makes you think you have the right to tell me what I can and can't do in my own house?"

He glared at her across the tiny dinette where they'd eaten breakfast. It sat in the dining nook attached to her kitchen, separated from the food prep area by a counter, in a space that hadn't been remodeled since her house was built sometime in the '70s. The brick ranch house had good bones. Large rooms, a full basement, and a solid foundation, but it needed work. Sera intended to do that work herself.

"Be reasonable, love." He tossed her list onto the table between them and watched her amusement grow into full-blown humor. "Even with me helping, you'll never get the carpet ripped out of the basement and the library, and get Petey's room painted, and get the deck stained. Plus mowing the yard, trimming the hedges, and..." He inhaled sharply, as much from exasperation as temper. "There's enough work here to last a full crew of men two weeks."

"My house," she said mildly.

Figured she'd say that. "At least let me hire..."

"No." Her cup thudded sharply onto the table and her expression turned mutinous. "My house, my money. I can't afford to hire laborers."

"I can."

Her face paled under her tan. "If I can't afford it, it doesn't get done."

"Be reasonable, love."

She stood abruptly and carried her coffee cup to the sink, brushing by his outstretched hand to get there. "It's not like I haven't done this work before. I help Dad and Jack out all the time."

"I bet they don't let you do the heavy stuff, though."

"There's nothing on that list that's heavy."

"Really?" He crossed his arms over his chest and leaned back in the chair. "How about the carpet? That's not a job for a woman."

"Chauvinist."

"Realist," he countered. "If you were bigger..."

Her hands came down on the rim of the sink in an impatient slap. "Don't start."

"Fine, I won't."

He rose from his chair, deliberately unfurling his long length slowly. Her eyes drifted from his bare chest down his shorts to his bare feet and her teeth nibbled on the corner of her lip. He stalked toward her, ignored the hand she held up and the soft murmur of his name, and snagged her, lifting her onto the counter in one easy heft. He wedged his hips between her thighs and yanked her close.

"Now, let's talk."

She hooked her fingertips in the waistband of his shorts. "You can't intimidate me into changing my mind."

"I'm not trying to intimidate you, half pint. I'm making a point."

Her eyes narrowed and glinted. "I can't believe you called me that."

"Get used to it, shorty." He wrapped his hand around her upper arm and squeezed. "Hmm. Nice, but kinda thin on muscle."

She raked her fingernails over his abs and returned his smug look with a glare. "Now you're just insulting me."

"Never." He kissed her hurt away, touched her forehead with his. "Writing doesn't build the kind of muscle needed to rip carpet out, love, and it's not something I want to spend my week doing."

He stopped her protest with another kiss. She softened and melted into him, and need ripped through him, hard and heavy and urgent. He eased it back, drew away from the soft promise of her lips, the warm welcome of her body. "It's my vacation, too."

"You don't have to spend it here." She buried her face in his throat and sighed. "And you don't have to help me either. I can do this, Levi."

"You're not doing it on your own, not while I'm here to help. Let me at least find some laborers to rip out the carpet. We can do the painting and the deck, and still have time to visit my berry farm and go shopping on Friday."

She stiffened. "You have a berry farm?"

"Hawthorne Hills, out on..."

"Blue Ridge Gap Road. I know where it is. Candi covets it every time we drive by."

"Then you can placate her with a trip next week, if you'll let me hire somebody to help."

She laughed softly. "That sounds like a bribe."

"Hey, whatever works."

"I pay for the laborers."

He rolled his eyes skyward. "For cripes' sake, Sera."

"My house, my money."

He let it go, satisfied with the compromise he'd negotiated. What had she been thinking? A woman on her own couldn't rip out the carpet and the padding for two large rooms in one week. He shook his head. Stubborn woman.

Later, they went into town for supplies, primer and paint for Petey's room and stain for the deck, and picked up enough groceries for the day. They made a good start on Sera's ridiculously long list of things she wanted to accomplish that week, and after, he grilled supper for her.

The next day, he drove into Clayton, hired a carload of transient Hispanics, and showed them what Sera wanted done in the basement. While they worked, he took her to the grocery store in Tellowee, set up an account for her on the sly, and introduced her to Heath's mum, who owned the store with her husband.

Evangeline took one look at Sera and muttered, "Does Hawthorne know about her?"

"No," he said. "And I'd appreciate it if you wouldn't tell her, either."

Evangeline tutted and fussed, but in the end, she agreed. Nobody wanted to face Hawthorne's wrath. Levi simply didn't want his nana to interfere.

He and Sera checked off items on her to-do list according to the time of day and amount of weather. The cooler mornings were spent outside staining the deck or tending her yard. Painting Petey's room and cleaning up once the carpet had been ripped out were saved for the humid heat of the afternoons and the near-daily summer rainstorms. He talked her into turning the radio on, inside or out, and caught her up in impromptu dances, kissed her every chance he got, and showered her with so much affection that by the end of the week, the casual touches no longer surprised her.

At night, they cuddled on the couch in her living room, watching a movie or talking, and when they went to bed, they made love, by turns fierce and tender, and held each other close while caught in sleep's gentle grip.

The week flew quickly by. Levi dreaded its inevitable end, when he'd have to return to Atlanta and his responsibilities there, leaving Sera behind. His stomach tied itself in knots every time his mind dwelt on it. Sleeping alone in his sterile apartment without her sly humor and the rapid taps of her fingers on her laptop's keyboard as she worked, his bed empty, his heart cold. He'd already decided to cut back on his workload after his current obligations were met. If he whittled down his work to only his position at Icenia and managing his personal investments, he'd have a helluva lot more time for her and Petey. Once he did, he intended to renegotiate their relationship.

By Thursday, they'd finished nearly every item on her to-do list, what he hadn't talked her into leaving for a later date, anyway. He coaxed her into a trip out to his berry farm that morning, introduced her around, and helped her pick blackberries for jelly and blueberries for muffins, enough to last the entire upcoming winter. She froze all of the berries, said she'd work up the jelly next week, and then they packed and headed to Atlanta.

She sat quietly in the passenger seat of his Coupe, holding herself eerily still on the leather-upholstered passenger's seat. They made it all the way to I-85 before he prodded her out of her silence.

"You can drive, if you want."

She paled and shook her head in short, quick jerks.

"It doesn't bite."

"I'm not..." Her mouth thinned into a pink slash across her

face. "I can't afford to replace it if I wreck."

"That's what insurance is for."

Her eyes rounded as she huffed out a laugh. "You say that like it's nothing. This car cost about four times more than my house."

"Yeah? So you got a good deal on the house, huh? Good for you." He waggled his eyebrows. "I like a woman who can haggle."

"It's not funny," she snapped.

"Money is never funny. Shouldn't be taken too seriously, either."

"Says the man who's never had to work for anything in his life."

He sucked in a breath. "Is that what you think of me?"

"No, I..." She closed her eyes and hunched her shoulders. "I'm sorry. I'm not trying to pick a fight."

"I work hard for what I have, Sera."

"I know. I know you do." Her hand eased across the space between them and grasped his thigh. "You're a hard worker. My dad will love you."

"Already does, in a roundabout way."

Her eyes popped open and she gaped at him. "What?"

"He contracts with my landscaping company, recommends it when he's building a new house. Don't think he knows it belongs to me, though."

"You own a landscaping company."

Traffic snarled ahead of them. He downshifted and slowed, merging right, avoiding the wrecked vehicles in the left lanes. "Started it when I was eight with another Son. Saved my money and bought the land for the berry farm when I was fourteen."

"On your own?"

He ignored the horrified note in her voice, or tried to. What was so wrong with a man knowing his mind at a young age and following up on it? "Da put up the house and signed the loan for me, but I made every payment. Colin, Heath, Jordan, and I cleared the land, planted the first bushes on it."

"When you were fourteen."

"Took us a couple of years, but yeah."

Her head dropped back against the seat. "Any other businesses you want to tell me about?"

"A dairy farm in Otto. Real estate holdings across north

Georgia, some inherited. A few other things." Gold and stocks and other things he was pretty sure would bore her to tears. He shrugged, aiming for casual, and failed miserably. "Told you I had a healthy investment portfolio."

"And a degree in finance."

"And an MBA, just finished."

Her eyes widened and when she spoke again, her voice was faint. "And you wear tailored suits and drive a quarter million dollar custom-made car."

"Somebody's been googling again."

"Google is the only way *somebody* has to learn about these things. When were you going to tell me?"

"About the money?" His fingers traced the knob of the gear shifter, memorizing a shape he already knew. "When I thought you could handle it."

"You mean, when you knew I wasn't a gold digger."

"No, I mean when I thought you wouldn't freak out and decide maybe you didn't want to deal with it enough to give me a chance." He sighed and sorted through his thoughts, striving for the kind of raw honesty she would appreciate. "Maybe for five seconds, I thought you might be after my money, but then I realized that a woman like you, you're not a gold digger. I wouldn't be with you if you were, wouldn't've continued to pursue you if you had been."

"Seems you know me better than I know myself." Her unsteady smile firmed and grew so big, she hid it behind her hand. "For a minute there, I was really tempted."

He cut a sideways glance at her. "Yeah? How so?"

"The berry farm." Her smile turned into a giggle. "Do you know how expensive berries are?"

He grinned. "So you can be bought for all the berries Petey can eat, huh."

"Berries, milk." She wiped her eyes and exhaled the last of her humor. "You wouldn't happen to own a herd of beef, would you?"

"Not yet."

"Has to be a good investment, given the price of meat these days." She laid her hand over his on the gear shift, rubbed her thumb across his skin. "No more secrets, Levi. Ok?"

"Just a few more," he murmured, and when her hand tightened, added, "Soon, I promise."

She settled into her seat and the tension eased out of his shoulders. She didn't care about the money or, at least, what he'd told her about it. The People, the Prophecy, and all the rest, those secrets could wait for another day. This day was for the two of them and he wouldn't let anything ruin it or come between them, not anything.

THEY SPENT THE NIGHT at Levi's apartment in Virginia Highlands. Sera hated it on sight. The hardwood floors were a nice touch, as was the view from the row of windows taking up the entire wall of his living room. The décor, on the other hand, was modern and minimalist, the kitchen so shiny, she couldn't picture actually cooking in it. She wandered around the rooms and tried to imagine her seven-year-old son not breaking the glass-topped tables or staining the white leather sofa.

"This is not you," she told Levi.

"You're right, it's not. I hired an interior decorator to come in and redo the place when I bought it."

"And she did this?"

"He." One corner of Levi's mouth quirked up. "Tomás did exactly what I asked. Upscale, professional, good for entertaining."

She narrowed her eyes. "What kind of entertaining?"

His smile evened out, lighting his whiskey eyes. "Business. I don't bring women here."

"I'm a woman."

"I noticed." He pressed a fleeting kiss to her mouth. "Remind me to give you a key so you and Petey can come visit."

She glanced at the furniture. Visions of child-created mayhem danced in her head, and she shuddered. "Maybe we should stick with you visiting us."

"Not a chance. You're coming down even if I have to send Colin up to fetch you."

She tilted her head, trying to follow the veer in the conversation. "Why would Colin fetch me?"

"He's a bodyguard and damn good at what he does." Levi's eyes went cold and hard. "I say fetch, Colin brings you down."

141

"Just like that. What if I say no?"

His smile thinned. "Colin won't give you a chance to."

She stared at that smile and realized he was deadly serious. "That take charge thing? It's starting to piss me off."

"I'll do what I have to, Sera. Remember that."

It sounded like more of a promise than a threat. "Sometimes, you make no sense whatsoever."

"It'll make sense, eventually."

"Let me guess. Another secret." She rubbed her forehead with the fingers of both hands. "How many more do you have?"

"A few." He crossed the room and wrapped his hands around her shoulders, kneading the tense muscles with deep, sure strokes. "My life can be complicated."

She let that sink in as she relaxed against his warm strength. "Dangerous?"

"Sometimes."

"So if Colin comes to the house and says duck, I should really duck, huh?"

He kissed her forehead. "Now you're getting the idea."

"And I can trust you'll never send him without a reason."

"You can always trust me to do what's best."

That's what she was afraid of, that he'd do what he thought was right regardless of her opinion. He acted like they'd been dating for months instead of a week, two if she counted their time in the Outer Banks, but try as she might, she couldn't dredge up enough energy to care. It felt like they'd been together for years, so quickly had they settled into a routine together. Their time had been filled with intimacy and laughter and not nearly as many adjustments and arguments as she'd expected.

She'd miss him when he returned to Atlanta. Her heart already ached with it, knowing they had only a few days left before his inevitable departure. Petey would be back the same day, filling her heart the way only he could, but somehow, a small chunk of it had broken off and named itself Levi's.

How had that happened so quickly?

She let him coax her into bed, opened herself to him, and welcomed him when he surged into her, loving her in a way no man ever had. After, they drifted into sleep with her heart beating in time to his.

The next day, they woke early and shared a quiet breakfast, then navigated the flood of traffic between his apartment and the high-rise housing Icenia, LLC.

Sera had chosen her outfit carefully for the morning she'd spend in Levi's office waiting for him to finish his meeting, tailoring her look to match his without being as formal. When her books had taken off, she'd invested in clothing nice enough to pass scrutiny at conferences and other professional venues. She'd found the raw silk, sapphire toned suit she wore at the Goodwill in Buckhead. Candi had helped her adjust the fit and length, then talked Sera into buying an ice blue silk tank top at the Mall of Georgia to wear underneath.

The tank top had cost way more than the suit, but it had been worth it.

She'd paired the suit with strappy heels and dangly silver hoops, and piled her hair on top of her head in artful curls. When she'd stepped out of the bathroom that morning, Levi's whiskey eyes had smoldered as his gaze raked over her. He'd slid his hands into the pockets of his charcoal gray slacks, and that's when she'd known exactly how much he wanted her.

Levi never held back unless his control was teetering on the brink of collapse. It was probably the most valuable thing she'd learned about him.

Well, that and the fact that he owned a berry farm.

She bit back her grin as they passed through security and rode the elevator to Levi's office. A young woman with large leaf green eyes and short springy blonde curls stood as they approached.

"Mr. Ewart. It's good to have you back."

"Good to be back." He nodded between her and Sera, his attention focused on the planner open on the woman's desk. "Janine, this is Sera Noland. She'll be working out of my office today. If she needs anything, please get it for her."

Janine's eyes widened and fixed on Sera. "I'll take good care of her, Mr. Ewart."

Levi nodded and led Sera into his office through a door that had two nameplates on it. One read *Levi Ewart,* and underneath, the other spelled out, in letters big enough to read plainly, *Vice*

President.

Sera shut the door behind them. "So. You're a Vice President."

He sorted through the mail, dropping it into piles on top of his massive oak desk. "One of a couple, yeah, and very junior."

"At twenty-two."

He glanced up and shrugged. "My great-grandmother owns the company."

She stood frozen at the entrance to his office. It was huge, with a full-blown seating area to her right and a bar in the far left corner. A door on the left was closed. Probably a private bathroom, she thought, a little dazed. His desk was situated so that when he worked, his back was to the bank of windows along that side of the room.

This man really loved his windows.

"I bet you earned your position here." She shook her head, attempting to clear the dizziness. Levi was so far above her, it gave her vertigo to think about it. "What exactly is it you do?"

He leaned his bottom against the edge of the desk and grinned. "This and that."

She huffed out a laugh. "Come on, Levi. Tell me."

"I oversee the hospitality properties and a couple of our charities."

"The young writers fund," she murmured.

"You have googled well, my young Padawan."

She snorted out a laugh. "And you've been infected by Petey's posters."

"Hey, I like Star Wars." He opened his arms, held them out as she crossed the room, and wrapped her tight against his chest. "How many times do we have to have this conversation?"

"What conversation?" she asked, though she already knew.

"The one where I reassure you that I don't think less of you because you don't have scads of money or power or social standing. That isn't what binds me to you, Sera."

"I know, really. It's just..." She turned her nose into his throat, careful to keep her make-up away from his shirt, and breathed him in, the sharp sensuality of his cologne and the underlying masculinity that was all him. "It's a lot to take in."

"Get over it, love. Please."

"It would've been easier if you'd told me all at once instead of making me dig to learn it."

"Maybe. On the other hand, learning it in bits gave you time to accept it." His hand gripped her nape, holding her still and close. "Now that you know, though, I expect us to not have to revisit this."

"There you go again, laying down the law."

"As if you'd ever listen." He pressed a kiss to her temple. "We're going shopping this afternoon and you're gonna let me spoil you."

"Levi..."

"No buts. Consider it payback for you cracking the whip all week." His breath feathered across her skin in a low moan. "That suit should be registered as a lethal weapon. This'll be the first time I've ever gone into a meeting with a hard-on."

"If the outfit kept you from lecturing me, I'd be more impressed."

"I wouldn't lecture if you wouldn't overreact."

"Says the man who threatened to sic Colin on me if I wouldn't come visit."

Janine poked her head in the door and cleared her throat. "Ten minutes, Mr. Ewart."

"Thanks, Janine."

When the door closed behind her, Levi touched his lips to Sera's, easing her into a kiss so gradually, she couldn't mark when passion wrested control and sent them both spinning into a free-fall of need, their hands clutching each other, bodies pressed tightly together. He eased back just as gradually, nipped at her lips as their breaths panted out of their chests and mingled in the space between them.

"I never get tired of that," she said.

"Goddess willing, neither one of us ever will." He patted her bottom playfully and held her hands as she regained her balance and stood on her own, away from him. "Help yourself to anything you need."

"I will."

"Be back as quick as I can."

"Mm-kay."

She walked to the sitting area on shaky legs and sank gratefully into the leather sofa. This one was a sturdy brown, designed more for wear and tear than show, unlike the one in his apartment.

Levi slipped through the door opposite his desk and came out a minute later, suit straightened, lipstick smudges cleaned away. He gathered seemingly random folders and stuffed them into his briefcase, kissed her forehead and murmured a goodbye, and then he was gone.

His scent lingered in the air behind him.

She closed her eyes and inhaled, taking him into her, holding him there for long moments while everything she knew shifted and resettled.

Levi held her in the palm of his hand, had since almost the moment they'd met.

And he was right. She had to quit picking at him about his life and accept him, as he'd so readily accepted her. Warm, fierce Levi with his barely restrained exuberance and the untamed rambles of his childhood still shining from his eyes.

Petey was going to love him.

The possibility should've bothered her, but somehow, it brought a smile to her heart instead. For the first time since she'd become pregnant, Sera knew she could trust a man, or that she could someday, if she didn't completely at that moment. Someday, she'd introduce him to Petey. Someday, her son and her lover would hit it off and become friends. Someday was at least six weeks off, though. She'd worry about it then and not a minute before.

Thirteen

TRUE TO HIS WORD, Levi spoiled Sera shamelessly after his meeting was finished. He took her to an upscale restaurant in Midtown where she lost her breath over the prices on the menu. After the waiter took their order, Levi leaned over and, with a gleam of humor sparking in his eyes, whispered, "I don't eat like this often, love."

Later, he escorted her to Memory, an exclusive boutique in Buckhead, and sat on an antique love seat while she tried on dress after dress, none with a price tag affixed. By the time she reluctantly chose an outfit, his expression had shifted from the politely indifferent mask he wore in social situations into hot, desperate need. The sales girl had caught sight of that look and blushed and giggled her way into a tizzy, and Sera hadn't been much better. How was a woman supposed to resist a man that looked at her the way Levi looked at her, as if he'd never wanted a woman the way he wanted her?

They drove back to Sera's house the next day, late after a day playing tourist in Atlanta, and fell into bed together. As she drifted to sleep, wrapped firmly within the strength of Levi's embrace, Sera replayed the two days in her head. It had been fun, more than she'd ever imagined the city could be. Maybe she'd take Levi up on his offer to visit, though she certainly wouldn't let him spend that kind of money on her again. And Petey would have to be very, very careful in Levi's apartment.

Sunday morning, Levi woke her with a whispered, "Get up, love. There's something I want to show you."

"Mmph." She shifted on the bed, snuggling into his embrace,

and dared a bleary glance at the window. "It's not even light outside yet."

"It will be by the time we get there." He patted her bare bottom, lingered for a caress. "Come on. If we don't hurry, we'll miss it."

Her grumbles weren't all good-natured, but she rolled out of bed, put on the shorts, tank-top, and sturdy walking shoes Levi suggested, and followed him to her car.

"Mine won't make it," he said. "You don't mind if we take yours, do you?"

"No. Where are we going?"

His expression wavered between vulnerable and hopeful. "The equivalent of church for the People."

"You're taking me to church." She glanced down at her casual outfit, then to his bare chest. She hadn't even combed her hair, for goodness' sake. "Dressed like this."

"Hey, we could go in our birthday suits. Speaking of." He started her car and backed carefully out of her parking area into the driveway. "There might be a few naked people there, some of the, er, older participants."

She dropped her head back against the seat and closed her eyes. "Oh, my God."

His hand covered hers and squeezed. "You don't mind going with me, do you? I mean, I figured since you weren't going to church and you didn't comment on all the goddess references you might be open to this."

She peeked at him through one eye. "I'm kind of a *to each his own* sort of person. Besides, I'm curious."

"Yeah?"

"Well, we hear all these rumors about the people living in Tellowee, how insular they are, how unless you want to get your ass kicked you shouldn't go there and stir up trouble, especially with the women."

"Many a young buck has received a hard set down from the women of Tellowee."

She laughed. "So I've heard. What about you?"

He grinned. "I'll never tell."

"Spoil sport."

He turned onto a poorly maintained Forest Service road, then onto a clearly marked private road in slightly better condition. When she realized where he was headed, Sera sat up straight in her seat, her grumpiness over the early hour forgotten. "This is private property."

"Sort of. It backs up to the IECS."

"The Institute for Early Cultural Studies?" She tried to align where they were with the institute's location and her brain fogged over. Drat him, he hadn't even let her have a cup of coffee before he'd dragged her out of the house, and it not even daybreak yet. "I've never been."

"I can arrange a tour if you want."

"Maybe later. You know, when I'm awake."

The road spit them out into a graveled parking area containing a dozen other vehicles. Levi parked in an empty spot and switched off the ignition. "There are a couple of things I need to tell you before we go up."

"More secrets?"

"Part of one." He shifted toward her and snagged her hand, holding it loosely between his, his elegant fingers stroking her skin. "You've heard me talk about the People, right?"

"Some. Ruby, too." She faced him and rested her head against the seat. "Y'all say 'people' as if you're a separate culture or something. I didn't want to pry, but..."

"You were curious, I know." He gently kissed her fingertips. "We *are* a separate culture, more distinct than most outsiders realize. The People descend from Seven Sisters who lived thousands of years ago. The short version is that these sisters avenged their parents' deaths and were cursed by a cruel god to live forever without love or the ability to bear sons."

"Forever as in immortal?"

His eyelids fluttered down, hiding his whiskey eyes. "The goddess Ki saw how unjustly the sisters had been treated and mitigated the curse, allowing each one and her female progeny to find peace in her own way. It's a long story, Sera, not one we have time for now."

"I'm still trying to understand the immortal part."

"Someday." His voice was scratchy, uncertain, as if he were

afraid she'd react poorly. "We come here to face the promise represented by the dawn and give thanks to the Lady Ki for her blessings and mercy."

And he wanted to share that with her, something obviously sacred to him and his family. Her own faith chimed in her head. *Thou shalt have no other god before me.* She wrestled with it, considering her individual promise to God and the tenets she'd been raised to hold dear, weighing them against his need and her own curiosity. "Do I have to participate or can I just watch?"

"Whatever you're comfortable with. I won't be disappointed either way."

"Can I pray to my god?"

His smile was gentle, kind, and more understanding than she would've believed. "We're kind of a *to each her own* sort of people."

"Ok, then." She leaned forward and touched her lips to his. "Don't let me violate your practices or anything."

"It's not that complicated."

They got out, leaving the key in the ignition and the doors unlocked. Levi held her hand and guided her to the trailhead behind two women in their mid-twenties, both dressed as casually as Sera.

The trail was spongy under her tennis shoes and shaded by the deep woods surrounding them. The sky lightened as they hiked the rolling hills through the humid air, gradually making their way higher in elevation with each one. He helped her across a railless wooden footbridge, around outcrops of granite boulders, and ever upward as the forest awakened with the coming dawn.

They reached the top twenty minutes later, joining nearly three dozen others on a knoll cleared of trees and undergrowth. Levi helped her onto a rock and wrapped his arms around her from behind, pulling her against his chest with his mouth next to her ear. They faced east looking across a heavily wooded valley toward a ridgeline whose name escaped her. No one spoke, though all stood still and tense, apparently waiting for the sunrise.

Levi brushed his lips along her ear and said, in a voice so low only she could hear, "When the sun tops the ridge, don't look directly at it. Lower your eyes and listen, or you can pray, if you want to. Others will be."

She nodded and placed her hands over his where they rested on her stomach. Others came in behind them or from side trails, joining the larger group without speaking. It was odd being there among so many people, standing as still as statues among the summer green of the woods, the only noises the occasional scuff of a foot along the ground and the birds chirping in the treetops above them.

Streaks of red and gold shot through the pale blue eastern sky, deepening as the sun rose and finally topped the ridge, gradually lightening the dark sky overhead. Sera shifted her eyes away, though not before noticing others bowing their heads. A woman standing at the front of the crowd on an outcrop of rocks jutting into open space raised her arms. She began a song in an unknown and oddly familiar language, and was quickly joined by a chorus of other voices, mostly female.

"Blessed Ki, have mercy on your children," Levi translated in a low whisper. "Protect us as we protect our own and grant us strength to endure the ages. Guide us with the light and love of your wisdom to the one who will release us from eternity. Blessed Ki, Lady Goddess, Mother to us all, we honor you. Blessed Ki, blessed Ki."

He stopped speaking, though the song went on. Sera kept her head bowed, listening to the voices merging into a single chorus, carried into the dawn by a light breeze. The song ended abruptly, and in the silence that followed, Sera found a reverence she'd seldom witnessed within the walls of the churches she'd attended in the past. It wrapped around her, lifting her into the sacred, and her heart followed, filling with wonder and awe in equal measures.

She didn't pray, not with the coherence or forethought others might've used. She'd always believed God heard what was spoken in the heart. That morning, her heart carried her enduring love for Petey and her family, and her worry over Levi. The quickness of their relationship, his leaving that day to return to Atlanta, and all the concerns she'd deliberately shelved in order to enjoy what little time they had together. Though he was of a faith so radically different from hers, she couldn't help the silent longing for his safety winging its way to her own god.

The rising sun warmed her skin long before low murmurs rose

among the people gathered around her. She opened her eyes and shifted around, facing Levi.

He was watching her carefully in that intense way he had, as if he wanted to memorize everything about her. "Thanks."

"I enjoyed it."

His arms tightened around her, melding his firmer form into hers. "Ruby's over there. Thought we could go say hello."

He made no move to leave, holding her close, his eyes steady on hers.

"Are you ok?" she asked.

"Mmm. It just occurred to me that I didn't explain everything."

"Like what?"

"Like what happens after for those that've found their mates." His mouth curled into a slow, wicked smile. "The more devoted take their lovers into the woods and thank Ki by celebrating their love."

Her heart tripped and stuttered. "You mean...?"

"Yeah, I mean." He rubbed the tip of his nose against hers. "Want to do that when we get home?"

She breathed out a laugh. "Levi, really. Haven't you had enough of that yet?"

"Never." His hands smoothed over her back in slow circles and a burning spark lit in his eyes. "In fact, I kinda wanted to try something new with you."

"What kind of something?"

"Something we've never done before. It takes a lot of trust. Will you?"

His hands wandered over her back and his eyes held hers, and heat began an answering dance within her. He wanted to have sex with her in a way that required more trust than what they were already doing. It sounded...deliciously kinky.

"Just think about it." He kissed her, hard and demanding, then eased back. "Let's go say hi to Rubes."

"Can I have a minute?"

"As long as you need."

She followed his sure stride across the clearing with her gaze, and chuckled. Ruby was clad only in tennis shoes and the yellow bikini she'd worn at the Outer Banks. Good ol' Ruby. Sera wrapped her arms around her waist, hugging close the peace she'd found during the service, if such a loose gathering could be called that.

It was odd how the unceremonious informality had seemed so much more holy than the church services she'd attended all her life. Maybe because they were in the middle of God's creation rather than boxed up in man-made walls, or maybe because everybody gathered there seemed so devout. Her gaze lingered on a couple of the women with tears drying on their cheeks. They held themselves unashamedly erect, never hiding the emotion that had driven them to cry.

Someone brushed by her, knocking her slightly off balance. She teetered on the rock and shrieked, and was caught by firm hands around her waist. She glanced up and her laughter turned to a smile. Ethan Phillips, a local doctor and a nearly lifelong acquaintance, was standing in front of her, helping her balance. He was at least as tall as Levi, though broader through the shoulders and tanned. His dark brown hair was tinged red and his clear green eyes were friendly in a face women sighed after wherever he went. He wore running shorts and no shirt, and she bit her lip as her eyes fell on the bare skin of his muscled chest. Wow. She didn't remember him being that buff when they were teenagers.

She deliberately fixed her gaze on his face. "Hey, Ethan. Thanks for catching me."

"Anytime." He smiled and drew back, though his hands lingered on her waist. "What are you doing here?"

"Oh, you know. Learning." She glanced around and tangled her fingers into a knot, all too aware of Ethan's hands warming her skin through her clothes. Levi was nowhere to be seen, neither him nor Ruby. "Do you worship the Lady Ki, too?"

"Yeah." His smile faded into obvious curiosity. "But you don't."

"Afraid not," she confessed. "I'm here with someone else."

"A male someone else."

"Um, yeah. Levi Ewart. Do you know him?"

"I do." Ethan's expression shuttered abruptly and his hands slid away from her waist. "I was under the impression you weren't dating."

She dropped her gaze and sighed. Good grief. Did everybody

think she was an old fogey? "It's a recent thing."

"How recent?"

"We've been dating a couple of weeks." Though dating was maybe not the best word for whatever she and Levi were doing.

"Must be serious if he brought you here."

She shrugged and told a whopper, more out of a need to not have her business spread along the rumor mill than anything else. "It's really too early to tell."

Ethan's laugh held just a hint of bitterness. "Trust me, Sera. If you're here, it's serious."

A hand slid along her lower back, startling her. She pressed a hand to her jumpy heart and turned toward her lover, smiling to cover her relief. "Levi, you know Ethan, don't you?"

Levi nodded. "Phillips."

"Ewart." Ethan's eyes flicked from Levi to Sera. "Tell Petey and your family I said hello.'

"I will," she said, and huffed when he turned on his heel and strode away without another word. "Well, that was odd. I've never known Ethan to be rude before."

"You've known him a while, then?"

"Since high school. We dated for, oh, three months or so." She laughed and shifted, facing Levi fully. "He took me to this dance at Tellowee, very swank, and then he went off to college. Nearly broke my heart in two."

"I see." Levi's gaze hardened and a raging heat gathered in his eyes, not the sensual heat she was used to seeing there, but a thinly disguised anger. "Pined for him, did you?"

"I was fifteen, no, fourteen. All teenaged girls pine for the boys that left them behind."

Her light words seemed to stoke his fury instead of diffusing it as she'd intended. "What's wrong, Levi?"

"Nothing we can't fix when we get home."

The razor sharp edge of his voice scraped over her, shaving away a sliver of the peace she'd claimed. He took her hand, holding her gently, and guided her solicitously down the trail. They drove home without speaking. During the short drive, she raced frantically over the morning's events, trying to pinpoint the cause of Levi's carefully restrained anger, and failed. The ritual had been poignant, moving, and a treasured glimpse into his life, one she had a feeling he hid carefully away.

When they made it home, he led her into her house and into her bedroom. Once there, he ran his hands down her arms and held her wrists in a tight grip. "So, we're not serious, are we?"

She gaped at him and tugged at her wrists. "That's what you're upset about?"

"I'm *upset* because you let another man touch you in a place sacred to the People." He backed her slowly across the room, guiding her with the strength of his body and the grip of his hands on her wrists. "You smiled at him and batted your pretty little eyes and told him you weren't serious about me."

The back of her legs hit the mattress. He pushed gently and she sat, then sprawled backward when he let go of her hands. His eyes gleamed brightly, twin spots of fury in the granite set of his expression. "I'm gonna show you exactly how serious we are, little Sera," he said, and his voice wasn't at all like the sweetly attentive man she'd come to know.

LEVI TRAPPED SERA'S KNEES between his legs and braced his hands against the mattress on either side of her head. Her eyes were wide, shining like pearls in the early morning light spilling through the window. She was still and watchful, appraising him with the same wary regard of a mouse confronted by a feral cat, though not a drop of fear tainted her expression.

She should be afraid. His anger burned and ached, roiling through his veins with the bitter sting of acid. How could she let another man touch her fresh from *his* touch? And in the sacred grove, after hearing the mournful promise of the Song of Ki? How could she betray him like that, deny him to her past lover, then throw her relationship with that man in his face?

What kind of woman did that to a man?

He could barely think around the raw fury clogging his throat, crushing the tenderness that had led him to take her there. He'd given her that tenderness over and over again, and it had gotten him nothing but a bruised and aching heart.

Time for Sera to witness the most important lesson a Son's

155

mate could learn.

"I'm going to the closet, and when I return, you'll be naked. Do you understand?"

She nodded, a jerky, short-lived gesture.

"Say it."

She bit her lip, then said quietly, "I understand."

"You'll be flat on your back in the middle of the bed with your head on a pillow and your arms raised above your head."

A pink blush suffused her skin and her breaths shallowed. "Levi..."

"Whisht. Your legs will be open, as wide as you can get them. I want to see your sweet little pussy." He dragged his thumb slowly over the curve of her lower lip. "If you're arranged like that when I return, I'll take it as consent for what follows."

She inhaled sharply. "What's going to follow?"

He pushed himself off the bed and stared down at her, deliberately using the cold gaze she hated. "A long discussion about what it means to be with a Son."

"Levi..."

"You've said enough, Sera." His voice broke on her name, echoing the crack in his heart. He pivoted away from her, leaving her to do as he'd asked or not. "More than enough."

He stalked to her closet and rifled through the scarves hanging from hooks along the wall. They smelled of her. He brought one to his face, rubbed it over his skin. The smooth fabric held a trace of her perfume, light, seductive. In her bedroom, the bed creaked and silence fell. He leaned his forehead on the wall and hitched in a breath. This wasn't anger, this amorphous wound throbbing through him. It was hurt, bigger than he'd ever imagined it would be for knowing her such a short time.

It's really too early to tell.

How could she have said that? How could she have dismissed him with so little thought?

Two weeks. He knew two weeks was too soon, even for an impetuous Son, but Sweet Goddess, it felt like a lifetime to him.

Try as he might, he couldn't remember her ever expressing anything outside of desire toward him. His mind flashed back to the moment when she'd told him why she was with him, sitting in her car in a rest stop on the other side of North Carolina. He treated her well. That's what she'd said. She was with him because he treated her well and the sex was good, and it apparently meant nothing to her beyond that.

He'd sworn to leave her only if she pushed him away, and had known when he'd made that promise that it was already too late. She held too much of him already, and he held none of her.

The bed creaked again and fabric rustled. She had to be tired of waiting for him, no matter what she'd decided.

He clutched the scarf in his fist. It was a pale, icy blue, nearly the same shade as the silk tank top she'd worn under her suit two days before, and a close match for her beautiful eyes. He slid it slowly off its hook with a steady downward tug and wrapped it around his hands. This would do, if she agreed.

And if she didn't, he'd persuade her, nice and slow and easy, like a man gentling the untamed heart of a wild creature.

He exited the closet and found her lying on the bed exactly as he'd asked, beautifully nude, her hands over her head and her thighs open. Desire slammed into him, hard and fierce, nearly overwhelming the hurt. He breathed through the need, expelling it as much as he ever could when he was around her.

She touched him so deeply, so effortlessly, and had since his eyes had fallen on her the first time.

He toed off his shoes and kicked them out of the way, then crawled across the bed.

Her gaze was solemn, tinged with a regret he knew all too well. "Be kind, Levi."

He loosened his grip on the scarf and gripped her chin. "I have been, love."

She closed her eyes and turned her head away, and left her limbs loose as he wrapped the scarf twice around her left wrist. He looped the long end through a spoke on her wrought iron headboard, then wrapped her right wrist twice and tied her hands together with a pretty bow.

"Wiggle your hands for me."

She did, jerking hard on the scarf. If she twisted her wrists, she could still get out, but this was good enough for their first try. He stilled her hands, smoothed her hair back, and brought his mouth close to her ear. "Before I'm finished with you, you're gonna beg me to let you come."

Her breath left her in a husky, panting moan. "Levi, please."

"Do you wish me to release you?"

"No."

Her voice was hoarse, wispy thin. He trailed his palm down her body, skimming over the hard peak of her breast, along the soft skin of her belly, and rested it over the hair protecting her sex. He slid a finger between the slick folds of her labia. She was ready for him, hot and wet and sweet, and he wanted to taste her there, love her for hours, soak up the cries of her passion. He circled her clitoris, teasing her with a feather light touch. Her hips arched upward and he withdrew.

"Still your hips."

Her eyes squeezed shut and her hips flattened on the bed.

"Do you know why you're here, Sera?"

"I never know why you do anything."

The frustration in her voice edged its way through the dark cloud gripping his heart, teasing out his humor. "Don't you?"

She shook her head, tangling the loose curls underneath. He levered himself over her and spread them out behind her, bringing each silky handful to his nose, breathing her in. Her eyes followed him, soft and no longer wary, needy in their own quiet way.

He grazed a finger down her cheek, surprised when she turned into his touch. "In the sacred grove, what did you tell your former lover?"

"We were never lovers..."

He silenced her with a finger to her lips. "Answer me."

Her expression turned mutinous, her silver eyes hot and angry. He removed his finger, and she said, "I told him I was there with you."

"And after that?"

"That we hadn't been dating that long."

He arched an eyebrow.

"He wanted to know if we were serious, and I said..." Her eyes slid away from his, fixing on the wall to her right. "I said we hadn't known each other long enough."

"You lied."

"It wasn't like that, Levi."

"I know what I heard, and I know what Ethan Phillips walked away from that grove believing." He straddled her stomach, resting all his weight on his legs and none on her. "How could you lead him to believe you were free with me standing right there, waiting?"

"I didn't..."

"You shamed me, Sera, shamed us both. You never wanted to claim me in public."

"That's not true!"

"Said I was too young for you, too much..." He bit his words off before the anger returned and spilled onto her. "Best be getting on with things, then."

He backed off the bed, walked to the end, and crawled toward her, sliding his hands and mouth up her inner legs as he went. She twitched under his touch, moaned when he hit a sensitive spot. He knelt between her thighs with his hands draped over her hips, thumbs rubbing along the creases between her legs and her sex, and memorized the way she looked lying there. Her hands gripped the scarf in the long sections between her wrists and the headboard. It glowed starkly against the tan she'd acquired the week before, a beautiful contrast. Her long sable curls were spread around her, flowing over the tender inner skin of her upper arms and along the tops of her breasts. They were full and round, pulled into firm peaks by the position of her arms.

Her eyes held both sorrow and desire, and begged him silently, sweetly.

She wanted a quick release and the tender touch of the lover she'd come to know. He refused her both.

Instead, he knelt and touched his mouth to the faint stretch marks on her lower abdomen. She twisted away from him and said, in a raw, agonized voice, "Levi, what are you doing?"

"Do you want me to release you?"

Her breaths echoed in the silence between them, sharp and short and harsh. "No."

"Then I do as I wish."

He held her hips down, pressing them firmly into the mattress, and explored the one area of her skin she'd denied him, ignoring her hitched breaths and nearly silent sniffles. Nothing would come between them, not even her reluctance to have him see her there. Didn't she realize how beautiful a man found a woman's body when she'd given birth, pushing life into the world through her sweat and love? How any man in his right mind would want to watch her grow round with his child, coddle and protect her, knowing she'd forever bear the marks belonging to her and him and the life they'd created?

His fingers drifted to the secret folds of her body, hidden from the rest of the world. He drew back and studied her, skimming his fingertips gently over her sweet beauty. When he'd memorized her, locked her image into a place in his mind where she'd live forever, he laid down flat on his stomach and slid an arm under one of her thighs, lifting it. He traced his tongue over the skin his fingertips had learned, licking into every inch of her, tasting her. She was shy here, bashful, and had only allowed him this prize twice, once when he'd taken her unaware their first night together, and a few days earlier when his fingers hadn't been enough to slake her need.

His heart twisted, thickening in his chest. She might not ever allow him this luxury again. He wanted to please her, desperately longed to wring pleasure from her body in a way that would drive thoughts of other men out of her head. Never again would she deny him. Never again would she downplay their relationship, not to strangers or kin, not even to him.

He traced one finger in random patterns along her sex and sucked her clitoris into his mouth, rolling his tongue over the tiny nub, nipping it. Her muscles tensed under him, raising her hips slightly into his caresses. He backed off, feathering butterfly kisses across her stomach and thighs, and when she relaxed, he put his mouth on her again.

Over and over he teased her, bringing her a little higher and a little closer to release with each pass, allowing her to calm between touches, then bringing her high again. Her shallow breaths alternated between sharp, irregular pants and low, greedy moans. When she edged close to the point of no return, he backed completely away and inserted a single finger into her, rotating it slowly in and out. She writhed beneath his touch and he let her, knowing she was close, knowing she needed very little to push her into a screaming release. Her body was hot, wet, and her flesh clung to his finger. He added a second and sunk them deep, exploring her until he found the spot that had her arching and rolling her hips.

"Oh, my God," she panted. "Oh, my God, Levi, please don't stop, please don't stop."

He crooked his fingers and sucked her clitoris into his mouth a final time, and held nothing back, pushing her hard and fast toward the climax she deserved, using his tongue and his lips and his fingers curling inside her. Her hips moved in frantic bursts against his touch, writhing helplessly beneath him. The first throb of her release tightened around his fingers, and she pushed her hips up and breathed his name as it rolled over her, consuming them both.

He gentled his touch, bringing her down slowly. Slipped his fingers out of her and licked her release into his mouth. It was perfect. Everything about her was perfect but that one thing, her refusal to see him for what he was and claim him before the world as a woman claimed the man she cared about.

He pushed himself off the bed and stripped his shorts and underwear off with his back to her. Retrieved a condom and rolled it on, protecting her from the conception of a second child, his child. He shrugged the thought away and rejoined her, stretching himself out above her.

Their skin skidded as he nudged the tip of his erection against her core. "This is what it means to be with me, Sera. Never forget this, not ever."

He slid into her, treasuring each brush of her breath along his skin as he moved over her, thrusting into her in long, languid strokes. He tangled his hands into hers, buried his face in her hair, and let go, loving her the way she'd wanted him to from the start, tenderly, eagerly, passionately. She wrapped her legs around his hips, and he whispered everything he'd held back, slipping into a brogue so thick, he was sure she'd never understand. How beautiful she was, how good it felt to be with her, how much he wanted her. He brought her high again with whispered words and gentle strokes, seeking his own release in the greedy clasp of her body, and found it moments after she reached her own in a harried rush of emotion that drained out of him as they fell down together, leaving him empty and weak and so very, very hers.

Fourteen

SERA GASPED for breath around the harsh thud of her heart. Levi had given her two out of this world orgasms before... She twisted her head, grazing her face along his heaving chest, and gave up trying to locate her clock. Before noon, for sure. He'd tied her to her bed and done exactly what he'd promised. She'd begged for release, begged for his touch. Her mind drifted over what had felt like hours of his love making, and she huffed out a laugh, sure she'd begged for a lot more than that before he'd driven her to that first mind-blowing orgasm.

He shifted above her, murmured that he'd be back, and the bonds around her wrists abruptly loosened. She left her hands there. Hell, they were numb anyway. A breathy bark of laughter edged its way out of her throat and tears sprang into her eyes.

He was going to leave her.

His intent had been there in every touch, as if he'd never be able to touch her again and was storing up the memory of every single inch of her body. If that hadn't convinced her, his words had, how desperate he was for her, how much he'd miss her, how he'd never forget the feel of her under him, the sound of her voice, her soft, passionate cries.

She rolled onto her side, turning her back to the bathroom door, and buried her face in his pillow, willing the tears not to fall. Why hadn't he listened to her? Why did he have to be so stupidly, stubbornly male?

The mattress shifted and his skin met hers. "There now, love. Don't cry."

A sob escaped the tight grasp of her throat. "You're leaving me."

His sigh feathered across her temple. "Not right now."

"You promised me you'd never leave. You *promised*." She peeked at him over her shoulder, and was shocked by the naked vulnerability in his expression. "I want to be with you, Levi, only you. Don't you get that?"

"Then why did you..." His mouth thinned and his shoulders tensed. "Here. Let me clean you."

She grabbed his hand, stilling his attempt to turn her over. "Tell me what you were going to say."

"Why did you lie to Ethan?"

He blurted it out in a rush, and immediately turned away from her, sliding his arm out of her grasp.

"It wasn't much of a lie, Levi," she said softly. "We've barely known each other two weeks. That's a little fast, don't you think? And I just wanted to keep it to myself a little longer, have time for our relationship to strengthen and grow before it's tested by gossips. 'Oh, look at Sera Noland, so desperate for a man she couldn't find one her own age.'"

"Fuck's sake, Sera. Are we back to that again?"

Her voice lashed out of her, sharp and angry. "No, we're not, but that's what people will say and we should both be prepared for it."

"I don't give a..." He inhaled through his nose and gripped her hand in his. "I don't care what other people say. This is me and you here, Sera, and we both know you have serious problems with me. My age, my wealth, my job, the fact that I'm affectionate in public. Hell, is there something you don't have a problem with outside of my dick?"

She blanched and flinched away from the hard contempt in his voice. "Those things are only a part of you, Levi, and a small part at that, as far as I'm concerned."

"Are they, now."

"And I can't believe you'd throw sex in my face after tying me to my own bed and making me beg."

"I made you beg as much to please you as to prove a point."

"Hunh. Some point. All I'm getting is how quick you are to leave when things don't go exactly the way you want them to."

His paled, going impossibly white. "I once told you I'd never run. I meant it then, I mean it now. I'll stick with you to the bitter end, if it's what you want, but I won't do it while you're shoving me away and parading your former lovers in front of me."

"Ethan and I were never lovers."

"Yeah?" He leaned close and said softly, "Not because he didn't want you."

God, he was obstinate. "Don't be ridiculous, Levi. He and I dated in high school more than a decade ago, and since then, we've barely spoken."

"He wants you, make no mistake, and he'll come after you while I'm away at work and not around to stop him." He maneuvered her onto her back. "Let me clean you."

"Fine. You do that." She opened her legs and stewed while he bent over her, running the cloth in gentle strokes over her sex, and all the things she'd left unsaid whirled and raged through her mind. They burst out in a heated flood in the middle of his ministrations, halting him in mid-stroke. "You don't trust me."

He glanced sharply at her, and she rushed on. "No, you don't. You don't trust me to know what I want and to stick by you. Let me tell you something, Mr. Big Shot. I'm not a quitter, either. You think it's easy being a single mom? Well, it's not. You have to do it all on your own and you constantly worry that you'll screw up big time, but you keep chugging along because he's your kid and he depends on you. And then you walk into the grocery store and people stare and whisper, but you hold your head up anyway because, damn it, he's yours and you love him."

"Sera, don't."

She choked down the tears clogging her throat and forced herself to finish. "And you meet men, sure you do, but they're not really interested in taking on a ready-made family, now, are they? And then one day, this bright sun god of a man walks into your life and he just happens to be way too young for you, but he makes you feel and ache and burn, and you say *what the hell* and give it a shot, only to realize that maybe things won't be that easy, but so what. He's one of the best men you've ever known and he's yours, if only for a little while, and you want to try, but it's always something, and you're being stupid, then he's being stupid, and for God's sake, I've never met two people who were so crazy stupid for each other, and I write romances."

Silence fell around them. Outside, car doors slammed in the distance, voices drifted in from neighbors' yards. Levi knelt beside her, his eyes on the washcloth he folded and unfolded in his hands.

"Say something," she said, and her voice came out all wrong, shaky and barely there and not at all like the woman who'd ranted at him moments before.

Over and over, his fingers worked the washcloth, holding his gaze. "You're crazy stupid for me?"

"I am."

"And you think I'm crazy stupid for you."

"A man who buys a woman a priceless dress better be crazy stupid for her."

The faintest hint of a smile touched his mouth. "I'm gonna get jealous, when a man comes around."

"Jealousy is a sign of insecurity," she said gently.

"Yeah, it is."

"You've got nothing to be insecure about."

"You smiled at Heath."

She huffed out a laugh. "I can't quit smiling at men because you're insecure."

He lifted his gaze to hers, narrowing his eyes as that dangerous glint crept into them. "You were flirting."

"He was charming and I smiled," she said firmly. "And then he asked me to test the sand with him. Does that mean that what I think it means?"

He flung the washcloth over his shoulder and stretched out beside her, propping his head on his hand with his other resting on her stomach. "I'm gonna kill him."

She grinned. "You will not. Besides, he was just getting your goat."

"Hunh. If you wanna believe that, go right ahead." His hand circled slowly over her belly, lingering along the proof of her motherhood. "You have no idea how sexy you are."

"Whereas you know exactly how hot you are," she said tartly, and wiggled her pinky, showing him right where he had her. "We both know who leads and who follows."

"You're a lot stronger than you think, Serafina."

Maybe she was, though probably not the way he was thinking. Where Petey was concerned, she'd take on all comers. Levi, though, left her weak and helpless with the simplest touch. She cuddled into him and drew a finger in random patterns along his chest. "I hate it when we argue, and it seems like we've done it so much."

"We're adjusting, not arguing. Sooner or later, we'll hit that perfect stretch of road where the bumps come from the outside, not the inside."

"There you go being all romantic again."

"There I go being a man with a healthy love of cars."

A laugh sputtered out of her. "Healthy is not how I'd describe your love of vehicles. I saw the collection of keys in your apartment."

"Hey, now, I only have five, and they're all important." His hand smoothed down her hip and back up again. "Speaking of vehicles, yours is..."

"No."

"But it's old and..."

"Nope, and that's my final say." She pounced on him, peppering kisses across his face until he laughed and caught her close. "Now, we're going to go take a shower and put on nice clothes and go get something to eat, and we are *not* going to argue or adjust or be jealous and insecure or doubting about anything, you hear me?"

"What was that you were saying about me leading?"

"Ha, funny. Get a move on, Legs. I'm in the mood for pizza."

His hands tightened on her, stopping her before she could roll away from him. "Sera, wait. I don't know where you got the idea that I was leaving you, but I wasn't."

She nestled her head in the crook of his neck, hiding the hurt burgeoning in her heart. "You told me when we were, um..."

"In the thick of things?"

His humor pulled an answering laugh out of her. "You said you'd miss me and it sounded, I don't know, like you were never coming back again."

"No, love, no," he said gently. "I told you I'd miss you because

I will, because we'll be apart for weeks. Why do you think I tied you up and did what I did to you?"

"Because you're a kinky bastard?"

His lips twitched into an almost smile. "Because I wanted to give us both something so strong, it would tide us over until we could be together again."

"And it had nothing to do with your jealousy."

"That, too." His voice was easy, accepting, his gentleness a balm for the hurt lingering in her heart. "Can't have you forgetting who you're with whilst I'm away."

As if she could ever forget the man he'd shown her he could be. She led him to the shower and gave him back something of what he'd given her. All the while, his words rang in her head and she stored them away, saving them for the lonely stretch of road looming in front of her.

THEY ENDED UP at Mama G's, sneaking in a scant ten minutes ahead of the after-church crowd. Sera enjoyed Levi's company, flirted shamelessly with him over a large pizza and a slice of rich, white chocolate cheesecake, and ignored the speculative glances from acquaintances and distant kin. Levi was right. Who cared what other people thought? What mattered was what they'd found. Though they'd only made the first steps toward something deeper, she intended to enjoy it as long as she could, and promised herself she'd do everything she could to see that he enjoyed it, too.

Late that afternoon, he slid a key off his keychain and gave it to her, then sat at the dinette in her breakfast nook and filled two sheets of paper with information.

"What's this?" she asked.

"The first page is contact information. My home phone, the company's number, and mine and Janine's direct lines. Addresses for home and work, and emergency contacts. My itinerary for the next eight weeks is under that."

She scanned it quickly and homed in on an interesting item. "You'll be at DragonCon?"

"I'll be filling in for staff at DragonCon," he corrected. "We own one of the venues, and because it's such an important contract,

I'll stick around all weekend and make sure everything goes smoothly."

She clutched the paper and debated her words carefully. "Petey would love DragonCon. Would it be a huge imposition if we stayed with you?"

"That's what the key's for, love," he said gently. "'Though it might be better if I rented a room so we can be on site."

"Oh, no, that's..."

"Not a bit of trouble, especially since we made a deal not to argue."

She grimaced. "You are..." *Stubborn. Mule-headed. Obstinate.* "Such a man."

He grinned. "That's not what you were gonna say. I'll take care of everything, ok?"

"I wasn't asking you to."

"No arguing," he reminded her. "Besides, I'm pretty sure the way to Petey's heart is through DragonCon."

"Levi, really. You can't buy a child's affections."

"I'm not trying to. I'm not, I swear," he added when she frowned. "I'm supporting his interests. That's completely different."

Her expression softened. What a sweet thing for him to say, and an even sweeter thing for him to do. "Thank you. He'll enjoy it, I know."

"Let's hope." He prodded the pages. "The second sheet is a list of places where I've set up accounts for you."

She flipped to it and goggled. "What do I need with an account at Memory?"

"Darlin', if you haven't figured out why I like that place, you're not nearly as smart as I thought you were."

Her cheeks colored as her mind detailed the purchases he made for her on Friday past, including the hand-painted, one-of-a-kind lingerie she hadn't mustered the nerve to wear yet. "Oh. Right." She studied the list more carefully and huffed. "I'm not letting you buy my groceries."

He cupped his hand to his ear. "What was that? I could've sworn I heard an argument coming from you."

She slapped the papers onto the table and glared. "Figures you'd use my own words against me."

"That's my finely honed negotiating skills at work." He scooted around in his seat and held out his arms. "Now, come send me off proper-like, woman."

She did, kissing him soundly, and after, she helped him pack his bags away in the surprisingly roomy trunk of his car. They stood in the open door of his car, clinging to each other.

When she could bring herself to ease away from him, she said, "Be careful. Traffic's horrible between here and there."

"No worries, love. I make this drive all the time."

"I know, it's just..." She swallowed the lump in her throat. "Text me when you get home, ok?"

"I will."

"And call soon."

"Every day after supper, if I'm able."

She buried her face in his chest and curled her fingers into his t-shirt. "I'll miss you. I know how stupid that sounds, to miss a man I barely know, but I will."

"Hey, now, none of that. We agreed that we're crazy stupid about each other, so the barely knowing each other thing is a bit of a moot point, yeah?"

"Yes, it is, and I don't know why I keep bringing it up."

"'Cause you're crazy stupid about me."

He kissed her one last time, then she stepped back and let him go, stood watching him drive away like a lovesick schoolgirl.

That's about how she felt.

A reluctant grin tugged at the corners of her mouth. When his car disappeared around the curve, she went into her house and dragged out her laptop. Her work had been neglected over the past week while they painted and stained, though she'd allowed for that in her writing schedule. Still, it was time to get back to it. She pulled up her work in progress, read over the last few scenes, and poured every bit of her worries over her relationship with Levi into the characters coming to life under the rapid clicks of her fingertips along the keyboard.

SERA'S REFLECTION in the rearview mirror followed Levi as he drove away from her. He rounded a curve, blocking her from view, and leaned his head against the back of his seat. She was supposed to've been a healthy flirt, nothing more, and now, two weeks later, he had to fight the urge to do a u-turn and race back to her.

Time apart would be good for them.

He repeated that mantra as he signaled for a turn onto the road leading to Tellowee.

A breather this early in their relationship would slow them down, allow them both to evaluate their feelings without the pressure of the other person's constant presence. Intellectually, that made perfect sense to him.

Emotionally, not so much.

His heart was a tangle of confusion and infatuation, overlain by an oversized dose of lust.

He clamped down on that thought and searched for his control, strangely absent during the past two weeks. His friends would laugh their arses off if they could see him now, all flummoxed and flustered, letting a slight woman nearly a foot shorter lead him around by his dick, all the while worried she might let go.

When had he ever worried over a woman? For that matter, when had he ever needed to? No woman had ever caused him as much doubt as Serafina Noland did. With her, he was never sure exactly where he stood, though she wasn't one to push and pull on a man just because she could, her own doubts aside. She was reasonable, steady, but try as he might to convince her otherwise, she still had deep reservations about the surface differences between them.

Two weeks hadn't been long enough to overcome her fears, wouldn't have been in any case, so he'd formulate a plan and execute it with the grace and style he'd inherited from his battle-hardened foremothers. All he needed was a good strategy built on sound tactics demonstrating his friendship, emphasizing their compatibility, and showing her that she could count on him to stick, just as he'd promised.

His mum was outside weeding her flowers when he pulled into his parents' drive. She rose gracefully into a stand and brushed dirt off her bare knees, stripped off her gloves, and opened her arms to him. He folded her into a hug, surrounding himself with the love that had been a constant presence during his childhood. The weight of his worries lifted, lightening under the comforting touch of his mother's embrace.

Noreen Ewart, daughter of Iniira, daughter of Hawthorne, was a tall woman, strong and flexible in spite of having lost her immortality a quarter century before to his father, Iain. She wore her black hair in a sleek cap, had for as long as he could remember, and had gifted him with the light brown eyes Sera found so beautiful.

Levi tightened his grip and buried his face in his mum's neck. "Missed you."

"Not so much you'd come and see me, and been near Tellowee a whole week, I hear." Noreen drew back and cupped his face in her slender hands. "Rumor has it you've taken up with the Noland girl."

He drew away from her and slid his hands into his pockets. "I'm sorry you and da weren't the first to know."

"Well, you're a grown man, have been for a while. I can't expect you to tell me everything going on in your life, much as I'd like to know."

His gaze fell to the sidewalk. "It's complicated, Mum."

"Love always is." She slapped her gloves against her thigh, bare below the ragged cuff of her cutoff shorts. "Come on. Your da will want to see you. The two of you can stand around the grill making man noises and brag about your prowess with women."

They followed the scent of grilling meat scattered by the breeze barely stirring the late afternoon air. Iain Ewart stood at the grill, a giant bear of a man with unruly copper hair, a bushy beard and mustache streaked through with blond and gray, and blue-green eyes that shifted color with his moods. He was as different from his elegant, refined wife as a man could be, hearty and hale and unafraid of demonstrating his temper, in stark contrast to his wife's controlled demeanor; yet the two had managed to have a happy marriage for nearly a quarter of a century.

Maybe he should've brought Sera here first so she could see how two people could manage to find love in spite of the wide gap between their backgrounds and personalities.

Iain greeted Levi with a hefty smack on the back. "Grab a beer and a chair. Supper's near done."

"Can't stay. I have some work to catch up on."

"Eh, is that it, then? Well, your mum tells me you've a woman. Right serious about her, are you?"

"Getting there." Levi shrugged, trying to settle the whip of emotion lashing through him every time he thought about Sera. "When did you know Mum was the one?"

Iain peered at Levi with one eyebrow crooked. "About two shakes after I met her. Took a while to come 'round to love, mind you, and an age and a half to convince her of it, but a patient man always snares the dove."

Levi snickered. "Mum's not much of a dove, Da."

"She was to me. Never gentle, not my Noreen, but she was tall and slim and had the fire of a warrior shinin' from her near golden eyes." Iain sighed gustily and prodded the ribs on the grill. "You should've seen her, lad."

Levi had heard the stories often enough. Noreen had been travelling in Scotland, literally singing for her supper as she wandered through the countryside. She'd ended up attending a bonfire in the village near where his father lived. Iain had talked her into staying longer than a day, then coaxed her into love. It had always been Levi's favorite story growing up, told in the thick brogue of his father's tongue, embellished only a little with each passing year.

Noreen slipped her arm through Levi's and rested her head on his arm, exactly over the *amaetien* hidden under the sleeve of his t-shirt. "You'll stay for supper. I insist," she said mildly, overriding his protest. "You can spare half an hour while you eat and tell me all about Serafina Noland, else my first errand tomorrow will be a visit to your nana's house."

He grimaced. That had always been the most effective weapon in his mum's arsenal. Nobody wanted to rile Hawthorne the Beheader, nobody. She had a habit of swinging first and asking questions later, even among family. Among the People, she had a fierce reputation, more frightening even than her daughter, Iniira, and his grandmother wasn't exactly known for her tolerance or patience.

Like mother like daughter, he figured. Thank the Lady Ki his own mum had mellowed after meeting his da.

He helped his parents put the finishing touches on the meal, then sat with them around the mission style table in their kitchen, his plate piled high with boneless ribs and a heaping salad filled with vegetables from his mother's garden.

A preemptory strike was always best, so he began the conversation with what his mother wanted to know. "I met Sera in Kill Devil Hills a little more than two weeks ago. She was on vacation, couldn't stay but a week. Since I had a few days free, I rearranged my schedule and drove home with her."

Noreen's hand paused with her fork halfway to her mouth. "When you say 'rearranged,' you mean you cancelled the rest of your plans with your friends, yes?"

Levi's fingers tightened around his knife. "I mean I rearranged my schedule for the week."

"You put off business for a woman you'd known a week." She lowered the fork, her stare neutral. "Please continue."

"We spent the past week together, here and in Atlanta."

Iain leaned forward, his eyes glowing. "You take her to that little boutique, whatsit? The one with the fancy knickers?"

The grin slipped through before he could contain it. "I bought her some of those fancy knickers, Da."

"Yeah? She wear 'em?"

Noreen's hand slapped onto the table beside her plate. "You spent your own money on a woman you barely know?"

"It's my money." Levi pinched the bridge of his nose, grimacing over the childish remark. He wasn't a damn kid who had to account to his parents for every penny, hadn't had that sort of childhood anyway. "She's not the kind of woman who expects you to do for her, if that's what you're worried about."

"I'm more worried that you took her to the peak after knowing her for two weeks."

Levi's appetite fled. He slumped into his chair and met his mother's stare evenly across the width of the table. "It was an impulse and not one I regret. She found something holy there. Isn't that the point?"

"I think the point here is that she welcomed another man's

173

touch. Mother wasn't pleased."

Fuck. He bowed his head and breathed through the nerves roiling in his gut. He hadn't seen Gran, hadn't thought to look for her. She could easily have slipped in and out of the group without him being the wiser, as large as that day's crowd had been.

"Sera and Ethan have known each other for a long time. She was being polite, and if you knew her, you'd know she can't be any other way." He glanced between his parents, noting the humor in his father's eyes and the worry in his mother's, and chose his words for the effect they'd have on his mum more than his da. "She's a good woman. Hard-working, self-sufficient. She has a son."

Noreen's eyes widened and her breath hitched. "A son?"

He wiped the triumph from his expression. Daughters always had a soft spot for male progeny, no matter the mother, and Mum was no exception. "Petey. He's seven. Haven't met him yet, but from what Sera's said, he's intelligent and kind."

"You're trying to bribe me." Her eyes narrowed, glinting with something close to admiration. "Just when I think you're all Iain, you do something like this."

"I'm merely pointing out that she's a good mum, much like my own."

"And flattery to boot." Iain smacked Levi's shoulder, knocking him off balance. "There's a good lad."

Noreen speared Levi with an imperious gaze. "You'll bring her and her son to supper next weekend."

"Can't. I'm working. It'll be weeks before I have a weekend to spare."

"And you plan to spend it with her, after taking her to the peak and no doubt spoiling her with your time, attention, and money." She picked up her fork and curled her lips into the cold smile of a warrior on the hunt. "Well, I suppose there's nothing left for it. Mother and I will pay the Noland girl a visit and see for ourselves what kind of woman she is."

"Butt out, Mum."

"Let her be, son. You wanted a different outcome, you should've brought the lass here first instead of letting the rumor mill carry the tale to your mum."

"I've known her for two weeks."

"Aye, and your heart's already tangled." Iain lifted a rib in the fingers of both hands and gestured toward Levi with it. "Eat your supper now, lad. There'll be plenty of time for your mother's fuss and bother after."

That's what he was afraid of. A Daughter's *fuss and bother* could range anywhere from a mild reprimand to a full blown war, usually the latter, especially when the Daughter in question had his mother's temperament. He picked at his own meal, ate as much as his stomach would hold around the knot lodged there. Sera deserved fair warning. He'd see she got it, but beyond that, there was nothing he could do to keep Noreen from inspecting the woman that had gained a foothold in her son's heart and mind.

Fifteen

EARLY MONDAY MORNING, Sera and Petey settled into their summer vacation routine. They ate cold cereal around the dinette in the breakfast nook, talking about whatever came to mind. Petey dominated the conversation, rambling in excited spurts, sharing his and his cousins' adventures from the past two weeks. Sera listened as she ate, nodding or contributing when the conversation called for it.

The room was oddly large, the dimensions somehow wrong. Levi had filled the space, dominating it with his size and the force of his personality. It seemed empty without him, as if he should be sitting there with her and Petey, sharing the start of their day.

Which was just ridiculous.

She nudged a chunk of cereal with her spoon and smiled at Petey acting out Dale's repeated trips down the waterslide. Even if Levi weren't two hours away working, she didn't quite feel right yet about letting Petey meet him. Soon, yes, but first, she had to explain Levi to her son and give him time to get used to the possible change in his young life. After watching the nightmares other single moms in the community went through juggling dating and kids, Sera wanted to proceed as cautiously as she could. It would be weeks before it became a problem anyway, but if she prepared Petey thoroughly for it, hopefully his introduction to Levi would go much more smoothly than it had for some of the other local kids in the same situation.

"Are you listening, Mama?"

"Yes. Dale said the slide felt like greased lightning under his butt." She reached across the table and gripped Petey's narrow hand, wiggling it for good measure. "What I want to know is why

176

none of the waterslide stories you're telling involve *you* going down one."

His silver eyes, so like her own, dropped to his bowl of cereal. He slumped over it and kicked his bare feet together under the table in a steady *slap, slap.* "I didn't wanna."

Sera stifled a sigh. It had been a year since he'd fallen out of a tree and broken his arm. A whole year, and he was still afraid. "I need to do a little work before Candi and the boys get here. Why don't you start sorting out your clothes so I can wash them later?"

"Yes'm." He squeezed her hand and lifted his eyes slowly to hers. "Can I ask you something, Mama?"

"You can ask me anything, Petey."

He heaved a sigh, pursed his lips. "Do you think you'll ever find me a dad?"

"Oh, my sweet boy. Come here." She scooted sideways in her chair and held out her arms, enfolding him in a huge hug when he climbed onto her lap. He was fine-boned and scrawny, might always be given her height and his father's. She breathed in his little boy smell, an odd mixture of sweat and soap, and kissed the top of his head. "I'm sorry your dad isn't around for you."

"I know. It's just, if I had a dad, maybe I wouldn't..." His hand clutched the fabric of her tank top, wrinkling it into a knot between his slender fingers. "Dale and Matty ain't scared of nothing."

"Dale and Matty are different people than you. Anyway, I bet they're scared of some stuff. Spiders and snakes." She lowered her voice, added a spooky Transylvanian accent, and said, " *Vampires.*"

"Mama." He dragged the word out to three syllables, the way only a Southern child could. "Ain't no such thing as vampires."

"How do you know?"

She goosed his ribs and laughed with him until his worries faded, then scooted him off to his room, her own worries sighing out of her. Now was the worst possible time for Petey to decide he needed a dad. The first time he met Levi, he'd fall head over heels, and then what would they do if things didn't work out? Levi would never hurt Petey, not intentionally. If she had even a doubt on that score, she'd never let the two of them meet. No, what worried her was that they would hit it off and become so tightly wound together, there'd be no separating them, regardless of what happened in the future.

She clapped her hands to her face and laughed. She must be the only woman on the face of God's green Earth who worried that her son and the man she was involved with would like each other too much.

After cleaning up breakfast, Sera turned on her laptop and checked her e-mail, deleting spam and noting important ones to deal with later. She opened Levi's last, swallowing down the excited flutter of her nerves, and smiled as she read it.

Knew you'd check this before checking your phone, so... Good morning, love. Missed you last night. I'd wish you here, but I'd rather be there, surrounded by you.

Her heart melted and purred, and she patted her chest, unable to control a grin. What a romantic.

I'll call tonight if I can. Have a late meeting and don't know when it'll wind up. Mum might call on you and she'll probably bring Gran along.

Oh, crap. Levi's mother, here? Thank goodness she'd cleaned the house thoroughly before going on vacation. That afternoon, though, she and Petey would go through it again, just in case.

Remember our walk to the peak and the legend I told you? You asked about immortality. Gran may be able to answer that question for you. I trust you to keep an open mind and consider the possibilities.

Well, that sounded ominous. Not good anyway. Sera mulled over his explanation of the People's origins. Seven sisters had been cursed to live forever. Surely that couldn't be true, not the immortality part, anyway. Nobody lived that long outside of legends and myths.

Did they?

Don't let them intimidate you. You've only me to please. No, scratch that. Isn't it the man's job to please his woman? I aim to, for as long as you'll let me. Make it a good long while, will you? I'm of a mind to spoil you.

A laugh spilled out of her, exasperated and charmed. If he spoiled her any more, she'd be rotten.

He signed the e-mail, *Ever yours, Levi.* She printed it off and made a folder for it, hiding it away like the women of yesteryear used to do with their sweetheart's love letters. Maybe she'd write him one on real stationery and send it the old-fashioned way, through the U.S. Postal Service. It would please him to receive it, especially if she tucked a picture of him and Ruby inside, one Sera had taken on the sly during their trip to Cape Hatteras.

She had several good shots of him, all snapped surreptitiously. For all his bold personality, Levi was camera shy. The night before, after he'd left, she'd uploaded the final set of pictures from her vacation onto her computer and organized them, then spent half an hour mooning over the ones she'd taken of Levi.

One in particular, shot after his bout with Ruby, had captivated her. He'd been standing at the grill with Colin, holding a beer in one hand, the other tucked into his pocket. A moment before, he'd been watching her take pictures of the ocean. She'd caught him doing it or she would never have known. As soon as she'd turned, he'd looked away, but his mouth had curled into that wicked smile and his whiskey eyes had smoldered with the heat of whatever had been running through his mind. She hadn't hesitated, hadn't even thought it through before she'd raised her camera and snapped the picture, perfectly capturing him in a moment when he'd been thinking of her. That one would go on her nightstand, protected by a frame decorated with a handful of the seashells she'd brought home. Every time she looked at it, she'd remember what was between them.

As if she needed a reminder. Her thoughts drifted constantly to him and the time they'd spent together. Her dreams had been full of him, his hands on her skin, their bodies entwined in passion, and she'd woken reaching for him. It had taken her a long moment to remember that he was in Atlanta, not out on an early morning jog or cooking breakfast for her in her sadly outdated kitchen.

She reread his e-mail, holding close the secret thrill of a woman with a new lover. Later, she'd answer it in kind, but for now she had chores. She clicked out of his e-mail into Facebook, posted a short note letting her fans know she was home from vacation, then closed her laptop and went to round Petey up.

FORTY-FIVE MINUTES LATER, she drove through the gates of Levi's berry farm. Candi sat in the passenger seat, gawking like a tourist while the three boys crowded together in the back seat of the Volvo. She was a slender woman, taller than Sera by a good four inches, with shoulder-length brassy blonde hair and bright blue eyes. Both of her boys had inherited their father's darker hair, the same rich shade of brown as Sera and Petey's, though Matty was otherwise the spitting image of his mother, mischievous eyes, pixie face, and all.

"How did you get an invitation here again?" Candi asked.

"I know the owner." Which she'd already told Candi three times. Her sister-in-law wouldn't be satisfied until Sera dished all the details, but there was no way she could do that while Petey was within earshot.

Sera parked next to the main building, escorted everybody inside, and introduced her crowd to Heath's sixteen-year old brother. Theo resembled his elder brother enough in looks for no one to mistake the relationship, though their personalities seemed miles apart. Not long after, he gave them a map and directed them to the best sections of the farm for harvesting blueberries and blackberries.

They walked out, the boys swinging the empty plastic ice cream buckets they carried, one in each hand, Sera and Candi lagging behind. The July sun had burned away the dew long before their arrival. Moisture lingered in the humid heat of the morning, already above seventy with the promise of a much hotter day to come.

The farm was neatly tended. Precisely trimmed sections of grass separated widely spaced rows of brambles and bushes. A dirt road wound through the property, branching off in sharp angles and curves, demarcating different areas of the farm. When they reached the first blueberry picking area Theo had recommended, they spread out, the boys skipping ahead, leaving their mothers to pick the first few bushes clean.

"How many gallons of each do you want?" Sera asked.

Candi flipped the buckets in her hands. "How many are you getting?"

"We picked what I needed last week."

"We?"

Sera focused on the thumbnail sized blueberries in front of her, ignoring Candi's raised eyebrows. "So, will five gallons of each be enough?"

"Who cares about that?" Candi lowered her voice and leaned closer. "I want to know if this *we* included a man."

Sera glanced around. Petey and his cousins had moved well out of earshot. She lowered her voice to a whisper anyway. "His name's Levi Ewart. I met him in Kill Devil Hills, first day there."

Candi gaped. "And you brought him home with you?"

Sera hunched her shoulders as heat flooded her face. "His parents live in Tellowee. He cut his vacation short so we could drive back home together."

"That's not all you did together, I bet. Oh, my God. You took a *lover.*" Candi grasped Sera's forearm and squeezed. "Spill the beans, sister, and spare not a single detail."

"I'm not telling you about that."

"Oh, come on. Give me something here."

Sera bit her lip, containing the smile threatening to spread across her face. "He's gorgeous, six one at least, and built like you wouldn't believe. Red hair, this odd, light coppery color, and the most beautiful eyes I've ever seen." She turned back to the berries, pulling off handfuls as she sorted through everything that had happened between her and Levi, condensing it into a version that would appease Candi's curiosity. "Very sweet and attentive. Thoughtful. Our first date, he took me on a walk along the beach, held my hand. God, it was gorgeous that night. The full moon shining down, this light breeze blowing in. We talked for what felt like hours, and after, he..."

Candi had fallen oddly silent, her head tilted to the side, her expressive eyes curious. "After, he *what?*"

"Treated me very well." How could Sera describe the potency of that first kiss and the way he'd made her feel? Beautiful, desirable, sexy, all with one kiss. "We spent the week together, mostly. Went sight-seeing with his friends. It seemed like the most natural thing in the world to bring him back here. He asked me first though, asked me to stay with him there, but I had chores here."

"And you're not one to neglect your chores, are you?" Candi murmured.

"Well, they have to be done by somebody, and since I'm the

only one around..." Sera shrugged. "Anyway, we did a few things around the house, then he took me to Atlanta. He works there. Corporate stuff. We went to this little boutique in Buckhead. There were no prices on the dresses. Can you believe that? And he and the clerk pushed me into trying on at least a dozen outfits." She halted the words flooding out of her. "Sorry. I didn't mean to go on like that."

"No, please. It sounds like you were about to get to the good part." Candi glanced away and back. "Tell me quickly. The boys are headed this way."

"He bought me a dress, this slinky silver thing with barely any back, and half a dozen pairs of hand-painted underwear. I swear, it's so beautiful I'm afraid to put it on."

"You let him buy you a dress?" Candi narrowed her eyes into glittering slits. "The woman who refused to take money from her family when she was pregnant and jobless let a man buy fancy underwear for her."

"I couldn't help it. His eyes went all hot and wild, and all I could think about was what he'd do to get me out of those clothes."

Candi inhaled sharply. "Oh, my God, my legs just went weak. Tell me he's good in bed."

Sera glanced around. The boys had crouched on the grass fifteen feet away, examining who knew what with the focus young boys reserved for icky things their mothers hated. She turned back around and said, "You have no idea. He tied me to my bed and...and *did* things to me."

"Things?" Candi breathed the question out. "What *kind* of things?"

"*Things.*" Sera lowered her voice until it was barely audible. "With his mouth."

"As in...?"

"Yes, *as in.* For about half an hour, maybe longer. I sort of lost track of time." Sera sucked in a sharp breath around the heat pulsing through her. "And then he made love to me and whispered all these beautiful things to me with his hands tangled in mine."

"Jesus Lord forgive me, but *damn*, Sera. Why aren't you dragging him to the alter?"

Sera focused on a leaf, fiddling it between her fingers. "He's only twenty-two."

Candi wheezed out a laugh. "And he knew how to do that with his mouth? Are you nuts? What does his age matter if he can take care of you, you know, when it counts?"

"It's not just that. He's young and wealthy as sin, and he's not a Christian. You know how Mom and Dad are. It's bad enough that I don't go to church anymore, but if they find out about Levi's religion, they'll freak."

"Who cares? Honestly, Sera, you have to stop living your life according to what other people think you should do." Candi tilted her head again, eyeing Sera thoughtfully. "But it looks to me like you've already made that decision where Levi's concerned."

"All but," Sera admitted. "He'll be away working for a couple of months, but I'm telling Petey about him this week. There's a place where Levi's family worships and that's where I want to tell Petey. God, it's beautiful there. They sing this song to the dawn, sort of a hymn asking for protection and guidance."

"You went to church with him."

"It's not like that. This was outdoors. After the song, there was this long moment of silence and then people sort of broke up and went their own way, some lingering with their friends and family. Some left with tears on their face. It was so..." Sera shook her head, unable to find an adequate way to express how she'd felt there, what it had meant for Levi to share it with her. "Standing there surrounded by him and these people who seemed so lost and hopeful at the same time, it seemed like the most holy place I'd ever been."

"You went to church with him." Candi shook her head and her blonde locks swung around her shoulders. "And you brought him home with you, let him spend money on you. Let him tie you to your bed, for cripes' sake, which I'm totally envious of, and you're telling Petey about him. Sera, honey, do you even realize how deep you're in with this man?"

"Oh, I know. Trust me, I know." She squinched her eyes closed and blurted, "He gave me a key to his apartment and opened accounts for me at a dozen different stores."

"Eh, come again?"

"I know. Ridiculous, right? I mean, it's not like I'm gonna use them or anything."

"I think you'd be crazy not to, especially that key." Candi snagged Sera's hand and held on tight. "Is that why we're here today?"

"He owns this farm, said I could bring you and Mom whenever I wanted. We get the family rate, as long as y'all are with me."

"Dang, Sera, hang on to him for the farm if nothing else." Candi's smirk faded into a worried frown. "Just, be careful, would you? I mean, I'm really happy for you and I'm dying to meet this gorgeous paragon of a man, but I'm worried, too. You've been hurt enough."

"I'm being as careful as I can." She swallowed the lump in her throat and her gaze fell on Petey. "Truthfully, I don't want to be. Every time he's close, I have this urge to throw my arms around him and never let go, but there's more than me to consider here."

"The things we do for our kids, huh? It'll all work out, if it's meant." Candi squeezed Sera's hand. "Later, though, you *will* provide details of this tying up thing. Us old married folks have to get creative to keep things interesting."

For some reason, Sera didn't think she'd ever have that problem with Levi, and if she did, all she had to do was bring out the underwear he'd bought her. The idea of what he'd do to her after shivered through her, the way he'd make love to her, yes, but also the way he'd hold her once passion swept them high. He never left her wanting there, curling around her as if he wanted to hold what they'd shared in the space between them. It warmed her as surely as thoughts of the way he touched her did, and she carried that warmth with her through the rest of the long, summer day without him.

LEVI PUT the final touches on the last of the paperwork he'd scheduled for that morning and stacked it into a pile with the other work his assistant would handle once he was finished. He punched at his phone. "Janine, are you eating out or in?"

"Out. I've got a hot lunch date with Mr. Macelroy's assistant's cousin."

He didn't wanna know. Really, he didn't. Janine was sharp as a tack, a hard worker, and always had a positive, sunny attitude. Where men were concerned, though, she was as fickle as a rattler under the hot July sun. No man passed muster long enough to make it to boyfriend status. Given her age, that might not be a bad thing.

Levi winced. Damn it, she was a year older than him and more than mature enough to know her own mind. Hadn't he made that point with Sera over and over again?

He refused to dwell on her doubts about their age differences, absolutely refused to. "Could you bring me the menu for Toni's?"

"Be right there," Janine said, her perky voice so chipper, it was nearly a song.

He opened his laptop, rewarding himself with a peek at his e-mail. Sera had answered him. His heart leapt into his throat and a secret smile curved his mouth. He clicked her e-mail open, his smile widening at her tart words. *You've already spoiled me too much, Levi.*

Janine walked in, a pert bounce in her steps, and stopped dead in her tracks, her mouth gaping. "Wow. Is that the smile you use on women you date?"

He tried to discipline his emotions, really he did. They slid through his attempts like air around a chain link fence and bounced through him, buoying his smile when he'd meant to contain it.

"'Cause if it is, I'm quitting so I can throw myself at you." She finished the trip to his desk and set the menu near his laptop, exchanging it for the pile of paperwork he'd set aside for her. "Unless you're serious about the woman you brought here the other day, in which case, *dayum* I lose again."

He grinned, couldn't help it. "You're not ready for serious."

"I would be if a man looked at me like that," she retorted, and sashayed away.

"Hey, be careful with Macelroy's whatsit."

She peered at him over her shoulder and waggled her eyebrows. "Aren't I always?"

He drew the menu in as she left, studied it for half a minute, and placed an order for delivery. The night before, after wending his way through his mother's less than subtle attempts to ferret out information about Sera and Petey, he'd made the tedious drive home, sat down in his sterile apartment, and planned a campaign to ease Sera's fears. Couldn't do that if they were apart, though he well understood the benefits of taking a breather. Still, too long and he'd have to start from scratch. Their trip to Winston-Salem had saved him a scant day three weekends from then. He'd juggled and negotiated with himself, calculating his responsibilities, shifting work to earlier or later, though it meant adding hours to each day until then, and managed to carve out two days and one night a couple of weekends later, just for her.

It wasn't much, but it was better than nothing.

During short work breaks that morning, he'd begun implementing his plan. Weekly deliveries of fresh bouquets to her home, a call to a friend of a friend who was a weapons expert, research into security systems and family-friendly vehicles. Sera wasn't as security minded as he was. Hopefully, it wouldn't take much to convince her that she needed to protect herself and Petey while he was away.

And the clincher, registration for the three of them to DragonCon and lodging in one of the suites reserved for family. Between the other weekend he'd carved out and the convention, his time apart from Sera would dwindle from an eight week stretch into visits every third weekend. After that, his schedule would settle.

No more side work. He had enough anyway, between Icenia and his own investments. He'd only ever taken other jobs to fill his time, out of habit more than anything. The People worked, everybody who was able. It was the only thing they'd ever known and had long since become an integral part of their culture. Now, though, he had another priority in a kind-hearted brunette and her son.

The chef's salad he'd ordered came while he stood at the windows behind his desk, gazing over the city, his mind on the future. He ate it standing and flipped through his e-mails, lingering on Sera's, checked Facebook for news on a distant cousin's impending birth, and found a notice from Sera's author page.

Back from the Outer Banks, which was crowded, but gorgeous. Had a blast, thanks to some very special people. Pictures of all the touristy stuff will be on the blog later, some here, too. Many thanks to everyone who attended the book signing, and to street team members Katie and Sandra for their help getting the word out. Got most of my to-do list around the house accomplished, thanks to a little help from a friend (ok, a lot). Now, it's nose back to the grindstone!

Several people had already commented. On a purely mischievous impulse, Levi clicked in and posted a comment, too. *Did you enjoy the souvenir you brought home?*

He finished off his salad, cleaned up, and was about to start on the afternoon's slate of work when he noticed other comments. One woman's read, *What souvenir?* Katie had responded with, *OMG, if it's what I think it is (and I'm pretty sure!), I wish I had me some! Does this souvenir have a brother? Or maybe I could have one of the other three??? Don't make me beg!*

He snickered and closed his laptop. Work first. Gossip later.

Sera everywhere in between.

An hour after, he checked her author page again, just to see if she'd commented, and grinned. The discussion had spiraled out of control, with people asking if she'd started dating, who he was, were they getting married, what did her son think. Sera had calmly responded with a blanket statement. *Yes, I'm dating. We met in the OBX. He's a great guy. I'm sure y'all will hear lots about him down the road!*

Her first comment, though, was to him. *Levi: Yes. I enjoyed my souvenir very much and am looking forward to enjoying it again. Soon?*

That had only incited her fans more.

He rubbed a hand over the ache in his chest, sweet and hopeful and light. She'd acknowledged him. On a public forum in front of hundreds of people, she'd openly admitted they were together. He tapped out a quick reply, *Sera: As soon as I can make it back*, then logged out, away from temptation.

She'd taken the first step towards reconciling herself to their differences. He buried himself in work, determined to make space for her in his life, the way she'd made space for him.

Sixteen

BRIGHT AND EARLY Tuesday morning, Wendell Noland knocked perfunctorily on Sera's front door and let himself in, calling for her as he wandered through the house.

"Back here, Dad," she hollered, and rose from her desk, placed in the tiny third bedroom she used as an office. In a few days, she'd begin ripping out paneling in the library, now that the carpet was up. Jack had promised to help her install sheetrock in its place, and once it was up and painted a soft yellow, she'd refinish the floor, a sturdy hardwood the previous owners had covered with lime green shag carpet for some bizarre and unknown reason. In a few months, if she was patient and worked hard, she could move her office there and redo this room as a guest room.

For that *souvenir* she'd brought home from the Outer Banks.

She met her dad in the kitchen, stood on tiptoes, and kissed his weathered cheek. He was a handsome man, young looking in spite his fifty-eight years and decades spent out in the sun building other people's homes. His silver eyes normally glittered mischievously, his buoyant humor highlighted by the laugh lines radiating away from them. Today, they were serious and sober, not a trace of mischief in sight.

She dropped onto her heels and choked down the worry gripping her throat. "What is it? Is Mom ok? Has something happened?"

"No, nothing like that." He yanked off his battered Atlanta Braves ball cap and beat it against his thigh. "You got a minute?"

"For you, I have lots of minutes."

She poured him a glass of sweet tea from the pitcher she kept in the fridge and perched on a seat across from him at the dinette.

"So, if it's not family, it must be business. Everything ok?"

"It's not that either." He ran a thumb down the condensation gathering on the side of his glass. "Candi let it slip to your mom that you're dating the Ewart boy."

She bit back a sigh. Her sister-in-law was the sweetest woman on the face of God's green Earth, but she had loose lips, something Sera should've remembered before spilling the beans. "He's not a boy, Dad."

"Says my little girl." His smile was gentle, teasing. "What are you now, fifteen? Sixteen?"

"A lot older than that," she retorted. "Levi's a good man. We haven't known each other long, but I've known him long enough to be sure of that."

"I know he is. Known his parents for years, remember? Coming from his family, he couldn't be anything but." His smile slid away, replaced by furrowed eyebrows and pinched lips. "It's his family that might be the problem. He tell you anything about his heritage?"

She sat back in her chair. "He said they were culturally distinct and gave me the abridged version of one of their legends. Seven sisters who were cursed to immortality. Why?"

"The folks in Tellowee are...different." He sipped his tea, set his glass down. Picked it back up and took a much longer swallow. "Not all of their legends are mythical, if that makes sense."

She nodded, then shook her head. "Not a bit."

"I was sworn to silence a long time ago. The only reason I been able to work in and around Tellowee is, I keep my mouth shut. I can't break that vow, not even for my baby girl, but there are things there among the People that might make you reconsider getting involved with young Ewart."

Her fingers tightened into a tangled knot on her lap. "What kind of things?"

"Nothing bad, not the way you're thinking. The People are mostly good. Got their share of rotten eggs to be sure, but they're a good-hearted bunch, tough when they need to be. Ewart'll protect you with his dying breath, if he's anything like his nana."

"Hawthorne?"

His gaze sharpened. "You met her?"

"Not yet. Levi said his mother and grandmother would come a-calling, but he seemed really reluctant to tell his nana."

"She's got a sword and ain't afraid to use it." Wendell's mouth twisted into a wry smile. "Hawthorne's not a woman you wanna cross."

"I gathered."

"He mention anything about..." His lips pinched together again. "Bad stuff?"

"He said his life was dangerous sometimes and if he sent a friend to get me and Petey, I should listen."

Wendell sighed and sat back in his chair, his hands splayed flat on the tabletop. "That's good then. You start locking your doors, you hear? And try not to go out much at night alone."

"For goodness' sake, Dad. This is Persimmon we're talking about, not Atlanta."

He speared her with the stare of a father who meant business. "It's either that or you and Petey have to move back in with me and your mom."

"Now you sound like him, laying down an ultimatum as if I were a child." She pinned him with her own *mother knows best* stare. "Which I'm not."

"That's my final say on it. A woman living alone ain't safe, especially one dating a Son. And I want you to keep your gun here now instead of in my gun safe."

"Petey's not old enough yet for a gun to be around the house."

"Sure as hell, he's old enough to know when to leave 'em alone." He stabbed a finger at her. "You think about that boy now, you hear? I ain't leaving the two of you alone here without something to back you up. Sass alone won't stop the kind of bad that haunts the People."

"Fine. I'll get the damn gun from you tomorrow." She gripped her thighs, biting back the urge to scream at him. She'd been an adult for over a decade, and still he treated her like a child, him and Levi both, and it was getting really old. "Anything else?"

"As a matter of fact, Barbara said to bring him to dinner."

Sera's eyes widened and she gaped at him. "Mom's cooking? Really, Dad, are you *trying* to run him off?"

His laugh rolled out of him, hearty and strong, and he slapped his hand against his thigh. "Lordy, no. Wouldn't do that to you. Candi'll cook, or me and Jack'll throw something on the grill."

Sera tutted and shook her head. "Had me going for a minute there."

"Us old folks gotta take our humor where we can find it."

"Yeah, right. You old folk, you."

She saw him out a while later after a good long chat over goings on. The whole conversation bothered her, start to finish, though she couldn't quite pinpoint her unease. Her dad had never been one to warn her away from men, though he should've at least once. The warning now, in spite of his belief that Levi came from a good family, made her rethink her stance on what she'd previously considered Levi's overreaction. Next e-mail, she'd ask him about it, that and the secrets her father had alluded to.

Someday, maybe Levi would trust her enough to not hold anything back, though she didn't hold it against him too much, not right then. Their relationship was still in its first teetering stages, fresh and new and bright, and trust was built on more than a budding friendship and outstanding sex.

She called Candi, had her send Petey over. Ten minutes later, he slammed through the house, calling for her the same way his grandfather had. She took one look at him and sighed. "Did you wallow in every mud puddle from here to Aunt Candi's house and back?"

He glanced down at his muddy feet, then at the floor behind him. "Oops."

"Oops, indeed, little man. You're not the one who just mopped that floor."

"We was playing with the water hose."

And he'd walked along the dirt trail between the two houses with wet feet, no doubt. "Go wash your feet off and clean up. I've got something to show you."

He went, grumbling good-naturedly, and she swept and mopped the mess away, leaving the floor as shining clean as the faded linoleum could get. Levi's mother hadn't made an appearance yet, but it was coming. A good Southern woman never let expected company into a less than spotless house. Family, sure. Company, never.

A few minutes later they were off, winding along the road toward the People's holy place. Petey was strapped into the backseat in the dreaded booster seat, staring out the window, his hair slicked back and a streak of dirt on his chin. Close enough to clean, she figured, especially since he'd taken the time to brush his teeth and put on a clean t-shirt.

A mom had to take her victories where she could.

She turned the radio off as they neared the parking area. A handful of cars were lined up in a neat row at the far end. As soon as she parked the Volvo, Petey scrambled out of his booster seat and stuck his head between the two front seats. "I don't like hiking."

"I know that, sweetheart, but this is something you'll like." She hoped.

His eyes met hers in the rearview mirror. He scratched the tip of his nose, wiggled it, and scratched again. "Don't like the woods neither."

"Open your mind a little, squirt. There's something special waiting for us at the top."

He paled under his tan. "The top as in *up high*?"

She stifled a sigh. Some things, even a mother couldn't cure. "Our feet will never leave Planet Earth, I promise. Come on."

They walked hand in hand up the trail, their steps slow and nearly silent along the spongy trail bed. Petey balked at the footbridge. She carried him over it, enjoying his weight cuddled against her. All too soon, he'd outgrow this, outgrow her. He balked again at the outcropping of rocks, brushed past them with his eyes wide and his fingers biting into hers.

At the top, Sera sighed out her relief and led him to the rock she'd stood on during the Sunday past, holding her son around his waist, away from the few people scattered around the clearing speaking in hushed tones. She pointed toward the ridge where the sun had risen each day for thousands of years, and would for thousands more. "In the morning when the sun comes up, it tops the hills and shines out across the valley below."

"I don't think I wanna see that, Mama, 'specially not the valley part."

His voice was thin and tired, and he leaned against her, his head close to hers.

"You don't have to, sweetie. I'm just setting the story."

"Like in your books?"

"Exactly. So, the sun rises over there, and when it does, there are people who come here to this very spot and pray. I came here this past Sunday with someone I met while you were in Orlando."

"A friend?"

"I hope he is. His name's Levi and he's very special to me."

His hand plucked at the back of hers. "Like me?"

"Not quite. You're the most special." She smiled and kissed his temple. "But he's special, too. We're dating and..."

He popped away from her, his silver eyes wide. "You went out on a date?"

"We went out on several."

"With a guy."

She firmed her lips against a smile. "Yes, with a guy. He works in Atlanta and he's very nice. I think you'll like him."

"Does he make pancakes and have a truck?"

"Um." Sera huffed out a bemused laugh. "I don't know."

He slumped against her again, his face as droopy as his shoulders. "Oh."

"I can find out. It's probably a safe bet that he owns at least one truck. He's kind of into cars."

"Yeah?"

"Oh, yeah. He likes Star Wars, too, and he's a much better cook than me."

He scuffed the toe of his tennis shoe along the rock. "I guess he might be ok, then."

They left not long after. Sera ignored the stares directed their way by the women in the clearing, coming and going as she and Petey wound their way back to the car. He barely gave the outcropping of rocks a second glance, and at the footbridge, he walked across without any help. Once in the car, he buckled himself into his booster seat, uttering not a single complaint about having to use it, and fell asleep with his head against the glass.

Hunh. Maybe he'd been too tired to protest the hazards of the trail or maybe the second time through them had been easier. He'd handled hearing about Levi ok, much better than she'd expected. Of course, reality would be a different story. Once another person snagged part of her time and attention, her son might not be so willing to share.

He woke as she maneuvered around a white van pulling out of their driveway. "Who was that?"

"No idea."

They walked to the steps leading from the garage into the kitchen and stopped. An artful arrangement of sunflowers sat on the top step, their round faces cheerful in the shade of the garage. Sera carefully tugged a small envelope out of the pick holding it in place and pulled the card out. *Ever yours.* She bounced on the balls of her feet and held the card to her chest, warming from head to toe.

"Who're they from, Mama?"

She whirled and lifted Petey up, cradling him in her arms. "Levi."

He wrapped his legs around her waist and glanced between the flowers and her. "Really?"

"Absolutely. He's just nice like that."

She set him back on the ground, snagged the vase of flowers, and centered them on the kitchen table where they'd greet her and Petey each morning. He shuffled past her, smothering a yawn with a haphazardly placed fist. She followed behind and tucked him into his bed under the Star Wars sheets he'd picked out for his last birthday.

His eyes closed as soon as his head hit the pillow, though a small smile lingered. "He gave you flowers."

"Yes, he did."

She kissed his forehead and went into her office, puzzling over the baffling conversations she'd had with two of the men in her life that day. Sometimes, it seemed like she was the only person in the world who didn't know what was going on around her.

EARLY ONE Saturday morning, Petey woke up sniffling. He squinched his eyes closed and nuzzled his face into his pillow, then sneezed. Snot ran out his nose and he sighed. If he didn't get up and blow it, he'd be in a *world* of trouble.

That's what Mama said when he didn't mind her, as if he had enough trouble in him to fill up a whole planet. He snickered at the idea, and the snot rolled down his upper lip. He grimaced and slid out of bed, shuffling toward the bathroom. Allergies sure were the pits. Everybody knew kids were supposed to sleep in on Saturdays. It was, like, a rule or something, but if he didn't blow his nose, Mama would be mad.

She *always* knew when he hadn't done something he was supposed to. *How* was a complete mystery, kinda like what kept the sun in the sky. *Nobody knew*, and he'd asked everybody. PawPaw and Uncle Jack had shrugged and said, "It's the sun," like it was supposed to just hang up there and make light and stuff and there was no questioning it. MawMaw and Aunt Candi had blinked and sorta stared at him, and Mama had said, "Go look it up, Petey."

He blew his nose, threw the tissue away. Washed his hands with soap and hot water, in case Mama asked later. He blinked sleepily at himself in the mirror, made faces, and held one showing the holes where his front teeth were supposed to be. He poked his tongue through and felt around for new ones.

Nope, not yet.

He left the bathroom and peeked into Mama's room. She was still asleep, lying on her stomach with one hand stretched across the other side of the bed. Her clock said 7:03. If he was really, really quiet, she'd sleep until at least eight and he could watch cartoons.

He tiptoed into the living room and froze, his heart pounding in his chest. A man was lying on the sofa sound asleep, dressed only in running shorts, the silky baggy kind Dale and Matty liked to wear. The guy was big, nearly bigger than the sofa, and his legs were really hairy. He had hair on his chest and belly, too, though not as much, and he even had some under his arms. All of it was a funny reddish color.

Petey pulled out the neckline of his pajamas and peered through it at his own thin chest, lifted an arm and checked his armpit.

Nope, no hair there.

He stared at the man. Should he go wake Mama up? He glanced at the TV, then at the man. If he woke Mama up, he wouldn't get to watch cartoons, and it's not like the man was doing anything, right? He was just lying there like a lump, breathing quietly, with one hand behind his head and the other on his belly.

On the other hand, he was one big dude and had lots of muscles and a tattoo on his arm, a string thingy with little dots floating above it. Petey bounced from foot to foot, torn between waking Mama up and watching cartoons. Dale said guys with tattoos were really bad, but this guy didn't look bad at all. He just looked *big*.

And the tattoo was pretty cool.

Petey edged closer and squinted at it, stepped another inch forward. What was it, anyway? It looked kinda like... He screwed up his face, trying to remember where he'd seen the dot thingies before, and grinned when it popped into his mind. Musical notes. He'd seen them in church, in the book that had all the church songs in it.

Did a tattoo feel different than plain skin?

What if he poked it and found out? Would the guy get mad and yell at him?

Maybe he should just get Mama and ask her. Then again, she hadn't known what kept the sun in the sky, so maybe she wouldn't know this either.

The guy shifted and opened his eyes. Petey yelped and scrambled away from him, tripped over his own feet, and landed hard on his butt on the other side of the coffee table.

"Hey, sorry." The guy swung his legs over the side of the sofa and sat up, yawning. "You ok?"

Petey blinked and ignored his throbbing bottom. "Mama's gonna be mad you broke into our house."

The guy grinned. "She showed me where the key was, squirt."

"Oh."

"I'm Levi." The guy rubbed his hand over his hair and rolled his shoulders. "A friend of your mum's?"

Petey squinted at him, angling his head different ways, trying to match the guy sitting on the couch with the pictures Mama had shown him of Levi. They looked sorta the same, far as he could tell. They both had red hair, anyhow, and lots of muscles. After she told him she was dating, Petey had waited and waited for Levi to visit, but he never had, and Petey had about given up on him ever coming over again. But this guy said he was Levi and he had red hair like Mama's Levi, so they must be the same, right?

After thinking it over long and hard, he said, "I'm Peter Zachariah Noland."

Levi held out his hand. "Pleased to meet you, Mr. Noland."

He scrambled up off the floor and shook Levi's hand and his eyes went round. Levi's hand just about swallowed his whole. Kewl. "You can call me Petey, sir. Everybody does."

"Petey it is, then."

Petey wrinkled his nose and swiped at it. Dang allergies. "You talk kinda funny."

"I was born in Scotland. Afraid it never leaves you."

"I wasn't making fun. It's just, you know, different." Kinda neat, really, once he thought about it. Uncle Jack and PawPaw had plain ol' accents, like him and Mama, nothing really special at all. Petey scrubbed a bare toe along the carpet. "Do you have a truck, Mr. Levi?"

"Just Levi, kid, and yeah, I do. It's in Atlanta, though. Brought my motorcycle up this trip."

Petey's breath left him in a rush and his eyes about popped out of his head. "You got a motorcycle?"

"Oh, yeah. A sweet cruiser, red as fire. Wanna see it?"

Boy, did he. Uncle Jack didn't have a motorcycle 'cause Aunt Candi said they were too dangerous. Wait 'til Dale and Matty found out that *his* mama's feller had one.

Except Mama would be mad if he went outside without telling her. Petey slumped and shook his head. "No, sir. I can't go outside 'til Mama's awake."

"Laid down the law, did she?" Levi grinned, showing crooked front teeth. "Tell you what. How about we compromise? You stand in the doorway and I'll explain what everything is. Since I'll be right there, I don't think she'll mind you opening the door. Sound fair?"

Petey rolled it around in his mind, looking for holes in Levi's plan. Mama was real particular about the rules. She always said that she didn't have many, but she expected him to mind them real good like. "I don't know. It *sounds* ok, but sometimes even when something sounds good, Mama gets mad."

Levi nodded. "That's 'cause she's a woman, and women work in mysterious ways."

"Uncle Jack says that, too, especially when Aunt Candi gets

mad at him."

Levi grinned and reached a long arm out, ruffling Petey's hair. His hand was warm and strong and big, and it felt kinda nice, and then he stood up, way, way up, and Petey dropped his head back and goggled at him. "You're..." *Absolutely humongazoid gigantic.* "Really big."

Levi laughed. "You're Serafina's kid, all right. Give me a minute and we'll look my baby over from top to bottom."

Levi went into the bathroom and came out a few minutes later, then they walked side by side through the living room into the kitchen. Levi's hand brushed Petey's arm every once in a while, and then they were at the door. Levi unlocked it, opened it wide, and pointed to the weather stripping. "Not a toe over that or your mum will have both our hides."

"Yes, sir." Petey peeked around Levi walking down the stairs into the garage and spotted the motorcycle. It was big and shiny and looked like it could go super fast. "Wow."

"That's what I said the first time I saw her." Levi opened a box on the back of the motorcycle, pulled out a small bag, and set it on the kitchen floor next to Petey. "Forgot to bring that in last night when I got in. So, you ever been on a motorcycle before?"

"No, sir. Uncle Jack can't have one and PawPaw says he's too old."

"Ah, well, you're never really too old for a motorcycle, though I suppose your gran wouldn't agree. Do you know the parts?"

Petey screwed up his face. "Tires and handlebars and a seat. What's the shiny silver thing?"

"The muffler. It can get hot, so never touch it unless I tell you to, ok? Now this is the rear fender and this is the engine. With me so far?"

"Yes, sir."

Levi pointed out the different parts of his motorcycle, explaining what each one did, then he went over them again and had Petey name them until he got all of them right. He never raised his voice when Petey made a mistake, never got mad if he got stuff wrong, and as Levi explained how the engine worked, a warm feeling gathered in Petey's chest. He bounced between his feet, trying to memorize everything Levi said. Who knew motorcycles could be so cool? And that his mama would date somebody who knew so much about them?

A noise in the kitchen startled Petey and he whirled around. Mama stood next to the stove with her fists on her hips, her eyes spitting fire. "Peter Zachariah Noland, what are you doing?"

Petey hunched his shoulders and glanced at Levi. "Uh-oh."

"I got this, kid." Levi jogged toward him and took the steps two at a time into the kitchen, then rested his hand on Petey's shoulder. "Hey, Sera. Don't yell at him."

"Levi." Her hands fell to her sides and her eyes went wide. "What are you doing here?"

"I had a couple of days free, so I thought I'd surprise you. Me and Petey here were inspecting my motorcycle while we waited for you to wake up."

"Your motorcycle." She laughed real quiet like and rubbed her hands over her face. "Should've known."

"You're not mad, are you?" Petey wound a finger into Levi's shorts and tried to look like he was sorry. "I mean, I didn't go outside and Levi was right there the whole time, looking out for me."

"I'm not mad, sweetie. You just startled me, that's all. It's not like you to break the rules." She opened her arms and drew him in for a big hug. "In fact, let's revise those rules right now. Any time Levi's here, you can go outside with him as long as y'all leave me a note on the fridge board. And, if he's here and awake, you can go outside on your own or over to Uncle Jack's or your grandparents' house, if you promise to tell either him or me first. Did you get all that?"

"Yes'm."

"Good then." She patted his bottom and scooted him toward his room. "Motorcycle lessons can resume later. Get dressed and I'll make us some breakfast."

"No, Mama, please." Petey glanced at Levi and whispered, "You'll burn the bacon again."

Levi snickered. Mama gave him her mean look, and Levi covered his mouth with his fist and coughed into it. "Me and Petey'll make breakfast. Cooking's man's work anyway."

Petey blinked at him, pretty sure Levi was pulling his leg. "It is?"

"When the man's the one that knows how to cook, yeah, it is. Go on, now, so your mum can greet me proper like."

Petey raced across the room. On an impulse, he paused in the doorway between the living room and kitchen and looked back. Mama stepped real close to Levi and wrapped her arms around his waist and laid her head on his chest.

"I didn't think I'd get to see you again for weeks," she said softly.

Levi hugged her close and kissed the top of her head. "Couldn't go that long without you."

"I'm so glad you're here."

"Me, too."

Levi glanced up and winked at Petey, and Petey grinned. This dating thing was turning out to be pretty cool.

Seventeen

A S SOON AS PETEY left the room, Levi swung Sera up, cradling her in his arms. "Mmm. That's better."

She laughed and rubbed her fingertips along his nape. "Put me down, you."

"Nope. I've got you where I want you and now I'm gonna get you."

He hefted her higher and strode through the house, ignoring her laughing protests. She seemed light in his arms, or maybe that was his heart, lifting them both up with the pleasure of seeing her. He paused at the threshold to Petey's room and poked his head inside. "Hey, Petey, you have something to do for a few minutes? Your mum and I need to have a little chat."

Petey pulled his shirt over his head and nodded, his silver eyes round in his tanned face.

"We'll be in her room. Make sure you knock before you come in, ok?"

"Yes, sir."

"I can't believe you just told him that," Sera hissed as they entered her bedroom.

He kicked her door closed, dropped her on the bed, and followed her down, bracing himself above her. "It's been three weeks, Sera. Have mercy on me."

She sighed against his chest and ran a foot down the back of his leg. "I'm not having sex with you while my son is awake in the next room."

"Key word being awake, I hope." Sweet Goddess, she felt so right under him, soft and giving and warm. He buried his face in her throat and breathed her in. "Wasn't planning on having sex with you now. Later, though, that's another story."

"Later, definitely. I can't believe you're here."

"I can't believe you haven't kissed me yet."

She turned her head, evading his mouth. "Haven't brushed my teeth."

He sighed and contented himself with her throat. "Soon, then. Very, very soon."

Petey knocked and said through the door, "Mama? Can I come in?"

Levi smacked a final kiss to her throat and rolled off of her. "I've got this. You go brush those teeth."

"Levi, wait." She grabbed his arm, her eyes serious. "I'm on the pill, have been since about a week after you left. If you want to, you know, without a condom..."

Heat shot through him, settling low in his belly. He hissed in a breath as his dick went from mildly interested to ready, willing, and able. Being inside Sera with nothing between them? Holy Mother, did he want to. "We'll talk about this later when I can prod all the details out of you, like what possessed you to tell me that right before I have to go cook breakfast with your incredibly observant seven-year-old kid while my body is clearly not behaving."

Her smile was entirely too knowing. "It seemed like as good a time as any."

"We need to work on your timing, love." He slid off the bed and opened the door. Petey was standing right outside, his face screwed up into a frown. "Good thing you knocked when you did, kid. I was about to have to spank your mum."

"Levi!" Sera hissed.

Petey's eyes went round as saucers. "You were?"

"Yeah. She broke the cardinal rule." Levi cupped his hands around Petey's ribs and hefted him onto one hip. "Keep her boys happy."

"Oh. You're kidding." Petey's arms tightened their stranglehold on Levi's neck. "You really gonna spank her?"

"Only if she wants me to."

Behind Sera whispered a hoarse, "Oh, my God."

Levi wrapped his arms around the thin little boy clinging to him and wandered into the kitchen, smiling. He swung Petey down, planting him on the floor.

As soon as he was free, Petey dragged a chair from the dinette to the counter separating the breakfast nook from the kitchen proper and scampered onto it. He knelt on the chair's seat and leaned his elbows on the counter, his gaze following every move Levi made. "Mama's face went all red when you said you were gonna spank her."

"That's why I said it, kid." Levi opened the fridge and scrounged for breakfast fixings. Bacon, eggs, an onion, a green pepper that had seen better days. It was still usable, so he grabbed it with the other items and nudged the fridge door shut "I thought your grandparents had a garden."

"They do. Mama hardly ever gets anything out of it, though. MawMaw says it's because she's too stubborn for her own good."

That was true enough. Levi dumped his finds on the counter and rummaged for a skillet for the bacon. "You might not want to carry too many tales, especially about your mum."

"Oh. Um." Petey's nose wrinkled above a frown. "What does that mean, Mr. Levi?"

Levi grinned. Yup, Petey was Sera's, all right. "Carrying tales is the same thing as gossiping."

"But if I don't tell Mama what MawMaw said, how's she supposed to know she's too stubborn?"

"You got a point there." Levi laid strips of bacon in the pan to cook and washed his hands, found the cutting board and set it on the counter Petey was leaning on. "I hear my mum came to visit."

"Yeah. She's, like, really tall. Not as tall as you, though. I mean, you're really big and you got lots of muscles." Petey flexed his arm, testing the muscle, then sagged against the counter. "I'll never get muscles like that."

"Sure you will. Just wait 'til you're a little older."

Petey stared at Levi's hands as he peeled and seeded and chopped. "Is it carrying tales if I tell you what your mama said when she was here?"

"I've already had it from her and your mum, and from my gran, so in this case, no, tell away."

"Well, first she was all like this." Petey tilted his head and looked down his nose, his face set in stone. "And she said, 'I've come to see your mother, child.'"

Levi stared at Petey, startled. "That's her all right."

"She was kinda scary, and then your gran came inside, and..." Petey picked at a chunk of diced green pepper. "Mama got this funny look on her face. I mean, she went all white and she stared at your gran and said, 'How old are you?' And then your gran said, 'Older than you would ever believe, little one.' And then Mama got kinda quiet and asked 'em to sit down."

Levi checked the bacon, flipped it over. Sera hadn't told him how she'd reacted to meeting his grandmother. Iniira Battlesong appeared to be his age, though she was centuries older. And it wasn't fair for him to pry that bit out of Petey instead. On the other hand, if the lad talked about it freely, it wasn't cheating to listen, was it? "Go on, then."

"Well, your mama was kinda mean to my mama. She said a mundane mortal wasn't good enough for her son. What's a mundane mortal?"

"Somebody born outside the People."

"Oh. I don't know what that means, either."

Levi ruffled Petey's hair. "You'll learn along and along."

Petey frowned, then shrugged. "Well, then *your* mama said it was too late anyhow 'cause you gave Mama your heart and she better treat it good or *your* mama would make sure *my* mama suffered, and then..."

Levi paused in the middle of gathering the chopped vegetables together. "Suffered or suffered the consequences?"

"The second, only I can't say it, but that's what your mama said."

"Big difference, kid."

Petey shrugged again. "Then your gran said, 'Leave her be, Noreen. Even a blind woman can see where her heart lies.'"

Sera hadn't told him that, either. In fact, it sounded like all three women had left significant chunks of the conversation out. Thank the Lady Ki Petey had a great memory and a knack for mimicry.

"Your gran made me come over so she could inspect me. That's what she said, *inspect.* She made me answer a bunch of questions, too, like did I know how to ride a horse and was Mama teaching me how to defend myself, and Mama got all quiet again, like she was sad or something." Petey wrinkled his nose. "And then your gran said I was supposed to call her Gran, and your mama said, 'No, he'll call *me* Gran.' And I said, why couldn't I call them Gran One and Gran Two, like Thing One and Thing Two in *The Cat in the Hat,* and then your mama got this really funny look on her face and said, 'Are you certain you're not Levi's son?'"

Levi snickered, turning it into a cough when Petey turned solemn eyes on him. "Sorry, kid. You were saying?"

"Well, Mama's face went red as the motorcycle and she said, 'He most certainly is *not* Levi's child.' And then she sent me over to Aunt Candi's so I wouldn't hear them argue, but I listened for a minute anyhow and, boy, was Mama mad. She used a dirty word and everything, and then she said she didn't appreciate your mama coming into *her house* and treating her like dirt, and if they didn't like her dating you, then *tough tooties.* I left after that, 'cause when Mama says tough tooties, it ain't good."

"I'll keep that in mind," Levi said, and cursed under his breath. Damn his mum and Gran both. He'd expected them to be a little hard on Sera. Nothing like what had happened, though. All three of them had glossed over that argument as if it were nothing, and there was no telling what else had been left out.

And he'd been wrong to let Petey ramble on about it, though Sera's son had the right of it. If somebody hadn't told Levi what had gone on in a conversation involving him, he never would've known and could never do anything about it.

When the bacon was finished and all danger of popping grease was gone, Levi helped Petey pull his chair over to the stove, wrapped him in an apron, and handed over a wooden spoon.

Petey stared at the onions and peppers sizzling in the skillet like they might bite him. "But I've never cooked before, Mr. Levi. What if I mess up?"

"You won't. Besides, I'll be right here helping you." Levi placed his hand over Petey's on the spoon and stirred the cooking vegetables, letting go when Petey got the hang of it. "I hear you'll start school Monday."

"Yes, sir. I'll be in second grade. I'm supposed to be in third except my birthday's late and Mama said she wanted to wait until my body was ready to sit still all day, only I didn't really understand 'cause it's not hard to sit still, but it sure is hard paying attention all day long."

"I feel your pain, kid."

"Yeah?" Petey stirred the vegetables in vigorous circles. "Did you have a hard time paying attention, too?"

"Sometimes, especially if the weather was nice. I'd rather be outside any day."

"Oh." Petey slumped and tapped the handle of the spoon against the rim of the pan. "I guess you like sports and stuff, too, huh."

"Sure. You?"

"Sometimes."

By the way he said it, Levi guessed what Petey meant was *not very much.* "It's ok to like some stuff better than others."

"Yeah?" Petey glanced at Levi out of the corner of his eye. "Mama said you like Star Wars?"

"Star Wars is awesome. Do you..."

Levi trailed off. Sera was standing in the doorway between the living room and kitchen, fully dressed and clean as a whistle, with her arms crossed over her stomach. She had a funny look on her face, as if she weren't sure what to make of the pair of them. Levi let his hand fall away from Petey's nape.

He hadn't even realized he'd been comforting her son.

"Sera. Hey. We were just talking." He stifled a wince and poured the eggs over the vegetables, began crumbling bacon into the whole while Petey stirred. "After breakfast, me and Petey can take care of the yard, unless you've got other plans."

Petey swung around and stared at Levi, his eyes wide, his mouth gaping.

"Just the usual," Sera said. "Straightening the house, grocery shopping. I thought we could rent a movie."

Levi nudged Petey back to his duties with a well-placed elbow to the lad's shoulder. "Mum'll want us over for dinner."

Sera nodded. "If you don't mind, I'll let Mom and Dad know you're here. They'll want us to come over tomorrow night, if you can stay that long."

"That'll be fine." He finished the bacon, eyed the eggs. Stuck his hands under hot water and scrubbed them good, waiting for Sera to say something, anything. When he finished cleaning up, she was still in the doorway, looking for all the world like she was lost in the middle of the woods without a way to get back home. "You're too quiet, love. What's wrong?"

"Nothing, it's..." Her gaze bounced between him and Petey, and her brow furrowed. "Harder than I thought it would be."

His heart twisted hard, taking his breath with it. Had he overstepped with Petey, done something he shouldn't have? He thought back and, except for coaxing the lad into detailing the whole conversation between their mothers, he'd been careful to treat Petey as Levi's da treated him. Kind, patient, firm, and always, always with love. "Do you want me to back off?"

"You would, wouldn't you." She paled and her head bowed. "You'd leave if I asked you to."

Petey jerked around, taking a spoonful of eggs with him. "You're gonna make Mr. Levi leave?"

"No, lad, she won't. She was only asking, though she already knows I'll always do what's best, for the both of you." He patted Petey's bottom, pointing him back to the nearly-done scramble, and snagged the paper towels. "I'll be careful, love. Does that satisfy your mother's heart?"

Her smile was small, but it was there. "Why do I get the feeling you just negotiated me into agreeing with you without your giving up a thing?"

"That's purely your imagination."

If he'd really negotiated that well, she'd never have brought it up in the first place, never felt the need to be protective of her son. Never hesitated to share him with Levi.

He cleaned up the eggs Petey had scattered, mindful of the quiet conversation between mother and son taking place around him. He'd never dated a woman with a child before, hadn't considered doing so would ever be a problem. Even if he'd married a Daughter with children, the chances of those children being older than him were staggering, so Sera's reaction wasn't something he'd anticipated. How did a man handle a mother wanting space between her child and her lover, especially considering where he and Sera were headed?

He had no clue, though he knew somebody who would, a man that had married a Daughter and successfully woven his life into the lives of his new step-daughters.

Sera set the table while he and Petey finished cooking. They sat together in the kitchen and made plans for the weekend and for the start of school the next week. Every once in a while, she settled a worried frown on Levi and Petey. By the end of the meal, Levi had made up his mind. He'd talk to his da as soon as he could. Between the two of them, surely they could figure out a way to handle Sera's reluctance to allow Levi into her son's life.

LEVI STEPPED into the shower in Sera's bathroom, bone tired and filthy. After breakfast, he and Petey had mowed the yard using her ancient riding lawn mower. Petey had sat on Levi's lap, steering while Levi kept one arm around the little boy and a hand at the ready under the steering wheel. The yard was huge and oddly shaped. It had taken the two of them the better part of the morning to care for it. They'd eaten sandwiches Sera had fixed for them, outside since they were both covered with grass, and then they'd tackled odd jobs she'd pointed them to when she returned from running errands. A screen door that didn't sit right in the frame, a stuck window, the leaning mailbox.

And, of course, he and Petey had had another go at the motorcycle. Soon as he could, Levi would take the lad to Iain's shop and show him around. No sense wasting a curious mind.

He adjusted the spray and turned his back to it, braced his hands on the far wall. The water was hot as it slid over him, loosening sore muscles, taking some of the past few weeks' stress with it. He'd worked his arse off to make time for this weekend, cheating himself of sleep and exercise and sometimes decent food, and now he was paying for it. A Son his age shouldn't feel the effects of a morning of barely rigorous yard work, four hours of sleep or not.

Just a few more weeks, that's all he needed.

The bathroom door opened and closed. "Is there room in there for me?"

He glanced around. Sera was tugging off clothes, stripping herself bare. Desire stirred and he nudged the shower curtain back. "Where's Petey?"

"I sent him to Candi's for a while so we could talk."

He smirked and helped her over the side of the tub, then pulled her close. "Is that what they call it now?"

"They call it lots of things I'm too old to keep up with." She leaned her head back and met his gaze evenly. "Petey's already half in love with you, you know."

Fatigue eroded his patience. He inhaled through his nose and reached deeper into his reserves. "I promised I'd be careful with him, Sera. What more do you want from me?"

"I don't know." Her smile was gentle and a shade rueful. "I didn't know this would be an issue. You're such a good man, so kind at heart when you're not being bull-headed, and I thought, he'll be perfect with Petey, and then you were and I..." She shook her head. "It's hard to think someone else might take my place in his heart."

"You're his mum. Nobody will ever capture that part of him." He ran a finger down her cheek, surprised as he always was at how soft her skin was, how beautiful she was. "If I'm gonna be a part of your life, a good, long part of it, then he and I are gonna have a relationship apart from you."

"I know. I want that, really." She circled a finger along his chest, scratched her fingertips over his skin, her gaze focused tightly on the movements. "At the same time, it hurts just a little, seeing the way he looks at you. I think, he just met Levi and already he's following after him like a puppy."

Levi huffed out a laugh. "That's what Jordan said about me."

"Did he really? Hmm." Her fingers shifted to his arm, tracing the lines of his bicep. "Do you really think we'll be together that long?"

Forever, his heart whispered, and he cut it off. It was too soon to think about forever, but it wasn't too soon to reassure her. He slipped a finger under her chin and tilted her face up. "You know how I feel about that. What did I say to you?"

"That you'd never run out on me."

"Do you believe it?"

Her eyelashes fluttered, and then her gaze held steady. "I do."

"Then why do you keep questioning it?"

"I'm not questioning. I'm testing the boundaries."

He grinned, and she laughed.

"Forget it, Levi. We don't have that much time."

"A man can hope."

He tested a few boundaries anyway, touching her, reacquainting himself with every inch of her skin as she scrubbed him clean with hands full of suds. They made it out of the shower in time to be mostly dressed when Petey slammed into the house. Sera scooted her son into a bath while Levi checked his e-mail. Halfway through, he gave up. The words blurred together and he couldn't concentrate on their meaning. He put his laptop away and stretched out on the couch, closed his eyes. Just for a minute...

The sofa shifted, waking him. Sera sat next to him, her expression soft and womanly. She brushed a hand along his forehead. "How much sleep have you been getting?"

"Almost enough."

Her lips thinned. "That's the first time you've ever lied to me, Levi, and it better be the last."

"Yes'm."

"Smarty pants." Her hand slid down and cupped his face, and her thumb stroked over his cheek. "Those dark shadows under your eyes shouldn't be there. Tonight, you're going to bed early."

He bit back exasperation. "You're not my mum, Sera."

"I'm your lover and I want you healthy and whole." She leaned down, close enough for their breaths to mingle. "You can have my bed."

"I'm not pushing you out of your own bed."

"My house, my rules. I'll sleep with Petey. We'll try not to wake you too early." Her lips touched his, comforting and sweet, and her hand tightened along his skin. "This is the part where you nod and say yes and help me find the perfect stretch of the road."

"I thought we already had." His hand skimmed along the long line of her back under her shirt, and he drew her strength and warmth in, winding it around the tender feelings he held for her deep in his heart. "I think a kiss might seal the deal, though."

"Would it," she murmured, and captured his mouth with hers,

tasting him with gentle flicks of her tongue, driving him slowly to the edge of need. Rapid footsteps sounded in the hallway and she drew back a moment before Petey burst into the room. "Later," she whispered.

LATER, THOUGH, they went to his parents'. His mum cornered Sera in the kitchen, peppering her with questions about Petey's school. Levi found his da by the grill and, in a hushed voice, relayed his concerns that Sera might not be willing to accept him having a role in Petey's life. "What can I do, Da?"

"What you've been doing. Love them, care for them. Show them the kind of man you are."

Levi glanced away. "I never said I loved her."

"If you didn't, you wouldn't care whether you had a place in the lad's life or not."

"Maybe I want him for himself."

"Aye, that's a part of it, but not the whole." Iain slapped Levi on the arm. "You've never been one to lie, not even to yourself. Don't hide from your heart now, lad. That way'll bring trouble."

They ate together as a family, gathered around his mother's kitchen table. Levi ignored the appraising glances his mother cast over him and Sera and Petey, and did as his father suggested. He cared for them, filling plates and wiping up the drink Petey spilled, pulling Sera onto his lap for a kiss when nobody was watching. And he acknowledged that maybe his da might've been right. Maybe love had crept in over the yearning and the desire and the friendship he and Sera were building. Maybe love had been the reason he'd known, after less than a week, that he'd never be able to walk away from her.

They returned to Sera's home after an evening that, though not quite easy, had been pleasant enough. Petey changed into his pajamas while Sera set the movie up.

Levi slouched into the sofa and draped an arm across her shoulders when she sat down beside him. "Thanks for making room for my parents."

"You'll be doing the same for mine tomorrow." She curled her legs over his and rested her head on his chest. "I'm so thankful you could make it."

"Me, too." He brushed a kiss over her hair. Why did it always feel so right to have her close, and so wrong to be away from her? "Y'all will come down in three weeks for the con. I won't have as much time, but we can at least see each other."

"I thought you'd forgotten about that."

"Hardly."

Petey bounded in and wedged himself between them. "What are we watching?"

Sera shot an amused glance at Levi over her son's head. "The new Star Trek movie."

"Awesome," Petey said, and then his shoulders slumped. "Only, you said I was too young for that."

"I decided to make an exception just this once, since we have company. But, if anything bothers you, you have to tell me right away, ok?"

"Yes'm."

Sera started the movie and turned off all of the lamps, leaving the hallway light on and saving the living room from complete darkness. Levi stretched a hand along the back of the sofa and toyed with a loose strand of her hair, relaxing as the movie played out across the screen. Beside him, Petey's eyes were wide, fixed on the TV as if he were afraid of missing a single second of the action.

Halfway through the movie, Petey's determination wound down. He yawned and slumped, and finally crawled into Sera's lap. Levi scooted over and pulled them both close, and his own determination to stay awake slipped a notch. It was nice being with the two of them, holding Sera while she cared for her son. Levi yawned and stretched his legs out in front of him. She was a good mum, as he'd suspected from the start, and Petey was a good son.

By the end of the movie, Levi was so relaxed, he wasn't absolutely sure he could muster the energy to move, or that he wanted to. Sera shifted next to him and that's all it took for him to remember why he'd be leaving the living room very soon and taking her to bed.

She smoothed Petey's hair back and kissed his forehead. "Time for bed, sweetie."

"Aw, Mama. Do I have to?"

"Afraid so. It's past your bedtime."

Petey rubbed his eyes, his expression as sleepy as it was grumpy. "Can't I stay up a little longer?"

Levi pressed his lips together. If Sera was upset about him hanging out with Petey, she'd flip a lid over him interfering. And damn it, he wanted that perfect stretch of the road, too.

"Not tonight, Petey. You know the rules."

Petey slid off her lap and stood facing her, his eyes mutinous beneath lowered eyebrows. "Dale and Matty get to stay up late on Saturdays."

"Dale and Matty aren't my children."

"That's what you always say." Petey's hands balled into fists at his side. "You never let me do anything, never. I never get to stay up and I never get to have any fun."

Levi sat forward, the end of his patience reached. "There now, lad. Don't sass your mum."

Sera inhaled sharply as Petey swung around, his eyes huge, his lower lip trembling.

"Your mum let you stay up to watch a movie she wouldn't normally have. Seems you might want to remember that before you say something you'll regret."

The way they looked at him cut right through his heart, Petey with a tear streaking down his cheek, Sera as if she'd never seen him before. He breathed past the hurt and stood. There were a lot of things a man could tolerate for a woman. Allowing somebody to be disrespectful of her wasn't one of them.

Even if the person being disrespectful was her beloved son.

"I've got my own orders from your mum to get to bed. Good night, love." He dropped a kiss to the top of her head, then one to Petey's. "Good night, Petey. Bright and early, we'll take apart your bicycle, see if we can fix it."

He made it to Sera's bedroom without falling, though he was numb from head to toe. That look. Sweet Goddess, that look. He dropped down on the edge of her bed and buried his head in his hands. A minute later, Sera and Petey walked by the open doorway and disappeared into Petey's room, their quiet conversation drowned out by the buzz in his head.

Sera reappeared not long after, sat beside Levi, and ran a hand over his back. "It's hard being a parent, knowing when to correct and when to let them grow."

"I wasn't trying to take your place, Sera."

"I know." She sighed and rubbed her cheek over his arm. "I know that."

He straightened and slid an arm around her waist. "I thought you were gonna ream me a new one."

"It was my first reaction," she admitted. "And then I heard your dad in your voice and I realized you were doing what you always do, and that if you hadn't, it would've eaten at you. It hit me that if I really, truly want that perfect stretch of the road, I have to quit asking you to hold back. You've done that a lot for me. No, you have," she said when he shook his head, "I can feel it in you, the patience coiled in your heart and the doubts you have that I'll accept you as you are. Do you remember our first date when you held my hand and told me you'd been raised to be a responsible gentleman?"

"I do." And he always would.

"Later, after I called you grabby and immediately regretted it, by the way, I thought, Sera, you idiot. He's a gentleman through and through, if you'll just let him be. Young and sometimes pushy, but a gentleman. And a gentleman would never sit back and allow a wrong to occur if he could prevent it. That's who you are, Levi. It rankles a little for you to discipline my child. I can't always promise to take it well, but I'm also not going to keep you from doing it." She smiled and added, "As long as you're reasonable."

His laugh rushed out of him on a sigh, more air than humor. "Trust you to put conditions on it."

"It's who I am."

"I know," he said, and bit his tongue again, containing the love welling up through the relief.

"He wants to talk to you."

Levi glanced at the door. "You sure that's a good idea?"

"Positive. You two boys have a good chat, clear the air. And then *you* are going to bed, mister."

"Not without you."

"If that's the only way I'll get you in."

He kissed her cheek and hugged her, hard. "I'm holding you to that."

When Levi peeked in, Petey was staring up at the ceiling, the covers tucked securely under his arms, his hands folded on top of his chest. Levi sat on the side of the bed and knotted the Star Wars comforter under his fingers, holding in the need to comfort. "Your mum said you asked for me."

"Yes, sir." Petey sniffed and blinked, his eyes fixed on the stars glowing on the ceiling above them. "I wanted to 'pologize for being ugly."

"Seems to me you're apologizing to the wrong person."

"I done 'pologized to Mama. She kissed me and tucked me in and said what she always says."

"What's that?"

A small smile tugged at Petey's mouth. "'Nobody's perfect, Petey, but we should try anyway.'"

Levi laughed. "You've got her down pat."

Petey shrugged and the smile slipped away. "Are you mad at me?"

"No, Petey. Never." Levi relented and covered Petey's narrow hands with his own. "I didn't like the way you spoke to your mum, though."

"She didn't much like it neither, Mr. Levi."

Levi squeezed Petey's hand. "I thought we agreed you'd call me Levi without the mister."

"Mama says..."

"Whisht. This is between you and me, Petey."

Petey blinked furiously. "Your voice gets all funny sometimes."

"And you'd notice that, wouldn't you." Levi stood and stared down at the little boy, tucked so carefully into his bed. "Bedtime now. We've chores in the morning and your grandparents Noland to visit in the evening."

"Yes, sir." Petey shifted onto his side, facing the door, and yawned. "I'm glad you're dating Mama. I just wish you had a pancake pan."

"Some wishes are easier to fix than others, lad. Get some sleep now."

Levi pulled the covers up and pressed a kiss to Petey's temple, and pulled the door partway shut on his way out. He stripped his shirt off as he stepped into Sera's bedroom, closed the door firmly. She was already in bed, Kindle in hand.

He undressed down to the skin and slid into bed beside her, ran a finger along her bare shoulder. "I don't remember seeing that camisole before."

"I've been saving it for a special occasion." She set the Kindle aside and shut off the lamp, then curled herself into him. "I've been waiting for this moment all day. Can you put off sleep for another quarter hour?"

He rolled her onto her back and covered her, nuzzling her throat with his mouth. "Woman, if you think I'm letting you go after fifteen minutes, you're crazy."

She laughed and wrapped herself around him, and accepted his touch for a good long while after.

Eighteen

BRIGHT AND EARLY Sunday morning, a hand woke Sera as it slid under her camisole and rested on her stomach, fingers splayed, palm warm and heavy. *Levi*. She smiled and sighed, and enjoyed the solid strength of his embrace. Petey would be awake soon, but for these last few moments, Levi was all hers, every inch of him.

Sera's eyes popped open on a gasp. *Petey*. She was supposed to've slept with him. He'd be awake soon, wondering what she was doing sleeping with Levi, and *God*, how stupid could she be? Hadn't she promised herself that when Petey was around, she'd never have a man in her bed through the night? What a terrible example to set for him, and it the very first time Levi stayed over.

The hand on her stomach tightened, holding her firmly in place. "Not so fast, love. He'll not wake for a while yet."

"How did you know what I was thinking?"

"You went from relaxed to jumping out of the bed in three seconds flat." He rolled her onto her stomach and kissed his way down her nape. "Plus, you're still here with me and not in bed with him, and the sun's up."

She wiggled under him, stilled when his erection brushed across her bottom, no less arousing for the barrier of her underwear. "I don't think we have time for this."

"Says the woman who only gave me fifteen minutes last night to please her." He slipped a hand into her panties and tugged, working them down over her bottom. "We've plenty of time."

"Are you going to use a..." His fingers slid along her clitoris, rubbing gently. Heat shot through her and she lifted her hips for him. "Oh, God, Levi."

His fingers withdrew and his teeth nipped her earlobe. "Are you sure about this, love?"

But he was already nudging at her core, pressing into her, filling her slowly. He shuddered, lowered his mouth to her ear. "Sera, love. You feel so good, so good."

He loved her slowly, thoroughly, taking her from behind, bringing her to a peak that left her breathless and panting and empty of everything but him, the muted throb of his release, his body holding her to the bed, and his softly lilting words. He slipped away all too soon, padding into the bathroom a moment before Petey knocked on the door.

"Mama? It's morning."

Sera laughed into her pillow. Boy, did she know it was morning. What a way to celebrate the new day.

Levi poked his head out of the bathroom, his beautiful mouth curled into a smile. "Ask him to go look under the couch."

Sera relayed the message and waited for the inevitable response, one eyebrow arched.

"But it's dark under there."

"That's what flashlights are for, Petey," Levi said. "Be a good lad and find one. If you do, there's something in it for you."

After a long moment, footsteps pattered down the hallway. She had just enough time to retrieve her panties and slide them back on before Petey burst through the door bearing a flashlight, still on, and a large present, his eyes shining as bright as the sun.

"Look, Mama. Santa Clause left a present for me under the couch and it's not even Christmas yet."

Levi's snicker filtered in from the bathroom.

Sera took the present and flashlight from Petey, and flicked the flashlight off. "I think it's for your birthday, and I'm pretty sure Levi brought it, not Santa Clause."

"Oh." Petey slid a sly glance toward the bathroom door. "Mr. Levi brung me a present?"

"Looks like." She patted the mattress. "Up and at 'em, squirt. Let's see what's inside."

He scrambled onto the bed beside her and pulled the box into his lap. "Mr. Levi," he hollered. "We gotta open the present now."

Levi opened the bathroom door. "Nice set of lungs there, kid. I'm pretty sure they heard you all the way in Tellowee."

Petey grinned. "You're kidding."

"I am." Levi stretched out across the bottom of the bed, his head on one hand, and wrapped the other around Sera's feet through the covers. "Open away."

Petey did, ripping through the Star Wars themed wrapping paper in a flash, smiling the whole time. Sera slit the tape with her thumbnail, and he opened the box and gaped.

"Mr. Levi," Petey whispered. He pulled out a backpack with a montage of Han Solo, Princess Leia, and Luke Skywalker in the foreground, and Darth Vader behind them, and held it in his hands like it was the most precious thing he'd ever seen. "How did you know?"

Levi's hand squeezed Sera's feet. "A little birdy told me. Couldn't let you go to school with a regular backpack, could I?"

Petey shook his head, then nodded.

"What do you say, Petey?" Sera prodded.

He looked up, his silver eyes shining. "Thank you, Mr. Levi."

"Just Levi, kid, remember? Better check the pockets, too."

Petey pulled zipper tabs back and forth, checking the backpack's pockets, and finally found a card. He opened it and read it to himself, his lips moving, his eyebrows lowered. "What's D-d-dra-g-g..."

"DragonCon." Sera ran her finger under the word and pronounced it again. "It's a place where a lot of people get together and talk about science fiction and fantasy. There'll be actors and writers and..." She glance at Levi.

"People in costumes and demonstrations," he said. "I'll be doing a stick-fighting exhibition with Nana on opening night."

Petey's eyes went round as saucers. "Really? And me and Mama can come see it?"

"Absolutely. You even get to miss a whole day of school so we can go." Sera patted Petey's thigh and wiggled it. "And now, I think we need to have a serious discussion about breakfast."

The rest of the day passed quickly. They ate breakfast at the tiny dinette off the kitchen, went outside to inspect Petey's bike. Sera sat on the steps leading from the kitchen to the garage, coffee cup in hand, watching Petey and Levi make man noises over the bicycle's loose chain and sticky brakes.

After, they all spiffed up and Levi took them to the new Mexican restaurant in Clayton. They sat in a booth in the upper seating area, Petey bouncing between Sera on one side and Levi on the other.

During one lull, Sera leaned across the table. "He's not usually this hyper."

"He'll settle down, once he gets used to everything."

Levi's soft smile told her exactly what he meant, but since *she* wasn't used to Levi yet, how could she expect her son to be?

It still thrilled her every time he walked into the room. Her heart jumped when he smiled at her, and when he touched her... She sucked in a breath and avoided his knowing gaze. Drat him, he knew exactly what effect he had on her.

And that didn't bother her a bit.

The afternoon was too pretty to stay indoors, so they changed into play clothes and headed out. Sera set up on the deck on a lounge chair with her Kindle and a tall glass of iced tea while Levi and Petey bounded into the yard. Her attention drifted from them to the book she was reading, and came out of it abruptly when Petey raised his voice.

"Nunh-unh, you cannot," he said.

"How much you wanna bet?"

Petey rubbed a finger across his chin, a perfect imitation of his Uncle Jack. "A whole quarter."

"That much, huh?" Levi hooked his hands on his hips. "All right, then. Shake on it."

They shook hands, man to man, then Petey scrambled out of the way. Levi took three running steps and launched into a round off, twisted into a series of backward handsprings, and ended with a no-hands back flip, landing on both feet.

"Whoa!" Petey raced across the yard and skidded to a stop next to Levi. "How'd you do that?"

Levi ruffled Petey's hair and grinned. "Practice. If you went to school in Tellowee, you'd learn that, too."

"Can you teach me?"

"Eventually, though it'd be better if we found a regular class for you, since I can't be around all the time."

Petey's shoulders sagged. He dragged a bare foot across the freshly mown grass and his voice dropped too low for Sera to hear. Levi squatted down beside her son and placed a hand on his shoulder, talking quietly. A moment later, Petey nodded and grinned, and all was right in the world again.

Levi had the exact same effect on her.

Maybe the People were really witches and their specialty was enchantment.

She shook her head, dislodging the whimsy, and turned back to her book, satisfied that her men were doing ok.

They ended their evening with a walk to her parents' home, through the woods behind Jack and Candi's house. As soon as they arrived, Petey slipped away, joining Dale and Matty at the swings in one corner of the yard. Sera introduced Levi to her father and her brother, and left the men to their grill talk.

Inside, Candi and Sera's mother were standing at the kitchen sink, their noses close to the window above it, looking out over the back yard. Their heads leaned toward one another, Barbara's gray-streaked brunette curls setting off Candi's brassy blonde bob.

"Very subtle, y'all," Sera said.

Candi waved at Sera, her gaze pinned to the outside view. "That's Levi?"

Sera rolled her eyes and scooted around them to the stove. Shucked and silked corn was stacked high on a nearby counter. On the stove, water bubbled and spit inside a tall, aluminum pot. Since Candi was otherwise occupied, Sera dropped the ears into the pot one by one. "No, it's the Easter Bunny. Who else would I bring to meet y'all?"

"He's a handsome devil." Barbara peered over her shoulder at Sera, her brown-green eyes bright. "I hear he's good in bed, too."

"Oh, my God." Sera slapped a hand over her eyes, not even bothering to hide her flaming cheeks. "I can't believe you told my mother about that, Candi."

Candi leaned closer to the window. "All I said was that he knew how to take care of you. I didn't even mention the tying up thing."

Barbara's eyebrows rose and her cheeks plumped into a grin. "You should've mentioned that first, sister."

Sera slid the last ear of corn into the water, then swung around and grabbed a beer out of the fridge, popping the top off with the opener stuck to the fridge. "I'm going outside with the civilized folks."

She slipped through the door just as her mother said, "My Sera really let a man tie her up?"

The men were still huddled around the grill. Sera handed the beer to Levi and wrapped an arm around his waist, settling against him under the arm he draped across her shoulders.

"There's a good-sized chunk for sale on the other side of our property." Wendell jerked a thumb over his shoulder, away from Jack and Sera's houses. "Sixty, maybe seventy acres, forty or so that's nearly flat, and most of that in pasture."

Jack sipped his beer. "Not quite adjoining. Some asshole from Florida bought five acres in between and built a god-awful house on it. Never quits bitching about the farms around here."

"Still, it's close enough." Wendell squinted at the pork chops on the grill and poked them with his tongs. "Not enough land for a big operation, but enough to run a few beeves, make a tidy profit, if a man was willing."

"I might be," Levi said.

Sera tilted her head up toward him. "Might be what?"

He sipped his beer, hiding his beautiful smile. "Looking for some land for that herd of cattle you wanted."

"I was kidding about that." She patted his lean stomach, couldn't resist touching him, though she didn't miss the way Jack's eyes narrowed on her hand. "The berry farm is plenty."

Jack's expression turned sour. "All I've heard since you took Candi to that damn farm is *why don't we put in brambles, Jack,* and *we've got room for some blueberries over there, honey.*"

Sera pressed her lips together around a smile she was sure her brother wouldn't appreciate. "I guess she didn't tell you about the dairy, huh."

Jack pointed the top of his beer bottle at her. "And neither will you, little sis, not if you know what's good for you."

The evening was much more pleasant than the previous one had been. Then again, Sera's parents had fewer objections to Levi than his parents had to her. His mother, anyway. Iain Ewart had always been kind to Sera, and that hadn't changed when he'd learned his son was dating an older woman.

Though if what Levi said was true, and she was beginning to believe it might be, his mother was much, much older than his father, possibly by centuries.

Sera hadn't quite wrapped her head around all of it yet, but meeting his grandmother, or the woman *claiming* to be his gran anyway, had put a whole new spin on the legend he'd told her. Of a certainty, it had given her something to think about.

THEY WALKED HOME as the sun was setting, throwing shadows along their path. Levi carried a sleepy Petey draped over his chest like a limp blanket. Once home, Sera ran a bath for her son and left the door to his bathroom open while she leaned against the doorway to her bedroom within easy reach of him.

Levi stood at her bed, stuffing clothes into a battered red backpack as he undressed. "I'll call as soon as I get home."

"I appreciate it."

"It's less than three weeks." He zipped the backpack shut and dropped it on the bed, then pulled on a sturdy pair of jeans. "A few more after that and I'll be able to come up nearly every weekend, if you'll have me."

"Say yes, Mama," Petey hollered.

"Little pitchers," Sera murmured.

Levi padded toward her on socked feet. Her eyes dropped to his bare chest and she nibbled on the corner of her mouth with sharp teeth, and he grinned. "I've a question or two for you, love."

Her eyes narrowed into silver slits. "Is there s-e-x involved?"

"I wish." He drew her into her bedroom and closed the door. "Would it be ok if I left some things here next time?"

"You mean clothes and razors and mysterious man gear?" She toyed with the sparse hair scattered across his chest, scratching her fingernails lightly over his skin. "This is one of those things women's magazines warn you about. It's a sign."

He brushed his cheek along her temple. "Of what?"

"I can't remember," she said, and her luscious mouth stretched into a crooked smile. "I just remember the warning signs. Leaving things at your house, refusing to have sex with you."

"Hey, now, that'll never be a problem, I promise."

"I wasn't worried for a minute." She sighed and leaned into him, wrapping herself around him just the way he wanted her to. "I can see how it would be convenient for you to leave things here. I'll clean out a couple of drawers for you."

"Planning for me to leave a lot, then?"

"As much as you need," she said easily. "What was the other question?"

"It was more of a request. I'll start it by reminding you that I'll be here more often in a few weeks and I'm not gonna let you use your own money to feed me."

"Ugh. Not this again."

"The food's of a better quality at Evangeline's, and it's healthier, too. Think how much better it'll be for Petey's allergies to eat food fresh from one of the People's farms."

She dropped her head back and stared at him, her expression oddly mild. "If I weren't positive you were concerned about him, I'd give you a good piece of my mind for trying to use him against me."

"I'd never do that, love, not ever." He tucked a stray curl over her ear, cupped her nape. "I'm worried about the both of you. He sniffled all weekend and the ragweed's not even blooming yet, and you, you're my lover. I want you healthy and whole."

She screwed her face into a grimace, reminding him so strongly of her son, he had to bite back a laugh. Even wearing her irritation so openly, she was beautiful, her goodness a light he held firmly to.

He hadn't expected to fall for her so hard so soon, but there it was. His heart was tumbling steadily into love and there wasn't a damn thing he could do about it, or would, either one. "Perfect road, remember?"

She laughed, soft and warm, and he hugged her close. Petey knocked on the door and Sera scooted out of the room, leaving Levi to finish dressing on his own.

He sat on the side of her bed and tugged on his motorcycle boots, lacing them tight.

She hadn't seemed too surprised at his concern for Petey or that her son's welfare was uppermost in Levi's mind. Caring for the fragile boy was a responsibility Levi was willing to shoulder, for the boy's sake as much as Sera's, and for his own. What kind of a man dated a woman, carried the feelings he suspected he held for her, and *didn't* want her child, too? That Petey was bright and friendly and intelligent only made the decision easier, without changing the core of Levi's responsibility and concern a whit. He'd be careful not to overstep his bounds, but beyond that, she should expect him to care and worry for Petey, just as he cared and worried for her.

Half an hour later, his gear was packed and stashed away in the motorcycle's trunk and saddle bags. He rolled it out of the garage Sera never used for her own car and reset the kickstand. Sera and Petey followed him out, their silver eyes solemn.

Sera laid a hand on Levi's chest over the protective layers of his jacket. "You look so tough and strong."

"Prepared," he corrected. "The armor in this jacket will protect my hide if the worst happens."

She shuddered. "Be careful, Levi. I only just found you and I'm not ready to let go of you yet."

"Would you be mad if I said I hoped you never were?"

She smiled. "You're such a charmer. Be safe for me."

"I will." He kissed her, hard and all too brief, and gave in to Petey's tugs on his jeans. Levi pulled away from Sera and peered down at the little boy. "Jealous there, lad?"

Petey wrinkled his nose. "I just wanted to say goodbye before you got all mushy and stuff."

"Goodbye it is, then." Levi stuck out his hand and shook Petey's much smaller one. "I'll see you in three weeks, yeah?"

Petey grinned, flashing the empty spot where his two front teeth were slowly growing in. "Mama said we'd be there."

"And if she said so, then it must be true."

Levi ruffled Petey's hair, pressed another kiss to Sera's sweet mouth, and tugged his helmet and gloves on. It was a long way from there to Atlanta, with dark coming on and tourists heading back into the 'burbs from their weekend in the mountains. He had work ahead of him, too, things that needed tending. It might be enough to distract him from thoughts of her, though he didn't really believe it.

He straddled the motorcycle and found his balance. Kicked the stand up and turned the ignition switch. Sera and Petey moved back. He waved at them, waited until they lifted their hands, and rolled out of the driveway and onto the street. Three weeks wasn't that long, less than, really, and they'd have fun at DragonCon.

He turned onto Highway 76 away from Tellowee, made it to Clayton without meeting much traffic, and took Highway 441 southbound, merging with late night travelers headed back home, as he was. Somehow, though, it felt like he'd left his home behind him with a kind-hearted romance author and her precocious son.

Nineteen

THE FIRST DAY of second grade went off almost without a hitch. Sera walked Petey to the bus stop, waited for him to board the big yellow bus, then spent the day catching up on the work she'd planned for the weekend.

No regrets there. Having Levi for nearly two whole days was worth the extra time she'd have to put in because of it.

She had a sneaky feeling he'd done a lot more than that to make time for the weekend spent with her and Petey. The shadows under his eyes worried her. She poured a cup of coffee and padded through the living room and down the hallway with it, dropped into her chair and logged into her e-mail. And smiled. Every morning, she received an e-mail that began the same way.

Hello, love. Miss you.

She checked the time stamp and pursed her lips. 5:45 a.m. His text the night before hadn't hit her phone until almost 10:30, and she knew for a fact he'd stayed up later. Well, there was no way around it. She was going to have to put her foot down. He needed more than five or six hours of sleep at night, and no matter how badly she wanted to see him, she refused to allow him to sacrifice his health for her.

And it was becoming clear that he would.

She sipped her coffee, read through his e-mail twice, just to have his voice in her head. Answered him in kind, with questions and stories and all the details they were learning about each other through the simple, daily communications.

Between logging out of her e-mail and logging in to Facebook, her mind drifted to Petey's father. Kyle Vincent had been a handsome man, charming and intelligent and witty, and outwardly a good catch. They'd met her second year at the University of Georgia, during her first journalism class, and over coffee and heaping slices of carrot cake, had bonded through a love of the written word. In the way of college students everywhere, they'd hung out together for weeks, moved from there into dating, and eventually wound up in bed together.

By then, she'd been so infatuated, very little could've pried her from his side, in spite of what she'd thought of as his need for space. The night Sera had told him she was pregnant wasn't the first time he'd skipped out on her. She'd heard rumors of infidelity, let them slide because she'd never seen proof, not at the time. Later, though, after he'd torn out of her life and ended his in a crash, the wool had lifted from her eyes. After that night, she'd understood exactly what kind of man he'd been, weak, immature, and not nearly good enough to be a father to her son.

Levi had his flaws, but those weren't among them.

He was one of the strongest men she knew, and she was beginning to believe, deep in her heart, that no matter what happened, he'd never leave her and Petey to fend for themselves the way Kyle had. Levi would stick by them, doing for them to the point of exhausting himself.

So, that line would be drawn, perfect road or not. A woman couldn't stand by while someone she cared about sacrificed so much, not if she could do something about it.

A compromise might help sway him her way.

She drowned her grimace in a sip of lukewarm coffee. If she gave in on shopping at Heath's parents' grocery store, maybe Levi would give in on pushing himself so hard. It was worth a shot, anyway. And if that didn't work, she'd tie him to the bed, though she might not let him sleep for a while afterward.

Her eyes drifted shut. Levi, stretched out on a bed, his hands tied tightly together above his head, his lean, nude length at her mercy. Her heart sped up and heat shot through her. Lordy, she'd love to have him like that, with his muscles straining against the bonds, his body arched under her mouth, his lilting voice murmuring lovely words to her. She shivered and opened her eyes. The image of him lingered in her mind, distracting her for a long,

long while as she busied herself with work.

The bus rumbled around in mid-afternoon, dropping Petey at the end of the road with a handful of other neighborhood children.

Sera met him at the edge of the driveway and frowned as he approached. "What happened to your backpack, sweetie?"

Petey dropped his gaze to the toes of his sneakers. "It was an accident."

She fingered the ripped section of one of the straps. It took a lot of force to damage such sturdy material, more than an undersized seven-year-old could accomplish on his own, even accidentally. She knelt beside him and cupped his thin shoulders in her hands. "Is there anything you want to tell me?"

He looked away and shook his head, his expression so miserable, her heart broke just a little.

If he didn't want to talk about it, she couldn't make him, but she could at least try to fix things. "I bet MawMaw's sewing machine is strong enough to repair this rip."

A small smile tilted the corners of Petey's mouth. "Yeah?"

"Won't hurt to try, will it?"

"Unh-unh." His smile slid away and his thin face wrinkled into a worried frown. "Do you think Levi'll be mad?"

"I don't think so, especially once you explain that it was an accident. You will tell him, though, since he went to so much trouble bringing this backpack to you in time for school."

Petey's shoulders drooped under her hands. "Yes'm."

She stood and sighed. Whatever it was her son was holding back, hopefully he'd find a way to talk about it while she could still help him sort it out.

They dumped his homework and books out on the dinette and walked to her parents' house, backpack in tow. Barbara set up her sewing machine and repaired it quickly, as Sera had suspected her mom would do.

After a good visit, Sera and Petey wandered home along the trail worn into the dirt mostly by the feet of three little boys eager for company. Petey's smile returned and with it his chatter. At supper, he skimmed over the school day in favor of more interesting topics.

Petey attacked his mashed potatoes with more zeal than finesse. "Miz Royal said she knows Levi. Did you know that?"

"I didn't."

Though she should've. Bev Royal was the sweetest teacher Petey had ever had. She was also tall, beautiful, athletic, and single, and not much older than Levi. Of course, he knew her, just like he knew a lot of other people in the area, including Sera's parents. Him knowing Bev didn't bother Sera a bit. Nope, not one bit.

She conveniently ignored the twinge of jealousy poking insistently at her heart.

"Levi said if I worked hard in school, I could do anything I put my mind to."

"Did he, now."

"Yup. And he gave me ten whole dollars for helping him with the yard work and said he'd help me 'vest it."

Sera's eyebrows shot up. She hadn't known *that*, and wouldn't have allowed it if she had. Petey already received an allowance. Paying him to do chores seemed like overkill, even if the chores in question weren't ones he normally performed.

"He said when a body does a man's work, he should expect pay for it, and when he gets paid, he needs to learn what to do with it. He said a bunch of other stuff, too, like this." Petey's voice dropped and took on the odd cadence of Levi's. "Petey, lad, if a man's old enou' tae earn his keep, he's old enou' tae pick up after himself. Yer mum's not yer maid."

Sera pursed her lips together, torn between amusement over Petey's dead accurate imitation of Levi and outrage at Levi's lecture on manhood. Honestly, Petey was years away from having to worry about that, and she was years away from wanting him to pick up after himself. He was still her little boy, wasn't he? Time enough for him to do for himself when he was a grumpy teenager.

"Levi said you were a good mum and I should mind you and look after you, because that's what sons do." Petey's eyes were bright as he scooped up a bite of meatloaf and chewed, swallowing hastily. "Ooo! And he said he'd teach me to fight because a man always learns to defend his own. That's what he said, Mama, and he said that it was better to use words if I could, but to be ready if words weren't enough, which is almost *exactly* what you say. *All. The. Time.*"

So when she said it, it was just Mama nagging, but when Levi

230

said it, it became divine gospel. Figured. "Is there anything Levi didn't say?"

Petey paused with a forkful of peas halfway to his mouth. "Um. No?"

"Uh-huh. Finish your dinner, *lad*, so you can start on your homework."

He giggled and rocked sideways, nearly taking his milk with him. "I love you, Mama."

"I love you, too, squirt. Now eat and maybe I'll let you talk to Levi when he calls, if you're still awake."

"Awesome!"

As Petey plowed his way through the rest of his meal, Sera began to see the potential in having Levi around. As a motivator, he was apparently better than a favorite toy, for both of them. She finished her own meal and got another earful of *Levi said*, half of which ended with some version of *Levi did*.

A tiny knot of dismay mingled with worry in her gut, though she couldn't pinpoint exactly why. It was natural for Petey to be enamored of Levi. Wouldn't her son fall for any man she dated, if she'd ever allowed him to spend time around those few men? Boys needed their fathers, and while Sera's father and brother had stepped in and filled those shoes as often as Petey needed them to, it wasn't the same as having a father to call his own.

And Levi wouldn't abandon Petey the way Kyle had. A flutter of nerves joined the growing tangle within her. He'd promised and Levi was a man of his word, just as his father was. It was there in his steady gaze and the strength of his touch, in the promise he'd made to her that day under the hard summer sun before they'd even known each other well enough to make promises.

Surely she hadn't made a mistake introducing her lover to her son.

Petey cleaned his plate, drank the last drop of milk in his glass, then carried his dishes to the sink, the tip of his tongue stuck through the gap in his teeth as he focused on the small chore.

A man picks up after himself.

Sera huffed out a laugh. Likely, Levi hadn't realized how literally Petey would take him, or if he had, he hadn't thought of his words as anything more than wisdom passed from one generation to the next. Hadn't she caught her father and Jack doing the exact same thing? Was it any different because they were her relatives and Levi was, well, Levi?

No, she decided. Wendell and Jack irritated her, too, when they imparted *man stuff* to Petey, as if she weren't a capable parent on her own and they needed to do an end run around her female brain. At least Levi was...

The thought trailed off. What was Levi, exactly? He hadn't been in their lives long enough to be a father figure. She thought back to the way he'd treated Petey over the weekend. Straight-forward, man to man, honest. More like a friend than anything, so that's what she settled on. Levi had mostly treated Petey like a friend, and maybe that was exactly what her son needed in his life right then.

Sera carried her own dishes to the sink and began the arduous task of putting away leftovers and cleaning up the kitchen. Petey laid out the bagful of paperwork he'd brought home and sorted his homework from the rest, his dark head bent over the task with the concentration of a man intent on finishing his work. The knot of worry lodged in her stomach unwound and in its absence grew something better. Deep in her heart, she'd always believed Petey would grow into a wonderful man some day. With Levi around, steadfast Levi whose firm morals outmatched her own, her son could only become an even better one.

No, it hadn't been a mistake to introduce the two of them to one another, and she'd remember that the next time Levi imparted man wisdom to her baby boy.

LEVI STRIPPED his suit off and dropped it into the dry cleaning bag. Twenty-four hours had passed since he'd said goodbye to Sera and Petey. It felt more like twenty-four days. He tugged off his tie and hung it up, unbuttoned his shirt and threw it into the dirty clothes hamper with his t-shirt and socks. Sagged onto the edge of his bed and, giving in to fatigue, sprawled backward onto the mattress. He snagged Sera's pillow, held it close to his chest, but her scent was long gone. His cleaning service changed his sheets every week whether he was there or not, and had long since washed the pillowcase Sera had slept on during her one visit to Atlanta.

Seventeen days until he could see her again. She'd promised to take Petey out of school early on the Thursday of DragonCon, hoping to avoid rush-hour traffic as they drove south. Seventeen days and she'd be here again, in his bed, wrapping herself around him, letting him make love to her without the barrier of a condom.

Heat slid through him, gathering in his groin, and his body hardened. He groaned and buried his face in her pillow. She'd trusted him to be safe, and he was. The People weren't generally susceptible to the same diseases other humans were, likely thanks to the immortal curse holding their daughters in its steely grip. He'd been careful through the years anyway, never taking a chance even when he was with an immortal Daughter who wasn't in her needing time, save the day he'd lost his virginity. Sera was the first woman he hadn't used a condom with since he was fourteen and first discovering the bliss of a woman's body.

He'd forgotten how good it felt to have that slick heat clinging to him.

He rolled onto his stomach, taking her pillow with him, and breathed through the need clawing at him. That one time without a condom hadn't been nearly enough, and he shouldn't have taken her then, not until he'd explained the peculiars of the People's physiology or at least offered to be tested. No, like a selfish dolt, he'd given only a token resistance before succumbing to the temptation of her soft, welcoming heat.

Where Sera was concerned, his discipline was long gone. He laughed into her pillow. And she thought he was the one leading her around. No, all she had to do to get her way was crook her delicate finger and he just about fell prostrate at her feet.

He drifted for a while, thinking of her, all of her, his beautiful Sera. His cell rang, waking him from the light doze. *Sera*, he thought, and pushed himself off the bed, groping for his phone. He checked the number and flopped back onto the bed. "Hey, Mum."

"Hello, Levi. I hope I'm not disturbing you."

He rubbed his eyes with the fingers of his free hand. She only used her formal voice when she was about to do something he wouldn't like, or when he'd done something she didn't like. "Never. You and Da ok?"

"We're fine. Thank you for bringing your young woman by."

He blew out a breath, grappling with his suddenly thin patience.

"Young Peter was quite the surprise." Iain's voice rumbled in the background over the static. Noreen's soft laugh followed, and when she spoke again, her voice was gentler. "That's why I called. Your father and I would like to have Serafina and Peter over for dinner one evening."

"You'll need to run that by Sera, Mum."

A sharp silence hung over the line. "Perhaps I misunderstood the nature of your relationship."

"She's not of the People. She doesn't follow our customs, and I wouldn't subject her to most of them, anyway."

Like the traditional marriage ceremony, if their relationship went that way. Sweet Goddess, what man in his right mind would put a woman through *that?*

"I see," Noreen said.

"Besides, I've only known her five weeks." Five weeks, two days, eight hours, and... He squinted at the clock on his nightstand. Twelve minutes, but who was counting? "That isn't enough time to lay claim to her, and I wouldn't speak for her anyway, not without her permission."

"Your father claimed me in less time."

Levi rolled his eyes. *Here we go*, he thought. "You and Da aren't me and Sera. She's her own woman, much like my mum, and I won't be telling her what to do when she's got a solid head on her shoulders." Unless it suited him to do otherwise. Stubborn woman. He sat up, snagged the pen and notepad he kept by his bed, and jotted down a note to remind her to shop at Evangeline's. In a couple of days, when it would seem less like nagging.

"A Son has certain duties..."

"Have I ever failed you?"

His mother's teeth clicked sharply together. "No child of mine would ever fail in his duty."

"Then there's no need to remind me of it, is there?" He sighed, already regretting the impatient tone he'd used. No matter how irritated he got with her, she was still his mum and one of the best women he knew. "I'll ask her about it tonight when we talk, though it would be easier if you'd call her yourself."

A chair creaked, fingers tapped against wood, and in the long silence that followed, Levi bit back a laugh. Sera must've really put his mum in her place the day Noreen and his gran had visited.

"Perhaps it would be better if you spoke to her first."

"I'll do that, then. Can I speak to Da?"

Noreen murmured her goodbyes and a moment later, Iain's laughing voice boomed over the line. Levi chatted with his father, wedged in a not-so-subtle hint about bringing Petey to the shop, and rang off, still bemused by his mother's reticence to approach Sera without an intermediary.

This from the woman that had faced more than one army with only a sword and spear and a handful of other Daughters as backup.

He clicked through his contacts and called Sera. She picked up on the first ring and said hello in that honeyed twang of hers, and tension seeped from his muscles. They talked for half an hour about this and that, little, every day things. Petey's first day of school and his upcoming birthday, the release of Sera's latest book later that week, the property next to her parents'.

He'd already decided to make an offer on it, whether he established a herd of cattle or not. The convenience of owning that piece of land, right in the midst of her family and so close to his own, was too tempting to pass by. He jotted down another note, reminding himself to contact a realtor, and ended their conversation with his mother's invitation to dinner.

Sera, unsurprisingly, was reluctant to go without him acting as a buffer, though she didn't put it quite that way.

"Levi, no. I know she's your mother and you love her, but I'm not subjecting myself to her condescension. When you're here, of course we'll visit your parents, but not without you."

He left it at that. Noreen had made a thorny bed when she'd treated Sera poorly in her own home, but that was a Daughter for you. The arrogance bred over centuries of immortality never bled out of them.

The days blurred by in a hazy hustle of work. Every morning, he set aside ten minutes to write Sera and every night he fell into bed with her voice in his ear, reciting the day's events in a slow, calm drawl, soothing and arousing him in equal measures.

In between, he juggled his schedule and negotiated contracts, smoothed over problems or solved them, ate better when he remembered to, which was hard to avoid. Sera had placed a pointed call to Janine and "had words with me," as his assistant put it. Now, every morning when he came into the office, Janine speared him with unblinking green eyes and asked if he'd eaten. Every day at lunchtime, she set proper food in front of him if he couldn't arrange it himself, and every afternoon before she left for the day, she reminded him to take time for a healthy supper.

He was pretty sure she was reporting exactly what he ate to Sera by e-mail, though he never actually caught her doing it.

Another man might've found their machinations annoying. He preferred to think of it as what Sera would do for him if she were there. Breakfast in the mornings before they headed to their separate jobs, lunch dates two or three times during the workweek, and a meal together in the evenings as a family, Petey's bright chatter joining with her softer one, filling his apartment with life.

They'd never be there, though, not on a permanent basis. He hadn't considered the possibility, not even in his dreams. Sera would hate living in the city, and Petey needed the fresh air and open spaces of the country. No, when the time came for change, Levi would be the one to make that adjustment.

When.

That word dwelt in his mind more frequently as the days passed. When DragonCon was over, he'd be able to slow down marginally, leaving more time for Sera and Petey. When summer passed into autumn, they'd spend their weekends together, raking leaves and gathering pumpkins for Jack O' Lanterns. When autumn's balminess turned to winter's chill, he and Petey would bundle up and practice basketball, a secret wish Sera's son had confessed in a quiet voice, his eyes downcast. When next summer rolled around, Levi would coax Sera into a vacation in the Outer Banks and they'd celebrate the love they'd grown into as the ocean crashed against the shore and the moon shone overhead.

When was a powerful hope he held close to his heart. It carried him through the long days at work and the shorter nights alone in his bed, curled around Sera's pillow as if it were her, and it anchored his resolve and determination. *Just a couple more weeks,* he thought as he pushed through another drawn out meeting. *Just a few more days,* he gritted out as yet another problem cropped up with the construction of a new hotel in Macon. *Just a few more hours,* he told her when they talked the Tuesday before DragonCon.

And then at last, *when* became *now.*

Twenty

S ERA HAD NEVER THOUGHT of a long car ride with her son as an onerous task. He'd always been such a sweet boy, only too happy to sink into the mysterious worlds he created in his mind, and when that didn't work, an audiobook, music, or conversation usually helped him pass the time easily.

Of course, that was before Petey met Levi.

"Are we there yet?"

Sera glanced in the rearview mirror. Petey sat stick-straight in the Volvo's back seat, silver eyes wide, his nose pressed to the window. The much-hated booster seat had finally gone the way of the dodo on his birthday. Without it, he was barely tall enough to see over the door panel.

"We still have a little way to go."

She'd picked Petey up from school at noon sharp, right after his lunch period, and headed straight down Highway 441 toward Levi's office. They hadn't made it from Tiger to Tallulah Falls before Petey grew restless and gave up on the car tag game. The closer to the Greater Atlanta area they got, the more clogged the roads grew. Between him and the traffic, her nerves were stretched thin. Thank goodness Levi would do all the driving during the coming weekend.

Petey kicked the seat with the backs of his shoes. "What about now?"

Sera merged onto I-85. An F-250 loaded down with construction supplies zoomed past her and shifted into her lane, leaving less than six inches between the two vehicle's bumpers. She gritted her teeth, waited for the truck to gain distance on her, then sped up slightly, matching the flow of traffic. "Still driving, Petey."

He sighed, long and heartfelt and very put-upon. "Can't you go faster or something? He's gonna leave without us."

"Levi promised he'd wait for us at his office and he never goes back on his word."

"Petey, lad," her son murmured, "a man makes a promise, he keeps it."

Sera firmed her lips against a smile. "Did he tell you that?"

"Unh-unh. It just sounded like something he'd say."

Boy, did it. Over the past two and a half weeks, Sera had gotten an earful of *Levi said*. Petey hadn't spent that much time around Levi, but apparently he'd soaked up every word his new hero had uttered and then some.

That was Petey, her little sponge.

A nerve-wracking forty-five minutes later, Sera pulled into the parking garage near the headquarters for Icenia, LLC, ushered Petey out, and locked the Volvo. Through their short walk, Petey ogled everything around him and asked at least three million questions, stopping only once they reached the floor for Icenia and wended their way to Levi's office.

Janine was seated at her desk answering a phone call. She grinned and held up a finger, and a moment later, hung up. "Hey, Sera. We were starting to get worried."

"Traffic was horrible."

Janine rolled her eyes, and Sera laughed.

"Yup, it was that bad. This is my son. Petey, this is Janine, Levi's assistant."

Petey held his hand out and said solemnly, "Pleased to meet you, Miss Janine."

"Aw, lookit." Janine leaned forward and shook Petey's hand, her smile soft. "Those are the best manners I've seen on a man to date. You're not married, are you?"

His eyes widened. "I'm only eight."

"You're breaking my heart, kid." Janine nodded toward the door behind her. "He's waiting for you, not very patiently, either."

"Thanks, Janine."

Sera took Petey's hand and pushed the door open, closing it as soon as the two of them slipped through.

Levi stood at the wall of glass behind his desk, looking out over the urban landscape. The sleeves of his crisp, white shirt were rolled up and the jacket of his suit, the shimmery brown one she liked, hung over the back of his chair. He glanced around and smiled. "Hey."

His smile hit her with the force of a Mack truck, taking her breath. It was warm and welcoming and soft, and carried the weight of every kiss they'd shared, every touch, every press of skin on skin. Her heart melted into a puddle of need and longing and an emotion she refused to examine. She swallowed past it and found her breath, and met him halfway.

He enfolded her in his arms and his body brushed against hers, reminding her of the night ahead. "I was getting worried."

"That's what Janine said." She rubbed her cheek along the silkiness of his tie and relaxed into him. He felt so good, so strong. All too quickly, he'd become her anchor. "Someone else was impatient for us to arrive."

"Yeah?" Levi eased back, leaving his arm around her shoulders. "Anxious for DragonCon, huh?"

Petey's gaze fell to the floor and he scuffed the heel of one tennis shoe along the carpet. "Maybe a little, sir."

"Understandable. I was excited the first time I went."

Petey slowly lifted his gaze. "Yeah?"

"Yeah. Still am." Levi squeezed Sera's shoulder. "I need a few more minutes."

She ran a finger down his tie, straightened it. "Mind if we use your bathroom?"

"Help yourself."

Sera scooted a suddenly shy Petey into the bathroom. When she would've followed him inside, a firm hand came around her middle, pulling her back, and another shut the bathroom door, closing her son in.

"Levi," she breathed.

He pressed a kiss to her neck. "Just for a minute."

She covered his hands where they rested, one on her stomach, the other on her hip, measuring his warmth with her fingertips. He nipped her skin and *mmmd* softly against her throat. Heat slid through her, steady and warm, and tiny, fluttering, needy throbs pulsed between her thighs.

"You taste so good." His breath feathered over her ear and his tongue followed, flicking along her skin. "Tonight, after Petey's asleep, I'm gonna taste every single inch of you."

She shuddered, already aching for him. "Why do you say things like that?"

"Because they're true."

His hand slid out from under hers and tangled in her hair, sliding through the silky strands to stroke the side of her neck. His fingers tightened and his mouth met hers, and she opened for him, blossoming for her sun god. He devoured her, slowly and thoroughly, as if he'd never get enough of her.

God, she hoped not.

Behind the closed door, the toilet flushed, water ran in the sink. Levi eased away from her, his eyes lowered, his breath panting across her mouth. "Tonight."

She nodded, grasped the handle of the door, steadying herself when he let go. Holy cow. How could a kiss get better every single time?

As soon as Levi finished his work, they left for his apartment. Sera followed him, mindful of her son in the backseat and Levi ahead of her in his ridiculously expensive sports car. Once there, Petey perched carefully on one of the straight-backed metal and wood chairs at the dining table, carefully writing out vocabulary words.

Sera sat beside him, half of her attention on him and the other half on Levi's open bedroom door, where she caught glimpses of her semi-nude lover packing a duffle for the weekend ahead.

Not that she was looking or anything. Nope, she absolutely had not taken more than a dozen lingering glances of his graceful body, nor had she admired his firm tush, clothed only in briefs, or his long, muscular legs.

She missed seeing those legs. Maybe she could talk him into another trip to the beach next summer, just so she could ogle them. *Levi, darling, honey pie, sweetheart,* she would say, *wouldn't a trip to the Outer Banks be lovely right about now? Oh, and, don't forget your swimming trunks.* Or maybe, *Hey, wow, how did that Speedo get in your bag?*

Half an hour later, they headed to the hotel in her Volvo, Levi behind the wheel. She'd handed over the keys before they'd even left his apartment, and ignored his knowing smirk.

The hotel was crowded when they arrived. Many of the attendees wore costumes, some recognizable, others more obscure. Petey's eyes grew rounder and wider as they pushed their way through to the front desk and checked in. All the way up to their room, he regaled them with continual tallies of the number of Star Wars characters he'd spotted.

Levi sent them off to supper with a light kiss for her and a good hair-ruffling for her son, while he stayed behind preparing for the exhibition. Not long after eating, Sera and Petey followed the map Levi gave them to the exhibit area and found seats near the ring set up in the center of the room.

Petey trained his eyes on the ring as if Darth Vader himself would make an appearance there. "This is gonna be *so cool.*"

Sera clamped down on her own excitement. She knew what to expect, sort of, after watching Levi and Ruby have a go at each other two months before. At least, she knew enough to know how beautiful the fight could be, and how vicious.

And his great-grandmother would be his opponent. Sera was curious about the mysterious Hawthorne. Was she the same woman whose pictures Sera had found through brief internet searches during her and Levi's visit to Winston-Salem? Would Levi introduce them or would he want his beloved nana to know his lover and her son?

She caught a motion out of the corner of her eye, distracting her from thoughts of Levi's nana. Levi stood at one corner of the ring talking to a tall, slender woman whose red spiky hair was shades darker than his, and whose face closely matched the pictures Sera had found of the fantasy writer named Hawthorne. She was young, her face unmarked by time, though her eyes were hard and brittle, much as Levi's grandmother's had been.

Levi's grandmother who appeared to be much younger than his mother, Noreen. Was there truly some substance to Levi's allusions that the People's women had been cursed to immortality, or was he playing her for some as-yet-unknown reason?

No, not Levi. He might withhold information, if he thought it best, but he never lied to her, never, and that left only one conclusion. If, as he said, Hawthorne was his great-grandmother, then either the best plastic surgeon in the world had doctored her face or she was immortal.

Sera rolled the idea around in her head only once before tucking it away. There was only so much a woman could process at one time. Now was not the moment to examine that idea.

She turned her attention back to Levi and Hawthorne, admiring the toned elegance of their bodies. The pair wore matching athletic clothing, black Lycra tights that covered them from waist to ankle. Levi had on a short-sleeved shirt made of the same fabric and the woman a tank-top. The material hugged their bodies. Neither appeared to have an extra ounce of fat anywhere.

Sera's heart tripped in her chest and liquid heat pooled low in her abdomen, and again she was struck by his beauty. She was so ordinary by comparison, short and rounded and blah, and he wanted her anyway.

Two young women sat down in front of Sera and Petey, both blonde and thin and attractive, and Sera's heart plummeted right to her knees. Those were the kind of women Levi should be with, not a nearly-middle-aged woman with too many curves and a son to care for.

Levi slipped his shoes off and swung himself effortlessly into the ring. He leaned his stick against one corner and faced Sera, meeting her gaze over the heads of the women in front of her, ignoring them completely. A small smile played around his sensuous mouth, as if he knew what she was thinking, or maybe he knew exactly what effect he had on her, dressed in clothes that left very little to the imagination.

She glanced down his lean form and inhaled sharply. He appeared to be completely nude under the thin tights. His muscles flexed and bunched as he launched into a series of slow stretches, their lines thrown into sharp relief under the exhibition hall's bright lights, and his sex was half-hard.

Nope, those clothes left not a thing to the imagination.

She flushed and lifted her gaze to his face. He was still looking at her, his expression impassive, his whiskey eyes burning bright. He was looking at her and Heaven only knew what he was thinking.

No, that wasn't right. She knew his thoughts revolved around the same thing hers did. *Tonight.*

She snuck a glance at Petey. His unblinking gaze was trained on the center of the room. When she looked back, Levi had placed his back to them, continuing his stretches with toe touches and yoga poses that showcased his athletic form. Desire raced under her skin with every shift of his lean body, with every turn of his head and every pass of his whiskey eyes over her. Levi had always been more than her. Younger and more beautiful, wealthier and more polished, so far above her in some ways, he might as well live on another planet, but he was hers, at least for a while.

A referee stepped into the ring. Levi retrieved his stick and winked at her and Petey, then he and the woman he'd referred to as Nana went at each other with moves so sure and quick, their hands were a blur of attack and counterattack.

THE METAL CHAIR was hard and cold under Petey's knees. He held on to Mama with one hand and stretched his neck as far as he could. The lady in front of him was tall and her hair was kinda poufy and she kept talking to the lady beside her, so no matter where Petey moved, he had a hard time seeing around her.

Levi and his nana were in the middle of a raised wrestling ring. They moved slowly around the mat, trying to hit each other with long, heavy sticks. When Levi had come to visit ages ago, he'd explained the whole stick fighting thing to Petey, how they weren't really fighting, just practicing. Petey had relayed the whole conversation to Dale and Matty, adding, "You know. In case they ever really *do* have to fight a bad guy."

Kinda like how Spiderman had to practice using his web stuff before he could swing from tall buildings. Or like how Luke had gone to Master Yoda to learn how to use the Force. Levi was just like that, only better 'cause he was *real*. And his costume was cool, too.

The lady in front of Petey moved again. He went the opposite way, just in time to see Nana hit Levi in the back of his knees, knocking him off his feet. He landed flat on his back, then popped right back up like a real live ninja.

"Kewl," Petey said.

Mama had her hand over her heart, patting it, and her eyes were real wide and kinda gooey looking. When Petey got into a fight with Dale or Matty, Mama fussed at him, but when Levi fought, she got all mushy.

Girls sure were weird.

Petey shook his head and turned back to the fight. Levi's hand was moving really fast, swinging his stick around, blocking Nana's swings and pokes, but Nana was faster, moving so quick, sometimes Petey had a hard time following her. She whirled around Levi, hit him three times in a row faster than you could say *spit*, and after, Levi held his hands up and grinned. Everybody stood up and applauded, even Mama, who had a big smile on her face.

Levi kissed his nana right on the mouth, which was just gross. What was it about grown ups and kissing anyhow? Couldn't they just shake hands or something? But no, every time he turned around, Uncle Jack was kissing Aunt Candi or PawPaw was kissing MawMaw. Petey had even caught Levi kissing Mama a couple times, when they hadn't known he was there.

It sorta made his chest feel all funny, like when Mama gave him a hug, except better. Now that Mama was dating Levi, Petey prayed every night that they'd get married so he could have a dad. Levi was nearly perfect, too. He hadn't made pancakes yet, but he had a truck *and* a motorcycle *and* a really cool car, and he sent Mama flowers and talked to her every day, and she smiled. *A lot.* Plus, he did all kinds of cool stuff, like fixing Petey's bike and doing handsprings and stick fighting, and he never made fun of Petey for liking Star Wars or being small or not having a dad, not like other people did.

Petey rubbed his shoulder and rolled it. Maybe Levi would teach him how to fight so the kids at school wouldn't pick on him all the time. Maybe one day, if he practiced hard enough, he'd be so big and strong, nobody would frog his arm or rip his backpack or shove him into the swings on the playground.

Levi stepped out of the ring and signed autographs. Petey bounced on his toes the whole time. What if Levi forgot about them? What if he just turned and walked away and didn't even think about him and Mama standing there waiting?

"Give him a minute, Petey," Mama said, real low and soft.

"He'll be here soon."

And sure enough, a few minutes later, Levi walked right up to them. Even standing on the chair, Petey wasn't as tall as Levi.

Levi scooped Petey up, holding him with one arm under Petey's butt. "What do you think, squirt? Ready to take on Nana?"

Petey curled his fingers into Levi's shoulder and tried not to look down. Levi was really, really tall, and the ground was a long way away. "She looks kinda scary."

Levi laughed. "She is, but only if you rile her."

Mama rested her hand on Petey's back. "Have you eaten yet, Levi?"

"What is it with you and food?" Levi cupped Mama's neck and kissed her smack on the mouth right in front of everybody, with Petey squished between them. "How 'bout I skip dinner and we go straight to dessert?"

Mama laughed. "What is it with you and dessert?"

"I like dessert," Petey said, and they both grinned at him. He wrinkled his nose. What was so funny about liking dessert, especially when Mama wouldn't let him have any except on the weekend? That wasn't funny at all.

Levi kissed Petey on the forehead and set him down on the ground, resting a heavy hand on his shoulder. "I'll grab a bite as soon as I say goodbye to Nana."

"We'll meet you in the hotel room." Mama held her hand out for Petey. "It's time for Petey's bath."

Petey sighed, though he didn't dare complain. Mama had let him miss a whole day and a half of school for DragonCon and he didn't want her to take it back. He grabbed her hand and held on tight, following her through the crowd of people out of the big room, onto the elevator, and to their hotel room. He got ready for a bath straight away, and after, he finished his homework without being asked.

A man always took his homework seriously.

Mama tucked Petey into bed in one of the hotel room's two bedrooms and began reading from *Charlotte's Web*, picking the story up where they'd left off the night before. Just as Avery was trying to knock Charlotte into a box, Levi came in and sprawled out on the bed next to Petey, resting his hand on Petey's stomach. It was heavy and warm and nearly covered Petey from one side to the other, it was so big, but he didn't mind. It was kinda nice lying between Mama and Levi while she read and he and Petey listened, almost like something a real family would do.

Mama finished the chapter and placed the bookmark at the start of the next one. "I'm going to talk with Levi for a little while, and then I'll be back in here to sleep with you, ok?"

"Ok, Mama." Petey squinched his eyes half closed, endured her kiss, and endured another one when Levi bent down and kissed his forehead.

"Long day tomorrow, huh, squirt?"

"Yes, sir." Petey watched them walk toward the door. Levi placed his hand on Mama's back, protecting her the way he said a man was always supposed to protect his family. A thought popped into Petey's head. "Levi?"

Levi glanced over his shoulder.

Petey opened his mouth, closed it. He'd almost said it, almost asked Levi if he could teach him how to fight soon, but it sounded so stupid he couldn't bring himself to say it. "Never mind."

Levi looked at him for a long time, just looked at him. "You sure, kid?"

"Yes, sir."

Mama cut out the light and she and Levi left, pulling the door almost closed behind themselves. Petey stared up at the ceiling, running Levi and Nana's fight through his head. Levi had told him all about how Gran Noreen had started teaching him to fight as soon as he could walk, and how Gran Iniira and Nana and Grampa Iain had helped. How at the school in Tellowee, all the kids learned how to fight, and if Petey went, he'd learn, too.

He wanted that more than anything, besides wanting a dad, more even than getting an Xbox One for Christmas. If he'd just asked, Levi would've understood. He would've helped. Shoot, he'd already promised to. He just hadn't been around enough to do it yet. And hadn't he said that a man always took care of his family? Wasn't Petey sort of part of Levi's family, now that he and Mama were dating?

Levi wouldn't say no. Petey just knew it.

He slid out of bed and tiptoed to the door, listening carefully.

The hotel room was nearly silent. He opened his door and listened again, then followed the quiet sounds of Mama and Levi talking to the other bedroom. There was a small crack between the door and the doorframe, just wide enough for sound to come out, not wide enough for Petey to see inside.

"Looks like he might need braces, though," Levi said.

"I've already started a fund."

The mattress squeaked. "Let me help."

"Levi, come on. Let's not do this again."

Uh-oh. That was Mama's *I've about had enough* voice. Levi better be careful or next thing, she'd talk to him real stern like, and then there'd be *trouble.*

"Do what? I have the money..."

"And I can take care of my own child." Mama sighed and the covers rustled. "I've been taking care of him on my own for a long time."

"I know. You're a good mum, Sera, and I know you love him. Maybe I think it's time you had a little help with him, that's all."

"Levi."

"Maybe I want to be a bigger part of his life."

A funny feeling wiggled around in Petey's chest and he got all warm and squishy inside. Levi wanted him, really wanted him? Like, maybe the way a dad wanted his son? How awesome would it be to have Levi for a dad? Petey opened his mouth, about to tell his mama to *say yes* when she spoke.

"We haven't known each other that long yet. I want to give him time to get used to you." The mattress squeaked again. "It's been just the two of us for so long and, God, Levi, you wouldn't believe what a nightmare it's been for other moms when they date."

"I'll never hurt him. You have to believe that, love."

"I do. You're such a good man, so strong and sure. You're just what he needs."

"And what about you? Am I just what you need?"

Mama's voice went soft, too quiet for Petey to hear, and his mind drifted. If Levi was his dad, Petey would be just like the other kids in his class. Even the ones whose parents were divorced still had a dad. They just didn't always live together, but Levi would. He'd live with them and come home from work every night. They'd eat supper around the kitchen table and talk about their days, and then Levi and Petey would go outside and do man stuff, the way dads and sons were supposed to, and Mama would smile and nobody would call Petey names and everything would be so much better.

"Put your hands above your head, love."

Levi's voice startled Petey. He jerked to attention and placed a hand on the door. If he told Mama he wanted Levi to be his dad, maybe she'd change her mind about waiting.

"Levi." Mama's voice sounded kinda funny, all low and quiet and kinda husky. "I'm not letting you do that to me while Petey's asleep in the next room."

"I'll hold you there."

The mattress squeaked again. What were they doing, bouncing on the bed? Geez. And Mama got so mad at him when he did that.

"Levi, mmm." Mama hissed in a breath. "Don't..."

Levi's laugh was just as low as Mama's voice. "Anything I want."

Mama groaned. "No, Levi, not that."

A sick feeling lodged itself in Petey's stomach, edging out all the good, and his hands curled into fists. What was Levi doing? He'd promised he'd take care of them. He'd *promised*, and a man never, ever broke his promise.

Petey opened the door and his eyes went wide. Levi was lying on top of Mama, butt nekkid, holding her hands above her head, and Mama was wiggling, trying to get away from him.

Petey's face went hot and his heart pounded so hard in his chest, he could hear it. "Stop hurting my mama."

Levi jerked away from Mama and yanked the covers over her.

Mama groaned and hid her face in Levi's shoulder. "Oh, God. What are you doing up, Petey?"

"I came to ask Levi something, but it don't matter." A tear rolled down Petey's face. He sniffed and swiped it away. Hadn't he taken a fist to the arm instead of letting Jeremy Ryan call Mama names? Hadn't he stood up for her when everybody made fun 'cause she wasn't married? And now Levi, who'd almost been part of their family, was hurting her. "You get away from her, you hear? I'm not letting you hurt her no more."

"Petey, no. He wasn't hurting me, I swear." Mama pushed at

Levi's shoulder. "Let me up, Levi."

Levi was half turned on the bed, watching Petey carefully. "I think me and Petey need to sort this one out, man to man."

Petey threw his shoulders back and met Levi's hard stare with one of his own. "Yes, sir."

Levi nodded, just once. "Wait for me in your bedroom."

This was it, then. Levi was gonna whoop him for sure or at least yell at him for sassing. Petey managed an answering nod, then turned around and headed back to the bedroom, his knees shaky and his hands numb. He sat on the edge of the bed and stared at the wall, his mind all crazy and mixed up. How could Levi hurt Mama? How could she let him hurt her? Why would she *do* that?

Levi came in a minute later dressed in shorts and knelt in front of Petey with his hands on his thighs. "So, you want to take a swing at me, do you?"

Petey looked at his feet, dangling in the air two feet above the carpeted floor. "I just don't want you to hurt my mama no more."

"I wasn't hurting her, Petey." Levi took a deep breath and let it out slowly. "When a man and a woman care for each other, sometimes they, ah, hold hands naked."

"She was making funny noises and wiggling."

Levi's lips twitched and he coughed into his hand. "Yes, she was. She likes to hold hands naked. I can see how you might think I was hurting her, but I wouldn't, not ever."

Petey narrowed his eyes. "Yeah?"

"I would never lie to you." Levi rested his hands on the bed, one on either side of Petey. "Your mum wouldn't either, would she?"

"No, sir."

"She said I wasn't hurting her."

"Yes, sir." Which meant Levi wasn't hurting her, 'cause Mama never lied. Petey kicked his legs against the side of the bed. "Can't you just hold hands with your clothes on or something?"

Levi grinned. "That's not nearly as much fun, kiddo."

Petey wrinkled his nose. "Seems kinda gross, having to be nekkid with a girl."

"When you start dating, I'm gonna remind you you said that."

Petey nodded, though he doubted that day would ever come.

Girls were stuck up and mean, and he couldn't imagine ever wanting to date one, let alone wanting to hold one's hand. "Did you mean it, the thing about caring and stuff?"

"I did. Your mum's a special woman and I care about her a lot."

Petey swiped the back of his hand across his nose. "Do you love her?"

Levi's face went all soft. "I do."

"Does she love you?"

"I don't know. I like to think so, though."

Petey's heart went all funny again. "Do you think maybe you could love me someday, too?"

"I already do. Come here, lad." Levi gathered Petey up in his strong arms, holding him close. "I'm very proud to have such a brave young man in my life. What you did tonight, standing up for your mum that way? That took a lot of courage. Not many men would've done the same."

Petey buried his face in Levi's neck and held on tight. "I was really scared."

"I know you were, but you did the right thing anyway." Levi cupped the back of Petey's head, stroking his hair. "You've a strong heart, Petey. Any man would be glad to call you his own."

Petey squeezed his eyes closed and blurted out what was in his heart. "I love you, Levi."

"I love you, too, lad. Now, scoot into bed or your mum's bound to skin us both."

Petey scrambled into bed and snuggled into the pillows, yawning around the happiness filling up his insides. Levi tucked the covers around him, kissed him on the temple, and padded silently toward the door.

"Levi?"

Levi paused with one hand on the light switch. Mama stood behind him in the doorway, her arms crossed over her chest, her face all twisted up like when she cried.

"Do you think you can teach me how to fight soon?"

"As soon as I can. Good night, Petey."

"Good night." Petey closed his eyes. "Good night, Mama."

"Good night, baby."

The light went off and Petey fell asleep, dreaming about all the things he and Mama and Levi would do once they were a real family.

THE WEEKEND PASSED QUICKLY, filled with the hustle and bustle of a convention. Petey grinned the whole time, even in his sleep, and raced from one exciting event to the next, gathering autographs, having his picture taken with his favorite costumed characters and actors. "Next year, I'm gonna come as Darth Vader," he declared.

Sera hadn't even thought past the end of this year's con, let alone had she considered the next one. Her head was still wrapped around the conversation Petey and Levi had had that first night, when Petey had misinterpreted sex as Levi hurting her. As soon as Levi had pulled on shorts and walked out of the bedroom, she'd gathered up clothes and followed, standing far enough away that Petey couldn't see her while she dressed, but close enough to hear in case she needed to intervene. What she'd heard had stunned her.

Levi loved her. He loved her and he loved Petey, and how was she supposed to feel about that?

He never said a word to her about it. Every night, he pulled her into bed and made sweet love to her, whispering beautiful words against her skin. How much he missed her, how good it felt to hold her. *Mmm, do that again, love,* but never word one about how he felt.

She was beginning to think she'd imagined the whole thing.

During the day, Levi was his usual attentive self. When he wasn't filling in for sick staff or putting out fires around the hotel, he wandered the con with them, holding her hand, carrying Petey when her son's energy flagged, and generally spoiling them both as rotten as she'd let him.

She did a little spoiling of her own, rubbing his shoulders at the end of the day, making sure he ate decent meals and exercised. A woman could worry about the man in her life, couldn't she? Whether she loved him or not.

And there, her thoughts stuttered to a halt.

It was hard not to care about a man like Levi, her bright, beautiful sun god with his tender heart and rakish grin, and she did, much more deeply than she would've thought for the short time they'd known each other. How could she not? He was one of the best men she'd ever known, sweet and intelligent, charming and thoughtful, and so very, very good to her and Petey.

She didn't love him, though, not yet. Maybe someday she would, probably in the not so distant future. Who could resist a man that went so far out of his way to put a little boy at ease? What woman could deny a man that looked at her as if the whole universe revolved around her?

He'd looked at her like that from day one.

She held the thought close as the weekend drew to a close. The night before the con ended, she crept into Levi's bed and loved him the way he so often loved her, with gentle caresses and slow kisses and a world of feeling locked inside her heart.

The next day, they packed their bags and checked out, wandered the con for a while longer. Levi treated them to lunch, and after, they spent the afternoon in his apartment, watching the tail end of a baseball game, all three of them cuddled together on the couch.

When it was time to leave, Levi walked her and Petey to the car and helped her pack the Volvo's cargo area with luggage and souvenirs. He slammed the lid shut, checked that it was closed tight. "I'll be up in two weeks, if it's ok."

"Come whenever you like." Sera smiled, couldn't help it. He looked so formal, asking permission to see her again, as if he were afraid she'd say no. How could he even think that, when she was so eager to see him again, she didn't want to leave? If Petey didn't have school the next day, she'd be tempted to stay. "You know where the key is."

"I do." He snagged Petey and hefted him up against his chest. "I think it's right here, in Petey's pocket."

Petey giggled and wriggled, evading Levi's tickling fingers. "It's not, it's not, I promise!"

"Coulda sworn." Levi planted a smacking kiss on Petey's cheek and swung him down to the ground. "Go buckle up, lad. I need a word with your mum."

Petey wrinkled his nose. "You're not gonna hold hands, are you?"

"Maybe a little. Go on now."

As soon as Petey scampered around the corner of the car, Levi dropped his hands to her hips and drew her close. "Thanks for coming down."

"Thanks for having us." She rested her hands on his chest, exploring it through the thin material of his t-shirt. "Petey had a blast."

"And what about Petey's mum?"

"Petey's mum had a *very* good time, day and night."

"We aim to please." His whiskey eyes fell to her mouth. "Kiss me now, woman, quick before he turns around."

His lips met hers in a kiss that was nowhere near being quick or light or easy. Her fingers curled into the fabric of his shirt, holding him close, and she arched into him, giving back as good as she got. Heat spiraled through her, rising swiftly, consuming her in the same fierce way that he devoured her.

He broke the kiss and pulled her into a hug, holding her tightly to him. "Call me when you get home."

"I will."

"Call me if you have to stop."

"Levi..."

"Do you want me to worry about you?"

I want you to tell me you love me, she thought, and bit it back. It wasn't fair to ask him to say what was in his heart when she couldn't honestly say what was in hers, but golly, did she ever want to hear him say it.

He watched them drive away, his hands tucked into the pockets of his shorts, his expression impassive. Tall and proud and beautiful, that was her Levi. His image and the words they'd left unsaid haunted her through the long drive home.

Twenty-One

THE STACK OF PAPERWORK on Levi's desk slowly dwindled as the morning passed. If he could maintain this pace, he might be able to free up a day on the weekend and sneak up to the mountains. He reviewed and signed a stack of letters Janine had typed for him, set them aside. Picked up another folder and pulled its accompanying file up on his computer.

Maybe he'd drive up early Saturday morning and surprise Sera and Petey. Four days after sending them home and already he missed them. They'd played family all weekend during DragonCon, the three of them, and Levi had been content with that, even as his heart had longed for more.

Sera hadn't said a word about his conversation with Petey, straightening out that little misunderstanding, though he knew she'd heard every word.

He sighed and clicked through to the contract for the hotel in Macon. She just wasn't ready yet, and he wasn't going to push. Why should he? They had time, more than enough for her to come around and for all of them to get used to each other. Time for Sera to understand that Levi would stick with her, if she'd let him, her and Petey both. Time for her to understand exactly what that meant when the man doing the sticking was a Son.

His cell phone buzzed, rattling against the top of his desk. He reached for it automatically, clicked through to a text message, and stilled.

Petey was in a fight.

Levi checked the sender. It was from Bev Royal, Petey's teacher and an old school-mate of Levi's. As soon as he'd learned that Petey would attend the local public school, Levi had investigated and learned Bev was teaching second grade there. It hadn't taken much to convince her to have Petey assigned to her classroom. Levi had been thankful to have Sera's son there under the protection of somebody with close ties to the People.

There was nothing like an immortal Daughter at your back when a situation went south.

Levi read the text again while he shut his computer down and stuffed folders into his briefcase. Petey was a lot of things, but he wasn't an instigator. He wasn't one to fight. Hadn't he asked Levi to teach him how? Levi had been planning on it anyway. Everybody needed to be able to defend themselves, especially anybody affiliated with the People, as Sera and Petey now were, but Petey starting a fight? It wasn't in him. Standing up for somebody he loved, absolutely. He'd stood up to Levi just fine, hadn't he, and Levi had never been more proud of anybody in his life.

He shoved his laptop into its bag and flipped his phone around, opening a second text from Bev.

Kids knocked him down on the playground. Somebody blacked his eye.

A slow anger burned its way through Levi's blood. He cursed under his breath, low and long, and dialed Sera. Her cell rang through to voice mail. As soon as the automated message ended, he said, "Hey, love. I just heard about Petey. I'm on my way north right now. Call me as soon as you can."

He hung up and texted Bev, thanked her, and asked her to forward news if she had it. Sera might be tied up for a while. No telling when she'd get back to him, and he needed answers. Who had hurt Petey, for one, and why.

Levi snagged his suit jacket, briefcase, and laptop bag, and strode out of his office, catching Janine in the middle of a coffee break. "Petey's been hurt. Nothing serious, but I need to head home."

Janine paused with the coffee cup halfway to her mouth, her green eyes wide. "Is he ok?"

"Probably. I'll know more when I get there." He dug around in his briefcase, pulled out the letters he'd signed, and placed them on the corner of her desk. "I need you to rearrange my schedule for today and tomorrow."

"Sure thing, boss." She set her coffee cup down and appraised him. "So when you say 'home' you mean....?"

"Sera's house," he said flatly. "I should be back Monday, maybe Tuesday. You know how to reach me if you need me."

She nodded. "Let me know if I can help."

He smiled, or tried to around the tangle of worry and anger lodged in his gut. "Thanks, Janine."

He went to his apartment first, packed enough clothes to last the weekend, and switched vehicles, garaging the Mercedes in favor of his Audi A8 and its roomy backseat, perfect for carting a little boy around.

Lunchtime traffic clogged the roads. Levi gritted his teeth and edged his way through busy streets and onto I-85. He tried Sera again, hung up when her phone went straight to voice mail.

A black eye.

Levi swallowed the words rising in his throat. A black eye wasn't life threatening, but it hurt like a mother.

Who would've hit Petey anyway? He hadn't said anything about having a quarrel with his schoolmates. Surely Sera would've told him if he had. She'd started doing that, talking over her concerns about Petey, sharing some of the load of raising her son with Levi, and he'd encouraged her to as unobtrusively as he could.

Well, as unobtrusively as he was capable of being.

His phone buzzed, signaling another text. He clicked through one-handed with a judicious eye on the road and read another message from Bev.

He'll probably be suspended.

Levi eased off on the gas and texted back. *Did he start it?*

Bev's reply was brief and to the point. *No.*

Fucking public schools and their zero tolerance policies. As soon as he and Sera started dating, he should've insisted she send Petey to Tellowee. At least there, he'd learn how to defend himself and he wouldn't be suspended for being the victim.

Levi slipped the phone into the cup holder within easy reach and sped up, driving carefully away from the city, northeast toward Sera's house.

After what felt like hours, he pulled into her driveway and

parked behind her Volvo. He got out and jogged to the door leading to the kitchen, rapped twice, and pushed it open. Sera was sitting at the dinette, her head in her hands, wearing faded jeans and a collared olive green shirt. She looked up when he entered. Her face was pale and blotchy, as if she'd been crying. He opened his arms, and she stood and walked right into them, burying her face in his chest.

"There, now." He stroked her hair, smoothing the long curls down her back. "What happened?"

"I don't know." Her voice was thin and soft, and nearly broke his heart with the pain it held. "He won't talk to me. All he says is that he got into a fight. He won't even tell me who with, and the school has been less than helpful."

"I gathered."

She stilled, then pulled away from him. "Wait, how did you know something was wrong?"

"Bev texted me."

Sera huffed out a breath. "Right. I forgot you knew her."

He cupped her face and said gently, "She shouldn't have been the one to tell me, anyway, should she?"

"I was going to call you tonight." He snorted out a disbelieving laugh, and she added, "I was. I just didn't want to interrupt you at work."

"When something's wrong, you need to interrupt me. Where is he?"

"In his room. He went in as soon as we came home and he won't come out."

"I'll talk to him."

Sera shook her head. "This isn't your problem, Levi."

He cupped her chin and tilted her face up, and let her see exactly what was in his heart. "Yes, it is, love."

He kissed her gently and let her go, walked through the living room and down the hallway with Sera following quietly behind him. The door to Petey's room was closed. Levi jiggled the handle and found it unlocked. "Petey, lad?"

A sniff came to him through the door. Levi eased it open and peeked in. Petey was lying on his bed curled into a ball with his back to the door.

"Go away," Petey said, his voice soft and raw and bitter.

Levi sat down on the edge of the bed and rested a hand on Petey's narrow feet, still encased in the tennis shoes he'd worn to school. "Turn around now, Petey, and tell me what happened."

After a long moment, Petey rolled over. A bruise blossomed around his left eye and another along his right cheekbone. In the daylight streaming in through the room's only window, the bruises were dark against Petey's pale skin.

The anger that had muted during the long drive north roared to life. "Who did this to you?"

Petey glanced from his mum to Levi. "Jeremy Ryan."

Sera hissed in a breath.

Levi twisted around and raised an eyebrow.

Her eyes went flat. "Preacher Ryan's son."

Levi didn't have to ask who Preacher Ryan was. He could read it in her face. "We'll get back to Preacher Ryan in a minute."

She hugged her arms around her waist and nodded.

Levi turned back to Petey. "How long has this been going on?"

"Since school started back." Petey's voice dropped to a whisper. "He keeps calling me names. Said I was nobody 'cause I didn't have a dad, but I told him it didn't matter none 'cause I had something better. I told him..."

Levi squeezed Petey's foot. "You told him what, lad?"

Petey took a deep breath and looked Levi straight in the eye. "I told him I didn't need a dad 'cause I had a Levi."

A strange ball of emotion rose in Levi, expanding through his chest and up into his throat, squeezing it shut. He held his arms out, and Petey launched himself upward off the bed, landing with a solid thump in Levi's lap.

Levi held the little boy close, rubbing his back gently as Petey's sniffles turned to great, heaving sobs. "There, now, lad. I've got you. You're safe now."

Sera sat down on the bed, her eyes red, her lips pressed into a thin line. Her eyes met his over Petey's head, and in them he saw a well of sorrow and something that looked an awful lot like defeat.

He tightened his grip on Petey and held out a hand to her. She took it and settled against his other arm.

"Ow." Petey's shuddered out a breath and wiggled under Levi's hand. "That kinda hurts."

Levi loosened his hold and drew back. "What is it, kiddo?"

"Right there." Petey twisted his arm around, pointing to his left ribs. "Kinda hurts."

Sera lifted Petey's shirt. Her eyes went round. She glanced at Levi, then tugged Petey's shirt up. "Off with it, Petey. Let's see all the damage."

Petey pulled his shirt off, moving gingerly, and as his thin body was revealed, so were the bruises dotting his torso and arms.

A red haze descended over Levi. He tamped it down, shutting his fury away until he could deal with it, though he was all too aware of it rumbling around in the tiny space he'd given it, waiting to break free. "When did this happen?"

"This morning, in the bathroom. Jeremy followed me in with some of his friends. They held me down and..." Petey's face crumpled and tears welled up in his silver eyes. "Are you mad at me, Mr. Levi?"

Levi met Petey's gaze evenly and softened his voice. "I could never be mad at you, lad, though I'm none too happy with you for hiding this from your mum. We can't help if you don't tell us what's wrong."

And he was pissed that such a thing had taken place at all. Where had the teachers been when Petey was being beaten, not once, but twice? Why had no one stepped in to help the frail lad or at least fetched an adult?

Levi prodded the bruises gently, found a couple of spots that were worryingly tender. "Anywhere else?"

"No, sir. Matty came in and stopped them, but I asked him not to say nothing." Petey's eyelids fluttered closed and his shoulders slumped. "I didn't want him to get in trouble."

Levi bit back a curse. With a zero tolerance policy, anybody involved could've been blamed whether they were trying to help or not. "Your mum's gonna call Doc Ethan, and while she's on the phone, you're gonna tell me every single thing that happened between you and Jeremy Ryan from the time school started to the time he popped you in the eye. Is that clear?"

Petey nodded. "Yes, sir."

Sera kissed them both and slid off the bed. "I'll be back in a minute."

"Take your time, love." Levi settled Petey on his lap. "This might take a while."

And as Sera's son began a detailed explanation of the events leading up to that day's fight, Levi listened carefully and began to formulate a plan for dealing with the situation.

SERA SAT AT THE DINETTE, stirring her cereal with a spoon. Her appetite had fled the minute she'd gotten the call from Petey's school to come pick him up, and it hadn't returned in the more than eighteen hours since.

Thank God Levi had come up. Otherwise, Petey might never have come out of his room and told her what had happened, and she'd be facing his principal today without a clue as to what was really going on.

Not to mention that she wouldn't have found the rest of the bruises until bath time, if she'd managed to coax Petey off his bed by then.

Principal Talbert had called a few minutes after she'd hung up the phone with Ethan's office. Gary was a few years older than her. They'd gone to high school together, as nearly everyone in Rabun County did, and though they'd never hung out with the same crowds, he'd always been friendly and courteous. Having his pleasant voice tell her that Petey had been suspended for fighting hadn't made it any easier to take.

Levi hadn't taken it well, either. His expression had gone as cold as she'd ever seen it, and then he'd told her they'd talk about it later *in depth and at length*. They hadn't the night before, but she knew it was coming. His anger simmered just below the surface, well-hidden from Petey, but there all the same, and she couldn't blame him. She was mad, too. Mad at Jeremy Ryan for beating up Petey. Mad at Tony Ryan for raising a bully. Mad at the school for not stepping in, and madder than hell that they were suspending Petey.

He hadn't even lifted a hand to defend himself, not that it mattered. The school absolved themselves of responsibility by refusing to sort out what had happened. It was so much easier to simply blame everyone involved than it was to figure out who had started it and why.

Most of all, though, she was mad at herself. She'd known something was going on with Petey, had ever since he'd come home that first day with his brand new backpack ripped. Why hadn't she pushed him to talk about it instead of allowing him to come to her on his own? Why hadn't she found a way to draw him out instead of letting him bottle all that hurt up inside his fragile little body?

She clunked her spoon into the bowl and drew in a deep breath, exhaling it slowly. Across from her, Levi ate the scrambled eggs he'd fixed himself and Petey, and listened as her son rambled on about little boy things in a voice far more subdued than normal. Their heads bent closer together, Levi with a small smile, Petey as if he were imparting the secrets of the universe.

The night before, Levi had done more than save her bacon when he'd stepped in and done her job for her. He'd saved her son. After going with them to the doctor and waiting while Petey was checked over, Levi had spent the evening calming them both down, caring for them in his own way. She and Levi had both sat with Petey until he'd fallen asleep, and then Levi had drawn her down onto her bed and held her through the tears she'd sobbed into his chest, giving freely of the strength he seemed to carry in endless reserves.

When the inevitable discussion about Petey came around, Sera vowed to listen rationally to whatever Levi said and consider it carefully. He wasn't her husband and he wasn't Petey's father, but she could no longer deny that he deserved at least a small say in what happened to them.

After breakfast, she and Levi dropped Petey off at Iain's shop outside Tellowee, leaving her son under the care of Levi's mother. Noreen took one look at the bruises on Petey's face and said, in a voice so cold it chilled from the inside out, "You will let me know who was responsible for this."

Levi nodded once, and that was that.

He drove her to Petey's school without saying a word, though his hand held hers against his thigh, over the khakis he'd paired with the brown and green striped dress shirt he'd worn on their first date. She'd unthinkingly pulled on an outfit he'd appreciate, a fitted dark brown skirt and a matching camisole topped by a thin cream colored sweater, dressing to please him so automatically, it should've alarmed her. Maybe if Petey hadn't needed her, she would've given it more thought, but the fact that she wanted Levi to see her was a blip in her mind among larger worries over her son.

Gary's secretary ushered them in as soon as they arrived. He rose out of the chair behind his desk, a slender man with a friendly smile worn on a face just shy of homely, and shook hands with both of them. Sera introduced the two men as they each took a seat.

Gary rested narrow hands on his desk and threaded his fingers together. "Sorry we have to meet under such difficult circumstances, Mr. Ewart. Petey is an outstanding student, bright and eager to learn, and never a disciplinary problem. I hate that we have to suspend him over a playground tussle."

"It was a little more than a tussle, Gary." Sera crossed her legs and folded her hands in her lap, digging her nails into her skin, fighting back the helpless anger holding her in its sway. "We had to take him to the doctor last night, he had so many bruises on him. Dr. Phillips said Petey was lucky to come away without a fracture."

Gary's eyebrows snapped together. "You should have Petey's medical records forwarded to the school for his records. If this happens again..."

"Again?" Levi crossed an ankle over his knee and held it there, his fingers tight on his leg, his knuckles white. "So you're saying that in addition to suspending Petey for a fight he didn't start, a fight where he was beaten badly, you'll have no part in protecting him from the boy that hurt him."

"We can't be everywhere, Mr. Ewart."

"I'm aware." Levi's voice was deceptively mild, his gaze as frosty as his mother's had been. "I'm also aware you're fostering an environment that encourages children to turn their heads when one of their own is being bullied."

Gary's gaze went hot, though his voice was even. "It's not a child's place to interfere in these situations."

"It is when adults can't be everywhere," Levi shot back.

Sera placed a calming hand on Levi's arm and refused to flinch away when he turned that cold gaze on her. "Levi, honey, Gary's just doing his job."

Levi snapped his mouth shut with a hard click of his teeth. He gazed at her for a long time before turning back to Gary. "Have Petey's school records ready by the end of the day. He won't be coming back here ever again."

Gary cleared his throat and glanced at her. "Are you sure?"

Sera inhaled a steadying breath. Well, she hadn't seen that one coming, though she should've. Levi was right. If the school couldn't protect Petey from the children that had bullied him, then this wasn't a good place for him to be. She didn't know what she'd do, maybe homeschool him or look into one of the local private schools, but he wasn't safe here. "Yes."

Levi's muscles jumped under her fingers, though he didn't speak. They said their goodbyes and left an apologetic Gary in his office. Levi held her hand as they made their way to Petey's classroom, interrupting his classmates' reading lesson. He spoke quietly to Bev while Sera gathered up the extra clothes Petey left there and some of the work he'd completed that hadn't made it home yet.

Not long after, she and Levi returned to his car. Her throat was raw and nausea roiled through her stomach. What was she going to do? What *could* she do? Her mind whirled and stuttered over the possibilities, refusing to hold a solid thought long enough for her to consider it. She slid into the passenger's seat and held Petey's things in her lap, her breath frozen in her lungs, her body near numb.

Levi settled into the driver's seat and rested his hands on his thighs. "He can go to school in Tellowee."

Sera squeezed her eyes closed. "I looked into that school when he was going into kindergarten. They wouldn't take him."

"Only children of the People are allowed to go to school there." Levi's breath shuddered out of his lungs and the back of his head met his seat's headrest. "I can get him in."

"How...?" She shook her head, pressed fingers to the ache blooming in her temple. "It doesn't matter. I can't afford to send him there. For crying out loud, Levi, the tuition's more than I make in a year."

He rolled his head toward her and speared her with a flat stare. "I'll pay it."

"No." She hissed in a breath. Of course, he'd offer, but that was going too far. Taking his advice, letting him help, those were completely different from him paying her and Petey's way. "If I can't afford it, he won't go."

"Be reasonable, Sera."

"I am. I'll homeschool him or maybe he'll qualify for a scholarship at Tallulah Falls, but I'm not letting you pay for him to go to school."

"It's the best school in the county. They have a different approach to education, small classrooms, and a unique way of handling bullies. Plus, he can learn to defend himself. Petey will thrive there." He rolled his head around and stared out the windshield. "I oversee a scholarship fund through Icenia."

She considered his carefully closed expression. "Are you saying Petey might qualify for a scholarship?"

Levi's hands tightened on his thighs. "I'm saying Petey deserves a chance at a healthy childhood where he's not in fear of being beaten because he's small and unable to defend himself."

"Don't you think I want that?"

"I know you do. That's why I'm asking you to think about this before you say no." He rubbed a hand over his nape. "I've already contacted the principal and asked her if we could bring Petey by today."

Sera gaped at him. "What?"

"It's just a tour, love. No commitments, just a chance for you to see how the school runs." He wrapped his larger, stronger hand around hers. "You don't have to make a decision today."

"But you'll talk until I give in, won't you." She shook her head and tried to stem the laughter that rose, part relief, part gratitude. "God, Levi. What am I going to do with you?"

One corner of his mouth lifted into a crooked smile. "I've got ideas."

"I just bet you do. Ok, then. I guess we need to go see Tellowee's elementary school."

He brought her hand to his mouth and pressed a kiss to her fingertips. "Thank you."

"For what?"

"For listening." He placed her hand on his thigh and started the car, backed carefully out. "I thought you'd be harder to convince."

265

"I'd already made up my mind to listen." He raised a skeptical eyebrow, and she laughed. "Oh, stop. I'm not that bad."

He huffed out a laugh. "Only when you're being stubbornly independent."

Which was most of the time, she thought, but she let it pass. Levi had earned a little leeway and a lot of faith over the past week. The least she could do was hand it to him graciously.

Twenty-Two

THEY PICKED PETEY up from Iain's shop and drove into Tellowee. The town was beautiful, the homes and yards well-maintained. The stores along main street bustled, even early on a Friday morning. Sera hadn't yet begun shopping at the grocery store owned by Heath's parents. She hadn't expected Levi to be at her house this soon for one, but she'd also been holding it in reserve as a bargaining chip.

Which was shameful, but a necessity around Levi, her smooth negotiator.

He parked in the compact asphalt parking lot outside of Tellowee's elementary school, a two-story brick building located inside the campus of the Institute for Early Cultural Studies. The school housed grades kindergarten through sixth, while the adjacent high school accommodated students from seventh through twelfth grades. The two schools shared a large, open yard that served as a playground. A swing set, a slide, and monkey bars were installed near the elementary school. A paved, half-sized basketball court ate up a good chunk of space next to the high school. A long, concrete sidewalk joined the two buildings, perfectly bisecting the lush lawn.

"Well, this is it." Levi switched the ignition off and twisted in his seat toward Petey. "What do you think, squirt?"

Petey's face twisted into a skeptical frown. "It looks kinda small."

"Not a lot of kids go here. Sometimes, that's a good thing, though."

Petey flopped his feet against the seat. "Did you like it when you went here?"

"I did." Levi reached through the gap between the two front seats and wiggled Petey's knee with his fingers. "The work is a lot harder than you're used to, but it's not all worksheets and lectures. And, you'll get to take gymnastics and learn to defend yourself."

Petey narrowed his eyes at her, then glanced at Levi. "Are the kids here nice?"

"Mostly, they're like kids everywhere. Some are good, a few are bad, but the one thing they don't do is pick on somebody smaller than them." Levi jiggled Petey's knee. "Come on, kid. They're waiting for us."

They walked in hand in hand, Petey between the adults. Sera studied every detail of the school and its environment. She'd been there before, to the elementary school when she'd applied for Petey to go there and with Ethan Phillips to the high school for a dance. Not many people were allowed inside the hallowed grounds, though, and since she was touring, she wanted to absorb as much as she could.

Levi led them straight to the principal's office, bypassing the main office next to it. He knocked and entered, and introduced Sera and Petey to the woman standing stick straight behind an uncluttered wooden desk.

Patricia Devlin was, like so many of the people living in and around Tellowee, tall and graceful and athletic. Her thick black hair was pulled into a chignon and her nearly black eyes swept over Sera and Petey in an appraising manner that was just shy of polite and well into curious. Her unlined skin held a hint of an olive undertone, nicely offset by the black tailored pants suit she wore with a burgundy silk shirt.

She assumed a seat on her chair with the grace of a queen on her throne, and with the same regal tilt of her head. "I never thought I'd see the day when Levi Ewart brought a Son into my school."

Levi smirked. "Only because you thought nobody would have me."

"There is that." Patricia turned a steady gaze on Petey. "Even without your explanation last night, I can see why you've brought such a precious gift to us."

Petey ducked his head and blinked at his jean-clad knees.

Sera clasped Petey's hand and squeezed it gently. Poor kid.

He'd been through so much lately. "Levi said you might have room for Petey here."

"We have room for any member of the People that needs us." Patricia slid a sly glance at Levi. "Is he of the People, Levi?"

Levi met her gaze evenly. "What do you think?"

"I think you're still the same headstrong boy Hawthorne brought here some sixteen years ago, expecting me to tame the wildness within you, though you're a bit bigger now." Patricia's smile held both humor and pride. "I'll need a Councilmember's consent."

"I'll have it to you by Monday."

Sera glanced between them. "Why do I feel like I'm missing something?"

Levi's smile was soft and intimate. "Trust me?"

Only as far as she could throw him, which wasn't an inch. *Leeway,* she reminded herself, and just to hammer it home, tacked on *perfect road.* If he could get Petey into a safer environment than the public school, what did it matter how he did it?

"I'm not sure how much Levi's told you about the way we operate here," Patricia said. "Students attend classes based on their progress within each subject. Our class sizes are usually small, and we believe the best way for a child to learn is by using his brain, not by filling in a box on a pre-made form."

"They don't use a lot of worksheets," Levi murmured.

Patricia nodded. "Books, paper, pencils, and a bright and eager mind. Students are expected to pay attention in class, to participate in discussions, and to have their work ready when they're asked for it. Self-discipline is emphasized above outside coercion."

Petey's voice was barely above a whisper. "I don't know what that means."

"It means you're responsible for your homework, not your mum." Levi ran a hand over Petey's head, ruffling his dark hair. "Think you can do that?"

"Yes, sir." Petey glanced from Levi to Patricia to Sera, then lowered his gaze to his knees. "I don't mind doing homework."

Patricia smiled. "That's good to know, young Peter."

Some of the tension drained from Sera's shoulders. "He's a good student."

"So I've heard. Beverly Royal has already e-mailed me with an overview of Peter's studies. We'll do our own assessments, of course, but for today, he's welcome to visit classes."

"Oh, well." Sera glanced at her son's bowed head. "I didn't expect to leave him here."

"He'll be fine, love."

Patricia raised an eyebrow and the humor returned to her expression. "We take care of our own, Ms. Noland, as I'm sure you've learned since meeting Levi."

Boy had she ever. Hadn't he all but charged to her rescue the night before? "Thank you for considering Petey."

"There's nothing to consider. As I said, the school is open to any member of the People that needs us." Patricia stood and nodded to Levi. "Second year maths is in session right now. I'm sure you remember the way."

Levi rose, a smirk edging its way through his serious countenance. "Yes, Maetyrm."

"Go on with you then," Patricia said. "Lead him well."

As soon as they were out in the hallway, Sera whispered, "What was that all about?"

Levi shook his head and scooped Petey up. "It's a People thing. I'll explain later."

He led them down one wing of the school, along a corridor with a dark brown, hardwood floor and freshly painted, cream colored walls. Framed posters hung at regular intervals, some of books, others holding portraits of various people overlaid by pertinent quotes. Levi stopped at a wooden door with a frosted pane of glass set into the top half and knocked lightly.

A young man in his mid-twenties opened the door, his blue eyes bright under a mop of dark brown hair. "Levi, wow. When Patricia told me you were bringing a Son to us, I thought she was joking."

"Afraid not. Randy, this is Serafina, Wendell and Barbara Noland's daughter, and this is her son, Petey." Levi set Petey down and rested a hand on his shoulder. "Sera, this is Randy Lowell, an old friend of mine."

"Pleased to meet you." Sera shook Randy's hand, unsurprised by the firm grip or the warm strength of his gaze. "So, you teach second grade math?"

"I handle math for most of the early grades," he corrected gently. "Come on in and you'll see."

They filed in behind him, Levi and Petey, then Sera, and faced a group of less than a dozen students, two boys and the rest girls. One of the boys took one look at Petey and jogged to the front of the classroom, the other boy trailing quietly behind. The first boy was a nearly a head taller than Petey with piercing hazel eyes, shaggy dishwater blonde hair, and a lean, tough build.

"Hey, man. I'm Zach and this is Charlie." Zach hitched a thumb over his shoulder at the other boy, who was two inches shorter and whip thin. "That's some shiner you got there."

Petey nodded. "Levi said it's gonna turn funny colors."

"Kewl. You get a punch in?"

Petey's hand squeezed Sera's. "Nunh-unh."

A knowing glance passed between Zach and Charlie. "We'll take care of that. Hey, you should come sit with us."

Petey looked up at Sera. "Is it ok?"

"Sure, sweetie. We'll be right here talking to Mr. Lowell."

He smiled, then followed Zach and Charlie into the knot of girls that had formed behind them. Zach introduced him around, and every single one, ranging from a sturdy girl who looked no older than five to a slender girl of maybe ten, tutted and fretted over his black eye, demanding to know what had happened.

"We have a fairly large age range in this group," Randy said, as if he'd read her mind. "Kids are placed in a particular year based on their ability to handle the material, not their age. We emphasize letting students work at their own pace as much as possible."

Sera kept her gaze on Petey. He lifted his shirt, showing his bruises to the class. Why hadn't he been that open with her? "How can you even do that? I mean, doesn't it get confusing trying to juggle so many kids in so many places in the text?"

"It's not as hard as you'd think, especially with a small class. Most of the kids are content to work at just above an average pace, so they're working on the same lessons at the same time as many of their classmates. Zach, for instance. He hates math, and though he's disciplined in every other subject, he refuses to advance in this one. He's in sixth year history and fourth year English and science, but math, well. Second year is as fast as he's ready to go right now."

"That's really..." *Amazing. Interesting. Unique.* "Nice." She ignored Levi's smirk. "Aren't you worried he'll never catch up?"

Randy laughed. "Are you kidding? These kids are competitive like you wouldn't believe. Sooner or later, Zach's competitive streak will kick in and he'll find his motivation, but he'll learn more if he's allowed to find it on his own."

"I can honestly say I've never heard of a teaching philosophy like that."

"It's one that works pretty well for us. Not always, but usually." Randy shrugged a slim shoulder. "Petey's fine here if you want to tour the rest of the school."

Levi draped an arm around her shoulders. "Thanks, man. We'll be by at the end of the period to pick him up."

"Or I can send him on to English with Charlie," Randy said easily. "Go see the library or something and come back for lunch."

So they did. Sera said goodbye to Petey, who beamed at her from among the protective knot that had formed around him. She and Levi walked down the hallway, his hand on her waist, and visited the library at the end of the corridor, then the cafeteria and the small auditorium. He took her by the gymnasium, where two classes were being held. On one end, younger children were directed through somersaults by two adults. At the other, a woman in form-fitting athletic clothes led an older group through a series of fighting stances. They observed until the classes broke, then went back to Patricia Devlin's office, where Sera found a sheaf of paperwork awaiting her. She tucked it into her purse and listened while Levi spoke with the principal, her mind buzzing with everything that had happened in the past two days.

Just before lunchtime, they found Petey in a science class sitting next to one of the girls from math class. "I'm ok, Mama," he said. "You can come back and get me when school's done."

Levi shot a triumphant grin at her. "Well, I guess that's that, then."

"It seems so," Sera said faintly. "We'll pick you up later, sweetie."

The girl turned solemn gray eyes on Sera. "Don't worry, Ms. Noland. We'll take care of him."

On their way to the car, Sera snagged Levi's hand and tugged, halting him in the middle of the sidewalk leading from one school to the other. "Are you ready to explain what's going on?"

He shrugged, his gaze fixed on the basketball court across the way. "There's nothing really to explain. Petey needs a safe place to learn and that's what he'll find here."

She eyed his casual stance. "Do you honestly think I'm going to accept that explanation? I mean, what was that about you bringing a son here and having to get a councilmember's permission and all that?"

He cupped her shoulders, smoothing his thumbs in soothing rubs over her skin through her thin sweater. "I promised I'd always do what was best for you and Petey. That's all I'm doing now."

She shrugged his hands off and glared at him. "You need to find a better way to explain this to me."

He returned her glare with a steely-eyed stare of his own. "Why can't you just trust me?"

"He's my *son*, Levi."

"He's my..." He bit whatever he was going to say off and his expression went flat. "Fine. You want a better explanation? How about we go back in there and take a look at Petey's face. How's that for an explanation, Sera?"

She hissed in a breath around the twinge in her heart. "Levi. God."

"I'm willing to do what I have to do to make sure he never looks like that again." He stepped back and jabbed a finger toward the school. "And this is just the start. I know you're his mum. I know he's not mine, not really, but after tonight, he'll never have to face a bully alone, and I'll make damn sure he never faces one again without knowing how to defend himself."

His whiskey eyes had gone hot and his face was flushed, and God, she didn't know what to do with him when he stood there with his shoulders taut and his voice as angry as she'd ever heard it.

"What are you going to do?" she asked softly.

"What I should've done the minute you took me to your bed."

She swallowed around the lump of nerves and worry lodged in her throat. "I wish you'd just tell me."

"I would, if I thought you were ready to hear it."

He pivoted and stalked toward his car in long, ground-eating strides, leaving her on the sidewalk staring after him, wondering which one of them really deserved to call Petey a son.

LEVI TREATED SERA to lunch at La Cabaña in Clayton. They'd just been seated when her father and brother walked in trailing part of their crew of construction workers. The two men split off and headed toward Levi and Sera's booth.

She leaned around him and smiled. "Hey. What're y'all doing?"

Wendell slid into the booth's opposite seat behind Jack. "Looks like we're eating lunch with my prettiest daughter."

Sera laughed. "I'm your only daughter."

Wendell winked. "Which makes you my prettiest one."

Jack's mouth twisted into a wry smile. "Also the ugliest, but who's counting?"

Levi held himself back from the conversation, listening to the three of them chat and gossip. Sera rested her hand on his thigh under the table, squeezing or patting from time to time, soothing him with her quiet attention, and eventually, the irritation bled out of him. Wondering when Sera would be ready to have him fully in her life was futile. It would happen when it happened and not a minute sooner, and in the meantime, he'd go on exactly as he meant to, protecting her and Petey, caring for them as much as she'd let him.

After their food arrived, he waited for a gap in the conversation and said, "Are y'all busy tonight?"

"Nothing special on our end." Jack forked steaming strips of beef, onions, and green peppers into a flour tortilla. "You and Mom got plans, Dad?"

"Well, you know your mother. Ain't a whole lot she tells me. Just like a woman, ain't it?" Wendell waggled his eyebrows at Sera. "Y'all got something in mind?"

"I have a little business to take care of," Levi said. "Thought the two of y'all might be interested in helping."

Sera went still beside him, her gaze frozen on the chicken quesadilla she'd ordered.

Jack speared Levi with a silver-eyed stare. "What kind of

business?"

"Preacher Ryan's son beat Petey up at school yesterday."

Wendell's bushy eyebrows lowered sharply over a hot glare.

Jack turned an equally irritated stare on Sera. "You don't say."

"We're taking care of it, Jack," she said quietly.

Levi covered her hand with his. *We.* Sweet Goddess, it was about time. "We're moving him to the school in Tellowee, but that won't stop the Ryan kid from bullying anybody else. Also won't keep his da from backing defenseless women into a corner and putting his hands on them."

"Levi," Sera hissed.

Jack's fork clattered onto his plate. "The hell, Sera."

"Well, I knew there was a reason you stopped going to church." Wendell wadded his napkin up in thick fingers, his wrinkled face set in tense lines. "I shoulda trusted you and left it at that instead of nagging you to go back."

"What time?" Jack asked.

"Eight or so. Thought we'd meet at Sera's and go from there." Levi rubbed her icy fingers between his palm and his thigh. "I've got some things to take care of before then, but after, I'll treat you to drinks at The Omega."

"The Omega, huh?" Jack grinned. "Never been, but I bet it could get interesting."

Sera groaned and hid her face in her other hand. "For goodness' sake, Jack. Don't bet him."

Levi smirked. "I guess she hasn't told you we met on a bet."

"Well, you've done it now." Sera rolled her eyes at him, humor shining through the mock sternness of her expression. "They'll never let us out of here without hearing the story."

And because it put a smile on her face, he launched into a well-edited version of how they met, beginning with her walking out on the beach under the strong Carolina sun. They talked over and around one another, laughing and correcting each other's versions, though he was careful not to mention anything that might embarrass her. Over the rest of the meal, her worry over Petey dissipated and her expression lightened. That he'd had a hand in helping her with both satisfied him all the more.

As soon as they arrived at her house, Sera went into her office to check her e-mail. Levi settled onto her couch and texted his mum and Ruby, asking them to meet him at Councilmember Isolde's house after he and Sera picked Petey up from school, then texted his da and asked him to be at Sera's house around eight that night.

Sera came in as he finished a call to Tellowee's tattoo parlor. She curled up on the couch beside him and rested her head on his shoulder. "Thank you."

He dropped a hand to hers, holding her gently, rubbing his thumb across the soft skin along the back of her hand. "I'd say you're welcome, but I have no idea what you're thanking me for."

"For being you." She tilted her head back and met his gaze. "For being my knight and for having patience and for caring about Petey."

"I care about both of you, Sera."

"I know you do. It's just..." She sighed and snuggled into him. "Don't do anything rash tonight."

He squeezed her hand. No chance of that. He'd been planning how he'd claim her and Petey since about five minutes after the first time she'd let Levi kiss her. "You're not gonna try and talk me out of it?"

"If I thought it would do any good, you bet I would. I know you'll do what you think is right, no matter what I think, and I'm trying to accept that." She turned her hand over and tangled her fingers with his. "I wish you wouldn't shut me out so much, though."

"I'm not, love, I swear." He pressed a kiss to the top of her head and breathed her in. Sweet Sera. She'd taken his heart so easily. "If it helps, think of it as man stuff. You know, protecting my woman, beating my chest, making big, manly noises."

"Manly noises." She huffed out a breath. "What am I going to do with you?"

"Love me," he said, and immediately regretted it. He hadn't meant to say it like that, hadn't meant to blurt it out when he wasn't prepared for her to turn her back on him and tell him to shove off.

"I will." She cupped his face in her hand and her expression went soft and dreamy. "Don't go all cold on me now, Levi. I can't stand it when you look at me like that."

"I know, love. I'm sorry." He pulled her onto his lap, held her as close as he could. "I'll be out most of the evening."

"Doing man stuff?"

"And People stuff."

She curled her fingers around his neck, warming him to the bone. "I guess I can accept that. For now. Soon, though, you need to let me in."

He kissed her, afraid if he didn't, he'd tell her exactly how far into his life and his heart she already was.

A FEW MINUTES before time to pick Petey up, Levi changed into comfortable jeans and a thin, light t-shirt. He drove Sera to the school, went in with her to find her son, then dropped them off at her house.

He walked them to the door and caught Sera before she could enter. "I'll not come in when I return." No need to mention that he might not be in any kind of shape to get into the house by then, especially when he still had business to attend to after. "Have your da and brother meet me out here at eight sharp."

She nodded, though her lips were pressed into a thin line. "What time do you think you'll be home?"

"After ten at least. Probably more like eleven." He kissed her beautiful mouth hard, memorized her sweet taste, threaded it through his blood to strengthen him for what he had to do. "Don't worry about me. I promise not to stir up trouble."

He left her standing on the top step leading into the kitchen from the garage, her arms wrapped around her waist, a furrowed crease marring the smooth skin of her forehead. Her expression, so lost and worried, cut him to the quick, but there was nothing he could do about it. She wouldn't understand what he was about to do, and she damn sure wouldn't approve.

At least she understood that he was doing what was best. That would have to be enough for now.

He met Noreen and Ruby outside Councilmember Isolde's massive Greek Revival home forty-five minutes later. Isolde had assumed her seat on the Council representing the line of Bagda, one of the Seven Sisters, when Hawthorne, Isolde's aunt, had passed it by. Though she'd submitted her will to her husband decades before and become mortal, Isolde's personality had never softened, as so many Daughters' did when they found love and broke the curse hanging over them. Isolde remained a canny, ruthless warrior, and had no problem holding others of her line to the exact letter of the People's laws.

Noreen stopped him on the steps leading to the front porch. "Are you sure you want to do this, Levi?"

"He's mine, mum, in my heart. Time to make it official."

"But Isolde," she murmured. "Couldn't you have gone to another Councilmember, one with some compassion?"

He shook his head. "Anybody else would tell Nana."

"Don't you think she should know?"

"Not until Sera accepts my claim." He took a deep breath, steeling himself for what had to be done. "Come on, before she changes her mind."

He shook off his mum's hand and rang the doorbell.

Isolde opened the door, a small smile lighting her pale complexion under the perfect knot she'd twisted her midnight hair into. "Well, well, well. Young Levi has come a-begging."

Noreen hissed at the other Daughter. "You'll treat him well or you'll answer to me, cousin."

"I am as bound to duty as you, Elenora Tibicina." Isolde stepped back, her navy heels clicking on the hardwood floor of the foyer. "I understand there's a time constraint."

"There is, Maetyrm," Levi said. "I appreciate your attention on such sudden notice."

"Pretty manners. You must get them from your father." Isolde pivoted on a thin heel, ignoring Noreen's cold stare, and stalked down the hallway, her navy skirt swishing with each step. "We should have plenty of room in my office."

Isolde's office was, like many Daughters of her status, a large room lined with shelf after shelf of books. A dark-stained secretary occupied one corner, wedged between tall bookcases along one wall. In the middle of the room, a large sofa upholstered in a solid burgundy faced two matching chairs. A mission style coffee table was placed in the space between. Assorted weaponry hung between shelves or rested in cases or large vases around the room, from swords and staffs to spears and bows.

"Ruby, be a dear and take notes, would you? I sent my assistant into Franklin on errands." The councilmember sank gracefully into one of the chairs. "Best to keep this in the family, yes?"

Levi took a seat in the middle of the sofa between his mum and Ruby. "I appreciate the consideration, Maetyrm."

"Of course." Isolde folded her hands together in her lap, her gaze coldly amused. "So. You wish to claim your mortal woman's son and bring him into the People."

"I do." Levi omitted the reasons behind it. They weren't important here, nor would they sway Isolde to leniency, and he'd already discussed Petey's situation with her.

"And you're prepared to assume the sins of his natural father?"

"I am."

"What of the boy's mother? Has she consented to his adoption into the People?"

Levi kept his expression impassive. "She doesn't understand our customs. I chose not to involve her, since her consent isn't needed."

Isolde arched an elegant eyebrow. "You say that as if you consider her opinion unimportant."

"I value Sera's opinion, Maetyrm. I simply know her limits." He allowed a small smile to form on his lips. "Someday, I'll claim her as my mate, but for now, I'm content to claim Petey as my son."

"So be it." Isolde rose and stared down at him, the humor wiped from her expression, leaving only the chill behind. "Sixteen lashes as Retribution, one for each year of the Son's abandonment plus one for each year of his removal from the People. Additionally, a flat fine of fifteen thousand dollars per year of abandonment, to be paid by you into a bank account for the Son's benefit and added to annually through his sixteenth birthday. All will revert to the mother should the worst fate befall him."

Levi stood and bowed deeply. "Your mercy is boundless, Maetyrm."

Isolde inclined her head. "Who stands for the Son's mother?"

Noreen stood. "I do."

"Who stands for the Son himself?"

"I do," Ruby said.

"Do you find these terms just?"

"What will be the instrument of Retribution?" Noreen asked.

"A cane." Isolde's smile softened her mouth for only a moment. "Levi is still a Son and my kin. I have no wish to inflict permanent damage."

"Then I find your judgment just and thank you for the flesh on my son's back."

"I thought you might. I suppose it's too much to ask for you to remember that the next time you disagree with my actions in Council." Isolde clasped her hands together. "Well, best get it over with. You will want to take a protective mark this afternoon, I imagine."

"I'd planned on it," Levi admitted.

"Good. I shall keep the blows low, then." She strode to a large vase and retrieved a yard-long cane, whipping it through the air with a swift swing of her arm. "I shall do my best not to cut your skin, though I cannot promise."

Levi bowed. "I hadn't expected otherwise."

He stripped off his clothes down to his briefs and piled them on the floor. Noreen and Ruby stood shoulder to shoulder with their backs to the back of the couch. He faced them with his bare feet spread shoulder length apart. His mum took his left hand in her right one and held it to her chest over her heart, gripping his forearm tightly with her other hand while Ruby did the same, his right hand in her left one, her right hand wrapped around his forearm.

Isolde cupped his shoulder, drawing his gaze. "If I had been blessed with a Son, I would have been proud to have one as honorable as you, Levi."

"I would've been honored to be your son, Maetyrm."

She smiled, and for the first time since meeting them at her door, her expression held genuine regard. "Spoken like a true Son. Claim the boy now."

Levi took a deep breath, exhaled slowly, and stared straight ahead at the space between Noreen and Ruby's heads. He dug his heels into the bare hardwood floor and forced his muscles to relax. "I claim the boy, Peter Zachariah Noland, as my son and offer him as a gift to the People."

Isolde stepped away. The cane whistled through the air and landed on his lower back in a bruising blow, pushing his body into the women holding him. Pain radiated outward, away from the thin line the cane had scored into his back. He gritted his teeth against it and forced his body upright.

"I claim the boy, Peter Zachariah Noland, as my son and offer him as a gift to the People."

The cane whistled and another blow landed, perfectly spaced half an inch above the other one. Sweat popped out on Levi's skin. He breathed through the fire racing along his back, taking the blows as they came, restating his commitment to Petey between each one.

His vision blurred and the strength sapped out of his limbs. Somewhere halfway through, the world around him faded to the blows landing on his back, the words he recited claiming his son, and the hands holding him upright. He focused on his memory of the bruises on Petey's thin, fragile body, blows a child his age should never have to take. The pain of the lashes Isolde dealt was nothing compared to that, nothing compared to the pain in Levi's heart that came from knowing he'd had the means to save Petey from such a fate, and hadn't.

"I know, child." Noreen squeezed his forearm. "Once more and it's done."

He nodded and unclenched his jaw, stumbling over the words that would make Petey his. "I claim the boy, Peter Zachariah Noland, as my son and offer him as a gift to the People."

The last blow came, little more than a pinprick among the raw agony left by the previous lashes. Levi bowed his head and breathed through it. He *would* stand upright. A Son never shuddered under life's blows, no matter what hand dealt them. He let go of Noreen and Ruby's hands and swayed as the world spun 'round. He shook it off and allowed soft hands to guide him onto the couch.

Isolde hissed. "I tried not to cut him."

"Shouldn't've checked those last few blows," Mum said.

Ruby's voice sounded close to his ear. "I've got the salve."

Something cold cut through the hot fire along his skin. The pain dimmed and his focus came back, enough for him to remember why he wanted the agony slowly consuming him. "If you're putting pain medicine on me, you can stop right now."

"Says the boy who cried for an hour over a paper cut."

"Give me a break, Mum. I was ten." Sweet Goddess, whatever

they were doing felt good, though. "I'll be fine. Sixteen lashes is nothing."

"Sure, if you're a drug runner in Singapore," Ruby said. "Come on. Let's get your pants on at least and I'll drive you to the tattoo parlor, Stubborn McStubborn."

Levi managed a shaky laugh. "Knew I could count on you, Rubes."

She grimaced, though she didn't protest the name. Probably glad he hadn't called her Underhanded.

He slid his legs into his jeans when they appeared in front of him and stood carefully, grateful for his mother's gentle fingers settling the waistband low around his hips, under the worst of the wounds. Ruby wrapped her hands around one of his arms and Mum the other, holding him in place, though he could've sworn he didn't need the help, even with the world listing slightly to the left.

Isolde escorted them out, and he thanked her properly, as a Son should. A few minutes later, he was in the passenger seat of his car, leaning on his left side facing Ruby.

"I have a son," he whispered.

She grinned and eased the car away from the curb beside Isolde's house. "I know."

He grinned back as the knowledge expanded within him, overwhelming most of the harsh sting throbbing through his back. He had a son, and now, Petey would never, ever be without a father again.

Twenty-Three

THE AFTERNOON WANED SLOWLY into evening. After Levi drove off to God only knew where, Sera and Petey walked over to Candi's house. Sera's mom was there, sitting at the kitchen table sipping coffee. Sera sent Petey outside to play with Dale and Matty, and plopped into a chair between her mom and Candi.

Barbara set her coffee mug on the table with a sharp rap. "Your father said Petey was in a fight at school."

Sera nodded and rubbed tired hands over her face. It had been a long couple of days, and now with Levi gone, the whole of it weighed on her, adding to the sick worry in her stomach. What was he planning on doing? Surely to God he wouldn't confront Preacher Ryan. "Jeremy Ryan and a couple of other kids held Petey down and beat him up pretty badly."

"And you didn't tell your mother, why?"

"Mom, come on. I barely had a chance to pick Petey up from school before Levi came home. Dealing with him was bad enough." Sera slumped in the chair and fixed her eyes on the ceiling, holding them as wide as she could. Tears pricked at her eyes anyway, damn them, though she did her best to keep them from falling. "You should've seen him. Levi talked Petey into coming out of his room, and if he hadn't, I might not've ever found the whole thing out. And afterward, he was just furious, absolutely *furious* about the school's reaction."

"You want a coke, sister?" At Sera's nod, Candi retrieved one from the fridge and plopped it down on the table in front of Sera. "Jack was, too, and he was a mite pissed 'cause you didn't tell him and Wendell about Preacher Ryan harassing you. For goodness' sake, Sera. What made you think you should handle that on your own?"

Sera popped the top on the can of coke and rolled it between her hands, letting the moisture seeping along its sides accumulate on her palms. "What could anybody do? And since I didn't go back, it wasn't really an issue."

"Well, your father's up in arms about it." Barbara lifted her mug and sipped. "He's planning on churching Preacher Ryan on Sunday."

Sera gaped at her mom. "Can he even do that? I mean, he's a preacher for crying out loud."

"That doesn't make him above God's laws, Serafina Noland, or man's either, and I'm ashamed of you for thinking so."

Sera's voice wobbled and a tear slipped down her cheek. "Mom."

"There now." Barbara reached across the table and patted Sera's arm. "It's the only time I've ever been ashamed of my daughter, and hopefully it'll be the last."

Candi snorted out a laugh. "God, Barbara. The least you could do is shame her for letting Levi tie her up."

"Now, why would I do that when I'm trying to talk Father into it?"

Sera and Candi goggled at Barbara. She regarded them calmly across the top of her coffee mug, her serene smile barely visible behind its rim. Candi snickered first, starting a chain reaction that ended with all three of them hooting so hard, tears streamed down their faces. Sera's stomach muscles ached and her throat hurt, with laughter and tears and relief, and she said a silent, thankful prayer for the women in her life, and for the men, too.

An hour before sunset, she hustled Petey along the path toward home, fed him a quick supper, and put him in the bath. Since it was Friday, she popped a big bowl of popcorn and let him pick out a movie. They cuddled together on the couch as Christopher Reeve brought Superman to life on their TV.

In the middle of Clark Kent's first transformation into Superman, Petey snorted around a handful of popcorn. "Capes are so lame."

Sera ruffled his hair and peered down at him. "When did you get so cynical, squirt?"

He wrinkled his nose. "Don't know what that means."

"Never mind." She couldn't resist kissing the cute crinkle of his nose. "I thought you liked Superman."

"I do, it's just..." Petey shrugged and dug his hand into the popcorn. "Levi's way cooler. I mean, even his costume is neat."

"Yes, but Levi's not a fictional superhero. He's a regular guy who just happens to do a couple of neat things."

"I know, Mama." Petey wiggled around and smiled up at her, showing the gap in his teeth. "I know he's just a guy, but the thing is, he's *our* guy, and that makes him kinda special, yeah?"

"You know what? It absolutely does." She patted his leg and scooted off the couch. "I think PawPaw and Uncle Jack just pulled up. I'm gonna go talk to them, but I'll be back inside in a little while, ok?"

Petey turned his wide-eyed gaze to the TV. "Okey dokey."

Sera hustled to the kitchen door and peeked out into the driveway beyond the garage. Levi's black sedan was parked behind her Volvo, the engine idling, its headlights on. She slipped quietly out the door, bracing herself against the night's slight chill.

The driver's side door opened. Ruby's blonde head appeared above the frame. She shot a wary glance at Sera and held a hand out. "Stay there, Sera. Levi's in no shape to deal with you right now."

Sera sucked in a breath. "I don't care who you are to him, Ruby, or what he's been up to, but I'm not letting anybody tell me I can't see him. You hear?"

"It's not up to me." Ruby twisted her head around and ducked into the car. A minute later, she turned back around and rolled her eyes. "Ol' fickle butt here says he wants to talk to you. Mind you, thirty seconds ago, he told me not to let you near him."

Sera walked to the car and took Ruby's place at the door. She leaned in and did a double take. Levi was facing her, braced sideways in the seat, his muscled chest bare and his legs encased in the jeans he'd had on when he'd left. They were unbuttoned and slung low on his waist, exposing the waistband of his briefs. His skin was three shades whiter than normal and dotted with sweat, and slight tremors shivered through him at irregular intervals. A piece of tape four inches long was just visible across the top of his right shoulder.

Her heart tightened in her chest and a breath shuddered out. She sank into the driver's seat and touched light fingers to his forehead. It was clammy and cold, as if he were on the downswing of a fever. "Levi, honey, what happened?"

He closed his eyes and bowed his head into her touch. When he spoke, his voice was rusty and low. "Can we talk about it later?"

"If that's what you want."

"I just need another hour. Just one more, ok?"

She ran her fingertips down his face. His cheeks flushed and his breath wheezed out of his lungs. "What's happening in another hour?"

"I'll be able to move." His mouth curved into a faint smile. "Have to before then, though. Is Petey ok?"

"He's fine, sweetie. I'm more worried about you right now."

"Don't be. I'll heal. The scars will fade, and you'll never have to worry about Petey again."

"Oh, Levi." She touched his forehead again. His skin was significantly warmer under her fingers, alarming her. "What have you done?"

His voice dropped to a hoarse whisper. "What I had to."

Ruby's hand fell on Sera's shoulder. "Come on, Sera. You're wearing him out and he still has a lot to do tonight."

Sera kissed her fingertips and pressed them to Levi's forehead, then eased out of the car on shaky legs. She pulled Ruby into the garage, away from Levi's car, and hissed, "What's wrong with him?"

Ruby's mouth thinned into a slash across her face. "If I tell you, he'll kill me."

"Don't give me that, Ruby. You know he won't tell me, and I need to know."

Ruby glanced toward the car and lowered her voice. "It's a ritual of the People, something that will bring Petey formally under our protection. If you want any more than that, you'll have to drag it out of him."

Sera pushed her hair behind her ear with trembling fingers. "At least tell me why he's white as a sheet and running a fever."

"Because he loves you, that's why." Ruby jerked her head around. "Who drives a Ford F-150?"

"Either my dad or my brother."

Ruby nodded. "That's my cue. I'll talk to you soon." She darted off at a light jog down the driveway.

"Wait," Sera called.

Ruby turned around, walking backward along the concrete. "Can't. The men'll take care of Levi. They'll be here soon. Just leave his back alone and he'll be fine."

Sera stared after Levi's cousin. Well. That was a fine how-de-do. As soon as Ruby's blonde ponytail disappeared into the dark, lights flashed along the road at the end of the driveway and a Ford F-150 turned up it, parking on the grass in the front yard. A motorcycle followed close behind and parked on the other side.

Sera went back to Levi's car and peeked in. His eyes were still closed and his breath came in shallow, even pants. Men's voices came from the front yard as Wendell and Jack greeted someone and were answered in a rough Scottish brogue. Her shoulders sagged and her breath whooshed out. Iain. Thank God. *He* would know what to do.

The three men ambled over, all smiles and laughter, and Sera wanted to hit them for it. "I need a little help over here."

Iain raised a ginger eyebrow. "Out cold, is he?"

"Am not." Levi shifted in the seat, his gaze firm on hers. "Go on in now, love."

"I need to get you inside." She curled her fingers around the car door's frame, steadying herself. "Please, Levi. Let me get you inside so I can take care of you. Whatever it is, I swear I won't be mad if you'll just let me help you."

His smile was much closer to the smirk he'd given her the first time they'd met. "You can, promise. We'll be back in a few hours, and then I'll let you take as much care with me as you want."

She huffed out a breath. "For goodness' sake, Levi, I wasn't talking about sex."

"I know, love. Doesn't stop me wishing for it."

Large, firm hands grasped her shoulders, pulling her back. She stepped away and scowled at Iain. "You better bring him back in no worse shape."

His blue-green eyes danced under his bushy eyebrows. "Aye, lass, that I can promise. Don't worry your pretty head. He'll be right as rain by the time he gets back to you."

She leveled equally stern stares on her father and brother. They ignored her and slid into the backseat, and a few minutes later, Iain backed Levi's car down the driveway into the late summer night. She curled her fingers into her palms, digging her nails in hard. Stubborn, obstinate mule of a man. He'd obviously been hurt, but would he let her help him? Oh, no, not Mr. *I'm the Man* Levi. So help her, if he'd gone out and done something stupid, she'd tear into him when he came back home, no matter why he'd done it or what shape he was in for the doing.

THE CAR BOUNCED into a pothole, its shocks no match for the rutted dirt road. The skin of Levi's back hit the leather of the passenger seat and fire shot through raw nerves. He hissed in a breath. "Ease up, Da, will you?"

"Sorry, lad. Road's a fucking mess."

Wendell poked his head into the space between the front seats. "Too much rain this year. County's having a time keeping everything maintained. Course, we wouldn't have to worry about it if Ryan Sr. and Jr. had kept their hands off my baby girl and her boy."

Levi grunted and shifted carefully in the seat, leaning his weight on his right side. Lots of things he wouldn't have to worry about if things had been different. If Sera had been a little younger or him a little older, maybe they would've met while they were in school and she would've fallen in love with him back then. Petey would've been his kid from the start, and Levi wouldn't've had to grovel to Isolde and go about making the boy his the hard way.

Wendell let out a low whistle. "You start the fight without us, son?"

Iain glanced at Levi, then at Wendell in the rearview mirror. "He adopted Petey."

"And had to take a beating to do it?"

"That and pay a fine. The People call it Retribution, the price paid for forsaking a Son."

Levi's seat shifted under Jack's hands and pain stabbed at him.

He closed his eyes against a wince. Isolde had a helluva swing. Thank the Lady she hadn't hit him hard enough to break a rib or bruise his kidneys, or worse.

"Son of a bitch." Jack's voice was pinched and thin. "How many licks did you take?"

"Sixteen, with a cane." Levi sighed and cleared the gravel from his throat. "Eight each for his age and time away from the People. Do it again, if it meant keeping Petey safe."

Silence fell inside the car. Levi slipped into a fitful doze, barely aware of the crunch of gravel under the tires or the murmur of conversation resuming around him.

The gradual cessation of motion woke him. He forced his eyes open and stared into the dark beyond the car's window, his brain fuzzy, his body racked with chills. Shock, probably. He filed the knowledge away until he could do something about it. The door opened and gentle, work-roughened hands helped him out of the car, guiding him where he needed to be.

The dirt road gave way to grass under his feet. It was cool and prickly, and tickled memory. Summers running wild in the woods around Tellowee. Young boys' laughter, the crack of a baseball against a bat. His mother's voice calling him in to supper. He shook his head, clearing memory in favor of now, and focused on the ground beneath his feet.

A hard fist rapped on a screen door and a moment later, Wendell said, "Howdy, Ms. Lottie. We've come to talk to the reverend, if you'd fetch him for us."

Levi lifted his head. A pretty woman in her early thirties stood in the doorway of a gray, neatly-tended two-story home. She wore a pink twinset over dark jeans and her eyes darted around the men standing in her front yard. "He's in the back, Wendell. Y'all want to come in? I can fetch you some sweet tea."

"Mighty kind of you, Lottie, but this here's not something you want dragged into your home," Wendell said, and his voice was far kinder than Levi would've managed. "We won't take up much of your husband's time."

"All right then. I'll send him on out."

She let the screen door slap shut behind her and left the front door open. Light streamed into the yard through it accompanied by the faint sounds of primetime TV.

Levi tilted his head to the night sky and found the moon. It hung low along the mountains, it's pale surface turned yellow through the thick atmosphere near the horizon. He'd kissed Sera the first time under that moon, kissed her and started down the path leading him here. The hands holding his arms shifted and twitched. He inhaled a shaky breath and shrugged them off. Some things a man had to do on his own, and one of them was standing upright in front of the man that had put his hands on your woman when she wasn't willing.

Tony Ryan stepped through the screen door onto the rock steps leading to it from the yard. He was a thin man with a pleasant face capped by neatly shorn dark hair, maybe half a head taller than his wife, and dressed with the same casual polish in a collared cotton shirt tucked into jeans. "Help you, Brother Noland?"

Wendell yanked off his ball cap and held it between his hands at his waist. "Begging your pardon, Reverend, but your son, Jeremy, has been bullying one of my grandsons. He beat Petey up pretty bad yesterday, so bad Sera had to take him to the doctor."

"I'm sorry to hear that." Tony loped down the steps into the yard and tucked his fingers into the pockets of his jeans. "Lottie and I spoke with Jeremy. He's promised not to do it again."

Levi stifled a snort. As if a bully ever stopped because of one good lecture. "We've moved Petey to another school, so the bullying won't be a problem anymore."

Tony turned a placid stare on Levi. "I'm sorry, but who are you?"

"Levi Ewart, Petey's da."

Tony glanced between the men. "I was under the impression Peter's father died before his birth."

Jack crossed thick arms over his broad chest. "Levi's in the middle of adopting Petey."

"Ah." Tony smiled thinly. "Congratulations."

Wendell cleared his throat and rotated the bill of his cap through his fingers. "Thing is, we're here on another matter, too. Apparently, you were bothering my daughter to the point that she decided to leave the church."

Levi strode forward, coming even with Wendell. The bruises

along his back stretched painfully with each step and his skin went cold again. He ignored the pain and faced the man that had hurt his Sera so badly. "She says you threatened to run her out of town if she didn't sleep with you."

Tony's smile remained steady. "An unmarried woman with an illegitimate child should expect to be treated like the whore she is."

Levi swung out lightning fast and popped Tony in the jaw with a solid left hook, ripping open the cuts on his back, sending a wave of agony through him. Tony's head jerked to the side and down he went, crumpling into a heap on the grass.

Levi dropped into a crouch next to the fallen man, fighting the blackness threatening to overwhelm him. He dug his fingers into the front of the preacher's shirt and yanked him up. "Sera Noland is my woman. I ever hear tell of you even breathing near her again and I'll do more than bruise your jaw." He shoved the other man into the ground and loosened his hold. "And keep that hellion of yours away from my son while you're at it."

He staggered to his feet and threw off his da's helping hands. By the Blessed Mother, he'd stand on his own two feet if it killed him.

Wendell knelt on one knee beside the preacher's prone form. "I've already called the other deacons and let them know what's going on. Hate to embarrass your wife, but I'm calling you out in front of church Sunday morning."

Tony sat slowly up, one hand to his jaw. "You do what you have to, Wendell. I'll be sure to mention this little visit while we're at it."

Wendell nodded and levered himself into a stand. "Reverend."

The four of them marched back to the car, Levi between Iain and Jack, Wendell trailing behind.

"Remind me to never be on the wrong end of your fist," Jack muttered.

Levi snorted out a laugh. Fire raced along his skin, and he winced. Had to remember not to make any sudden moves.

They bundled into the car and headed toward The Omega, Tellowee's one and only bar. Levi's head had cleared by the time they arrived and the pain in his back had settled into a dull roar. He managed to stagger out of the car and teeter inside on his own, still shirtless and barefoot. Iain pushed his way through to the bar on the far side of the room, cutting a path for the other three men, and commandeered a spot near one end, away from the jukebox.

Levi curled his hands around the bar's edge and caught the eye of the bartender, Will Corbin, a tow-headed Son several years Levi's elder. "Start a tab for me, Will. We're celebrating."

Jack snorted. "Is that what you call taking a beating, getting a tattoo, and knocking down a man of the cloth?"

Levi managed to focus on Sera's brother through almost clear vision. "The People have gained a Son. That's always call for a drink."

A female voice on the other end of the bar called out, "A Son! Is he old enough to marry?"

"Marry, hell," another female said. "I need fresh meat."

Wendell's face reddened under his thinning hair. "Is it any use telling 'em Petey's only eight?"

Iain grinned. "They're willing to wait another eight years for him to grow into his manhood."

"God a-mercy," Jack muttered. "The women we've worked with in Tellowee have always been, ah..."

"Married," Wendell said. "We always work for the married ones, mostly anyhow. Heard the immortal ones were a bit difficult, 'specially the young'uns. Had no idea how much, though."

"This is tame," Levi said. "Wait until Petey's old enough to bed. Watch the unmated Daughters teem outta the woodwork then. They'll go after Dale and Matty, too, since they're close kin and of good stock."

Will lined four shot glasses up on the bar in front of them and filled them with amber liquid. "First round's on the house."

Levi nodded to Will and lifted a glass high in the air. "To Petey. May he live a long and happy life among the People."

"And to his da," Iain said. "May he find peace with the woman he loves."

Wendell raised his glass. "Amen to that."

They tossed the whiskey back and ordered another round. Levi flexed his hand, stretching the cuts on his knuckles where they'd grated along Tony Ryan's jaw. The numbness spread by the alcohol was a blessing, easing the agony in his back, but this pain, earned taking down a man that had put his grubby paws on Sera, was one he wanted to savor for a while.

He turned to the crowd and pitched his voice above the hum of laughter and conversation and the music beating out of the jukebox. "I have a son," he shouted, and the crowd's roaring cheer echoed the joy in his heart. "Drinks are on me."

He endured the congratulations and slaps to his upper arms with unsteady grins.

Jack eased his body between Levi and the crowd, deflecting some of the blows. "When are you gonna tell Sera?"

Levi tossed back another drink and hissed around the trail of heat it burned down his throat. "Not until I have to."

"She's gonna fuss."

"Then she'll have to fuss. Petey needs a da."

Jack nodded. "You love her?"

Levi met the other man's stare evenly. "So much it hurts."

"She'll come around, then." Jack wrapped a steadying hand around Levi's upper arm and hauled him upright. "Man, you got it bad. You sure you don't wanna go back to Sera's?"

Levi pressed a shaky hand to his forehead, unsurprised by the dry heat radiating off his skin. "Soon. Promised her I'd be home around eleven."

"Home, huh?" Jack shook his head and a grin grew steadily on his face. "Hot damn, man. I reckon we finally found somebody who's almost good enough for her."

Levi peered at Jack through one bleary eye. "You're still pissed about the berry farm, aren't you."

Jack's silver eyes, so like Sera's, glinted in the low light of the bar above the grin stretched across his face. "Yeah, I kinda am. Don't worry, though. I won't let you forget it."

Levi laughed, half humor, half air. "Another round?"

"Hell, why not. It's not every day a man becomes a father."

Will obligingly set another round of shots in front of them. Wendell offered a toast, and they all drank to the night and the family a man made with the promises of his heart.

Twenty-Four

PETEY FELL ASLEEP on the couch in the middle of *Lilo and Stitch*. Sera let him stay up late, as much to keep her company as anything. When she realized he was fast asleep, she turned off the movie and carried him to his bedroom, tucking him beneath the covers with her mother's hands.

Her brave little man. He'd only complained about the bruises dotting his body once, though he winced when he lifted his right arm too high. She smoothed his hair down and kissed his forehead, then wandered into her office.

Checking her e-mail took all of fifteen minutes. She answered one from a fan, sent a brief note to her agent in response to a request for clarification of a previous one. Logged in to Facebook and posted a message that she'd be away from her computer through the weekend. She glanced at her watch and groaned. Levi wouldn't be back for at least half an hour, and more like an hour and a half.

God, what had he done to himself? She leaned back in her chair and chewed on a thumbnail. He'd made a habit of holding back certain parts of himself since the first time they'd talked that day on the beach. Her eyes drifted to the picture of him and Petey she'd tucked into a corner of the message board hanging above her desk. She'd caught them talking, their heads bent close together as they discussed serious man stuff. Levi had heard the whir of her camera and looked around, a soft smile on his face, and she'd clicked again, catching him hovering protectively over Petey, guarding her son as if he were Levi's own, and Petey staring up at

Levi as if he'd hung the moon.

As far as she could tell, he had.

For the first time in Petey's life, she'd had someone to lean on during a hard spot. Her parents and Jack and Candi were good in a pinch, but they had their own problems to worry over. Levi had been there for her and Petey, really been there, just when she'd needed him the most.

He'd promised to stick, and boy, had he ever, so why did he still feel the need to shut her out?

She glanced at her watch and nearly growled. 9:48. Why didn't he come home already? What could possibly have taken the whole afternoon and evening for him to do?

She snagged her laptop and toted it into the living room where she could keep a better ear out for his car. She opened up an old title she'd decided to re-edit and tried to focus on it. The minutes ticked slowly by. 10:13. 10:27. 11:05, and still no Levi. She gave up on work and retrieved her Kindle, opening it to the Nalini Singh novel she was reading, and stared blankly at the screen. 11:16. 11:32. 11:49.

At just after midnight, a car pulled into her drive. She set her Kindle aside, hurried into the kitchen, and flung open the outside door.

Noreen stepped out of the driver's side door and waved her over. "I'm glad you're awake. It'll take both of us to get him inside."

Sera bounced down the steps and over to the car. Iain was sprawled along the backseat, his head lolling against one of the windows. "Where're Dad and Jack?"

"Your mother came and picked them up from the bar. Drunk as skunks, the lot of them." Noreen shook her head and slipped around the front end of the car. She opened the door, ducked into it, and murmured, "Come on, baby. You're almost there."

Levi shifted in the passenger's seat and turned toward his mother, his body shadowed in the low light cast by the car's interior fixture. Noreen pulled him out of the car into a wobbly stand. He leaned into the hands she wrapped around his arm and staggered with her around the car and across the driveway. His cheeks were flushed and his eyes unfocused through half-closed eyelids, and even from a few feet away, he reeked of alcohol.

Sera wrinkled her nose. "Is he drunk?"

"I wish." Noreen staggered to the side under Levi's weight, then jerked her chin at Sera. "Get the door, would you?"

Sera hurried to comply, holding the door open while Noreen manhandled her son through the doorway. She put her foot on the bottom step once they passed and her eyes caught on the mass of welts and bruises marring Levi's once flawless back. Her stomach twisted and bile rose in her throat. "Oh, my God," she breathed. "What happened?"

"Retribution. Which way to a bed?"

"To the left through the living room. Hold on."

Sera squeezed around them, careful not to touch Levi, and led them through the house, pushing the coffee table out of the way to clear a path. She turned the covers down on her bed and, when Noreen directed her to, tugged Levi's jeans and underwear off. His skin was hot to the touch, and no matter how careful she was, he flinched every time her fingers brushed across him.

She knelt on the bed and helped Noreen ease him down onto his stomach. A heavy ache pushed its way through the nausea, settling in her chest and throat, squeezing the breath out of her. "Why didn't you take him to a doctor?"

"It'll pass. In the morning, he'll wake up clear-headed and stiff as a dry log, but he'll be fine."

"How can you be so casual about this?" Sera's fingers hovered over the tender flesh of his back. "Someone beat him and you just shrug it off?"

Noreen's amber eyes hardened as she stared down at Sera. "I held him while he was beaten, held him while he claimed your son as his own, all the while muttering that the beating he took was nothing compared to the one he could've prevented."

"He claimed Petey? What..." Sera blinked through the tears clogging her head. "What does that mean?"

"That your son is now Levi's in the eyes of the People. That Levi is responsible for him, and through him, you." Noreen's gaze drifted to her son and softened. "Have a care with my son's heart, Sera. Once given, it will never be his again."

"I'll do my best."

"See that you do." A faint smile graced Noreen's elegant

features. "I'll see myself out."

"Wait." Sera held her hand out, halting Levi's mother. "How do I take care of him?"

"I'll leave some salve in the kitchen for you. Apply it every couple of hours, sooner if he gets restless. Be sure to wash it off in the morning."

"And the fever?"

"It'll take care of itself, though if it gets too high, call me. Cover him if he gets chilled." Noreen smiled again, this one as gentle as the last. "You've tended Petey through worse, I'm sure."

"Not quite," Sera murmured.

Noreen left quietly. Sera ignored the kitchen door opening and shutting as the other woman came in and out, and focused on Levi. The bedside lamp threw a thin stream of light over the sweat glistening along his forehead. She touched timid fingers there and bit back a curse. He was cold and clammy, and a fine tremor ran through him. She rushed into the bathroom and wet a cloth, cleaned his feet (What had he been doing, running around without shoes all night?), and covered him to a few inches below the lowest mark on his back.

He shifted on the bed and stretched a questing hand out, eyes closed tight. "Sera."

She cupped his hand between both of hers. "I'm right here, Levi."

"Missed you." A rattling breath shuddered out of his chest. "Don't worry. It'll pass."

"I know. I know, baby." She ran her fingers over his hair, brushing the silky strands off his forehead. "Your fever's breaking now."

"Shock," he mumbled. "Hurts."

"I'll get the salve."

He tightened his fingers around hers. "Don't leave me, Sera. Please don't leave me."

"I'm not. Shh." She sighed and stretched out on the bed next to him. The salve could wait, at least for a while. "I'm here, Levi."

He pulled her hand closer, tucking it under the firm muscle of his shoulder. "Love you."

She eased herself as close to him as she dared. "Shh. Rest

now."

His muscles relaxed and his grip on her loosened, and soon his breaths evened out. She watched him through the long night, caring for him as best she could, and prayed to God he'd really be ok when he woke with the new day.

LEVI FLOATED to awareness along softly ascending plateaus. Birds twittered and chirped outside the window. He listened to them for a while, content with their chatter and the warm body he'd curled himself around. *Sera.* He strummed a thumb along her stomach through the t-shirt she'd worn to bed and rubbed his chin over the top of her head, immersing himself in the floral scent of her shampoo. Beautiful, sweet Sera, his woman and the mother of his first child. He loved waking up to her every day.

The light in the room brightened, noticeable even through his closed eyelids. It was morning. He should go for a long run, and after, he and Petey could cook breakfast and tend the yard while Sera supervised. They could go to the lake that afternoon, catch the last warmth of summer before fall swept in and cooled the water. Or he could start working with Petey on basketball. Registration for rec ball was just around the corner. Maybe he and Jack could coach a team together.

First, though, he'd make love to the woman nestled so trustingly in his embrace. He stroked a hand down her stomach, tugging at the muscles in his back. A dull ache rippled through him and the fog of memory descended, blurred by pain and shock and a few too many sips of Will Corbin's best whiskey. Claiming Petey. Bruising that ass Tony Ryan's smooth jaw. Knocking back shot after shot with his da and Wendell and Jack at The Omega, and proclaiming to everybody within earshot that he had a son.

He smiled and tightened his hold on Sera. He had a son, and soon, he'd have a wife, too. Every day, he worked hard, showing her how much he cared for her, how much he ached to have her by his side, and every day, she softened a little more toward him. Surely by the winter solstice she'd be ready to admit that he held a piece of her heart. Surely by then, he could talk her 'round to allowing him a permanent place in her life.

She stirred in his arms and wiggled around to face him, moving slowly. Dark circles marred the smooth skin under her eyes and a furrow appeared between her eyebrows. "You're awake."

"Mmm."

She cupped his jaw and caressed her thumb over his cheek. "I didn't think you'd wake up today."

"It wasn't that bad."

Her eyes widened. "Good Lord, Levi. Your back is a mass of bruises and it was oozing blood last night. You ran hot and cold all night and mumbled in your sleep and, God, I was so worried you wouldn't be ok."

"I'm sorry, love." He tucked her into the curve of his body, comforting her. "I should've told you what to expect beforehand so you'd be prepared to deal with it."

Her sigh feathered over his chest. "Yes, you should've. I can't believe you keep leaving me in the dark. Do you really trust me that little?"

He drew back and frowned down at her. "Of course, I trust you, Sera. You're just not ready to accept some parts of my life yet."

"How can you know that? How can *I* know I'm ready when you hold so much back?" Her silver eyes searched his, seeking answers he wasn't sure he could give her. "Your mother had to tell me about the beating you took. Your mother, Levi. That should've been you, and you should've asked me before you did it. You should've explained what you were doing and why, and I shouldn't be wondering what's going on, especially when my son's involved."

He sighed, knowing she was right, knowing part of the reason he held back was out of his own insecurity. What if he told her everything and she rejected him? What if she couldn't accept him as he was, his duties and responsibilities to the People, and his need to love and protect her and Petey, even when it meant going behind her back to do it?

Still, it wasn't fair for him to keep her in the dark. She'd eventually learn anyway. "Ok, love. Help me up and I'll explain what I can."

She eased away from him off the bed and pulled and tugged while he pushed his way into a seat on its edge. The dull throb in his back morphed into a slow burn and sweat popped out on his skin.

She turned toward the bathroom, and he caught her hand, halting her.

"Wait. I need your help before you leave."

"I'm not leaving, Levi." She shook her head and laughed, and his heart caught on the bitter note underlying the sound. "Last night, you kept asking me not to leave, over and over again, as if I ever would."

He dropped his gaze to the floor, afraid the fear eating through him would show in his expression. "You don't love me."

"I care for you, enough to know I could never leave you. You've had me since that first night on the beach when you held my hand and listened to me ramble, and after, you kissed me senseless and didn't take advantage of my weakness."

"Only because you weren't ready for me to." He rolled his shoulders, easing some of the ache in his back, stretching out the stiffness. "You think I'm too young."

"Oh, that again," she said, and he glanced up sharply at the humor in her voice. She cupped her hands around his face and kissed his forehead gently. "I know you're too young for me, Levi, but I stopped caring a long time ago. You're more of a man at twenty-two than most men are at forty. I'm so thankful you took those bets and wiggled your way into my life."

"Yeah?"

"Yes," she said firmly. "Now, let me get a cloth to clean your back."

"I'd rather have a shower, if you'll take this stuff off my shoulder."

She hesitated, then crawled gingerly onto the bed, settling behind him. Her fingers plucked at the tape holding the protective plastic over his new tattoo. "The cuts have finally scabbed over."

"Another day and they'll close up completely." He stifled a laugh at her cautious tugs on the tape. "It'll hurt less if you rip it off."

"I'm not doing that, not when your back's still in such bad shape."

He rolled his eyes skyward. "Rip the damn tape off, Sera. Please. Just get it over with."

"God, you're such a man." She lifted a corner of the tape and yanked, pulling the covering off in one vicious swipe. "There.

Happy now?"

"Actually, yeah, I am." And he was, in spite of everything. A son and soon her, forever. Did she know how much she'd blessed him the day she'd accepted him into her life, even as tentatively as she had? "I guess you want to know what it is."

"Any idiot can see it's a sun," she grumped.

He snickered. Sweet, little Sera had her dander up, didn't she, and it tickled him to hear it in her voice, pleased him to know she was that way out of concern for him. "It's a symbol for Petey, since he likes science so much, and because he's the brightest part of your life."

"Oh." Her fingertips circled lightly around the stylized sun on his shoulder. "That's really kind of...sweet."

There she went again, editing her words. What had she omitted in favor of the milder word she'd chosen to share? "Traditionally, Sons wear little clothing, so the tattoos show who we belong to and who belongs to us. When I get married, my wife's mark will go on my left shoulder blade, and when we have more children, their marks will go to the side of Petey's."

"I see." Her fingers dropped away and her voice went quiet. "Have you... Are you engaged?"

He frowned. Why would she ask if he'd already committed to somebody, when his heart so clearly belonged to her? "No."

"Do you know who your wife will be? I mean, does your family pick her out or something?"

"If I hadn't found somebody by the time I was, say, thirty, Nana or Gran would've picked somebody out for me, probably based on alliances that would benefit our family." He shifted around on the bed, facing her. "As for my future wife, yes, I know who she'll be."

Her eyes slid away from his and an odd expression flitted across her face. "Do you need help in the shower?"

"Wait." He caught her chin and turned her face back to his. "What's going on in that pretty head of yours?"

Her gaze remained stubbornly shuttered. "I'm wondering if you need help with a shower."

"Come on, Sera. Tell me what's wrong."

"Nothing." Her voice was unsteady, belying the denial. "Let me clean you up and get some breakfast in you, and then I want to hear all about why you took it upon yourself to endure a beating for my son."

He let her chin go as she slipped off the bed and out the bedroom door, checking on Petey. What had he said that would leave her so cautious? He thought back over the conversation, trying to pinpoint his error, and came up empty. Maybe she was unsure about the customs of the People and worried that Nana would force him into another match, but hadn't he all but told Sera he wanted to marry her? Couldn't she see that as much as she claimed to be his, he was equally hers?

He rubbed his hands over his face and grimaced at the sticky feel of his skin and the stench of alcohol seeping from his pores. He levered himself slowly off the bed and shambled carefully into the bathroom, thankful for his nudity. If it weren't for the people he was sure would be dropping by all day long, he'd wander around in his underwear, but no. A Son had come to the People and word would get out. He paused in the doorway and sighed. He needed to warn Sera about that, too. Maybe she wouldn't mind so much. Mortal Southerners celebrated life about the same way.

She slipped into the shower not long after he stepped under the warm spray, and scrubbed him from head to toe, washing the tender flesh of his back with her hands, gently cleaning off the salve his mother had spread across the wounds. While she washed, he explained the ritual for claiming a Son, how the People valued male offspring both for their rareness and as a symbol of a Daughter's mortality, and how the penalty for abandoning a Son was high precisely because they were so valued. He glossed over his assumption of the sins of Petey's father, when the man had chosen to walk out of Sera's life rather than accept responsibility for his own actions. Her hands paused in mid stroke, like she'd understood exactly what Levi was saying.

He didn't remind her that he'd done what he had because it was best for Petey to have a father in his life, best for Petey to be among the protection of the People, best for Petey to attend school in Tellowee where he'd be welcome. What Levi had done was best for all of them, really. As far as he was concerned, they were a family. Whatever steps he had to take to show the world that, well, that's what he'd do.

She helped him over the edge of the tub and dried him off, and when she was finished and his explanation was as complete as he could make it, she stood before him with her head bowed and the towel hanging from her hand. "Just tell me one thing."

He cupped her slender shoulders, willing her to look at him. "Anything, love."

"You'll never abandon Petey, will you?"

He huffed out a laugh. What kind of question was that? Hadn't he just explained what Petey meant to him? "Of course not. He's my son now. Even if I hadn't formally claimed him, I wouldn't just leave."

"Even if you never get married?"

His hands tightened on her skin. Was that what worried her, that he'd abandon her and her son if she didn't do what he wanted her to do, when he wanted her to do it? A quiet humor rose in him. She was so much stronger than she believed herself to be. How could he love her if she weren't? "Even then, love."

Her shoulders rose and fell on a shuddering breath, lifting his hands. "Thank you, Levi."

"For what?"

"For being what we need. For sticking by us when things got a little rough." She stroked her palms lightly over his chest, curling her fingertips into the hair scattered across his skin. "You have no idea what that means to me, and to Petey."

He was beginning to, though, just as she was beginning to believe in him. "Mum should be here soon. Breakfast."

A small smile tugged at her mouth. "I'm not that bad of a cook."

"Never said you were. It's traditional. Besides, there'll be people in and out all day. You'll be busy playing beloved mother."

"Beloved mother, huh." Her smile stretched into a grin. "The People have some strange customs, Levi."

"Speak for yourself. I've attended foot washings and snake handlings and..."

"Those aren't my customs," she said primly, and he laughed and wrapped himself around her and let her talk him out of going back to bed, only because his mother's voice already mingled with Petey's in the kitchen. Later, though, he'd pull her into bed and show her how much he looked forward to the day they'd be married, aching bruises on his back or not.

PART THREE

Knowing

Twenty-Five

TEN PENCILS SCRATCHED math problems onto paper as Mr. Lowell recited them. Petey wrote every problem down exactly the way his teacher called them out, careful to get everything just right. Since starting school in Tellowee, he'd learned a lot of things. One of the biggest was how important it was to get the details right. At his old school, his teacher would've given him a worksheet already full of problems, but here, Petey was responsible for writing them down. If he didn't get the problem right, he'd get the answer wrong and Mr. Lowell would write a red x next to it.

Mama fussed if Petey got too many red exes, and that made his chest go all funny inside, like it did when she fussed 'cause he didn't mind like he should. What bothered him the most, though, was the look Levi would get on his face, all stern and serious. "Petey, lad," he'd say, "your grade isn't as important as the lesson you missed."

Petey hated missing lessons almost as much as he hated disappointing Levi.

Everything had changed when Mama had let Petey go to school in Tellowee. Here, nobody made fun because his real dad died before he was born. Lots of the kids didn't have dads in Tellowee, especially the girls. Nobody snuck punches at him in the bathroom and nobody but nobody held him down on the playground and beat him up. Plus, Maetyrm Holly was teaching him how to fight, though he had to go in with the little kids 'cause he'd never learned how before and had to start from scratch.

But that was ok. Nobody made fun of him for that, neither. And, *way cool*, Mama bought him a costume just like Levi's and Petey got to wear it every day.

School sure was harder at Tellowee, though. Petey stuck his tongue between his front teeth, all grown in now, and wrote down another problem. The first day he'd been a real student, he'd spent all afternoon in Principal Devlin's office taking tests, and part of the next day talking about them with the principal and Mama and Levi. He'd ended up in sixth year reading, which was way cool but really hard, and fourth year math, but when he'd said he wanted to take second year math with Zach and Charlie, they'd let him. How awesome was that? Sometimes Mr. Lowell gave Petey different work, but mostly, he got to hang out with his new friends, and they were just as nice to him as Dale and Matty.

"Petey," Mr. Lowell said, "are you paying attention?"

Petey continued writing. "Yes, sir."

"Then I'm sure you won't mind telling me what I just said."

"No, sir." Without thinking, Petey repeated Mr. Lowell's last words in his teacher's Yankee twang. "Seven cahs were red, six were blue, and nine were white. What is the ratio of blue cahs to red, and white cahs to the total?"

Mr. Lowell cleared his throat. "And before that?"

Petey put a question mark at the end of the world problem. "Ratios ah not a joking matter, Zacheus."

The room fell into silence. Petey glanced up. Everybody was staring at him, even Mr. Lowell. His teacher had a funny look on his face. Uh-oh. Petey's cheeks heated. He laid his pencil on top of his notebook and stood up beside his desk, facing Mr. Lowell head on. Petey squared his shoulders and prepared himself to receive a good talking to over whatever it was he'd done wrong.

A man never hid from his mistakes. Levi had taught him that.

Mr. Lowell's shoes rapped against the tile floor. He knelt in front of Petey, his blue eyes soft and kind. "Where did you learn to do that, Petey?"

"Um. Do what, sir?"

"Mimic the way someone speaks."

Petey shrugged one thin shoulder. "I don't know, sir. It just comes natural like, I reckon. I didn't mean no sass."

"I didn't think so, though I can't let it pass. Too much temptation for your classmates." Mr. Lowell smiled. "Do you mind doing something for me?"

"Ah, no, sir."

"Can you remember what I said at the beginning of class?"

"Um." Petey thought back and dutifully recited, " 'Class, today we shall continue working with ratios.' And then Zach went like this," Petey pulled his face into a grimace, "and said, 'Gawdess, not more ratios.' And Charlie said, 'Give it a rest, Zach.' And you said, 'Boys, leave your discussion for the break, when it's appropriate.' And Annabelle rolled her eyes and..."

Mr. Lowell laughed and his eyes crinkled at the corners. "Ok, ok, I think I get it. You're better than a recorder."

"I didn't mean no..."

"Sass. Yes, I know. Are you sure you don't want to move up in math?"

Petey peeked at Zach and Charlie, the best friends he'd ever had except for Dale and Matty. "I like second year math, sir."

"Ok, then. Stay after class for a minute so I can assign extra work." Mr. Lowell sighed and stood up. He was really tall. Not as tall as Levi. Almost nobody was as big as that, but Mr. Lowell was still a lot taller than Petey. "The first person I hear trying to do what Petey just did gets a double load of homework for a week. Is that clear?"

A chorus of *yessirs* echoed around the classroom. Petey slid into his seat and picked his pencil up. Zach hissed at him and caught his eye. *Later,* his friend mouthed, and Petey grinned. That was the signal for a get-together at recess on the playground, where they'd laugh and joke and tell stories, which was the best thing *ever.*

What was even better was when Zach and Charlie helped him learn to fight and he helped them with math and reading. Friends were supposed to help each other out. It was, like, a rule or something, only he'd never had friends before, not really. That was the bestest thing about going to school in Tellowee. Here, he had friends, real friends that talked with him and wanted to hang out, even though he sucked at sports and wheezed when he ran too fast. Sometimes, they even came over to his house after school or he went over to theirs, and they hung out and played video games and ate junk food when their mamas weren't looking. How cool was that?

But the bestest most magnificentest thing ever was Levi. Ever since the day Jeremy Ryan beat Petey up, Levi had spent more and more time with them. Sometimes he could only stay for a day, but sometimes he stayed three or four and worked at his desk in Mama's new office in the old library while Petey was at school. And when Levi was home, he'd take Petey outside and teach him how to dribble and shoot the basketball. Mama had signed him up on the same team as Matty at the Rec Department, and Levi and Uncle Jack were gonna coach them. Petey worked real hard and practiced every single day, and sometimes, he even hit the rim of the goal with the basketball.

Even better than all that was Mama. She smiled all the time now, especially when Levi was home. It was almost like they were a real family, just like he'd been praying for ever since Levi first came to visit. Any day now, he expected Mama to tell him they was gonna marry Levi, and then everything would be about perfect. Levi would be his dad and Mama would be happy, and maybe they'd even find a brother for him in the cabbage patch, where Mama said she found him.

Mr. Lowell finished saying the last problem, then dismissed the class. Petey stuffed his notebook and pencil into his Star Wars backpack, high-fived Zach and Charlie, and promised Annabelle he'd sit with her in science. She liked to hold his hand sometimes. He didn't mind so much, as long as he didn't have to be nekkid to do it.

No matter what Levi said, Petey didn't think he'd ever want to hold hands nekkid with a girl, especially not Annabelle. She was bigger than him and could beat everybody in school in fight class, even Zach. She was nice and all, but that was kinda scary.

Petey stopped at Mr. Lowell's desk on the way out. "I'm ready for my extra work, sir."

Mr. Lowell smiled. He had a good smile. It went right up into his eyes and stayed there for a long time after. "Three paragraphs on Euclid of Alexandria by Monday. Good-sized paragraphs, too, not Zach-sized ones."

Petey grinned. Zach was sneaky sometimes, especially when it came to getting out of math homework. "Yes, sir."

"And Petey? Tell your mother I'd like to speak with her about that memory of yours."

"I will, sir."

"Go on, now. Zach and Charlie are likely waiting on the playground for a report on how hard your extra homework will be."

Petey dashed out of the classroom, slowing to a normal walk when Principal Devlin rounded the corner. She nodded to him and said, "Eknon," the People's word for student, and he nodded back and said, "Maetyrm," which always made her smile, then put his backpack away in his locker.

Zach and Charlie and Annabelle and everybody else from second year math were waiting for him outside. Petey raced down the stairs right into the group, just like he was a real Son and everything, and didn't even mind when Annabelle slung her arm around his shoulders and planted a big one on his cheek.

SERA SPENT THE DAY after Halloween in a mad rush of errands. Her latest manuscript had absorbed all her time for the entire week and now they were out of everything, just everything. Since Petey had started school in Tellowee, his appetite had doubled, maybe from all the exercise the kids there got. If it wasn't one thing, it was another. Two periods of PE during the day plus recess and extra classes for the kids wanting them. On top of that, basketball was about to start and Petey spent at least half an hour every day outside practicing. He'd also been doing a hard sell for riding lessons, egged on by Levi's grandmother. So far, Sera had managed to hold firm, mostly because her son was already eating her out of house and home. How much worse would it be if he added yet another activity?

Not that she minded so much. For the first time since he was a toddler, Petey was gaining weight and adding muscle to his thin frame. And he was *happy*. Every day, he came home from school with a smile on his face, no matter how much homework he had. He'd become fast friends with a handful of children in his classes and got along well with everyone else. Sera had even started letting him walk to his friends' houses after school once a week or so. As Levi had pointed out, it was Tellowee. The community was so close-knit, a stranger never passed through without drawing attention. Petey was safe there, safer than he'd ever been anywhere else except

311

running between their home and her family's property.

Tonight, he'd be going to his first sleepover ever, at a girl's house, no less. Petey's friend Annabelle had turned nine on the twenty-eighth and most of the school-aged kids in Tellowee under twelve years were turning out for the party. Later, a handful would spend the night in Annabelle's rambling Victorian house under the strict supervision of her mother, Grace. The immortal Daughter's cold eyes scared the ever living hooha out of Sera. One thing was for sure. As long as Grace was there, the kids wouldn't get up to any funny business, the only reason Sera had allowed Petey to attend the sleepover. What kid in his right mind would dare disobey a woman better known as Bloodbringer?

Zach and Charlie, Petey's closest friends at his new school, knew Dale and Matty from the various sports they all played. It made for an entertaining couple of hours when the two came over to hang out with Petey. Sera had gotten to know their parents and the parents of some of the other kids, and through them, she'd begun to learn more about the People. A couple of the mothers had volunteered to act as sources for a historical romance Sera had been toying with writing for a few years. What better way to gather research than from someone that had actually lived through an historical era?

Once she got used to the idea of people being cursed to immortality, Sera had found it easy to accept the rest. So the People of Tellowee were a little odd. As Levi had pointed out, mortal humans were, too, especially in their religious beliefs. By comparison, the People were fairly tame, Retribution excepted.

Nearly two months later, she was still trying to wrap her head around the fact that Levi had claimed Petey as his son and taken a severe beating to do it. What kind of man endured such great pain for a child outside of his own blood kin?

Sera parked outside of Ingles and dashed inside, list in hand. She snagged a buggy, her thoughts caught on the question she'd asked herself every single day since Levi had come home that night, unable to care for himself, with deep bruises and a new tattoo on his back. The answer was the easy part. Levi was that kind of man. The whys of it all were the real crux of her problem.

She zipped through the wide aisles, smiling at people she didn't know, stopping to chat with the ones she did. In between, she filled the buggy with enough food for a family twice hers in size. Well, twice the size of a mortal family. Sera had learned fairly quickly that Sons had high metabolisms, and once she had, she'd been grateful Levi had set up an account for them at the grocery store in Tellowee, especially once Petey had started following in Levi's footsteps.

Though she still tried to talk Levi into letting her pay him back for her and Petey's share, an offer he'd flatly refused again and again, usually accompanied by his *I'm the man* stare. If he had, she'd be at Evangeline's in Tellowee right then instead of at the Ingles in Clayton, buying half of their month's groceries so Levi wouldn't bear the entire burden of feeding them.

In the checkout line, Sera checked the time on her watch and grimaced. If she hurried, she could get the groceries home and the cold items stashed safely away before she had to pick Petey up from school. Drat her stubborn hide, and Levi's, too. Why was he so resistant to letting them each pay their own way?

When Sera pulled into her driveway fifteen minutes later, Levi's Audi was parked in his spot. Her heart leapt into a rapid patter and warmth pooled within her. Nearly four months after meeting him, knowing he was nearby still had that effect on her. Maybe it always would or maybe it would mellow over time, but she hoped not. He meant too much to her for her to want the odd rush of desire he stirred to ever fade.

She popped the trunk on her station wagon and gathered up a box of bagged groceries. As she was lifting it, Levi stepped out of the house wearing a pair of navy blue athletic shorts and running shoes, the rest of him bare and beautiful.

He jogged toward her, his toned muscles bunching and flexing with every step. The bright November sun glinted off his fiery hair. "I'll get that, love."

"No, I'll get it, if you'll just walk back to the door and jog to me again."

His mouth twisted into a familiar smirk. "So, that run at the beach was what won you over, huh."

Oh, if he only knew. The memory of him jogging away from her that day, his long legs eating up the distance, his back muscles rippling under his pale skin, was enough to shoot heat spiraling through her. God, he was sexy, and he knew it, too. "Aren't you cold?"

He shrugged and slid his hands around the bottom of the box, lifting it easily away from her. "The house is warm."

"So you stripped down." She shook her head and snagged a smaller box. "I've never met anyone who dislikes clothes as much as you do."

"Hate being confined." He pivoted toward the house. "'Sides, the fewer clothes I wear, the easier it is for you to have your way with me."

As if. He was usually the one to instigate sex, and she never turned him down. Their time together was too precious to her. Her eyes fell on the faint scars along his lower back and the stylized sun tattooed into the skin over his right shoulder blade. *Levi* was precious to her and for more than just sex. He was the closest friend she'd ever had and he was slowly becoming the father Petey had yearned for since he was old enough to feel the lack.

They dropped the groceries on the counter, and Levi immediately tugged her close, burying his face in her throat. "Sweet Goddess, you smell good. Is that a new perfume?"

She cupped the back of his head in one hand and curled the fingers of her other hand into the taut muscles of his shoulder. His mouth trailed hot kisses along her skin, and she nearly lost track of his question. "Ah, no. I'm not wearing perfume."

"Mmm." He tilted his head and licked the pulse at the base of her throat. "Taste good, too. How much time before school is out?"

Sera checked her watch and stifled a mild curse. "Less than fifteen minutes. I need to get the groceries out of the car and put them away."

He sighed and drew back. "I'll do it if you want to take the Audi."

She pressed her lips together, holding back her automatic refusal. Instead, she rose on tiptoes and kissed him full on the mouth, lingering longer than she should've. "I love your mouth, I really do, but I gotta go or I'll be late."

"Later," he promised.

Boy, would she hold him to that. She dashed out of the house

314

at a near run, adjusted the Audi's driver's seat for her much shorter legs, and made it to the school just as Petey was walking out the front door, his hand held tightly in Annabelle's. Sera would worry, but she'd seen how affectionate the kids in Tellowee were. The teachers never let it go beyond casual hugs and kisses, not even in the high school, though outside of school was another matter, if Levi could be believed.

She had a feeling he'd given her a highly edited version of his own days at school.

Sera waved at Annabelle. The young girl nodded solemnly, then kissed Petey's cheek. He grinned and raced to the car, his thin body slightly more graceful than it had been two months before. He bounced into the backseat and buckled up. "Hey, Mama. Mr. Lowell wants to talk to you."

Sera backed out of the parking lot. "Anything serious?"

"I got in trouble for saying stuff back to him the way he said it. I wasn't sassing, promise. And then, he asked me what he said at the beginning of class and I said all that back to him, too, and he said maybe he should talk to you about my memory." Petey shrugged. "I thought I said it all back ok, but he seemed kinda worried about it. You think my brain's got a hole in it or something?"

She pressed her lips together, hiding a smile. "I don't know. Maybe I should take you to Doc Ethan and have him check you over."

Petey's eyes widened. "Really, Mama?"

"No, sweetie. I think Mr. Lowell understands that you have a good memory and wants to find the best way to help you use it." Much like Petey's other teachers. They were coming to know Petey very well and worked hard to tailor his education to his specific talents and needs. "So you have extra homework this weekend?"

"Yes'm. Three paragraphs due on Monday." Petey slumped into his seat and stared out the window. "I really like Mr. Lowell."

"Me, too." And she did. She liked all of Petey's new teachers. She liked the school and the administration, and she liked it very much that Petey was happy there, really happy. Thank God she'd listened to Levi.

As soon as she turned the ignition off, Petey was out the door and inside the house, hollering for Levi. She followed at a more sedate pace and found them huddled together at the kitchen table, Petey's dark head nearly touching Levi's brighter one, Levi's hand on Petey's smaller shoulder. Anyone seeing them together would think them father and son. In a way, they were, at least as far as Levi was concerned, and that didn't bother her at all. She'd once thought it would, having someone else interfere in her son's life, but with Levi, there was never a question in her mind that he loved Petey as much as she did, and would do everything in his power to protect the little boy.

For once, she was glad Kyle Vincent had run out on them. If he hadn't, she might never have met Levi, and without him, she and Petey would be lost.

She scooted Petey off to pack for the sleepover and slid into Levi's arms, settling on his lap with his arms loose around her. She tugged his head down and touched her lips to his, lingering for long, sweet moments. His arms tightened around her and he *hmmd* deep in his throat, and it felt so right she could hardly bring herself to stop.

He pulled away and peppered kisses along her jaw, down her throat, skimming his mouth in a hot line above the neckline of her shirt. "You really don't have a new perfume?"

She laughed softly and rubbed her fingertips over his chest. Touching him, having him near, holding him; that never got old. "I really don't."

"How long until Zach's mum picks Petey up?"

"A couple of hours."

"A whole night alone." He touched his forehead to hers and his breath shuddered out of him. "The things I'm gonna do to you, Serafina."

His eyes were hot and wild, need burning brightly in them, and she smiled, even as that wild need began to burn in her. "Is that code for *I want to tie you up and do wicked things to you?*"

"It's code for, I can't wait to be inside you." He kissed her lightly and patted her bottom. "Think I'll go for a run."

She slid off his lap, regretting the loss of his embrace as soon as she was out of it. "Put some clothes on. It's getting chilly outside."

He shook his head and stepped outside wearing only the silky shorts and running shoes he'd greeted her in. "Best get some of this out of my system before Petey leaves, else I'll have you flat on your back the minute he's out the door."

She snorted out a laugh. Like she'd object. "Don't be long."

He turned, walking backwards, and smirked at her. "Be ready for me when I get back."

"Go on with you, then."

She stared after him through the glass panes in the kitchen door as he loped away, and lost sight of her beautiful sun god when he hit the end of the driveway. Humor and desire warred within her. She'd be ready for him, all right, ready and more than willing to love him through the night ahead. Petey hollered for her, and she grinned. In the meantime, she had one little boy to feed and prepare for his first party without his mom. After that, though, Levi was all hers.

Twenty-Six

A BREEZE SPRANG UP as the sun's lower edge skimmed the mountaintops, chilling Levi's sweat-soaked skin. His feet pounded on the asphalt, his pace quick and even. An hour running from Sera hadn't done a damn thing to tire his need for her. It burned through him, stronger than it ever had, so strong he'd been half an inch away from lifting her onto the table and sinking into her soft, welcoming flesh, Petey down the hall or not.

By the Lady, he needed to get a grip on his body. It was one thing to lose control when they were in bed together, and something else when they weren't. His control had always been shaky around Sera, but this was ridiculous. Sooner or later, the urgent need tugging at him had to mellow into comfort, didn't it?

He wound his way along the roadways, circling around, letting his mind drift and his muscles loosen, finding peace in the steady thump of his feet on the road. Sera, beautiful Sera. Four months ago, before he'd even met her, he'd only dreamed of wanting a woman the way he craved her, and prayed the woman he found would want him the same way.

She was coming around to that, slowly accepting him in her life.

He grinned and sprinted the last fifty yards to the bottom of her driveway, then slowed to a walk, cooling off as his breath panted in satisfying heaves in and out of his lungs. A white, late model Jetta wagon was parked behind his Audi, exactly the kind he'd been eyeing for Sera as a replacement for her decade-old station wagon. He circled the Jetta, examining it from every angle. Six speed, diesel engine. Roomy trunk space and backseat. Likely got great gas mileage. She might like it if he could ever wear down her stubborn intent to hold on to the Volvo until it fell apart.

He slipped into the house and was greeted by gentle female laughter. Tamara Hunter, Zach's mother, sat at the kitchen table across from a smiling Sera, her sharp hazel eyes sparkling under a cap of tawny hair. The women turned toward him as he entered.

"Hey, Levi," Tamara said, but his gaze went to Sera's and held there. He could smell her gentle scent from eight feet away. Need slapped at him, taking his breath, and his body hardened. He slid into the kitchen, poured himself a glass of water, and hid his lower body behind the counter separating the dinette from the kitchen proper.

"Hey, Tamara." He swallowed a meager sip and lifted his glass toward the door. "That your wagon?"

Her grin was quick and easy, and an awful lot like her son's. "Yeah. I love it. Lots of room, plus great gas mileage, and I don't have to fill it up that often."

Levi nodded at Sera. "Trying to talk her 'round to one."

"Not this again." Sera rolled her eyes. "I have a perfectly serviceable car that's going to last me another five years at least, according to *his dad*, but no, that's not good enough."

"The Jetta's more reliable." He tried to sound reasonable over the laughter he held back. "It'll be more cost effective in the long run."

"Says Mr. Finance Major," Sera muttered. To Tamara, she said, "Do you know what it's like being ganged up on by two financial whizzes in my own house?"

Levi smirked. "If you objected to Petey learning how to manage his money, you should never have let me teach him about the stock market."

"Maybe he'll teach Zach." Tamara pushed herself out of her chair. "I'll just gather the boys up and take them on now so you two lovebirds can have fabulous make-up sex."

Sera's cheeks flushed pink. "We weren't even arguing."

Tamara waggled her eyebrows. "That's the best part about it. Don't worry about picking Petey up from Annabelle's tomorrow."

"Oh, but I promised Petey he could have Zach over."

"Next weekend," Tamara said easily. "In fact, I think Zach wanted Petey to stay the night. No time like tomorrow."

"But..." Sera twisted her mouth into a wry smile as Tamara left the room. "Boy, these Daughters don't know how to take no for an answer, do they?"

"Nor do Sons." Though he did know when to back off. "I'll be in the shower."

Sera stood and came around the end of the counter. "I'd better add some more clothes to Petey's backpack, if Tamara really wants him over."

They walked back together, her light scent teasing him all the way through the house. He said goodbye to a beaming Petey and slipped into Sera's bedroom, then into the shower, scrubbing himself clean. Two whole nights, the longest they'd had alone together since those first two weeks. No having to worry about Petey climbing into their bed in the middle of the night catching them sleeping together without, as Sera put it, the benefit of matrimony. No having to sneak out in the morning before Petey woke up. Sex whenever they wanted it, wherever they wanted it, and no other obligations to distract them.

He owed Tamara Hunter big time.

He grinned and cut the water off, stepped out and dried off. The house was nearly silent, the sounds of young boys' chatter no longer ringing through the air. He hung his towel up and strolled into the bedroom nude, his energy rebounding on the promise of the night ahead.

Sera was standing at the edge of the bed with her back to him, folding laundry, placing it in careful piles according to type and belonging, Petey's, hers, Levi's.

He came up behind her, gripped her hips in his hands, and rubbed his chin over the top of her head. "I told you, you don't have to do my laundry."

"It's no bother." She lifted one shoulder in a casual shrug and tossed a folded pair of Petey's socks into his pile. "Besides, you help us out so much. The least I can do is take care of your laundry for you."

"I do those things because I want to, not because I expect something in return."

"I know." She picked up a t-shirt, snapped the wrinkles out. "What do you want to do tonight?"

"Pretty much doing it," he said, and she laughed. He tugged her sweater up and ran his hands under it, cupping her bare stomach, and a familiar need surged through him. "Want some help?"

"I've got it. Thanks, though."

He undid the snap of her jeans and pulled the zipper down. "You don't need these, do you?"

"Kinda, yeah." Humor mixed with exasperation in her sweet drawl. "I'm not nearly as warm-blooded as you are."

"I'll keep you warm."

He slid his hands into the waistband along her hips and pushed the jeans down over her luscious ass. Underneath, she wore a pair of pale yellow, lace bikinis. He sucked in a breath and knelt behind her.

She twisted in his hands and peered down at him. "What are you doing?"

"Keeping you warm." He kissed the back of her thigh as he pushed her jeans down to her ankles. "Don't mind me."

She laughed and turned back to the laundry, and stepped out of her jeans when he urged her to. He touched her slowly, building her passion with tender kisses pressed to her soft skin. Even here, along her firm arse and the backs of her legs, she was smooth and sweet. He explored every inch with his fingertips and lips and tongue, learning her all over again, teasing her, taking as much pleasure as he gave. Her breath came in pants and she abandoned her chore, holding on to his hands with hers, steadying herself against the urgency of his caresses.

He tugged her panties down and off, and bent her over the bed, baring the slick folds of her pussy to his gaze.

She clenched the bedspread in her fists and buried her face in the unfolded laundry. "God, Levi. Please."

"I'll please you, love," he murmured, and stood, sliding into her tight, wet heat in one smooth stroke. His fingers found her clitoris, rubbing over it as his hips set an urgent rhythm, taking them both high so quickly, his release caught him by surprise. He shifted his caresses along her clit, and she followed, spasming around him with a soft cry of his name, prolonging the pleasure he'd found with her, and at last, he stilled his hips and shoved the laundry out of the way and eased her down onto the bed, curling up behind her.

"There, now. Are you warm?"

She laughed and slid her hand over his where it cupped her stomach. "Am I ever. Do you think it'll always be that way?"

"I hope so." His fingers unerringly found the stretch marks etched into the skin of her lower belly, tracing each reminder of the son she'd given him. "I love Petey."

She glanced over her shoulder, her expression puzzled. "I know."

"It's just." He sucked in a breath and chose his words carefully. "I wondered if you'd want more kids down the road."

"I did, before I had Petey." She turned her gaze away and snuggled into him. "When I was younger, I always thought I'd have a houseful, and then Petey came along and everything changed."

"If you had the chance, would you have more?"

"It's not like you to pussyfoot around a subject, Levi. I take it you want children of your own."

"Petey *is* my own, as much mine as any other could be." He tightened his hold on her and pulled her into him. No matter how close she was, it always seemed so far away. "But yeah, I'd like more."

A little girl with her mother's heart or another boy, if that's the blessing they received.

Sera was quiet for a long time, and when she spoke, it was in a gentle whisper. "With me?"

"Who else?" He kissed her temple and his body stirred, readying itself for her again. "I don't wanna rush, but you'll be thirty soon, and frankly, I don't want to spend our golden years chasing teenagers."

She sputtered out a laugh. "Our golden years? Geez, Levi. You make it sound like we've got one foot in the grave or something."

"Whisht, woman," he said, but he didn't mean it. Her laughter smoothed over the rough parts of his heart, the ones that had been waiting just for her. "Think about it, will you?"

She settled back against him with a contented sigh. "I will, when we hit the perfect stretch of the road."

He turned her to him with gentle pulls and tugs, and covered her willing body with his own. "Sera, love, we've been there for a while now."

She held him close as he loved her, and her gentle sighs filled him with the promise of the life they'd build between them.

THAT WEEKEND, Sera reveled in her time with Levi. She'd missed having him all to herself, though she certainly didn't mind sharing him with Petey. Still, it was difficult to have adult conversation with a young'un around and nearly impossible to share any kind of intimacy, even once said young'un was supposed to be in bed and sound asleep.

They opted for cuddling together on the couch in front of a movie, taking a long walk around the neighborhood hand in hand, and cooking meals together in her tiny kitchen. Mostly, though, they simply enjoyed being with one another. Levi pulled her into kisses at the drop of a hat no matter what they were doing and usually talked her into making love with him right there on the spot.

It was sheer bliss, even if she'd never look at her kitchen counter the same way again, or the dining room table, her office chair, the office floor, or various bare walls throughout the house. Levi had a way of making every moment special and he never left her unfulfilled, not in heart or mind or body.

Maybe it was just as he'd said. Maybe they already *were* on that perfect stretch.

Tamara brought Petey home Sunday afternoon. He ran straight to Levi, who swung Petey high into the air and gripped him in a bear hug.

Sera walked out to Tamara's car and stood beside the driver's side door next to Tamara. "Why is it that women do all the hard work raising children and men are the ones who reap the benefits?"

Tamara grinned. "Because they're a lot more fun than we are."

"True." Sera tucked her hands against her ribs, warding off a chill. "Thanks for having Petey over. Let us take Zach next weekend. Petey'll be in hog heaven."

"So will I, trust me." Tamara glanced over her shoulder at her son strapped into the backseat of the Jetta, then turned a sly look on Sera. "I love my son, wouldn't trade him for anything, but sometimes..." She shook her head, sending tawny hair flying. "I know you know what I'm talking about. At least my husband is home every night. Levi running back and forth to Atlanta must be hard, especially on your sex life."

Heat crept into Sera's cheeks. She'd known people would guess the nature of her and Levi's relationship. It was hard not to connect the dots with his car parked in the middle of her driveway every time he came to visit. It was something else to have it openly discussed. Other than Levi dropping some very pointed hints about what he wanted out of life, they'd never discussed the future. She didn't know what she wanted. Out of life, sure. Petey happy and healthy, a stable income, good health and the same for her family. But from Levi? She couldn't imagine not having him in her life. Other than that, she just wasn't sure.

Tamara touched tentative fingertips to Sera's shoulder. "Hey, I'm sorry. Whatever I said to make you uncomfortable, I didn't mean it."

Sera shook her head. "It's not you. It's just... Levi and I aren't married."

Tamara tilted her head to the side, studying Sera with her sharp-eyed gaze. "I know."

"He's kind of hinted he wants to. You know, down the road."

A slow smile stretched across Tamara's mouth. "With that body and the way he moves? You'd be crazy not to."

A laugh sputtered out of Sera. "Oh, my God, Tamara. I can't believe you said that."

"I'm married, not blind." Tamara ducked into the Jetta and slid behind the wheel. "I'll call in a few days so we can arrange for Zach to come over next weekend. Believe me, I appreciate the chance to have a hot date with my own boy toy."

Sera clucked her tongue as she stepped away from the car and watched it roll backwards out of her driveway. Boy toy, indeed.

Strong arms wound around her waist and tucked her into the warm presence of her lover. "Lusting after another woman's husband?"

She snickered. "Don't you mean *boy toy*? Honestly, Levi. Is that how people see us?"

"I don't care how other people see us. Now, the way you see me, that's different." He pressed nibbling kisses along the side of her neck. "Am I your boy toy, love? Do I need to take you in the bedroom and do wicked things to you?"

"You did that already, all weekend long."

"Tired of me so soon, huh." He smacked a final kiss to her cheek, then tugged her toward the house. "Come on. Petey swears he's starving. I promised to throw some steaks on the grill for supper. A man needs solid food when he's growing."

"Geez, Levi, don't tell him that or it'll be all I'll hear for the next week."

He slid an arm around her shoulders and smirked at her. "What? We're both still growing and a man..."

"Needs solid food. Ok, ok, I get it." She leaned her head against him and reveled in the joy zipping through her from his simple touch. "I'm so thankful you're part of our lives."

He glanced down at her, ginger eyebrows arched. "Where did that come from?"

She shrugged. "It just seemed like a good time to say it."

"Well, it's about time, woman. I thought you'd never come around."

He swung her up into his arms and spun her around, and she clung to him, shrieking laughter into the cool November air. Petey ran outside, a huge grin on his face. "Me, too, me, too," he cried, and Levi obliged, swinging her son around until they were both dizzy and grinning like the monkeys they were.

Sera shooed them inside, happiness swelling up inside her and bubbling over, feeding her own grin. Her boys. That had a nice ring to it. She wouldn't mind being able to call them both that for a long time to come.

Twenty-Seven

NOVEMBER ROLLED BY in a blur of activity. Bobby Upton's kidnapping sent shock waves roaring through the People's communities and the repercussions were astounding. Daughters locked their families down at home, every establishment owned and operated by members of the People tightened their security. Nobody went anywhere without at least one weapon on hand. For the Daughters, that was nothing new, but for those that had married into the People, the necessity added layers of stress and tension everybody would've preferred to avoid.

With visible proof of the Shadow Enemy on the move and rumors of the Eternal Order's reawakening spreading like wildfire, Levi finally managed to persuade Sera of the dangers the People lived under. He took a leave of absence from Icenia and escorted her and Petey wherever they needed to go, and he made damn sure she knew how to operate the handgun and shotgun she retrieved from her father's gun safe.

Thanksgiving evening, after enjoying a late lunch at the home of Sera's parents surrounded by her kin, near and distant, Levi gritted his teeth and did what he should've done months before. He rounded Sera and a protesting Petey up and drove them to his great-grandmother's house.

Sera was quiet during the short trip from Persimmon to Tellowee. Her hands were folded in her lap and her head rested against the back of her seat, and a small frown puckered the skin between her eyebrows.

Levi signaled for the turn onto Tellowee's main street. "Relax, Sera. She's not that bad, once you get to know her."

"It's not that." She sighed and shifted on the seat, facing him. "Ok, maybe a little. Why now, Levi? I mean, you could've introduced us to your nana a hundred times already, and you wait until a holiday to do it. It seems like bad timing."

"Maybe."

He rolled his shoulders, throwing off some of his anxiety. If he told Sera he'd deliberately waited until a lot of people were around precisely so Nana wouldn't pitch a shit fit, she wouldn't understand, not at all, and it might hurt her, when all he'd meant to do was protect her.

He glanced in the rearview mirror at Petey slouched into the backseat, his silver gaze dreamy, his mind likely in a galaxy far, far away. Levi lowered his voice anyway. "I wanted to present us as a solid unit, not individuals she could wedge apart. You don't know Nana like I do, Sera. She'll do whatever she thinks is right, whatever is best for her family, and she won't hesitate to do what she needs to in order to protect us, even from ourselves."

"Sounds a lot like somebody else I know," Sera murmured.

Humor pushed the last of his tension aside. "You know I'd do anything for you, but yeah, if I think it's best, you're damn straight I'm gonna act to protect you whether you like it or not. You know how I feel about you, Sera."

"I know, Levi." Her hand slid across the space between them and rubbed the top of his thigh. "Sometimes, you overdo it, though."

"Not this time, love, I swear." He eased to a stop behind his da's aging work truck and switched the ignition off. "This will work out. You'll see."

He led them inside, one arm around Sera's shoulders, Petey's hand tucked into his larger one. Hawthorne was holding court in the living room. As soon as he entered, she stood and fixed an icy stare on Sera and Petey. To Levi's utter shock, Petey tugged his hand out of Levi's and met Nana's gaze evenly, his shoulders thrown back, not a hint of shyness or fear in the little boy's expression.

Pride rose sharp and swift within Levi, followed closely by the full sweep of love. How lucky he was to have a son like Petey, one so brave he stared down a dangerous warrior, one so strong, he'd taken on the man that would one day be his father in order to protect his own mother, in spite of the fear shining on his young face.

Nana turned her cold gaze on Levi. "I expected you earlier, child."

"We had other obligations." His arm tightened around Sera's shoulders, reassuring himself as much as her. "This is Sera Noland and her son, Peter."

Lali tumbled out of the lap of Aaron, Hawthorne's lover, and threw her arms around Petey's waist. "Petey! I been waiting and waiting for you."

Petey's silver eyes widened, and Levi bit back a smile. "Petey, this is my cousin, Lali."

"Um, hi?" Petey gently patted Lali's back. "Maybe you could not squeeze so hard."

Lali stepped back and beamed up at Petey, and what followed was the most bizarre conversation Levi had ever heard from his young cousin, and that was saying something. Apparently, she'd been letting a strange woman she called *the pretty lady* into her room at night, and boy was Nana pissed about it. She snapped out orders, sending Aaron with Lali and Petey to fetch the pictures Lali had drawn of the intruder, and whipped out of the room following a demand for an audience with Levi, her temper clearly visible to all who knew her well.

Levi knuckled the sharp throb in his temple. Sweet Mother. Maybe he should've waited another year or two to introduce Sera to the rest of his family.

Sera's fingers squeezed his waist. "You ok?"

"Yeah." He hugged her tight, savoring the soft give of her body against his. "Let me introduce you around, then I have to go talk to her. Otherwise, she'll storm back out here with her sword and I'll have to fight her."

Sera buried her face in his chest and murmured, "We wouldn't want that, would we," and he laughed, exactly as she'd intended.

He left Sera in the living room and wound his way through Nana's house to her office, closing the door firmly behind him. He planted himself in front of her desk, arms crossed over his chest, and returned her hard stare with one of his own.

"Have a seat."

He curled his upper lip into a deliberate sneer. "I'll stand, thanks."

"Why did you not tell me you had formed a relationship with a mortal woman?"

He laughed. "Seriously? You have to ask that question? Every time you even think I'm considering a woman, you interfere. Who I date is my business, Nana, not yours."

Emotion flickered across her expression, so fleeting he almost missed it. "That woman is unacceptable."

"*That woman* is my future wife."

"I forbid it."

Levi snorted. Blessed Ki, that was rich. He'd never let her control his life, and never would. "Like you have any say."

The muscles in Hawthorne's jaw tightened ominously. "She is mortal and not of the People."

"Hypocrite. How dare you throw her mortality at me when you're living with a mortal man?"

"Our situation is different."

"Not a bit," he retorted. "Do you think you're the only person in this world entitled to love?"

"You could at least have found a Daughter, mortal or not."

"I looked, hard," he said flatly. "And you know what I found? Not a single one I wanted."

"You're young still, barely a man."

He laughed, hard and bitter. "I've been a man since I was sixteen, and treated like one for a lot longer, and you question the direction my heart takes?"

"It is not a question of the direction so much as your state of mind, your vulnerability. How do you know this mortal has not latched on to you in order to siphon your wealth into her own coffers?"

"Because Sera's not like that." He dropped his arms and stared down at his great-grandmother, hurt in spite of himself, in spite of knowing ahead of time how she'd react. He'd hoped this time would be different, hoped that as soon as Nana saw the woman he loved and the son he'd claimed, she'd understand why he was with them. "I should've known better than to bring Sera here, should've known you couldn't just be glad I'd found somebody. As long as you've searched for your heart, I thought you'd be happy I found mine."

The door swung wide and Aaron came in followed by Sera, Petey, and Lali. He fanned several colorful drawings across Hawthorne's desk, diverting Nana's attention away from their conversation.

Sera came straight to Levi and slid into his embrace, and his heart melted into a warm puddle in the center of his chest. His sweet, beautiful Sera. So what if Hawthorne never approved? It was his life and his heart, and damned if he'd let anybody dictate where it should linger.

They endured the rest of the evening there. Levi warned his nana away from Petey. By the Goddess, she'd leave his son alone if she wanted to spend any time around him, and her wish to do so was plain as day. Every time Hawthorne's gaze fell on Petey, her expression softened, and Levi almost felt sorry for her. Nana was nearly two thousand years old, and for most of that time, she'd longed for a son, making do with the sons her daughters and granddaughters bore. Now that Levi had Petey, he had a feeling grandchildren, as precious as they were, would be a poor substitute for the little boy that had wound his way through Levi's heart.

Between school and extra-curricular activities and the crush Lali had developed on him, poor Petey had enough to handle without adding Hawthorne's attention to the mix. Levi's cousin trailed the little boy wherever he went, though he tolerated it with a good-natured grin and the easy grace of a child that knew what loneliness felt like. No, Nana wouldn't get her immortal claws into Petey, not if Levi could help it, and she would come to accept Sera in Levi's life no matter what he had to do to gain his beloved nana's acceptance.

ON THE FIRST FRIDAY in December, Levi curled around Sera, enjoying the quiet comfort of holding her. She stirred in his arms and groaned. Levi ran a hand down her arm, soothing her. The alarm hadn't gone off yet. She still had a few minutes to rest, and he hated to wake her so early. He could wake Petey up and get him ready for school, and often did, but Sera liked to send their son off with the special hugs and kisses only a mum could give.

Two weeks. He smiled and pressed a soft kiss to the side of her neck. The winter solstice was in two weeks. He'd already planned what he would do. Jack and Candi would take Petey for the night while he and Sera went out to Mama G's. Over dessert, he'd tell her how much he loved her, how he wanted to spend the rest of his life with her and Petey, and ask her to marry him.

She'd love the ring he'd picked out for her, a simple pear-shaped diamond, not so big it was tasteless, not so small it would get lost on her hand. They could plan a July wedding and honeymoon in the Outer Banks. Petey could come along. What would it hurt? They were a family now and always would be. All she had to do to make it official was say yes.

The alarm buzzed. Levi reached across Sera and flipped it off. "Don't get up, love. I'll get Petey."

She mumbled an incoherent *mmph* and buried her face in her pillow. Levi grinned and rolled out of bed, then shut the bedroom door behind himself and padded to Petey's room. He veered into the hallway and cut the heat up to a decent level, tuned an ear to the aging furnace, and nodded when it cut on. Damn thing was temperamental. He'd tried to talk Sera into replacing it. She'd stared him down and said no, though her silver eyes had sparkled and a small smile had played around her sweet mouth.

It might not be an issue anyway. He was closing on the property next to her parents soon and hoped to build a house there, a bigger one with modern fixtures, a real office for each of them, and more bedrooms for the children he hoped they'd have through the years. They could renovate this place, rent it out, and stash the money into a college fund. He had it all worked out, the time it would take, the contractors they could use. Now he just had to convince Sera it was the best plan.

She'd come around, the same way she'd come around to accepting him in her life. He was sure she loved him as much as he loved her. She'd never said it, true, but she showed him every day how much she cared for him. A woman didn't do a man's laundry unless she loved him, did she?

He leaned a shoulder against the doorframe and grinned. Petey was propped up in bed reading a book by the light of his bedside lamp, his slight body curled under a layer of quilts. "Morning, lad. Getting a head start on your homework?"

"No, sir." Petey flipped the book shut and slid out of bed. "I figured if I let Mama sleep in, maybe she'd be in a better mood. She's been kinda grumpy lately."

Levi swung Petey into a hug. "She hasn't been sleeping well. That makes people grumpy."

"It makes me grumpy," Petey admitted. "You reckon she's ok?"

"She's probably just got a lot on her mind. The new book's been a little hard on her."

Petey laid his head on Levi's shoulder and wound his arms around Levi's neck. "That's what you always say."

"It's usually true. What do you want for breakfast?"

"Pancakes?"

"With eggs." Levi smacked a kiss to Petey's cheek and settled him on the floor next to the hallway bathroom. "A man needs protein to go with his carbs."

Petey flashed a grin, showing two fully-grown, crooked front teeth, and ducked into the bathroom. Levi made a mental note to find an orthodontist, and he was paying for it, whether Sera liked it or not. A man paid his child's way, and Petey was his now in every way that counted.

Levi eased the door to Sera's bedroom open and poked his head inside. The bed was empty. Something that sounded suspiciously like retching came from behind the closed bathroom door. He frowned. The flu had hit the area pretty hard lately. Sounded like it had paid a visit to their house, too.

He tapped on the closed door. "Sera, love, you ok?"

"I'm fine," came the muffled reply.

"Can I help?"

"Go away."

Levi rolled his eyes skyward. "I'm making Petey eggs and pancakes for breakfast. You want some?"

A muffled groan sounded, followed by another bout of retching. Levi took that as a *no*. "A Sprite might settle your stomach."

"Um." A long, shuddering sigh. "Ginger ale?"

He rested his forehead on the door's cool surface. "Anything else?"

"No, just..." A sniffle, another sigh. "Just go away, please. I'll be fine."

He tamped down the worry. She didn't sound fine. His first instinct was to break down the door and do everything in his power to change that. She wouldn't appreciate it, though, so he'd get a ginger ale and take care of Petey while she rested, and hope that was enough.

He scrubbed a hand over his nape. Soon, he'd make the vow to love her for better or worse. Loving her would never be a problem. Keeping himself from smothering her with that love, well, that was something else entirely. He forced himself to walk out of the bedroom. She'd holler if she needed him, and in the meantime, Petey needed his breakfast.

SERA DRAGGED HERSELF back to bed and hid her head under the pillow, ignoring the distant sounds of Levi cooking breakfast for Petey and getting her son off to school.

Panic rippled through her, hard and shaky, adding to the queasiness still roiling around inside her. The last time she'd been sick like this, she'd been pregnant, but no, that couldn't be the problem now. She took that little pill every morning like clockwork, hadn't missed a day the entire time she and Levi had been dating. He'd stopped using condoms a long time ago, but the pill on its own was nearly one hundred percent effective.

Maybe she had the flu.

A gentle rap hit the door. "Mama?"

She sighed. A day without Petey wasn't much of a day at all. She just wished her stomach and head were cooperating so she could enjoy him. "Come on in, honey."

Petey stuck his head in the bedroom and stared at her, eyes round and uncertain. "Levi's taking me to school now. He said I shouldn't come too close 'cause you probably had the flu and I didn't want that, not with Christmas right around the corner."

"You probably don't," she murmured.

He worried on his lower lip with his brand new front teeth. "You reckon Santa Clause'd still come see me if I was sick? I mean, I wouldn't want him to catch nothing, but with it being Christmas and all, I sure would hate for him not to come. You reckon Mrs. Santa Clause'd make him skip me?"

Sera pressed a hand over her mouth, hiding her humor and quelling a little of the nausea. "No, baby. Santa Clause will still visit whether you're sick or not. You've been a good boy this year, haven't you?"

"Oh, yeah," he agreed, nodding emphatically. "I got straight As and I been doing all my chores and everything. Levi said I had to be the best son ever."

And if Levi said it, it must be true. A fresh wave of queasiness rolled over Sera. She curled into a tighter ball and clenched her eyes shut, gritting her teeth against the urge to throw up.

"Come on now, lad," Levi said gently. "Your mum needs her rest."

"Yes, sir. Bye, Mama."

"Bye, baby," she croaked out.

"I'll be back in a little while, love," Levi said. "Try a sip or two of that ginger ale while I'm gone."

He shut the door softly. Sera scrambled out of bed and headed for the toilet, too miserable to care why she was sick.

She rested until mid-morning, dozing lightly in starts and fits. Levi propped the bedroom door open as soon as he came home from dropping Petey off at school, then let her be for the most part, and for that, she was grateful. It had given her time to pull herself together and decide on a path, whether she wanted to face it or not. Maybe it really was the flu or a stomach bug or something equally innocuous, and maybe it was something more.

She dragged herself into the shower, dressed in warm clothes, and let Levi know she was up. He was working in their office, his head bent over something or other on his computer. She huffed out a breathy laugh. Probably something to do with money. He seemed to have the Midas touch where his investments were concerned and had passed it on to Petey, whose summer yard money was growing nicely.

Her stomach rumbled. Dry toast and another ginger ale shouldn't hurt. She stuffed two pieces of bread into the toaster and leaned against the counter, rubbing her gritty eyes as the machine whirred through its cycle.

A gentle hand touched her waist. "What can I do?"

"Nothing." The word came out tight and thin. "I need to go into town later."

"I'll drive. Better, I can go while you lay down and rest."

She shook her head. Pain throbbed through her temples and she winced. Why had she moved? "This is something I need to do."

Not to mention it was something she was too embarrassed to have anybody know about. Maybe it was a false alarm.

Deep in her heart, though, she knew it wasn't. A sob escaped. She bit her trembling lip and wiped away tears. What was she going to do? What *could* she do?

Levi pulled her against his chest and wrapped his arms around her. One hand rubbed small circles over her back, warming her, comforting her. "Shh. Don't cry, love. Everything will be fine as soon as this bug runs its course."

She choked on a hastily indrawn breath. Lordy. If he only knew, he'd...

Her fingers tightened in his shirt. No, she was getting ahead of herself. There was no need to worry Levi when she wasn't sure herself what was wrong. It could be nothing. It could really be the flu and her panicked mind seeing something that wasn't there. She'd go into town and get a test, and if it was positive, well, *then* she'd worry about it.

The toast popped up. She pulled reluctantly away from Levi. Her rock. What would she do if he walked out on her? How would she ever make it through another pregnancy without the friendship, love, and support of the baby's father?

She pushed the thought away. That wasn't something she could face, not now, and it wasn't something she wanted to think about until she had to.

Twenty-Eight

THE NEXT DAY, Levi woke to the sound of Sera being sick in the bathroom. He pushed himself out of bed and knocked gently on the bathroom door. "You ok, love?"

A long silence followed. "Can you take care of Petey for me, please, just for a little while?"

"Sure. I'll make him some breakfast and then we'll go to basketball practice." He waited for her to say something else, anything that would let him know what was wrong. He wrapped his hand around the knob and turned. It was locked. Levi rested his forehead against the door. She'd never locked him out before. "Open up, love. Let me help you."

"Just take care of Petey for me."

"I'd do that anyway."

A sniffle. "I know."

His gut knotted into a tight wad of misery. Why wouldn't she let him help her? "Need anything?"

"Ginger ale?" Another sniffle, the soft bang of a cabinet door. "Maybe some saltines."

"Anything else?"

"I'll be fine, Levi. I'll..."

The word broke on a quiet sob. Levi tried the knob again and cursed low and long under his breath. So he'd play it her way for a while, fetch her something to calm her stomach, take Petey to basketball practice. Later, though, he'd take the fucking lock off the door. Privacy was one thing. Locking him out when she needed him was something else. Did she really think he'd sit by and watch from the sidelines while she was so sick she couldn't take care of her son? Nothing had ever kept her from doing that, not deadlines or Levi, not anything as far as he could tell. If she was that sick now, she didn't need to be alone.

"Is Mama ok?"

Levi whipped around. Petey was standing in the doorway, his expression as miserable as Levi felt.

"I don't know, Petey. She's awfully sick right now."

Petey swiped the sleeve of his pajamas across his nose. "You reckon she'll be ok?"

Levi crouched on one knee in front of his son. "She needs to rest and take care of herself for a few days. After that, she'll be good as new."

"Promise?"

"Promise. How about pancakes for breakfast?"

Petey's mouth turned down at the corners. "Two days in a row?"

"You'll run them off at practice." Levi ran a hand over Petey's hair, smoothing down the sleep-tousled spikes. "Come on. Let's leave your mum in peace."

The two of them talked quietly over cooking and eating breakfast. Levi sent Petey to get ready while he cleaned the kitchen. He kept hoping Sera would come out, but she never did, and worry ate at him. The day before, she'd seemed to rebound fine. She'd been pale and a little shaky all day, but she'd eaten a light lunch and a heavier supper, and had chatted with Petey in an almost normal voice. And now she was sick again?

He mulled it over during the drive between her house and the Rec Department, and during practice. Afterward, he and Jack took Petey, Matty, and Dale to eat at Dairy Queen. Jack volunteered to take Petey for the afternoon so Sera could rest. Petey pleaded so hard to go with his cousins, Levi didn't have the heart to tell him no. He followed Jack's F-150 from Clayton to Persimmon, alone with his thoughts and the nagging worry that maybe Sera was sicker than she'd let on.

He parked his Audi behind Sera's Volvo and tiptoed into the house.

Sera was sitting at the dinette wearing a loose, long-sleeved t-shirt and fuzzy pajama bottoms. She smiled wanly at him over a steaming mug. "How was practice?"

He shucked his jacket, hung it on the back of a chair, and sat down across from her. "Noisy. How's the stomach?"

She paled and glanced down at her cup. "It's not my stomach. Well, it is, but..." She blew out a breath. "Do you have a minute?"

He reached across the table and laid a hand on hers. "I have whatever time you need."

"It's just, I don't know how to say this." A tear streaked down one cheek and she swiped it away with impatient fingers. "I'm pregnant."

Levi's heart leapt into a runner's pace. He stared at her, his sweet lover, the woman he wanted to spend the rest of his life with. That's why she'd been sick and had insisted on going into CVS on her own the day before and had been unable to care for Petey in the mornings. A giddy wave of relief flooded him, sweeping away the worry.

He was going to be a father. Blessed Ki, he was going to be a father. He'd have to learn how to change diapers and help Sera breast feed the baby. He'd missed all that with Petey, that and him learning to talk and walk and a hundred other tiny things kids did that parents enjoyed seeing. Not with this one, he swore. With this one, he'd witness every minute, from the first doctor's visit to the time it was born.

Sweet Mother. Sera would be giving birth. He'd never been around the birth of a child before, but he'd heard plenty of stories, of the blood and the pain and the complications. The blood drained from his head and he swayed in his chair. "You're sure?"

"Pretty sure. I took the test this morning and it was positive, and..." Her lower lip trembled and her hands tightened around the mug under his hand. "It's yours."

He drew back, startled. "Of course, it's mine. Who else's would it be?"

Her gaze fell to the floor and the happiness bubbling up inside him sank under the sorrow pressing her shoulders down. He went to her, knelt between her legs, and rested his head gently on her stomach, over where the babe grew. His baby, a new member of their family, a perfect union of him and her. "I'm not like him, Sera."

"I know." She sniffed and laid a hand on his head. "I know

you're not, Levi. It's just, what am I going to do? It was bad enough having Petey on my own, but a second child? I don't think I can do it."

"You don't have to do it on your own, I swear." And he wouldn't have to wait until next year to claim her, not with the baby on the way. They could be together now, the way he'd been dreaming of for months, him and Sera and Petey and the little one. He pulled away and pressed a tender kiss to her forehead. "Hold on. I need to get something."

He trotted into the office and pulled the ring he'd bought for her out of his desk where he'd hidden it for safekeeping. The nervous hope he'd lived with since buying it fizzled, superseded by the giddiness of her news. They could get married now, live together without having to hide their relationship from Petey. He could tell her all the things he'd been bottling up in his heart, waiting for her to be ready, and she could feel secure enough to tell him how she felt, too.

When he walked back into the kitchen, she was huddled in her chair, arms wrapped around her waist. He opened the black velvet box and set it on the table in front of her, then sat in the chair next to her. She stared at the box and her skin, already pale, drained completely of color.

He laid a hand on her knee. "I was gonna wait until the solstice to give this to you."

Her mouth opened, closed again, and her leg shifted under his hand. She cleared her throat and said softly, "It's beautiful."

"It's for you. I had it all planned out, how we'd go out and I'd tell you how I feel and ask you to marry me, but now with the baby on the way, it seems stupid to wait." He rubbed a thumb along the bridge of his nose and bit back the grin trying to break free. If he smiled even once, he was pretty sure he wouldn't be able to stop. "I love you so much Sera, you and Petey both. Marry me. Make a family with me." He laughed and the grin he'd been trying to hold in check burst free. "A bigger family. Say you will, Sera. Say you'll have me."

Her face crumpled. She covered it with both hands and rocked away from him. "I can't marry you, Levi."

His grin faded and the happiness lifting him high burst and sent him plummeting. "What?"

"I can't marry you. I can't do that to you."

"Do what to me?"

Her hands fell into her lap. Her expression held a bleakness he'd never seen in her before, not even on the day she'd told him about Petey's da. "Saddle you with a woman like me. I'm not the kind of woman you need in your life, Levi. I've known it from the first."

He huffed out a bewildered laugh. "Exactly what kind of woman are you, then, that you're not good enough for me to love?"

"A single mother with an illegitimate son," she said flatly. "A woman with no backbone and no prospects, no connections in society, no wealth or influence, a woman who's entirely too old for you with too many responsibilities and nothing left to give."

"I told you, none of that matters to me." He leaned forward and grasped her cold hands in his. "I love you, Sera, you, a sweet woman with shy eyes and a good heart. Every day, you give me so much of yourself, your laughter and your son and a dozen little things most men never even notice. I can't imagine not having you in my life. Tell me you don't feel the same way."

"How I feel doesn't matter."

"Yes, it does. How can you even say that?" He squeezed her fingers. "You swore you'd never be able to leave me."

"I can't," she whispered. "That doesn't make what we're doing right, what we've been doing, and now we're paying the consequences."

He slumped into his chair and scrubbed his hands over his face. "Fuck it, Sera. If the consequences of loving you include getting you pregnant, I'm happy to oblige. I thought you wanted more children."

"Not like this."

"Then marry me."

"I can't," she wailed. "Don't you see? Marrying you won't make being pregnant right. All it does is drag you down with me."

"I've never considered being with you dragging me anywhere that wasn't good and right. I can't believe you don't feel the same way, after everything we've been through, after taking me into your life and sharing Petey with me." The ugliness of her words scratched at him, festering in the silence stretching between them. "You don't love me."

Her gaze slid away from his and fixed on the floor. "I care for you."

"But you don't love me."

"We haven't known each other that long..."

"Long enough, Sera." So long he'd fallen headlong into love, opening himself without reserve. He swallowed the bitterness clogging his throat. Not once had he ever considered that she might not come to love him the same way. "I'll move into the spare bedroom tonight."

"You're not leaving me?" she asked, and her words sank the last hope he had of ever having her the way he'd dreamed.

He stood and stared at her, and one by one, he shut his feelings down, closing himself off from the woman that had taken everything he had to give and thrown it back in his face. "You're the mother of my children. I'll not leave you to fend for yourself."

He forced himself to walk away from her, forced himself to leave her at the tiny table when everything inside him screamed for him to pull her into his arms, make her see reason, and never, ever let her go.

SERA HAD NEVER lived with someone so determined not to interact with her before. Levi avoided her whenever he could, slipping out when Petey was gone, hiding in the office or the spare bedroom during the times they normally spent together as a family. His nearly daily jogs ran over by half an hour or more and the weights he'd installed in her remodeled basement became a refuge.

Not that she blamed him for hiding. She'd handled their conversation so poorly, shame burned through her every time she replayed it in her head. Why hadn't she found a better way to turn him down? *Not now, Levi*, she could've said. *Maybe soon when I'm not in shock*, or even, *I care for you so much, Levi. Please give me more time.*

But no, she'd had to reject him. She'd allowed her horror over becoming pregnant again to push her into something she never would've done outright. Now, whenever she walked in one door, he walked out the other, right when she needed him most, and it was her own fault for pushing him away.

The next Thursday, she dragged herself to the health clinic in town for an official pregnancy test. Not that she needed one. Between the morning sickness and the two home tests she'd taken, she was positive she was carrying Levi's child. The folks at the clinic would have recommendations for OB/GYNs or nurse-midwifes, though, and that would save Sera a ton of research looking for the best one.

She was sitting in a room waiting for the results when a quiet knock fell on the door. She glanced up. Ethan Phillips poked his head in the door and smiled.

"Hey, Sera." He waved the stack of files in his hand over his shoulder. "I heard you were in for some routine tests. Everything ok?"

She gritted her teeth together. Small towns had their perks, like knowing everybody in a twenty-five mile radius. Handy when your tire blew on the side of the road in the middle of the night. Not so great when you were pregnant and wanted to keep it a secret. "It's nothing. How have you been?"

He slipped inside, closed the door behind himself, and sat down on the rolling stool next to the bed Sera sat on. He was dressed in street clothes, a dark green, collared shirt and khakis, and wore a visitor's badge clipped to his shirt pocket. "Busy. Since Bobby Upton's kidnapping, I've been running day and night."

"We heard about that. Levi..." She pressed her lips together, cleared her throat. "We went on lockdown for a while."

Ethan's light green eyes fixed on Sera. "You're still seeing him?"

"I was. We've had a...misunderstanding."

"I can't imagine a misunderstanding bad enough to make a Son miss his girlfriend's doctor's visit, not when she's pregnant."

Her cheeks warmed, scalding her as surely as hot water would. "It's not like that, Ethan."

"Yeah?" His expression hardened and he threw the files down on the counter running the length of the wall behind him. "Tell me what it's like, then. Did he abandon you?"

"What? No! He asked me to marry him."

"And you said...?"

She rubbed a hand over her eyes, hiding them from his astute gaze. "I turned him down."

"You don't love him."

"What is it with you men? I care for him. Why isn't that enough?"

"He's a Son, Sera," Ethan said gently. "We never do anything halfway, not at work or play, not with our hearts. He'd be a good father, a good husband."

Her hand thumped into her lap. "So now you're defending him. A few months ago, the two of you looked like you were about to have a go at each other, or was that my imagination?"

Ethan braced his forearms against his thighs and scrubbed a hand over his close-cropped, auburn hair. "It wasn't. I guess you told him you and I dated in high school."

"He didn't take it well."

"He shouldn't have."

Her eyes widened and she laughed. "That was ages ago, Ethan, and hardly anything serious."

"Are you sure?" he asked softly.

The smile faded from her face. "We were kids and we went out, what, a handful of times? And then you went off to college and I never heard from you again."

"I went to your dad not long before I left." Ethan slouched on the stool and crossed his arms over his chest. "Told him I wanted to court you, that I was serious about you, that I knew you were the one for me. He told me you were too young, said I should wait until you got out of college and to leave you alone until then. You needed to grow up, he said, and were too smart to waste your life getting married so young."

Sera gaped at him. "That's the first I've heard of it."

"I can't imagine he'd want you to know. Temptation." He snorted and glanced away. "So I waited, and I heard about your being pregnant with Petey, and I waited some more, trying to give you time to find your balance. After Petey broke his arm and you brought him to the emergency room, I tried to run into you for weeks, tried to find a way to ask you out again, and when I finally did bump into you, you'd already met Levi."

She shook her head slowly, too numb to truly process his words. "Why are you telling me this, Ethan? I mean, why now when you could've come to my house and asked me out or whatever it is men do when they're interested in someone? Why did you wait so long?"

"I damn well wish I hadn't, Sera." He stood and gathered his files together. "I wish I hadn't let your dad talk me out of dating you. I wish as soon as I heard you were pregnant with Petey that I'd found a way to talk you into marrying me. I wish I'd done a hell of a lot of things differently instead of sitting back and watching you get hurt over and over again. I'm not doing that anymore."

"I don't..." She rubbed her hands down her thighs, loosening some of the nerves pinging through her. "What are you saying?"

"I'm saying you have options." He smoothed her hair back and touched his forehead to hers. "If things don't work out with Levi and you need a friend or someone to help you through this, call me. I'll be there for you, the way I should've been all along. You don't have to be alone anymore, ok?"

"Ethan." She swallowed and curled her fingers into fists, pressing them against the bed to keep from reaching for him, to hold the tears clogging her throat at bay. The weight of the years they could've had bore down on her, years when she could've had a steady friend helping her through the tough times, sharing the burden of raising her son, years she'd never have because they'd both been too young when they'd met. "Thank you. You have no idea how much it means to have your support."

"But you won't marry me, will you?"

She jerked back and met his steady gaze with her own. "I didn't know that was an option."

"If Levi doesn't, I will." His smile was small, but it was there. "You know how to find me if you need me."

She nodded and listened to his quiet footsteps as he walked to the door. He was almost there when a thought occurred to her. She glanced over her shoulder and arched her eyebrows. "Isn't it a little unethical to ask your patients to marry you?"

"There's a reason you and Petey could never get appointments with me, Sera. I'm here today as a friend, not a doctor. Think about that while you're considering what to do next."

She huffed out a laugh. Trust a Son to find a way around a problem. The door clicked shut, leaving her alone in the tiny room, somehow lighter for talking to an old friend.

Twenty-Nine

HAT NIGHT, Sera sat on a hard bleacher at the Recreation Department next to Candi, watching Petey and Matty's team play basketball. Sera's gaze was drawn again and again to Levi. He'd taken a backseat to Jack, the official head coach, and kept stats, handed out water, or shouted encouragement to the boys as they ran up and down the court.

Longing twinged through her. Damn it, she missed him. She missed having his warmth beside her through the night and seeing his wicked smirk across the breakfast table in the morning. She missed watching him laugh with Petey and talking things over with him and holding his hand and, God, did she ever miss kissing him. She missed it so much, she was about ready to give in and do whatever he asked if it would get things back to normal between them.

Candi elbowed Sera's arm. "Those are the two handsomest coaches east of Tallulah Falls, aren't they? I swear, more women are watching them than the game."

"Maybe those women should keep their eyes on their own men," Sera muttered.

"Is that the green-eyed monster I hear?"

On the floor, someone called a time out and the boys from each team obediently trotted toward their separate benches. Sera glanced around. She'd managed to find a spot far enough away from the rest of the crowd to give her and Candi at least a semblance of privacy. No one was sitting within ten feet of them, thank goodness, and she really needed a friendly ear. She leaned closer to her sister-in-law and said, "We've had a falling out."

Candi glanced surreptitiously around and lowered her voice. "But he's still living with you."

"He was never living with me, Candi, just, you know, visiting."

Candi's expression turned skeptical. "Yeah, visiting so much he sleeps with you every night and keeps half his clothes at your house. Tell me another one, sister."

"Well, it's just..." Sera twisted her fingers together and glanced around again. "I'm pregnant."

Candi drew back and studied Sera. A slow smile spread across her face and she threw her arms around Sera, hugging her hard. "That's awesome, Sera. Oh, my God! When did you find out? What did Levi say? Tell me everything."

"Shh. Ow. Ok, that hurts."

Candi eased her hold and rested her temple against Sera's. "Sorry. I'm excited, is all. After Petey was born, we thought you'd never date seriously. I mean, not those dweebs you dated when he was a toddler, but a real man, somebody who'd take care of you and love you, and now, you have Levi and..."

Sera squeezed her hands around her knees. "I don't exactly have Levi anymore."

"What? But you're pregnant." Candi's eyes narrowed into angry slits. "Let me guess. He decided he couldn't handle having a baby with you."

"Er, no. He asked me to marry him."

"And yet you wear no ring."

"Your keen skills of observation always astound me."

Candi smirked. "Smarty pants. Seriously, though, what gives? He's handsome and smart and pretty dang funny, if you ask me, and he obviously loves you and Petey. I can't believe you didn't grab hold of him with both hands and drag him to the nearest preacher."

"I just couldn't, Candi. He's so, well, you know him. He has his flaws, God knows he does, but he's such a good man." The buzzer rang and the teams ran back out onto the court. Levi's gaze strayed to the stands and kept right on moving, and Sera's heart dipped and pinged. "He has so much going for him and he has his whole life in front of him. I couldn't do that to him, couldn't saddle him with my mistakes. He'd come to resent me eventually, and I don't think I could bear it."

"Wait, let me get this straight. You didn't marry him because you're not perfect, because you've made a couple of mistakes in your life? Do you even realize how insane that sounds?"

"But he's..."

"Unh-unh, no way," Candi said, and her eyes went flat and hard. "You listen to me, Serafina Eulene Noland. You're a good woman with a helluva lot going for you in your own right. I can't believe you'd let having Petey out of wedlock, which wasn't a mistake by any measure, keep you from grabbing hold of a great man with both hands. I can't believe you think so little of yourself that you'd allow that nut job Kyle Vincent to grind you into the dirt eight years after the asshole killed himself running from the best thing that ever happened to him."

Sera hunched her shoulders around her ears. "Candi..."

"I'm not finished by a long shot," Candi snapped. "That man loves you so much he can barely keep his eyes off you. He endured a beating to protect *your son*, a beating, Sera. Jack told me what Levi's back looked like that night, and don't think I haven't seen those scars and that tattoo myself. He loves you, just about as much as I've ever heard of a man loving a woman, and I know you love him, too. Don't try to tell me you don't."

"But what if..."

"Don't even go there." Candi sucked in a breath and jabbed a finger at the opposite side of the gym where Jack and Levi stood on the sidelines, cheering on the boys. "You find a way to make it right with him, Sera, or so help me, I'll do it myself. I'm not watching you wallow in misery another two decades trying to raise those kids on your own when you could have more happiness with him than most people ever dream of. Don't you dare let that go. Don't you dare."

Sera waited a beat. "Anything else?"

Candi blew out a breathy laugh. "Wasn't that enough?"

"I reckon it was." Sera threaded her arm through Candi's. "I miss him so much, even though he's right across the hall from me every night. How can that be?"

"Maybe it's because you love him, Sera," Candi said gently. "Did you ever consider that?"

"What if it's not enough?"

"Have some faith, sister, and hang on to the love. It's gotten me and Jack through ok."

That it had. Sera settled down to watch the game, her mind tumbling over everything Candi had said, her heart filling with a curiously buoyant emotion she suspected might be hope.

THE NEXT MORNING, Levi walked into Sera's house after taking Petey to school. She was sitting at the kitchen table in her pajamas sipping a can of ginger ale. Déjà vu, he thought, and shut the door against winter's chill.

He shrugged his jacket off and hung it over the back of the chair, resigned to speaking to her. For the past week, he'd done everything he could to leave her be. It was what she wanted, probably what she'd wanted all along. He was the one who'd intruded in her life. He was the one who'd insisted on starting a relationship with her, and now, she was the one paying the price.

He dropped into the chair, weariness eating him from the inside out. Even if he had a chance to do things differently, he wouldn't. He loved her, so much he could barely function without her, though he wished he could've spared her the hurt she was going through now. Maybe things would've been different if she could've found it in herself to love him back.

"You're up early," he said.

"I needed to talk with you." Her voice was scratchy and hoarse. She cleared her throat and wrapped both hands around the can of ginger ale. "I went to the health clinic yesterday and had them do another test. I'm officially pregnant."

His heart bumped in his chest. "I can't say I'm not happy about it."

"I know."

"Have you picked out an OB/GYN?"

"I thought you might like a say." Her gaze slipped away from him and fixed on the can, and she cleared her throat again. "I mean, it's your baby and I wouldn't mind having someone along, so I thought, you know. If you have time."

"I appreciate that."

An uncomfortable silence stretched between them. The furnace rumbled on, hissing warm air through the vents. A car drove by, the swish of its tires along asphalt clearly audible inside the tiny kitchen. Levi's throat tightened, choking off the words he wanted to say, how he loved her and didn't care if they got married, if she'd just say she wanted him again. How he'd settle for whatever she could give him, if she'd only let him hold her, take care of her, comfort her.

She thumped her can on the table and laughed, the sound so short, it was nearly humorless. "I ran into Ethan Phillips yesterday."

"Yeah?"

"He said you'd be a good father."

"You told him," he said flatly.

"He found out. I guess he read the test results." She shrugged and sipped her ginger ale. "He offered to marry me."

Levi placed his hands flat on the table. His heart twisted into knots in his chest, stealing the breath from his lungs, and it was all he could do to sit there across from her, knowing any hope he had of reconciling with her was slipping away. "What did you say?"

"What could I?" She shook her head and laughed. "I mean, c'mon, Levi. You wouldn't believe some of the things he said about when we were kids, how he went to my dad and wanted to court me and knew I was the one for him. It was crazy."

"Not so much," he whispered. Hadn't he recognized Sera from the start? It wasn't such a leap to believe somebody else felt the same way about her.

She sat up and reached toward him, a frown furrowing her brow. "Are you ok? You just went pale as a ghost."

"No, I'm..." Not fine. He couldn't tell her that. It would be a lie and he'd sworn to never out and out lie to her. "I'll be fine." Eventually, maybe. If he was lucky. "I have some things to do in Tellowee. Will you be ok for a while?"

"I guess. I was hoping we could talk some more." She pressed her lips together. "If you have time later?"

He managed a shaky smile and patted the hand she'd left stretched across the table. "I'll always have all the time you need from me."

Her pretty face lit with a genuine smile. She stood and walked around the table toward him, and pressed a sweet kiss to his cheek. "I was hoping you'd say that. I've missed talking to you, Levi. You have no idea how much."

He'd missed her, too, but there was nothing he could do about that now. She'd decided for another man, one older and more to her suiting, and Levi would just have to learn how to live without her. She slipped out of the room as he fumbled for his phone. A Son had been forsaken, and now, somebody had to pay the price.

SERA DRESSED SLOWLY, careful not to bend over too quickly or press anything against her tender stomach. It had taken half a sleeve of saltines and a can of ginger ale for her stomach to settle long enough for a talk with Levi and she didn't want to spoil the reprieve by pushing her body where it didn't want to go. She tugged her running shoes on and tied the laces, then eased upright. Since she was up, she might as well go grocery shopping and run errands, and she'd do it all in Tellowee using the store accounts Levi had set up for her, accounts she'd never used before on her own. It was well past time for her to give in there, baby or not.

Levi had listened to her.

She nibbled on her lower lip around a smile. They'd had a whole conversation together and he'd let her kiss him and said they could talk later, and the relief was so great, it nearly sent her flopping back onto the bed.

They'd be ok. She just knew it. Now that he understood she wasn't pushing him away, they'd really be ok. She stood and dug through her underwear drawer, and pulled out the black velvet box holding the ring he'd given her. Her smile widened and flutters of nerves or happiness or both zinged through her. She'd talk to him tonight, and after that, he'd understand that she just wasn't ready for marriage yet. Soon, yes, God, yes. What had Candi said about holding on to the love? Levi loved her, so much she could see it in him every time he looked at her, and maybe she loved him, too.

She just needed a little time to get used to the idea, was all, just a little more time to make sure him joining his life to hers wouldn't come back to haunt him down the road.

The ring tempted her, even hidden in its box. One peek wouldn't hurt, would it? It was such a lovely ring, after all, and it might be hers soon. She opened the box and stared at the simple, pear-shaped diamond, and touched nerveless fingers to her chest over the racing thud of her heart. He'd picked this out for her, and in doing so, had proven how well he knew her. It was nothing fancy, nothing gaudy, just a simple diamond beautifully set.

Could she really marry him? Could she and Petey really have a family with Levi, one that would last forever through all the ups and downs life would inevitably throw at them?

On an impulse, she plucked the ring out of its box and slid it onto her left ring finger. It was a little loose, though maybe that was a good thing. If she could work up the nerve to say yes before the baby came, she'd want to wear it every single day no matter how swollen her fingers became or how hard it was to work on and off her finger. Or she could get a necklace and wear it around her neck where she could feel it when she needed a reminder of how much Levi loved her.

As if he'd ever let her forget.

What a fool she'd been to push him away the way she had. Never again. Tonight, they'd talk and straighten the whole mess out. Things would go back to the way they were before. Levi would sleep with her at night, his whiskey eyes would smile at her whenever she walked by, the way they used to, and Petey would stop looking at them as if they were both crazy.

She traced one fingertip around the edges of the diamond. She should really take it off now and put it away for safekeeping, until the time was right. "Soon," she whispered, and started to slide it off her finger.

Her phone rang, startling her into bobbling the ring. With a laugh, she pushed it back onto her finger and picked up her phone. "Hello?"

"Sera, thank the Lady," a female voice whispered. "You've got to get over here."

Sera pulled the phone away from her ear and checked the number. "What's wrong, Ruby?"

"It's Levi. Sweet Mother, he's at Nana's and he's spilling his guts about how you're pregnant and you've forsaken him, and holy shite, Sera. He's about to take Retribution in your place."

"Retribution?" Sera sank down onto the edge of her bed. The happiness bubbling through her melted away, swamped by a sinking darkness. "I didn't forsake him. I mean, I told him I didn't want to get married, but I didn't... I don't understand. We were just talking not half an hour ago."

"He said something about your finding somebody else. Look, that's not important," Ruby hissed. "When a Son is forsaken, it's a major deal. Nana could impose physical Retribution and by the look on her face, she's ready to impose the max."

"The max," Sera said slowly, and her mind skipped back to the mess Levi had been in the night he'd come home, bruised and bloody and so weak with fever, his mother had had to brace him upright. Nausea erupted in her stomach. She scooted backward on the bed and laid down, curling into a tight ball, swallowing down the acidic bile burning her throat. "How bad?"

"Bad. One stroke for every year he's forsaken, and Levi's young. Seventy strokes at least, plus forfeiting his property and trust funds and his position at Icenia. He'll be nearly penniless, if he survives her whip."

A whip. Dear God, Hawthorne was going to use a whip on her own kin, and all because Sera hadn't found it in herself to marry Levi the first time he'd asked. Sweet, precious, hard-headed, stubborn as a mule Levi, his beautiful skin mutilated, his body broken. She inhaled slowly and forced herself to think around the sick twist in her gut. "What can I do, Ruby?"

"Get over here now." Ruby rattled off the address, then sucked in a sharp breath. "Great. Noreen's here and, boy, is she pissed. I won't be able to stall for long."

"No, I'll be there. Just do what you can. Please, Ruby." Sera's voice broke on a sob. She lifted a trembling hand and dried the tears sliding down her cheeks. "Please don't let her hurt him again."

Sera hung up and pushed herself off the bed. Levi needed her. Sweet Lord above, what if she didn't get there in time? She rushed through the house, grabbed her keys off the kitchen counter, and bounded toward her car, not bothering to lock the house. She slid into her Volvo and pulled the seat forward. Levi's long legs. God. She leaned her forehead against the steering wheel. It was cool and firm under her skin, a stark contrast to the panic racing through her. He had to be ok. She'd get there in time and she'd do whatever she had to in order to stop Retribution, and he'd be ok.

She fumbled for the correct key and inserted it into the ignition, turned it. Nothing happened. She tried again, and again nothing happened, and she stared at the steering wheel as the panic twisted into horror. The Volvo had never failed her before, never, but Levi had warned her it was getting too old to be reliable, and she hadn't listened, had she. Oh, dear Lord, why hadn't she taken his advice and gotten a new car when she'd had the chance?

She scrambled out of the station wagon and broke into an unsteady jog, searching for Candi's number on her phone with one hand as she stumbled through the back yard and into the woods. Her sister-in-law picked up on the second ring. Sera's words tumbled out, overlapping Candi's cheery hello. "Candi, oh, my God, are you home?"

"Ah, sure, Sera. What's wrong?"

"It's Levi. No, it's..." Sera's voice broke. She swallowed and rushed on. "I need to get to Tellowee right now and my car broke down and I really need your help."

"Ok. Just calm down, honey. I can be there in five and we'll get you where you need to be."

"No, stay there. I'm on my way. Just, please start the car and I'll be there in a jiffy."

Sera hung up and glued her eyes to the trail as she hurried down it, her mind caught in a litany of prayers. *Please let him be ok. Please let me get there in time.*

Candi was waiting in her car with the nose pointed toward the street and the engine idling. Sera jumped in, slammed the door behind herself, and gave Candi directions to Hawthorne's house.

"I know where that is." Candi shifted the car into gear and rolled down the driveway. "Now will you please tell me what's going on?"

Sera jerked her seatbelt on and fastened it. "Levi told his family I dumped him and now he's going through Retribution."

Candi frowned and eased the car onto the main road. "What the heck is that?"

"You know those scars on his back? Something like that, only worse." Sera scrubbed her hands over her face, surprised when they came away wet. She swiped at the tears seeping out of her eyes and sniffed back a sob. "Ruby said he's going to be flogged and he'll lose all his property, and oh, God, Candi, how could his own family do that to him?"

Candi slammed on the brakes and swiveled around, facing Sera. Her eyes went wide and her tanned skin paled. "They're going to flog him?"

"Don't stop, Candi. We need to go, very, very fast." Sera gripped her thighs as Candi set the car in motion again. "I don't know all the details. All I know is, I can't let that happen to him, not again. Not for me, Candi. Sweet Jesus, he doesn't deserve that."

"Nobody deserves that," Candi said faintly, and that was the last word the two of them spoke during the short, tense drive to Hawthorne's house.

Thirty

LEVI SLUMPED into a chair in front of his great-grandmother's desk and stared her down. He'd been there less than half an hour and already, he'd repeated himself half a dozen times. For some reason, she couldn't seem to grasp the finer points of the situation he found himself in. Maybe becoming mortal had sapped her intelligence. She *was* nearly two thousand years old.

He gritted his teeth and dug his fingers into the arms of his chair. "Why are you making this so hard? I thought you hated Sera."

"I merely thought her unworthy of a Son of your standing and breeding," Hawthorne said mildly. "Perhaps I was correct in my judgment, perhaps not. What remains unclear to me is your insistence that she holds no love for you in her heart. Love shone from the woman you brought into my home on Thanksgiving."

"That wasn't love..."

She slashed a hand through the air, silencing him. "I know what love is, Levi. Hers for you was visible to anyone caring to look."

"She cares for me," he acknowledged. "She's not the kind of woman to have sex with somebody she doesn't have feelings for, but that's not the same thing as loving me. Look, Nana, she as good as told me she wants to be with Ethan Phillips."

"I find that hard to believe. If you insist, however, I shall render judgment upon your mother's arrival."

"Thanks." Levi heaved a sigh and slid an inch lower in the chair. This would work out. He could still build a house on the land he'd bought next to Sera's parents. Petey could visit whenever he wanted, and when the baby came, Levi would take them both as often as Sera would let him. He had no legal claim to Petey, though if Sera married Ethan, the other man would honor the People's rites and not stand between Levi and Sera's son.

Blessed Goddess, he'd miss them. He rubbed a hand over the ache in his chest, right where his heart should've been. It was lost under the sea of sorrow he'd slipped into when she'd rejected him, maybe forever. He had a funny feeling even time wouldn't numb that wound.

Ruby flounced into the room and flopped into the chair next to him, her mouth stretched into a smug smirk.

He eyed that smirk warily. When Ruby smiled, about half the time it meant she was up to no good. "Where have you been?"

"Busy with things that needed tending." She crossed her legs and batted innocent gray eyes at him. "Your mother's here."

The knot in his gut tightened. He should've been relieved, should've been happy he was giving Sera what she wanted. Why did what should've been the right thing to do feel so wrong?

Noreen entered Hawthorne's office and settled herself on the edge of the desk facing Levi. "What's this about Serafina rejecting you and why is this the first I've heard of it?"

"She's found somebody else, Mum."

Noreen's dark eyebrows shot up and she laughed. "Are we talking about the same woman?"

"Why does everybody keep asking me that?" he muttered. "She got pregnant. I asked her to marry me. She said no and a week later, she told me Ethan Phillips asked her to marry him instead. What's so hard to understand there?"

"Maybe the fact that Serafina hardly acts like a woman on the verge of marrying another man." Noreen's voice was flat, matching the hard glimmer in her eyes. "If you don't want her anymore, there are better ways of handling the situation than Retribution."

Something ugly and fierce welled up inside him and he stood abruptly, facing his mother with his heart oozing and raw. "I fucking love her, Mum, so much it's tearing me up to leave her like this, when I swore I never would. I swore that before I even knew her, before I knew Petey, and now you're wondering if I'm making the right call? She doesn't love me." His voice broke, and to his shame, tears clogged his throat. He spun away from his family and stared at the ceiling, willing his heartache to stay where it was. "Maybe she never even tried."

"Levi, darling." His mother threaded her arm through his and rested her head on his shoulder. "I think you're wrong here, so terribly wrong, but if you think this best, I'll support your decision."

He covered her hand with his and squeezed. "Thanks, Mum."

"Judgment, then," Hawthorne said. "Seventy-eight lashes, one for each year of your expected natural life, as well as sixteen for the unborn child."

Ruby sucked in a breath. "Ninety-four lashes. I told her it'd be harsh."

Levi rounded on her, dislodging his mother's hold. He draped an arm around his mum's shoulders and leveled a hard stare on Ruby. "Told who?"

"Nobody." Ruby leaned back in her chair and faced Hawthorne. "Sorry, Nana."

Hawthorne folded her hands together on top of her desk. "Given your standing as a mortal and someone your family cherishes, I shall waive all save one of those lashes. When your trust fund matures in three years, the entirety will be pooled into a fund for Peter, the unborn child, and any others you may have with Serafina."

Levi shook his head. "That's not likely to happen."

"You challenge my judgment?"

"Never that."

"Good. You will further support Peter, the unborn child, and any other children you may have with Serafina in a manner the two of you deem appropriate, to include providing for their education, health, and welfare."

Levi waited for her to continue. When it became apparent she'd finished rendering judgment, he said, "That's it?"

"Is that not sufficient?"

"You're being awfully lenient."

"I hope the two of you reconcile. It is apparent to all who know you that the two of you hold great love for one another."

"I wish you were right." Blessed Ki, did he ever. "Can I take the lash now? Sera's at home alone and she's got morning sickness like you wouldn't believe."

Hawthorne exchanged a pointed glance with his mother. "You

358

continue to reside with her?"

"She doesn't need to be alone right now." Levi squeezed Noreen and dropped his hand, then stripped off his t-shirt. "Make it official."

Hawthorne stood and nodded. "Very well. Who speaks for the mortal, Serafina?"

Ruby stood. "I will."

"I speak for the Son," Noreen said. "Though I really think you're rushing this, darling."

Levi rolled his shoulders, shaking off his irritation. "I tried giving her time, but she's made her choice. Seemed happy about it, too."

Noreen regarded him steadily, a slight frown marring the smooth lines of her face. "I wish things had worked out differently."

"Yeah, me, too," he said, and braced himself for the blow that was nothing compared to the one Sera had delivered to his heart.

CANDI BROUGHT HER CAR to a screeching halt outside Hawthorne's house on the outskirts of Tellowee. Sera tumbled out of the car, nearly falling on the concrete sidewalk edging the winter-brown grass.

"Careful!" Candi called.

"Got it," Sera said, and hurriedly righted herself. She rushed up the walkway leading to the house with one hand over the frantic beat of her heart. *Hurry, hurry, hurry,* it seemed to say, pressing her into panic. What if she wasn't on time? What if Hawthorne really hurt Levi before Sera could stop the whole, crazy Retribution thing?

She took the wooden steps to the porch two at a time, scarcely aware of a car door slamming shut behind her or the soles of Candi's shoes pounding up the walkway. Sera rang the doorbell and, not content to wait, banged on the front door.

Footsteps sounded in quick patters from inside. The door opened on a sturdy cherub with blonde curls and huge gray eyes. The little girl gasped and threw herself at Sera's legs, wrapping herself around them with the strength and agility of a monkey. "Petey's mommy! You comeded. I wished and wished for you and Petey, and here you is."

Sera patted the little girl's head, smoothing back a stray wisp of hair. "Hello, Lali. I really need to find Levi. Can you tell me where he is?"

"I'll show you." Lali scrambled down and held out her hand. "Where's Petey?"

"He's still in school." Sera grasped Lali's hand. "This is kind of an emergency, sweetie."

"I know what that is." Lali turned and led Sera through the house. "My puppy told me all about them. He said when we has the 'mergency, I has to go find a 'dult and mind real good *or else*, but his or else ain't scary like Nana's."

"I imagine not," Sera murmured. After meeting the formidable Daughter and matriarch of Levi's family over Thanksgiving, Sera had no wish to be on the receiving end of any action Hawthorne chose to take, especially one succeeded by a stern *or else*.

Lali halted in front of a set of double doors. "Here we is. Levi's talking to Nana 'bout something 'portant, so we has to be really, really quiet."

"Thank you, Lali. I need to go in so I can help, ok?"

Lali shrugged. "Okey dokey. Me and the stranger woman can go make a snack with my puppy."

Candi gasped out a strangled laugh. "Well, ok then."

A sharp *whish* came from inside, followed by a low male grunt, and the color leached from Sera's face. "Oh, no. No, no, no." She tugged on the handle and after what seemed like ages, finally forced the door open. She burst inside. Levi stood with his back to the door, his arms held securely in front of him by Noreen and Ruby, his torso bare. A thin, red welt ran parallel to the waistband of his jeans along his lower back. Sera's heart nosedived into the sick roiling around in her gut. They'd already started. Oh, God. What would she do now?

Hawthorne stood to one side holding a long, slender stick. She turned toward Sera and arched one perfect eyebrow. "This is a private meeting."

Sera shook her head, sending hair flying around her face. She shoved it back and faced Hawthorne squarely. "I'm here to take Retribution."

Levi jerked around. "What the fuck, Sera? You're supposed to be at home resting."

"Ruby called. She said you were taking Retribution because you thought I'd forsaken you." She inhaled and pressed a shaky hand to her stomach. "Which I didn't, by the way."

Levi faced away from her. "Yeah, right. You seemed all hot to take Phillips up on his proposal."

"What? I never..." Sera's hand dropped as she gaped at him. "Is that what this is about? You think I threw you over for him?"

"Didn't you? Fuck's sake, Sera, you should've seen your face when you told me about him this morning, how happy you were, how..."

"No! God, Levi, that wasn't it at all."

"Enough." Hawthorne's quietly spoken word echoed through the room. "Judgment has been rendered. Retribution must be made. This man has agreed to take it in your place."

She raised the hand holding the long cane and, with a quick sideways slash, brought it down on Levi's back. He hissed in a breath and yanked at his arms, held firmly by the two women he faced. "What are you doing, Nana?"

"Allowing the child to see exactly what forsaking a Son means."

Hawthorne drew the cane back and hit Levi again. He grunted and cursed low under his breath, and Sera stared at the three welts on his lower back, right next to the scars he already bore there. The panic that had pushed her there, the fear, the horror at what he was undergoing because of her mistakes, all coalesced into a hard, resolute knot in her gut. Levi hadn't earned the punishment he was taking, but she had. Hadn't she rejected him? To save him, yes, to keep him from paying for the decisions she'd made, to give them both a little time to be certain marriage was what they wanted. Noble intentions apparently meant nothing to the People, and less than that to the hard-faced woman raising her hand for another blow.

"Wait."

Hawthorne paused with her arm arched back. "Why?"

Sera swallowed and lifted the hem of her sweater with trembling fingers, pulling it over her head and off. "It's my punishment to take."

"Sera, no." Levi jerked at his arms. "If the two of you don't let go right now, I swear, I'll never forgive you."

Noreen regarded Sera coolly over Levi's shoulder. "She needs to know the sacrifices you're willing to make for her."

"Not like this." Levi tugged again and a thread of panic entered his voice. "Fuck's sake, she's pregnant. Doesn't that mean anything to y'all?"

Sera laid her sweater over the back of the couch and strode across the room. She wrapped herself around Levi, protecting his body with her own as an odd calm settled over her. His skin was warm under her hands. He was so beautiful, so good, and he'd given her everything. She pressed her face into his back, exhaled slowly, and said, "I'm ready."

"Very well," Hawthorne said. "Three lashes have been dealt. Ninety-one remain."

"Oh, God," Sera moaned. Ninety-one lashes. That would kill her or leave her permanently disfigured, her back broken, unable to care for herself or Petey. A tear slid down her cheek. She tightened her grip on Levi, holding him as he struggled to free himself from her and Noreen and Ruby.

The cane whipped through the air and sliced into Sera's back, raising a streak of hot pain along her skin. She bit her lip, containing an agonized cry.

"Goddamn you, Nana," Levi said. "Don't hit her again."

"She wishes to take Retribution, child."

Another swish of air and a second blow cut into Sera's back. She jerked and nearly lost her grip on Levi. Fire ran along her back, etching its way through skin into muscle. The scars on Levi's back flashed through her mind. He'd taken sixteen licks when he'd claimed Petey, suffered through sixteen strokes like the two she'd been dealt, and he'd done it gladly.

Because he loved her.

In that moment, clarity struck. All along, she'd told herself she was holding back because she didn't want to hurt him, because they didn't know each other that well, because they needed more time, when deep down, she'd been terrified his love wasn't strong enough to last. Deep down, in her heart of hearts, she'd been so sure he'd be the one to run out on her. He'd be the one to let her down, the way Kyle Vincent had nearly nine years before, yet she was the one that had failed him. Over and over again, she'd forced Levi to prove himself to her. She'd doubted him and pushed him away, and through all of that, he'd stood beside her and loved her, even as she'd thrown his love back in his face.

She wasn't just a fool. She was a complete idiot.

Levi twisted in her grip. She allowed her hands to fall away and covered her face, hiding her grief from him and his family. She hadn't been able to trust him, hadn't found it in herself to believe in him, and look what a mess she'd made. She'd ruined everything out of her own insecurities.

Gentle hands lifted her high, cradling her against Levi's chest. "There now, love," he murmured. "I've got you."

She slid a hand around his nape and rubbed her cheek along his warm skin. "Oh, Levi. I'm so, so sorry."

"Shh, now. There's nothing to be sorry over." He laid her down on the couch and pulled a blanket over her. "You made your decision. I won't hold it against you."

She swiped the moisture from her eyes and met his impassive gaze evenly. "You've got it all wrong. I shanghaied you this morning because I missed you, missed being with you. Look." She held out her left hand, flashing the ring she still wore, his ring, the one he'd picked out especially for her. "I did make a decision this morning, but it didn't have anything to do with Ethan."

Levi ran his fingertips along her hand, circling the ring. "You put it on."

"I did." She twined her fingers through his and held on tight. Her rock. He'd always been that for her, since the day they'd met. Why had she ever doubted him? "I told you once that I'd never be able to leave you. How could you forget that?"

His mouth thinned into a hard line. "Ethan proposed to you."

"In a way, yes. That doesn't mean I want to marry him."

"But you didn't want me."

"Of course, I want you, Levi. God." She inhaled sharply and shifted on the couch, easing the pressure on the fading pain in her back. "I love you so much. I was just scared, that's all. I thought you'd understand, thought I'd explained it better, but I wasn't rejecting you."

He glanced away. "It felt like it, felt like no matter what I did, you'd never love me."

"I'm sorry I made you feel that way, especially when it's not at all true." She placed her hand on his cheek and turned his face toward her, and looked into his whiskey eyes, so sweet and warm. "I never meant to hurt you, not ever. You and Petey, you're the best part of my life. It would kill me to lose either one of you."

The beginnings of a familiar smirk tilted his beautiful mouth. "I wasn't going very far."

"You swear?"

"I never could, love. I thought about all the things I could do to care for you and Petey and the baby, trying to figure out how to live without you." He touched his forehead to hers and their breaths mingled in the space between them. "Don't ever make me do that again."

"Not ever." Sera kissed his fingertips and brushed her cheek over the back of his hand. "Marry me, Levi. Be my family."

He smiled and kissed her, lingering for a long, sweet moment before he pulled away. "I already am. I love you, Sera, have for so long. It's been hard holding that back from you."

"You never have to again, I swear." She squeezed his hand and tucked it into the space above her heart, right where he belonged. "What do I need to do to stop Retribution?"

"It's done. You're wearing my ring, you've placed yourself in front of me." He raised his voice slightly. "The People will recognize your intentions."

Hawthorne stepped into Sera's line of sight. "So it shall be."

"Blessed be Ki," Noreen said.

"Blessed be Ki." Levi smoothed Sera's hair back and pressed a tender kiss to her mouth. "Marry me, Sera. Now, before Santa gets here and Petey gets distracted with presents."

Sera laughed and held on tight to the love shining from his whiskey eyes. "Yes, let's. It'll be the best Christmas ever, I swear."

"It will," he agreed, and he kissed her again, the way he had the first time, like a man that had discovered his heart and never intended to let her go.

Epilogue

PETEY STOOD on the edge of the Atlantic Ocean, the toes of his tennis shoes inches away from the waves rolling onto the beach. Levi had told him to be real careful not to step in. The tide was too strong for Petey to swim through it, but maybe it wouldn't always be. He worked hard every day, eating the veggies Mama and Levi made for him, even the ones he didn't like, and practicing basketball like crazy so his arms would maybe look like Levi's when he grew up.

Petey flexed his bicep, poked his scrawny arm, and sighed. No muscles yet. Soon, though. He was halfway to sixteen, and when he got there, he'd be a man among the People. Surely by then he'd grow some.

"Petey!" Mama called. "Time to come in."

He squatted and dipped his hand into the water. It was real cold, almost as cold as ice, and kinda gritty. He ignored the chill and faced it squarely. "Someday, I'm gonna be a man, and when I am, I'm gonna come back and swim and I won't be afraid of you none."

He stood and nodded at the ocean, and in his mind, the great figure of Poseidon rose from among the waves and nodded back, man to man, kinda like Levi did when they were talking real serious like. A man always treats others with respect. Petey didn't need Levi to tell him that to know it was true. It sure was nice hearing it from him, though.

A gentle hand fell on his shoulder. He looked up, way, way up, and grinned at his new step-dad. "Hey, Levi."

Levi grinned back. "Your mum's calling."

"I heard. I was just..." Petey shrugged. No way would he tell

Levi he'd been talking to the ocean. It sounded kinda stupid, now that he thought about it, and the one thing he never wanted Levi to think of him as was stupid. "The ocean's really big here."

"It is. We'll come back in the summer when it's warmer and you've had some swimming lessons." Levi swung Petey up into his arms and settled him against his chest. "Best mind your mum now, lad. She'll skin us both if we don't hop to it."

"Yes, sir." Petey wrapped his arms around Levi's neck, not 'cause he was scared. He'd been right about that all along. Having a dad made you unscared of almost everything, especially a dad like Levi. He was always there for Petey, no matter what. No, he wasn't scared of heights no more. He just liked to hug his new dad. "You reckon she'll get mad 'cause I was too close to the water?"

"We were watching you, son."

Petey pressed his face into the side of Levi's neck, hiding a grin. Ever since Mama and Levi got married, Levi had called Petey *son*, like he was really Petey's dad and everything. And the best part was that Mama and Levi both said Petey could call Levi Dad whenever he wanted. How cool was that? After all this time, he finally had a dad. Everything was exactly the way he'd wished. Levi lived with them all the time and brought Mama flowers and kissed her about every time she turned around.

Petey wrinkled his nose. That was kinda yucky, but maybe it was ok, as long as they didn't hold hands nekkid or nothing.

Levi made pancakes at least once a week and was teaching Petey all about man stuff, and Mama smiled all the time and kept them in line, the way mamas were supposed to. Shoot. They was even gonna get another kid soon, maybe a brother so he'd have somebody to play with all the time, like Dale and Matty had each other. Mama told him it was growing in her belly and said when it was bigger, he could put his hand there and maybe feel it moving.

Though why they couldn't just get the baby out of the cabbage patch where Mama had found Petey was a puzzler, but adults were all the time doing crazy stuff he didn't understand, like taking a vacation to a really cold beach over Christmas break. Levi had said something about things coming full circle, but no matter how hard Petey had looked on the beach, he hadn't seen a dang circle anywhere.

"There you are," Mama said.

Petey unburied his head from Levi's neck and looked down at her. "Sorry, Mama. I was watching the water."

"It's ok, sweetie. Lali woke up from her nap and wants to play."

Petey hid a grimace. He liked Lali and all, but she was just a little kid, not a half-grown man like him. "I'll go play with her."

Levi set Petey down and swatted his bottom. "Stay where we can find you."

"Yes, sir."

Petey scampered up the trail leading between two sand dunes. At the top, he glanced back. Sure enough, Mama and Levi was holding hands and smooching, the way Uncle Jack and Aunt Candi was always doing. Petey shook his head. Grown ups. A body never could figure them out.

He broke into a jog and raced toward the condo, pushing himself in spite of the slight wheeze settling into his lungs. Christmas sure had been great this year. He'd gotten that Xbox One he'd asked for, Levi and Mama had gotten married, and Petey finally had a real dad just like he'd always wanted. He grinned and hopped up the apartment building's outside stairs. Yup, everything was better now that he had a dad, and now that Levi was his, Petey sure didn't mean to give him up.

He turned around and spotted Mama and Levi and waved his arms real big. "Hey, Dad! I love you!"

Levi grinned and waved back. "I love you, too, son."

Petey didn't need to see Mama's smile to know it was there. He felt it clear down to his toes every time he remembered how she'd said yes to Levi and given Petey the best dad in the world, showing Petey that she loved him more than anything, just like she always said.

About the Author

Lucy Varna lives in the Blue Ridge Mountains of northeast Georgia, surrounded by her large, extended family. Visit her online at:

www.lucyvarna.com
www.daughtersofthepeople.com

The Daughters of the People Series
Book 1: *The Prophecy*
Book 2: *Light's Bane*
Book 3: *The Enemy Within*
Book 3.5: *Tempered*
Book 4: *In All Things, Balance*

The Sons of the People Series
Book 1: *Say Yes*

The Cullowhee Heritage Series
Book 1: *A Higher Purpose*
Book 2: *A Wicked Love*

Coming Soon
The Choosing (A Novel of the Pruxnæ)
Sanctuary (Daughters of the People, Book 5)